CHAPTER & HEARSE

"Filled with action . . . Lorna Barnett has written a delightful amateur sleuth filled with red herrings and false leads that keep reader interest from the explosion till the explosive climax." —*Genre Go Round Reviews*

"There's misdirection, miscommunication, red herrings, and plot twists galore . . . Tightly plotted and paced to keep you turning the pages, this series is indeed getting better with each book." —*Gumshoe Review*

"Well-plotted and there are a few good suspects . . . Best of all, there is plenty of book talk sprinkled throughout and even a few of Angelica's recipes." —*The Mystery Reader*

BOOKPLATE SPECIAL

"The third top-notch Booktown Mystery is a cleverly plotted cozy with everything a reader could want: mystery books, delicious food, and bad guys. With its bookstore setting and small-town charm, this series is bound to be a favorite for cozy readers." —*Romantic Times*

"Get ready to pop a lot of popcorn, cuddle up under a blanket, and spend a little time with Tricia Miles and crew. Ms. Barrett, queen of the cozies, has a winner here!" —*Feathered Quill Book Reviews*

"Once again, Barrett has written an interesting, plausible murder mystery with an amateur sleuth that not only entertains but educates . . . Another excellent installment in this series." —*Gumshoe Review*

"Barrett is skilled at making her characters flawed and fully believable. This book-based book is a perfect autumn read—right down to those smashed pumpkins—for mystery aficionados." —*Richmond Times-Dispatch*

continued . . .

BOOKMARKED FOR DEATH

"Interesting characters, growing interrelationships . . . It's like visiting friends and having an adventure rolled into one book after another."
— *Gumshoe Review*

"A series that will quickly gain a dedicated readership. If anyone has the formula for a frolicking fun mystery down pat, it's Lorna Barrett. The read is light and sheer entertainment. A good rollicking read."
— *Roundtable Reviews*

"A good cozy. The characters are likable and the puzzle is intriguing."
— *Mystery News*

"Clever twists . . . take readers on a journey through the intricate layers of book publishing . . . A mystery to be cherished."
— *Merrimon Book Reviews*

"Fans of Carolyn Hart and Denise Swanson rejoice! The latest [Booktown] gem . . . sparkles. This first-rate cozy artfully blends crime, cuisine, and even bookselling in a cheerful, witty, well-plotted puzzler."
— Julia Spencer-Fleming, Edgar® finalist and author of *One Was a Soldier*

MURDER IS BINDING

"[A] smart, fast-paced novel with likeable characters and enough plot twists and turns to keep things interesting."
— *Suite101.com*

"Charming . . . The mix of books, cooking, and an engaging whodunit will leave cozy fans eager for the new installment."
— *Publishers Weekly*

"Move over, Cabot Cove. Lorna Barrett's new cozy creation, *Murder Is Binding*, has it all: wonderful old books, quirky characters, a clever mystery, and a cat named Miss Marple!"
— Roberta Isleib, author of *Asking for Murder*

"Everything a cozy lover could want and more. Bravo!"
— Leann Sweeney, author of *The Cat, the Lady, and the Liar*

SENTENCED TO DEATH

Lorna Barrett

BERKLEY PRIME CRIME, NEW YORK

THE BERKLEY PUBLISHING GROUP
Published by the Penguin Group
Penguin Group (USA) Inc.
375 Hudson Street, New York, New York 10014, USA

Penguin Group (Canada), 90 Eglinton Avenue East, Suite 700, Toronto, Ontario M4P 2Y3, Canada
(a division of Pearson Penguin Canada Inc.)
Penguin Books Ltd., 80 Strand, London WC2R 0RL, England
Penguin Group Ireland, 25 St. Stephen's Green, Dublin 2, Ireland (a division of Penguin Books Ltd.)
Penguin Group (Australia), 250 Camberwell Road, Camberwell, Victoria 3124, Australia
(a division of Pearson Australia Group Pty. Ltd.)
Penguin Books India Pvt. Ltd., 11 Community Centre, Panchsheel Park, New Delhi—110 017, India
Penguin Group (NZ), 67 Apollo Drive, Rosedale, Auckland 0632, New Zealand
(a division of Pearson New Zealand Ltd.)
Penguin Books (South Africa) (Pty.) Ltd., 24 Sturdee Avenue, Rosebank, Johannesburg 2196,
South Africa

Penguin Books Ltd., Registered Offices: 80 Strand, London WC2R 0RL, England

This is a work of fiction. Names, characters, places, and incidents either are the product of the author's
imagination or are used fictitiously, and any resemblance to actual persons, living or dead, business
establishments, events, or locales is entirely coincidental. The publisher does not have any control over
and does not assume any responsibility for author or third-party websites or their content.

PUBLISHER'S NOTE: The recipes contained in this book are to be followed exactly as written. The
publisher is not responsible for your specific health or allergy needs that may require medical supervi-
sion. The publisher is not responsible for any adverse reactions to the recipes contained in this book.

SENTENCED TO DEATH

A Berkley Prime Crime Book / published by arrangement with the author

PRINTING HISTORY
Berkley Prime Crime mass-market edition / June 2011

Copyright © 2011 by Penguin Group (USA) Inc.
Excerpt from *The Walled Flower* by Lorraine Bartlett copyright © by Penguin Group (USA) Inc.
Cover illustration by Teresa Fasolino.
Cover design by Diana Kolsky.
Interior text design by Laura K. Corless.

ISBN: 978-0-425-24186-8

BERKLEY® PRIME CRIME
Berkley Prime Crime Books are published by The Berkley Publishing Group,
a division of Penguin Group (USA) Inc.,
375 Hudson Street, New York, New York 10014.
BERKLEY® PRIME CRIME and the PRIME CRIME logo are trademarks of Penguin Group (USA)
Inc.

PRINTED IN THE UNITED STATES OF AMERICA

10 9 8 7 6 5 4 3 2 1

For Jeannie Rigod,
who refused to accept a death sentence.

Long may she live!

ACKNOWLEDGMENTS

Every book is an adventure—for the author and her readers. I couldn't have survived this adventure without a little help from my friends. My thanks go to Krista Davis, Sandra Parshall, Kelly Raftery, Tyra Blackshear-Dedam, and Pat Remick for assistance with legal, language, police procedures, and local color issues, not to forget my eBay buddy, Nancy Ziefel, and Doranna Durgin, who was very helpful with doggy info.

Michelle Sampson, director of the Wadleigh Memorial Library in Milford, New Hampshire, continues to provide a wealth of useful information and local color.

Leann Sweeney served as my manuscript buddy. Both on tight deadlines, we encouraged each other (and compared notes on a daily basis to see who would finish her manuscript first). Colleen Kuehne kept me on my toes as my first reader.

My pals on the Cozy Chicks blog, www.CozyChicksBlog.com, and all the Berkley and Signet Girls at Cozy Promo have been there cheering me on, too.

My thanks go to my editor, Tom Colgan, his terrific assistant, Niti Bagchi, and the whole group at Berkley Prime Crime. My wonderful agent, Jessica Faust, gives me great advice and keeps me on track.

I hope you'll visit my Website, www.LornaBarrett.com, and sign up for my periodic newsletter.

ONE

Founders' Day weekend. What else could Bob Kelly, the head of the Chamber of Commerce, come up with to try to draw a crowd to the little village of Stoneham, New Hampshire? Tricia Miles shook her head at the notion and resettled the weight of the warm, sleepy—and sweaty—toddler against her shoulder. "Booktown, NH," as Stoneham was often referred to, had risen from the ashes of near extinction thanks to Bob's efforts when he'd enticed some ten or so booksellers to locate to the village. It had put Stoneham back on the map and had made Bob quite a handsome profit, too. Tricia hadn't done too badly either, with her own mystery bookstore, Haven't Got a Clue.

A small single-engine aircraft buzzed the town with a long banner trailing behind it announcing STONEHAM FOUNDERS' DAY—WWW.STONEHAMNH.COM behind it. Trust Bob to think of that, too. However, Tricia wished it wouldn't buzz quite so close, as it made conversation nearly impossible, and in only minutes her friend, Deborah Black, the architect of the celebration, would be on deck to give her welcoming speech and to open the festivities.

It was Deborah's child that Tricia held, since Deborah was otherwise occupied. Little Davey wasn't impressed by all the hoopla, and the warm August morning had sent him straight to dreamland, which was okay with Tricia. A fall had given the toddler a broken right arm, now encased in a purple cast that he sometimes not so playfully used as a club.

Tricia looked around the crowd, hoping Deborah's mother would soon make an appearance so she could give up the boy, who hadn't wanted to sit in his stroller—voicing that opinion with tears and screams. He'd found her to be a much more comfortable place to nap.

Tricia stood across the street from Stoneham's square, home to a Victorian-era stone gazebo with a lovely copper roof that had aged beautifully. The small park was crammed with carnival rides and colorfully tacky trailers with vendors ready to sell greasy, fattening foods. Loitering among them were the local merchants, townspeople, and tourists—exactly the crowd Bob had hoped to attract. Tricia could just picture Bob standing along the sidelines, rubbing his hands together in miserly fashion. That he'd suckered Deborah to do most of the work was yet another accomplishment. He'd share some of the glory with her but would no doubt take the bulk of the credit for coming up with the idea in the first place.

"Quite the turnout," Russ Smith said, almost in Tricia's left ear. Where had he appeared from? She stepped to her right and frowned at him. She and the editor of the *Stone-*

ham Weekly News had once been lovers, but that had been more than a year ago. Despite the fact he'd originally dumped her, he now wanted what he couldn't have.

Too bad.

"Shouldn't you be stationed closer to the action?" Tricia asked. After all, he did have his Nikon camera hanging from his neck. He'd need pictures of Deborah giving her speech for the next issue of the paper. Russ had contemplated selling the *Stoneham Weekly News* when he thought he could get back into reporting for a big metropolitan newspaper, but that hadn't happened, either. Still, Tricia found it hard to feel sorry for him—not after he'd stalked her for a time. Thankfully he'd gotten the message, and although he hadn't completely accepted the fact, his advances had backed off. He was trying for friendship; at least, that's what he'd said.

"Tricia!"

Tricia turned to see Deborah's mother, Elizabeth Crane, hurrying toward her. At last, she could surrender little Davey to another shoulder. He was getting heavy.

"Did that boy sucker you into holding him?" Elizabeth said, and held out her arms for the boy.

"I'm afraid so."

"He's an operator," Elizabeth said, and shouldered the child, patting him on the back. Davey didn't even stir. "Deborah has spoiled this kid. But then, she works so hard, when she's not at the shop, she likes to spend every minute she can with him."

Deborah and her husband both worked hard. David Black had two jobs and not quite so jokingly claimed he held the second one to keep his wife's shop afloat. That wasn't exactly true. Sales at Deborah's business, the Happy

Domestic, had picked up since she'd added a line of greeting cards and stationery to the retail mix. She was in the black—not very far, mind you—but any shade of that color was better than seeing red on a balance sheet. Deborah did, however, admit that David got a bit irritated at having to watch the baby on weekends, but they'd both agreed upon it when they decided to start a family. That said, he was nowhere to be found this day.

"Hello, Russ," Elizabeth said. "Are you going to take pictures of Deborah giving her speech?"

"I sure am."

"Get her from the right, it's her best side," Elizabeth said, and laughed.

The aircraft did another low circuit around Main Street. Russ grabbed his camera and snapped off a couple of shots. It was impossible to hear anything else until it had moved out of earshot.

"Nice banner," Russ commented. "I hope I got a good enough shot of it to print in the paper."

"If you didn't, it'll be around again in another couple of minutes," Tricia said, and pulled at the shoulder of her blouse where little Davey had drooled in his sleep.

Russ glanced at his watch. "The show's going to start in a few minutes. I'd better go up by the podium. See you later, Tricia?"

The man just didn't give up. "Good-bye, Russ."

Elizabeth turned her attention back to the gazebo. "I'm so glad Deborah was able to hire Cheryl Griffin part-time in the shop. I wouldn't have wanted to miss this."

"I admire Deb's stamina. She's really worked hard on the whole Founders' Day event." Of course, Bob had tried to foist the job off on Tricia—and several other members of the Chamber of Commerce—first, but she'd been more adept at dodging his constant nagging. After much badgering, Deborah had given in just to shut him up.

The aroma of freshly made popcorn wafted on the slight breeze. Tricia noticed Ray Dempsey standing beside his lunch truck, all decorated in red, white, and blue bunting. Despite protests by the owners of Stoneham's two lunchtime eateries, the Board of Selectmen had approved Dempsey's permit request to set up shop with what he called his mobile kitchen. That Tricia's sister, Angelica, was the owner of one of those establishments—Booked for Lunch—brought the dispute a little closer to home.

As if she could smell the popcorn from afar, Angelica, dressed in her white waitress togs, crossed the street and approached Tricia and Elizabeth. Despite being a nationally bestselling cookbook author, Angelica still enjoyed waiting on customers at her café a couple of times a week. And it was even more imperative that she do so of late, since she'd recently lost her short-order cook to the Brookview Inn's reopened kitchen and needed to supervise her new hires.

"Good morning, ladies," Angelica said, but her attention was focused on Dempsey. "So, he's added popcorn to the mix. What's next? Cotton candy and funnel cakes?"

"Someone's already selling those in the park. I love funnel cakes," Elizabeth said wistfully, but her sappy expression soon turned to chagrin at Angelica's baleful glare. "How's business at your café?" she offered as a form of appeasement.

"Not as good as it used to be," Angelica said, and turned her attention back to Dempsey's truck. "There's a reason they called those things roach coaches."

"Angelica!" Tricia admonished, although she had to admit the only food she'd ever partaken of from a street vendor was roasted chestnuts at Christmastime in Manhattan. Nothing else compared.

"Shouldn't you be getting ready for your lunch crowd?" Tricia asked.

"Bev can handle today's setup," Angelica said, volunteering her new waitress. "I thought I should come out to support Deborah." *And keep an eye on Dempsey*, Tricia thought.

"Thank you," Elizabeth said. She'd started swaying back and forth, rocking little Davey. "I'm so proud of Deborah. I always wanted to do something with my life, like she has, but I never had the opportunity. I got married right out of high school and had three kids," she said with a sigh. "We never had any money—Deborah put herself through college. She's my pride and joy." Deborah was the youngest of Elizabeth's children and, from what Tricia had deduced, Elizabeth's favorite.

A smiling Deborah stepped up to the podium, tapped on the microphone to make sure it was live, and leaned down to speak. "Good morning, everyone, and welcome to Stoneham's first annual Founders' Day celebration."

The crowd broke into applause, accompanied by whistles and cheers.

Again, the plane buzzed overhead, and Deborah had to wait until it was out of range to speak again. "It was back in 1822 that Hiram Stone first opened one of New Hampshire's biggest granite quarries and established the village where we are gathered today. It's with great pride that we—"

The plane buzzed even lower this time, and Tricia, Angelica, and Elizabeth involuntarily ducked as it drowned out Deborah before it zoomed into a steep climb.

"What kind of an idiot did Bob hire?" Tricia demanded of Angelica, who could only shrug in answer. Angelica and Bob had been seeing each other for almost two years, although of late their relationship had cooled somewhat.

Deborah cleared her throat and continued with her speech. "Hiram Stone was a visionary, and his gifts to the village named after him in life, live on in—" But no one was listening to her. Their eyes were riveted on the sky.

A sudden, horrible sound erupted from the crowd, and people began pushing, shoving—running away from the gazebo.

Elizabeth had turned her back to the village square. "What's wrong?" she cried, over the noise of the crowd.

And then Tricia saw it—the small aircraft plummeting to Earth, heading straight for the Stoneham Square and the gazebo. Tricia grabbed her sister's arm, pulling her as she began to run, with Angelica struggling to keep up. There was no sound of an engine as the plane dove at the ground. It hit the gazebo as if it had a red target painted on it. The squeal of ripped metal and shattered plastic tore through the air.

The plane exploded through the other side of the gazebo, ripping out the support pillars that held up the roof. It collapsed in a heap, and a plume of dust shot into the air. The plane skittered across the lawn and finally came to rest where at least one hundred people had been standing only a few seconds before.

TWO

Elizabeth screamed, waking little Davey, whose mouth opened wide as he mimicked his grandmother's shrieks. Tricia hurried to Elizabeth, who tossed the child at her and ran toward the gazebo.

"Elizabeth, no! The plane might explode!" Tricia warned, but there was no stopping her.

The plane looked like a broken toy with is wings ripped off. Its crumpled fuselage lay on the ground, steam escaping from where the propeller had been, but there was no sign of fire.

Angelica was on her phone, screaming at a 9-1-1 dispatcher, demanding they send a couple of ambulances, but surely there could be no survivors.

Davey's wails had already quieted, but he tried to pull away, struggling to get down to the ground to follow his grandmother.

Elizabeth had already reached the wreck of what had been the village's once-beautiful gazebo. She fell to her knees in the grass, her face drawn, her mouth agape with heart-wrenching wails.

Tricia struggled to hold on to Davey's hand. "Nana, Nana!" he cried, and Tricia cried, too. Tears streamed down her cheeks, and suddenly Angelica was beside her, rubbing her back.

"There's no chance Deborah could've—" Whatever else Angelica meant to say was lost in a sob.

Swallowing hard, Tricia picked up little Davey and turned away.

"I just can't believe it," Ginny Wilson said for at least the hundredth time. Her eyes were red from crying, the skin around them puffy. Most of the bookshops on Main Street had closed—there was little point in staying open when the north end of the road was closed to vehicular and pedestrian traffic and access to the municipal parking lot was blocked. But Tricia's employees, twenty-something Ginny and elderly Mr. Everett, had been reluctant to leave the store. Mr. Everett looked shell-shocked. Tricia's little gray cat, Miss Marple, sat on his lap in the reader's nook, quietly purring, offering the only kind of comfort she could give.

A dry-eyed Tricia stood at the far end of her big display window, her gaze fixed on the roadblock, as though staring at it would give her some kind of reassurance that her world hadn't gone completely off kilter. That her friend wasn't dead. That the small village park did not now resemble a war zone. She'd already cried a river of tears and knew there'd be more later, when she was alone.

A figure passed the window and paused at the door, where a CLOSED sign hung from it. The man tried the handle, found it was open, and entered. "Ginny?" Antonio Barbero called, ignoring the others in the store.

Ginny flew across the room and into the arms of her handsome new boyfriend.

"I came as soon as I heard," Antonio said, his voice soft but the lilt of his Italian accent strong. He held her close and patted her back.

"She's dead—poor Deborah's dead," Ginny sobbed.

"What will happen to her store?" Antonio asked.

Ginny pulled back, her face stricken. Tricia was just as appalled by the question.

Antonio shrugged. "It's a legitimate question."

"Only if you're a vulture waiting to pick the bones of some poor dead animal," Ginny said, and pushed him away. "I suppose you already told your boss about it and *she* wants you to put in a bid for the Happy Domestic."

"Of course I told her. But she did not ask me to put in a bid on the business. Only to keep my ears open in case it should come on the market. She sent her condolences," he offered lamely.

Nigela Racita Associates was *the* new game in town. The developer had not only bought the empty lot that once housed the history bookstore that had been blown to smithereens several months before, but it had bought a half interest in the Brookview Inn, which was currently under renovation. After the inn had lost its decorated chef, the new management had recruited—of all people—Angelica's short-order cook, Jake Masters, to head up their formerly award-winning kitchen. Of course, Jake was a trained sous-chef—but it seemed incredible that they'd given such a position to someone with such limited experience. The fact that Jake was also an ex-con made the appointment even harder to believe.

Angelica had taken the news as well as could be expected, and Jake had at least helped her interview candidates to take over the grill at Booked for Lunch. But even the mention of Nigela Racita Associates could send Angelica into a ranting rage.

"Look, everyone, why don't you all go home. Or, in your case, Antonio, back to your office. It's not likely we'll hear any more about this tragedy until the Sheriff's Department can piece together what happened."

"More likely the National Transportation Safety Board," Mr. Everett suggested, gently set Miss Marple down on the floor, and stood.

Tricia nodded. "Come on, Ginny, go home. Read a good book, and go to bed early."

"Yes, I will make sure she goes to bed very early," Antonio said, his expression and tone solicitous. Ginny glared at him.

Tricia stepped behind the counter, found Ginny's purse, and handed it to her. "Go home," she said gently.

Ginny gave her a hug and turned for the door, which Antonio held open for her.

"I'll be leaving, too, Ms. Miles," Mr. Everett said. He did not offer Tricia a hug but gave her a solemn nod.

The phone rang before Tricia had a chance to lock the door behind him. She picked up the receiver. "Haven't Got a Clue. I'm sorry, but we're closed—"

"Don't you think I know that?" came Angelica's voice. She sighed, and softened her voice. "Come on over to the café. I've made soup."

Although the day was warm, soup was Angelica's second-favorite comfort food—after ice cream, of course. It wasn't surprising she'd turned to cooking for consolation.

Two minutes later, Tricia found herself sitting on a stool at the counter in Booked for Lunch. She usually ate lunch at Angelica's café, but today she hadn't had the time or the inclination. Now the aroma of something heavenly took her back to her childhood.

"Deborah was my first friend here in Stoneham. I just can't believe she's gone," Tricia said, pressing a tissue to her leaky left eye. She had a feeling the tears might be about to make a return visit.

"And what a way to go," Angelica agreed, shaking her head. "Squashed like a bug."

"Oh, Ange!" Tricia admonished. "Deborah was my friend!"

"I'm sorry," Angelica said, and she truly did sound it. "She was my friend, too. But you have to look at it this way. It was quick. She never saw it coming, and she never suffered."

No. Not like their grandmother. That unhappy experience would haunt Tricia for the rest of her life. "But it's so unfair."

"Yes, she was just starting to turn a profit on the shop," Angelica agreed.

"I'm sure that wasn't the only thing topping her bucket list. She'd have much rather lived to see her son grow up, get married—and enjoy her grandchildren."

"Grandchildren?" Angelica wailed. "Her son wasn't even two years old—I'm sure she hadn't even considered grandchildren." She stepped behind the double doors that separated the tiny kitchen from the dining room, and came back with a bowl. She set it on the counter, pushed it in front of Tricia, and handed her a spoon. "Eat. You'll feel better."

"I'm not hungry."

"It's Grandmother's chicken soup recipe. I made it myself," Angelica said, her voice taking on a singsong cadence on the last words.

Tricia knew their grandmother had never written down this particular recipe. In fact, she rarely worked from a recipe. She boiled a chicken carcass for hours and tossed in whatever veggies she had on hand, and added salt and pepper to taste. It always tasted delicious and it never tasted the same.

Angelica placed a napkin and a couple of packets of saltines on the counter and handed Tricia a spoon. She dutifully plunged it into the bowl, fished out a chunk of chicken and a piece of green bean, brought the spoon to her lips, and burned them. "Hey!"

"Oh, I guess I should have warned you. It's hot."

"No kidding." Tricia put her spoon down on the paper napkin beside her bowl. She hadn't planned on mentioning Antonio Barbero—but in a fit of pique, decided to do just that. "Ginny's boyfriend came around just before she and Mr. Everett left for the day."

As predicted, Angelica winced at the reference to the man. "Don't tell me. He's already fishing to buy Deborah's store."

"He denied it, but from all the gossip going around the village, you just know that's what's going to happen."

"Do you think David would sell?"

"Not if Elizabeth has anything to say about it. But that's

the trouble—she probably won't. I'm sure Deborah left everything to David in her will. Isn't that what most married people do? That's what Christopher and I did."

"My last two marriages had prenups—neither Drew nor Gary were taking any chances. But then I made sure I was covered and did okay, anyway." Angelica leaned both elbows on the counter, resting her head on her hands. "And now that you're divorced, to whom have you left everything?" she inquired sweetly, and even batted her eyelashes.

Tricia frowned, but answered honestly anyway. "You— and a couple of charities."

Angelica's smile was beatific. "Me? You *are* my dear sweet sister. Have I mentioned lately how much I love you?"

Tricia's gaze narrowed. "I read a lot of murder mysteries where people are killed for inheritances, so don't suddenly invite me to go sailing in Portsmouth Harbor or anything else nefarious."

"Me, nefarious?" Angelica rolled her eyes. "If it makes you feel any better, I have left all my worldly possessions to you, too. And . . . maybe a few charities."

Maybe?

Tricia blew on her soup before commenting. "Great minds must think alike, after all."

The door to Booked for Lunch opened, and Bob Kelly stepped inside. "Am I interrupting anything, baby?"

Angelica sighed. Since she'd found out Bob had cheated on her earlier in the summer, her ardor had cooled considerably. But they still occasionally went out to dinner, and Bob tried unsuccessfully to mooch lunch off of her on a regular basis. Tricia turned back to her soup. By the look on Bob's face, he was about to start whining.

"What a day," he said, and took the stool next to Tricia. He sniffed the air. "Boy, that soup sure does smell good."

Angelica ignored the hint for a freebie. "What's up, Bob?"

"This has to be the worst day ever for Stoneham," he said, shaking his heard wearily.

"I'd say so," Tricia said, taking a spoonful of soup.

"I can't stop contemplating the slew of lawsuits that'll come from this mishap."

"Mishap?" Tricia asked. "There are two dead people— one of them my friend—and all you can call it is a mishap?"

"And all you can worry about are the lawsuits?" Angelica asked, just as incredulous.

"There's the whole bad PR angle to consider as well," Bob added, and reached for one of Tricia's packets of saltines on the counter. She slapped his wrist, taking back her crackers.

"I don't think you realize the position I'm in," Bob went on. "I hired that pilot. I suggested we hold the Founders' Day celebration. That leaves the Chamber of Commerce, the Board of Selectmen, and the whole village at risk of litigation."

"Who do you think will do the suing?" Angelica asked.

"David Black, for one. There's already talk that he's seen a lawyer."

"What?" Angelica asked. "His poor wife's only been dead a few hours."

Bob shrugged. "That's what I heard."

"Has anyone seen David?" Tricia asked. He wasn't her favorite person, but at the very least, she needed to offer her condolences.

Bob's gaze was intent upon her soup. "Not so far. At least he wasn't at the . . ." He paused, hesitating. "Accident scene."

"Some accident," Angelica said. "I've been wondering, why didn't the plane explode on impact?"

"That's the crazy thing. It looks like it was out of fuel."

"You're kidding," Tricia said.

Bob shook his head. "The firefighters were all set to hose down the area, expecting there to be a gas leak, but there wasn't any fuel on the ground."

"The plane ran out of gas," Angelica repeated, as though she couldn't believe such stupidity.

"Who was the pilot? Was he local?" Tricia asked.

"Monty Capshaw. He flew out of a grass airstrip north of Milford."

"Monty Capshaw," Angelica repeated. "Sounds like a movie star from the silent era. Did he wear a leather helmet and a bomber jacket?"

Bob shrugged. "He had on grease-stained coveralls the last time I saw him. Can I buy a bowl of soup from you, honeybun?"

Angelica's expression was bland. "Sorry, Bob, Tricia got the last bowl."

A flat-out lie. Still, Tricia took another spoonful of broth and closed her eyes, savoring the flavor. "Mmm-mmm, good."

Tricia left Booked for Lunch, intending to go straight home, but up ahead on the sidewalk she saw her friend Captain Baker from the Hillsborough County Sheriff's Department. Unfortunately, he was speaking to Russ Smith.

Still, Tricia decided to plunge ahead and picked up her pace to intercept them.

Fire and rescue trucks, and half the Sheriff's Department cruisers, lights still strobing madly, along with TV vans from Manchester and Nashua, still surrounded the village square. Ray Dempsey's lunch truck was also still in evidence, and by the crowd around his shiny chrome vehicle, it looked like business was booming.

Captain Baker looked up, saw Tricia approach, and the corners of his mouth quirked up.

"Hello, Grant," she said in greeting, ignoring Russ.

Baker sobered. "I'm so sorry about your friend, Tricia."

"Thank you." That he'd even remembered she and Deborah were friends said something about him. No wonder she liked him so much.

"They've taken the bodies away," Russ volunteered.

Not something Tricia was interested in knowing. She turned her attention back to Captain Baker. "Mr. Everett said you probably wouldn't head the investigation."

Captain Baker nodded. "We're glad to help with crowd control and the cleanup, but it'll be up to the National Transportation Safety Board to determine the cause of the crash. From what witnesses have said, the plane's engine had shut down. There was no explosion, no fire. From the looks of it, the pilot simply ran out of gas."

"Can I quote you on that?" Russ asked.

Baker frowned. "No."

Again, Tricia ignored Russ. "That's pretty much what Bob Kelly said. I don't understand how that could have happened."

"It's a known fact," Russ said. "More light aircraft

crashes are attributed to lack of fuel than any other cause, including pilot error—although if you ask me, not filling the gas tank is the biggest error a pilot could make."

Nobody asked you, Tricia was tempted to blurt, but thought better of it. Russ was really beginning to irritate her.

Tricia looked back to the fire and rescue trucks that blocked her view of the carnage. From where she stood, the gazebo wouldn't be in sight, anyway. Would she ever be able to walk past the once-charming park without thinking of Deborah and the terrible way she'd died? Unbidden tears began to form in Tricia's eyes, and she swallowed hard to keep them from spilling over.

"Mr. Smith tells me you witnessed the crash," Baker said, his voice soft.

Tricia nodded, and lowered her gaze so she didn't have to meet his eyes. "It was . . . horrible."

"Did you notice anything out of the ordinary before . . . ?" He let his words hang.

Tricia shook her head. "Only that the plane kept buzzing the crowd. I suppose so everyone would see the banner behind it."

"Have they tracked down the pilot's wife yet?" Russ asked.

"I wouldn't be at liberty to say," Baker said.

Russ shrugged. He'd find out somehow. Probably make nice with the reporters and crew from the TV stations—buy them coffee and plead that his weekly was hardly a threat to their up-to-the-minute coverage.

If Mrs. Capshaw was smart, she'd tell every member of the press "no comment" and take an extended vacation until the whole thing blew over. Then again, what would she have to tell him? If what Russ said was true, these kinds of crashes happened all the time. That fact brought Tricia no comfort—nor, she suspected, Deborah's survivors, either.

Baker looked back toward the crash site. One of his deputies signaled him. "If you'll excuse me," he said, and jogged toward the park again.

Russ waved a hand in front of Tricia's face, to pull her attention away from Baker's retreating form and back to him. "Tough day," he said.

"Very tough," she agreed.

"You should spend the evening with friends. How about me? I'll take you to dinner. It doesn't have to be here in town."

"No, thank you." He was the last person on the planet she wanted to be with. "I think I'll just go home to my cat and lose myself in a good book."

Russ nodded toward Haven't Got a Clue, where several people stood clustered around the entrance. "It doesn't look like you're going to get a quiet evening, after all."

Tricia recognized the women standing in front of her shop and barely said good-bye to Russ before jaywalking across the street. Before she even made it to her doorstep, Frannie Mae Armstrong lunged forward and burst into tears. "She's dead. Oh, Tricia, Deborah's dead!"

Tricia found herself patting Frannie's bony back, as the other women clustered around her. Nikki Brimfield, owner of the Patisserie, and Julia Overline hurried close, and Tricia found herself in the middle of a group hug, with much snuffling and wiping of eyes with damp tissues. The three women were all members of Haven't Got a Clue's Tuesday Night Book Club, as Deborah had been—not that she managed to make it to many meetings. But the women—and Mr. Everett—had shared a lot in the past two years. It was only natural they'd come together in their grief as well.

After what seemed like a full minute, Tricia managed to extricate herself from the warm, weepy mass of women and jangled her keys. "Come on inside and we'll commiserate."

Frannie tried to pull herself together, and the women waited for Tricia to open the door, turn on the lights, and usher them inside.

"Coffee, anyone?" she called.

Nikki raised a hand. "I'll make it." She'd done it before on nights when either Mr. Everett or Ginny had been unable to attend the club meetings, and Tricia let her. Tricia led the other two women to the reader's nook. Miss Marple had been sleeping on a pile of magazines. She raised herself, stretched, and began to purr as Frannie and Julia took their seats.

"I just can't believe it," Frannie said, and another tear seeped from her eye. Tricia was determined not to start crying, but just in case, she figured she'd better retrieve the box of tissues she kept under the cash desk.

"Now, now," Julia said, trying to comfort Frannie. "Deborah wouldn't want you tearing yourself up like this."

"I spoke with her only yesterday," Frannie said. When she was upset, her Texas twang grew more pronounced. "It was about the Founders' Day ceremony. I apologized because I couldn't be there. Now I'm so glad I wasn't. I don't think I could live with the memory."

Tricia winced. She was going to have to learn to live with that particular memory, and the thought of hashing it out again and again held no appeal, and she said so.

"Oh, Tricia, I had no idea," Frannie apologized, and Tricia took the third of the chairs, flopping into it. Immediately, Miss Marple crept across the table and arrived on her lap, giving her chin a friendly head butt, and revving her purrs into overdrive. Tricia petted the cat, wishing she could just go upstairs to her apartment, pour herself a glass of wine, and stop thinking about the day's events.

"I was in the Happy Domestic just this morning," Julia admitted. "I bought the cutest little decoupage waste basket, and a book on organizing the home." She sighed. "Poor Deborah. She was in such a state."

Nikki reappeared from the washroom with a pot full of water for the coffeemaker. "Why was she upset?"

Julia shrugged. "She was on the phone when I got there. I didn't hear much of the conversation—although she was whispering really loudly into the phone. And then she slammed down the receiver. She was so flushed, I thought for a moment she might faint, but when I asked if she was okay, she said she just needed a glass of water. She went in the back of the store and stayed there for the longest time. There were a couple of customers that needed to be waited on, and I found myself trying to help them find what they wanted. Finally, I had to call Deborah from the back room to take care of them. I wouldn't have felt right trying to use her cash register."

"What did she say when she finally came back into the store?" Tricia asked.

Julia shrugged. "Something about having to take care of the baby. But you know, I didn't hear him back there. And I could've sworn after I left that I saw Deborah's mother with the stroller walking up Main Street."

"That's odd," Frannie said, and looked thoughtful.

"Could you tell if it was a man or a woman she was talking to?" Tricia asked, curiosity getting the best of her.

Julia shook her head. "Deborah had her back to me through most of the conversation, and of course I didn't want her to think I was eavesdropping."

Tricia stifled a laugh. Knowing Julia, she must have been straining to hear every word.

"Do you remember anything she said?" Frannie asked. "It could be important."

Julia frowned, her brow furrowing in concentration. "Seems to me she said something about a gate. I have no idea what that would have meant."

That didn't make sense to Tricia, either.

"Tricia, I thought I saw you outside the Patisserie when it . . . when it happened," Nikki said, and choked on the last word. "You had little Davey, so you must've spoken to Deborah before the accident. Did she seem okay to you then?"

Tricia frowned. "She seemed nervous. I figured it was because she had to give a speech in front of half the village and a bunch of tourists. But maybe she *was* upset about her phone call. I guess we'll never know."

Nikki brought a tray with Haven't Got a Clue's paper cups that Tricia supplied for customers, some packets of sugar and sweetener, some nondairy creamer, and stir spoons. She set the tray on the nook's large square table, and passed out cups to everyone, before taking the only empty seat. "How about a toast to Deborah?"

The others nodded and looked toward Tricia to do the honors.

I will not cry. I will not cry.

She lifted her paper cup, and the others followed suit.

"To Deborah. We didn't know her as long as we would have liked—or as well. But she was our friend, and she will be terribly missed."

The others nodded, touched cups, and then drank.

They were silent for a long time, each of them mourning Deborah in her own way.

Tricia kept thinking about what Julia said. A gate. Why on earth would Deborah be talking about a gate, and why was she so angry?

Sadly, they would probably never know.

THREE

The next morning, Tricia awoke with the dawn, and leaving a sleepy Miss Marple in bed, she got up, dressed in sweats, and ran her usual four miles on the treadmill. She glanced at the clock. It had been twenty hours since Deborah's death. She had a feeling she'd be marking that occasion in hours and days for some time to come.

After showering and changing for the day, Tricia switched on her TV to find the Nashua TV stations had begun their newscasts with the crash story, although the reports didn't tell Tricia much more than she already knew or had seen for herself. As expected, the story topped that morning's *Nashua Telegraph*'s front page, too, along with several other related stories found on the inside pages. They, too, were of little value.

A look out Haven't Got a Clue's big display window proved that not much else had changed in Stoneham overnight. Amy Schram, from the Milford Nursery, watered the hanging geraniums that decorated Main Street. Customers were already flocking to the Coffee Bean for their first caffeine jolt of the day before heading to work.

Life went on without Deborah Black.

Tricia turned to take in her shop. Her first task: get the coffee ready. Maybe immersing herself in the mundane would insulate her from the pain of losing her friend—at least for a little while.

Ginny arrived some fifteen minutes before Haven't Got a Clue was to open. She was dry-eyed but pale. Had she, too, spent the night lying awake, thinking about the plane crash? "Good morning," she said, with none of her usual enthusiasm.

"Good morning. At least, let's hope it's better than yesterday afternoon," Tricia said.

"Amen," Ginny said, and stepped up to the cash desk. "You were much closer to Deborah than I was. If you don't feel like working this morning, I can handle things here in the shop."

"Oh, no. I'm fine."

Ginny frowned. "Tricia, sometimes I get the feeling you don't trust me."

Tricia's mouth dropped. "What?"

"I mean, I've been working for you for over two years. The only time you let me open and close for you was when Angelica broke her ankle and you had to take care of her. But since then, you haven't asked me to open or close once. I've never gone to the bank for you. You've never even given me a key to the store."

Tricia swallowed and felt her face flush. "Oh, Ginny. I . . . I don't know what to say."

Everything Ginny had said was true, but it wasn't a lack of trust that kept Tricia from giving her more responsibility. "I'm always here," she explained. "It didn't seem necessary to—" *Excuses, excuses*, a little voice inside Tricia said. Ginny had never before voiced a grievance. What had brought this on?

And then Tricia realized what—or rather who—was behind this.

Antonio Barbero. As the in-town representative of Nigela Racita Associates, he'd already poached Angelica's short-order cook for the Brookview Inn—what was he planning now? And then she remembered. He'd already voiced an interest in obtaining the Happy Domestic for his employer. Was he considering installing Ginny as manager? Did he feel she was too loyal to Tricia? Was Ginny more likely to leave Haven't Got a Clue if she felt unappreciated or undervalued?

Since Antonio and Ginny were romantically involved, it wouldn't do for Tricia to criticize him in any way. Instead, she spoke from the heart.

"I'm sorry, Ginny. It hadn't occurred to me that you might want more responsibility. You already do so much around here. I've been very happy with your work."

"And you pay me very well, I'm certainly not complaining about that. It's just that . . ."

Tricia tried to ignore her annoyance. Damn that Antonio for filling Ginny's head with the seeds of dissatisfaction so that he could swoop in and . . .

Ginny crossed the store and set her purse under the glass display case that served as a cash desk. "I was surprised to see the Happy Domestic is open this morning," she said, changing the subject.

"What?" Tricia crossed to the window. Sure enough, the lights were on inside Deborah's shop, and the CLOSED sign had been turned to OPEN. Tricia bit her lip and considered her options. Stay here with Ginny and continue a conversation that needed resolution, or escape and find out what was going on at the Happy Domestic.

"I think I'll head over and see what's going on across the street. If you don't mind."

"If you trust me to handle things here while you're gone," Ginny said, somewhat testily.

Tricia ignored the remark. "I'll be back as soon as I can."

Ginny nodded, and Tricia headed out the door, already dreading her return.

She turned the brass door handle and pushed open the heavy wood and glass door to the Happy Domestic. Cheerful harp music played on the store's stereo system, belying the sadness she felt at entering the comfortable, eclectic shop she knew so well. Deborah had done a wonderful job with her displays, and the scent of potpourri was never overpowering. Everything was perfect—just the way Deborah had left it the day before.

Elizabeth stood next to a set of glass display shelves, feather duster in hand. From somewhere in the back of the store, Tricia heard little Davey singing an unintelligible version of the alphabet song.

"Elizabeth?"

Deborah's mother turned, her eyes bloodshot and puffy. She looked as though she hadn't slept in a week. "Tricia. Thank you for coming over." She lurched toward Tricia and embraced her in a tight hug. Tricia patted her back, not knowing what else to do.

At last, Elizabeth pulled back and wiped her eyes.

"I was surprised to see the open sign," Tricia said.

"David wanted me to close the doors for good, but I just couldn't. I didn't know what to do with myself, either. I mean, it's up to David to make the"—her voice broke—"funeral arrangements." Fighting tears, Tricia reached out, rested a hand on Elizabeth's arm, waiting for her to recover. She sniffed and straightened. "He's made it clear he doesn't want any input from the rest of Deborah's family."

"When will the service be held?" Tricia asked.

"David's scheduled it for tomorrow morning at nine over at the Baker Funeral Home."

"Tomorrow?" Tricia repeated, disbelieving.

"That hardly gives my girls Paige and Terry time to get here to say good-bye. Although . . . it won't be an open coffin." Elizabeth's lower lip trembled and her eyes filled with tears.

Tricia reached out again and placed a comforting hand on Elizabeth's arm. She didn't even want to imagine the horrific injuries Deborah had incurred. The rescue workers had shrouded the crash site with tarps, keeping the curious at bay, and then removed the bodies in black zippered bags.

Scheduling the funeral an hour before all the stores opened meant the owners, many of whom did not have employees to cover for them, would not have to forgo the service or close their stores.

A stuffed blue bunny sailed through the air and landed at Tricia's feet. A baby gate held little Davey penned in the small office at the back of the store. She picked up the toy and returned it to its owner, who promptly began to chew its ear.

Tricia studied the wooden baby gate that stood about

three feet tall and kept Davey from entering and destroying the delicate glassware and other items on the shop's shelves. Could that be the gate that Julia had mentioned the day before? It didn't seem likely.

Elizabeth wiped her eyes and sniffed. "Davey lost his blankie a few weeks back, and it takes real effort to get him off to sleep. Last night was the worst. I don't know if it's just because he misses Deborah or he doesn't like being in a strange crib at night."

"Strange crib?"

"He's been with me since . . . since yesterday."

"Shouldn't he be with his father?" Tricia said, then instantly regretted it. Her tone had held a touch of reproach.

Elizabeth shrugged. "David says he can't deal with the baby right now. Not with everything else on his mind. I can't say I blame him."

That seemed wrong on so many levels.

Elizabeth sniffed again, turning to look down on her grandson. "Any day now, Davey's going to figure out how to scale that barrier, and then I don't know what I'll do. I can't watch him *and* run the store."

"I thought Deborah had hired help."

"I had to let Cheryl go. Until I know what'll happen with the store, I can't afford to spend money foolishly."

Tricia remembered a conversation she'd had with Mr. Everett earlier in the summer. He'd been willing to help out at Deborah's store. She imagined he'd be even more eager to help out now. Back in June, he'd won the New Hampshire Powerball lottery and had since been hounded by people looking for handouts. "I spoke to Deborah at the beginning of the summer about loaning her one of my employees at no cost to her. That offer's still open."

Instead of replying, Elizabeth leapt forward and hugged Tricia once again. "Thank you. I don't know how I can ever repay you, but I'll gladly take you up on it."

Tricia pulled back. "As it happens, Mr. Everett is looking for a change of scenery in the short term. This should work out well for both of you."

Elizabeth managed a weak smile. "Thank you for being Deborah's friend. She always spoke well of you."

Tricia fought back a tear. "I'm glad I can help." She swallowed hard, trying to appear strong. "I'd better get going. I have a store to run."

Elizabeth nodded. "Thank you for stopping by. And thank you for sending Mr. Everett. I can sure use the help."

She walked Tricia to the door and closed it behind her.

Tricia looked right and left, intending to cross the street, then noticed someone standing within the cordoned-off village square. The NTSB investigator? There was only one way to find out. Tricia struck off for the park.

The carnival rides and other equipment had already vacated the small park, leaving behind trampled grass and scattered litter. Tricia paused on the sidewalk to watch as a man with a clipboard walked the perimeter of the park. He jotted down a note and then raised the camera that had been slung around his neck. "Hello," she called.

The man looked up.

"Are you the NTSB investigator?"

The man frowned, and his gaze shifted suspiciously. "Why do you ask?"

Tricia's gaze moved to the rut in the ground where the plane had ripped up the sod before coming to rest. "My friend was killed here yesterday."

The man stepped closer. "Mrs. Black?"

Tricia nodded, and held out her hand. "I'm Tricia Miles. I run the mystery bookstore here in the village—Haven't Got a Clue."

The man shook on it. "Steve Marsden. Sorry about your loss." The words were mechanical, what everyone who deals with the bereaved is trained to say. Still, Tricia appreciated hearing them said.

"Have you determined what happened?" she asked.

Marsden's cell phone rang. "Hang on a minute. I've got to take this call," he said, opened the phone, and turned away. "Yeah, what have you got for me . . . ?"

Tricia sighed. He wasn't going to get away without answering some of her questions. She turned, looking for one of the benches that wasn't within the roped off perimeter, and saw Cheryl Griffin sitting on one. Tears streamed from beneath the woman's glasses. She held a damp tissue against her nose, her gaze focused on the bare patch of ground where the plane had come to a sudden halt the day before.

Tricia felt herself drawn to the grieving woman, who'd worked for Deborah for the past month or so. She didn't know her well but had met her a couple of times when she'd stopped in the Happy Domestic. "Cheryl," she called softly. "Are you okay?"

Cheryl looked up. "Tricia?"

Tricia sat down next to her. "Can I help?"

"Not unless you've got a job opening."

The question caused a chill to run down Tricia's neck. "Sorry, not right now."

Cheryl nodded and blew her nose. "I talked to every bookseller on Main Street before Deborah hired me. I doubt they have openings, either. Deborah could only afford to pay me minimum wage, but at least it was money coming in, you know?"

Tricia nodded, feeling sorry for the thin, pitiable woman—and a little guilty. She had to be about the same age as Tricia. Deborah had commented that she had little in the way of marketable job skills, but that she was better than having no one working with her at the Happy Domestic.

Maybe it was the ill-fitting clothes Cheryl wore or her slouching posture and too-large glasses that screamed "GEEK!" But then Tricia could identify with that. She'd worn glasses for years before undergoing Lasik eye surgery, and she'd been branded a nerd by the more popular girls in high school, who wouldn't have been caught dead reading for pleasure, let alone reading vintage mysteries. Thankfully, she'd blossomed in college, where nobody seemed to care much about what she read or did. She doubted Cheryl had ever visited the halls of higher education.

"Is there a reason you don't look for a job in Nashua or even in Milford?" Tricia asked.

"Oh, yeah—a big reason. I don't have a car. The Bank of Stoneham repossessed it in April after I lost my job at Shaw's in Nashua and couldn't make the payments."

Tricia refrained from asking why Cheryl had been let go. Probably just the slowdown in the economy. Lots of establishments had had to trim staff. She was glad she hadn't had to do that.

"I've got three weeks to find something before my rent is due," Cheryl continued. "It's too bad they don't pay you for blood anymore. That, I have plenty of. And I haven't got anything left that I can sell after all I've been through this past year."

Tricia swallowed and felt guilty because she was so well off, without a financial care in the world. And yet, bailing out Cheryl would only be a temporary solution. Should she offer her help, or would Cheryl take it as an insult?

"You know why there's a problem finding jobs?" Cheryl said with a knowing nod of the head. "Illegal aliens took them all. I heard on TV that there are millions of them living among us right here in the US of A. All I can say is, they've got really good disguises, 'cuz I haven't seen any that look like ET or Vulcans or Klingons or nothin'."

Tricia covered her mouth with her hand, trying to keep a straight face, because it was evident Cheryl was dead serious. "I don't think the news media was talking about extraterrestrials."

"I don't care what they've got extra—I just don't want them to capture me and encase me in carbonite or make me a slave, mining borate on some distant planet."

"Ohhh-kay," Tricia said, and realized how Deborah had gotten away with paying Cheryl only minimum wage. The poor woman was clueless, if not delusional. She'd never be able to appreciate the clever puzzles laid in most mysteries. Heck, had she even read a Nancy Drew novel?

Tricia let her gaze wander back to the investigator stomping through the square's grassy expanse. Finally, Marsden folded his phone and looked back down at the clipboard in his hand.

"If you'll excuse me, I need to speak to the NTSB investigator," Tricia said, grateful for a chance to escape.

"The who?" Cheryl asked.

Tricia pointed at the man across the way. "Him."

Cheryl stood. "Thanks for talking to me, Tricia. I feel

better now. Maybe I'll call the unemployment office to see if anyone in Stoneham has posted a job."

Tricia patted Cheryl's arm. "Good luck." She watched as Cheryl headed down the sidewalk and turned left, heading out of town on foot, and then Tricia marched across the lawn to catch up with Marsden once again.

"Mr. Marsden!" she called. He looked at her as if he'd forgotten they'd met only minutes before. Again, she introduced herself and repeated her question. "Have you determined what happened?"

Marsden stared at her. "Ma'am, it's been less than twenty-four hours since the crash. It'll be months before I make my final report."

"I realize that," Tricia said. "I mean, does it look like it was strictly pilot error?"

"I've hardly had a chance to gather many facts, let alone make that kind of determination."

Tricia pursed her lips. She should have known better than to expect any answers from a federal bureaucrat.

"Months, you say?" she tried again.

He nodded, looking a little bored.

Tricia sighed. It was no use even trying to engage the man in conversation. "I'll let you get back to your work."

"Thank you." He turned without acknowledging her further and again consulted his clipboard.

Tricia turned and headed back for Haven't Got a Clue.

Months. It could take months before a determination was made about the accident.

Tricia felt heat rise from her neck to color her cheeks. Maybe she was impatient, but she didn't want to wait that long to hear whatever it was Steve Marsden and the NTSB had to say about the crash. What kind of idiot of a pilot lets his plane run out of gas? And just because Russ said it happened all the time didn't mean it happened to Monty Capshaw. He wasn't a kid, and presumably he'd been flying for years without incident.

Bob Kelly had to know something about the man. After all, he'd hired him. Tricia reversed course and started north once again, heading for Kelly Realty. Bob had to know a lot more than he'd admitted the afternoon before. Somehow Tricia was going to have to get him to talk.

Or else.

FOUR

 Bob Kelly's car was parked in front of his real estate office, but the locked door and CLOSED sign hanging in the window indicated he wasn't in. Tricia backtracked two doors down to the log cabin that housed the Stoneham Chamber of Commerce. Bob had been its president for at least a decade and often held court there. As owner of most of the real estate on Main Street, he controlled the rents and was the recipient of most of the prosperity that had come to Stoneham.

Prim, proper, and middle-aged Betsy Dittmeyer, the Chamber's secretary for almost eighteen months, was not as friendly as her predecessor, Frannie May Armstrong. Nor was she a fount of useful information. A stickler for rules and regulations, she seemed to have memorized the Chamber's bylaws, as well as some receptionist's handbook, and played more of a gatekeeper's role—shielding Bob from those he didn't want to see. Tricia might well be on that list, so she decided it would be best to act as sweetly as possible when dealing with Betsy.

"Good morning, Betsy. Lovely day, isn't it?"

Betsy's mouth drooped, her eyes narrowing. "How can I help you, Ms. Miles?"

She was as cold as a day in January.

"I'd like to talk to Bob."

Betsy lifted the receiver. "I'll see if he's in."

Of course he was in. Tricia could see him behind the glass divide, hunched over his desk, intently staring at the papers scattered across it. The phone buzzed, and Bob picked it up.

"Ms. Tricia Miles is here to see you, Mr. Kelly."

Tricia watched as Bob's shoulders sagged. He looked up, saw her, and without enthusiasm motioned her to come in. He mouthed something to Betsy, but Tricia didn't wait for the reception's permission to move. She walked past Betsy's desk to Bob's office door and entered.

"Am I disturbing you, Bob?" she asked, and closed the door behind her.

He gestured to one of his guest chairs. "No." His tone was more weary than welcoming.

Tricia decided to drop the pretense and get straight down to business. "I just spoke with the investigator from the NTSB."

Bob nodded. "I talked to him earlier." He didn't offer anything else on the subject.

Tricia looked over the sheaf of stapled papers spread across Bob's desk. Contracts? He'd said he was worried about liability; no doubt he was checking the exact wording. Had he already spoken to the Chamber's legal counsel?

"I can't tell you how upset this whole situation has made me. I know you must feel the same." But for entirely different reasons, she knew. "Did you personally know the pilot, Monty Capshaw?"

Bob's gaze dipped to the papers on his desk.

"It's going to come out eventually, anyway," Tricia said.

Bob sighed. "Monty and I were old school pals. I hadn't spoken to him in at least five years when we talked about the Founders' Day celebration."

"And what did the conversation entail?" Tricia asked.

"We talked about him flying the banner over the village. He wanted to supply it, too, but I nixed that. The Chamber gave the job to one of our members, Stan Berry, the guy with the sign shop in his garage over on Pine Avenue."

"I met him at one of the Chamber breakfasts," Tricia said, mentally putting a face to the name.

"He did a real good job on it. Too bad it got torn all to shreds. We could've used it at other functions."

Tricia had to bite her tongue not to chastise Bob for being so cheap. Losing the banner was the least of the losses from that plane crash. She let it go. "Tell me about Monty," she said, her voice soft.

Bob shrugged. "He had a little puddle jumper outside of Milford. He told me he needed the work. I guess things hadn't been going well in the air transport business of late."

"What kind of services did he offer?"

"Mainly picking up parts or contracts and ferrying them to nearby cities. Back in the day, he flew to Boston on a regular basis, taking off from all the little strips around here. He was based outside of Milford but flew to Rochester and Concord all the time. Then the market tanked and . . . well, you know how it goes."

She sure did. Too many people lost their livelihoods when the economy took a nosedive. Tricia had been among the few who had not only hung on but somehow made a profit. Angelica had done the same. Sadly, not all their fellow Chamber members had been so lucky.

"Did you know much about Mr. Capshaw's experience? I mean, you did check his references and the like, right?"

Bob's gaze dipped once again. "He was an old school pal. I hadn't heard anything bad about him—and believe me, I hear all the dirt. As far as I knew, everything was on the up-and-up. This was just a tragic accident, Tricia. And I'm sure the NTSB is going to rule it as such."

Then why had he been intently going over contracts and insurance forms?

Tricia saw the letterhead for CAPSHAW AERONAUTICS on the top pile of papers. Oh, how she longed to just snatch up the papers and run with them, but even she wasn't that eager to suffer Bob's ire. She tried another tack.

"I'm sorry, Bob. I didn't know Mr. Capshaw was your friend. You're probably suffering just as much as the rest of us who are mourning Deborah's death."

"She was my friend, too, you know." Bob actually sounded hurt, as though no one had considered his feelings. The fact that he seldom showed any emotion might have had something to do with that, but Tricia decided to be charitable. "The funeral is tomorrow morning at nine."

He nodded. "I'll make a point to be there."

There didn't seem to be much more to add to the decidedly one-sided conversation. Bob could be tight-lipped when he wanted—and now seemed like one of those times.

Tricia stood. "I'd better get back to my store. Elizabeth

needs help over at the Happy Domestic, and I promised to loan her Mr. Everett."

"That's very generous of you Tricia. You've always been a kind person."

Tricia swallowed. It wasn't like Bob to hand out compliments. Part of her was willing to take his words at face value. The other part . . . wasn't so sure.

Mr. Everett had arrived by the time Tricia made it back to Haven't Got a Clue. Ginny was busy helping a customer, and Tricia made her way to the back of the store and the biographical shelves, where Mr. Everett was busy with what seemed like his favorite pursuit: dusting.

"Good morning, Ms. Miles. And how are you this lovely day?"

"Still sad, I'm afraid."

Mr. Everett nodded. "Yes, as am I and Grace. Mrs. Black was a lovely woman."

"Yes, she was." Tricia waited a moment before continuing. "Mr. Everett, back in June we talked about you helping out at the Happy Domestic. Would you still be willing to do so? Mrs. Crane, Deborah's mother, could really use your help."

"I'd be very happy to help out."

He looked like he was about to say something more, when the woman Ginny had been speaking with raised her purse and waved it at Tricia and Mr. Everett. "Yoo-hoo! William Everett! May I speak to you for a moment? It's about my son." She hurried forward, her face flushed, her eyes gleaming like those of a rabid raccoon. "He's a brilliant boy—and his scholarship money was canceled. Those

idiots at Avery Metal Fabricators decided to yank the financial rug right out from under him, and—"

Mr. Everett sighed. He listened for a moment more and
then interrupted the woman, handing her a business card.
"I'm sorry, ma'am, but you'll have to make your request in
writing. There are forms on our Website."

"But I want to tell you in person just how deserving my
boy is—"

"I'm sorry, ma'am, but I don't make the determination
of who gets how much. The chairman of our gift-giving
committee makes the decision based on need. Now, please,
unless you wish to make a purchase here at Haven't Got a
Clue, I'm afraid I cannot help you."

The woman took the card with bad grace, shoving it into
her purse. "Well, of all the selfish, hard-hearted bastards,"
she growled, turned on her heel, and stalked toward the exit.

A dejected Mr. Everett sighed. "Ms. Miles, I'm sorry
that all these . . . these money grubbers keep showing up
here at Haven't Got a Clue. Since the newspapers and TV
stations reported where I live and work, I can't get away
from them. Winning that lottery money was the worst thing
that could have happened to us."

People looking for a handout had become more than a
slight inconvenience, and Tricia felt sorry for Mr. Everett
and his wife, Grace. They'd been the victims of boorish
behavior far more than she had. It was Grace who'd set up
the Everett Charitable Foundation, took care of the Website, and gave out the grants, while Mr. Everett did his best
to keep a low profile.

"Don't worry about it. Now, getting back to the subject
of the Happy Domestic, would you mind going over there
right now?"

"Not at all." He surrendered his Haven't Got a Clue apron, put away his lambs'-wool duster, and grabbed the Red Sox baseball cap he'd recently taken to wearing. "If anyone asks for me, please don't tell them where I've gone—unless it's Grace, of course."

"You have my word," Tricia promised, and smiled. "But I can't guarantee people won't go looking for you. It's happened before."

Mr. Everett sighed. "That's true. I do wish I could don a disguise. I wonder, should I grow a moustache?"

"How about one like Hercule Poirot's," Tricia suggested as she walked him toward the exit.

Mr. Everett scowled. "I was thinking more like Tom Selleck."

"That would look good, too," Tricia agreed, and tried not to laugh.

"I think I should have started back in June." He paused at the doorway. "Would you like me to report in here at Haven't Got a Clue this evening after I leave the Happy Domestic?"

"That won't be necessary."

"Then I shall have Mrs. Crane verify my work time."

"Very good," Tricia agreed.

"I'd be happy to work there tomorrow, too," he said.

"Deborah's funeral is planned for tomorrow. I don't think they'll be opening."

"So soon?" Mr. Everett asked. Tricia nodded. "What about Sunday?" he asked.

"If Elizabeth decides to open, I can always ask Ginny to work here, and if she can't, I'm sure I can manage on my own for a day. I'll call you later should anything change."

Mr. Everett nodded and then pulled his ball cap down

low on his brow and opened the door. He poked his head outside, took a furtive glance around, gave her a quick good-bye, and then exited the store, pulling the door shut behind him.

"Sorry about that," Ginny apologized. "I tried to steer that woman toward Grace's Website, but when she saw Mr. Everett standing there . . ."

"I'm sure it's not the last time it'll happen. I feel so sorry for both of them. All Mr. Everett wanted to do was pay off his debts. And now he's being hounded night and day by a bunch of deadbeats."

"Alleged deadbeats," Ginny clarified. Tricia wasn't sure if she was being funny or serious. "Did I hear you say something to Mr. Everett about me working Sunday?"

"If you wouldn't mind."

"I'd be glad to. Antonio is going to be busy all day, so it'll give me something to fill the hours."

Busy how? Tricia wondered. Any time Antonio was too busy to spend a weekend with Ginny, that meant things were heating up at Nigela Racita Associates.

And why did the thought worry her so?

The lunch crowd at Booked for Lunch was long gone by the time Tricia showed up for her customary late lunch. This day, she was *very* late.

"I didn't think you were going to make it today." Angelica said, and got up from her stool, scooting around the counter. She hadn't waited for Tricia, as evidenced by the plate covered with whole wheat crumbs that sat on the counter. She'd spread out the manuscript pages of her next cookbook and had been going over them with a red pen.

Angelica stooped to retrieve something from the little under-the-counter fridge and set the plastic-wrapped plate in front of Tricia.

"Thanks. Got any soup left?"

"Sorry, Tommy already cleaned the kitchen. There wasn't much chicken noodle left, so I think he dumped it."

Tricia frowned.

"Believe me, much as I loved Jake, he thought of himself as a chef, not a short-order cook, and he didn't do a lot of cleanup. I'm thrilled that Tommy doesn't mind washing dishes and scrubbing pots."

"So you've gotten over the Brookville Inn stealing Jake?"

Angelica scowled. "It wasn't the Brookville Inn that stole him from me. It was Nigela Racita Associates."

"Ah, yes," Tricia said, and uncovered her lunch, balling up the wrap and setting it aside. "But you said it was a good career move for him."

"Of course it was. And I was the first to be served dinner the night he started there. I like to think it was me who set him up for greatness."

"Jake? Greatness?"

Angelica frowned. "Obviously you haven't eaten at the inn since he took over the kitchen. Their last chef was pretty damn good. Jake is better."

"You know I haven't eaten there lately."

"Then I will take you there and treat you. What are you doing tonight?"

"I don't know that I want to go out. I think I'd rather stay home and read."

"You've been doing a little too much of that lately. Pining over Captain Baker maybe?"

"No! It's just . . . Deborah's death has really depressed me. I don't feel like going out and celebrating—anything. By the way, I loaned out Mr. Everett to Elizabeth for a few days. *And* Ginny's upset with me."

Angelica blinked. "Because you loaned out Mr. Everett?"

"No. She thinks I don't trust her."

"Okay, I'm confused."

Tricia stabbed a forkful of tuna and related the conversation she'd had with Ginny that morning.

"You've always said she was the best assistant in Stoneham. And if that's true, doesn't it seem rather suspicious you haven't given her more responsibility?" Angelica asked.

"It isn't a question of trust—or even responsibility. I'm on the premises most of the day. I don't stray very far from the store—which is also where I live, I might add. There's simply been no reason for her to open or close for me."

Angelica leveled a narrow gaze at her sister. "You're a workaholic."

"I am not!"

"You're worse than Daddy ever was."

"That's not true," Tricia said, but it did seem to be the one trait she'd inherited from their father.

"Admit it, you can't stand to sit still—unless you've got a mystery in your hands, and then the world stops. If you ask me, you've dug yourself into a rut. If you want to go out with Captain Baker—ask him to take you out, or you invite *him* to dinner."

"You know I can't cook much of anything."

"That's why the Brookview Inn has a catering menu, dear."

"They do? How do you know?"

"I make it my business to know what every other eatery in the area is serving and what other ventures they're involved in."

That made sense. Tricia took another bite of tuna. Tommy made it differently than Jake. She couldn't put her finger on just what it was—not so much the taste . . . maybe the texture. There weren't as many crunchy bits. Yes, Jake had added more diced celery. Tricia had gotten used to it that way and now found she missed it. Not that she'd ever let Tommy—or Angelica—know it.

Angelica slipped on her reading glasses that had been hanging from a cord on her neck, and turned her attention back to her manuscript. "Have you heard anything else about the crash investigation?"

"Only that it'll take months before they make a determination."

"That's ridiculous. Bob said the plane ran out of gas. End of inquiry."

"If only it was that easy." Tricia sighed and set her fork aside. "I feel like I should be doing more," she said.

"What? Helping the cops figure this out?"

"Don't be silly. And, anyway, it's not the Sheriff's Department that'll be investigating. It's the National Transportation Safety Board."

Angelica waved a hand in the air. "Whatever."

"I thought David might have called me—maybe asked me to help plan Deborah's service. But, then, he hasn't even asked any of Deborah's family for input."

Angelica sighed in exasperation. Looking over her glasses and down her nose at Tricia, she leveled her index finger at her. "See, I told you you're a workaholic. So what if David hasn't asked for your help. You've given Mr. Everett to Elizabeth to work in the store. That will bring in income until David decides what to do with it—and knowing you, you'll be paying Mr. Everett's wages. Short of adopting little Davey, what else can you do?"

Tricia thought about it for a few moments. "I could collect money for Davey—maybe set up a scholarship fund for him."

"Unless he's a boy genius, the kid won't be going to college for at least sixteen years," Angelica pointed out.

"That'll give the money time to accrue interest."

"Not at the ridiculous rates banks are offering these days." Angelica stared at her sister for a long moment and then shrugged. "Whatever," she said again. It was beginning to annoy Tricia.

"Will you donate something?" she asked.

"Sure, I can spare fifty bucks."

Tricia gave her sister the evil eye.

"Okay, a hundred. Are you going to go door to door like you did when Jim Roth died?"

"Probably. And I'm going to hit up Antonio Barbero for a very big contribution. If Nigela Racita Associates is plotting to take over Deborah's store, the least they can do is contribute to her son's education."

"Isn't that kind of a double whammy? I mean, won't Davey be on the receiving end of whatever his father gets for the business?" Angelica asked.

"Not necessarily. The louse could remarry or blow the money on fast cars and fancy women."

Angelica scowled. "You really *don't* like David, do you?"

"Not especially." Tricia lifted her hand and rubbed her

fingers together several times. "Come on, write out a check?"

Angelica got up and stomped around the counter once again. She pulled out her purse from underneath and reached for her checkbook, then paused. "Who am I supposed to make it out to? You? The Davey Black Education Fund?" She placed the checkbook back into her purse and stowed it under the counter again. "Maybe you need to think this through before you rush into it. It might be that you should hit the bank first and set up an account for the kid."

"That's a good idea. I could make Elizabeth the trustee, and then no matter what happens with David in the future, Davey will be all set."

"Don't you think you'd better ask her first?"

"Do you honestly think she's going to refuse?"

"No. But it doesn't hurt to ask. Besides, it's just good manners."

"I guess you're right. I'll give her a call and see if she can meet me at the bank sometime soon."

"Why wait? Do it now." Back out came the purse, and Angelica handed Tricia her cell phone.

Two minutes later, it was a done deal. With Mr. Everett willing to cover for her, Elizabeth agreed to meet Tricia at the bank in fifteen minutes.

Tricia folded Angelica's phone and handed it back to her, then picked up her fork and continued to eat her lunch. Angelica shuffled her pages and stacked them in a neat pile. "I'm not getting any work done here. I may as well go home."

"The book not going well?" Tricia asked.

"It would be going a lot better if I weren't doing another

Easy-Does-It cookbook. I thought I'd be getting my foot in the publishing door with the first one, and then they'd let me do something a little more creative. But no. Now they want the same thing, only different. Why did I have to be so successful my first time out?"

Tricia laughed. "I'll bet that's a problem a lot of authors would love to have." She'd certainly heard it enough at the author signings she'd hosted over the past two years.

Angelica stood. "Have you thought about what you're going to say to David when he finds out you've made Elizabeth guardian of Davey's scholarship money?"

"Why do I have to tell him anything?"

Angelica raised her arms as though in surrender. "It's going to get around, and I don't think he's going to be pleased. Everyone knows he doesn't like you."

"Who's everyone?"

Angelica sighed, but didn't bother to reply.

"Besides, I don't like him, either. And after Deborah's funeral, I never have to put up with him again."

"Stoneham is a small village," Angelica pointed out, "and you know how things get ugly when the townspeople stick up for one of their own and shun the newcomers."

"David and Deborah were originally from somewhere on Long Island, not natives of Stoneham. And the villagers have hardly embraced the booksellers."

"They're coming around," Angelica said. "And I'm counting on them eating here at Booked for Lunch when the winter rolls around and the tourists stay home until spring."

Tricia ate her last bite of tuna and pushed the plate away. "You worry too much."

"With all the bodies you've found in this town, I'd think you'd be a little more concerned."

Tricia blinked, taken aback. "Do you honestly think David would threaten me over something as innocuous as setting up a scholarship fund for his son?"

"Of course not. But you've already interfered by loaning Mr. Everett to work in Deborah's store—a store David wants to close as soon as possible."

"Where did you hear that?"

"Everybody's talking about it."

Tricia was getting tired of hearing about *everybody*—especially if Angelica wasn't willing or able to identify who they were. "I'm not afraid of David Black."

"Well, maybe you ought to be. Deborah was," Angelica said casually. "And now she's dead."

FIVE

 Tricia stared at her sister, unable to believe what she'd just heard. "Aren't you the one who told me the crash was an accident?"

"Of course it was," Angelica said. "And wasn't it handy that it came at a time when the Blacks were having marital problems?"

"They argued about the amount of time Deborah spent at the store—I'll grant you that. But they weren't on the verge of divorce, either."

"That's not what Frannie says."

"Frannie?"

"Well, she lives on the same street as Deb and David. All the neighbors knew about their shouting matches— usually at night when people wanted to sleep."

Tricia wasn't sure how to react to that news. She'd thought Deborah had told her everything. She'd certainly complained about David often enough, but she hadn't mentioned that their marriage was as strained as Angelica—more likely, Frannie—had indicated. And why hadn't Frannie mentioned it the previous evening when members of the Tuesday Night Book Club came to Haven't Got a Clue to commiserate?

Tricia glanced at her watch. She had to meet Elizabeth at the bank, so there was no chance she could talk to Frannie any time soon. And she couldn't ask Elizabeth such a question in the bank for everyone to hear.

Tricia pursed her lips, angry at herself for succumbing to idle gossip. And if what Angelica said was true, she felt a little hurt, too, that Deborah hadn't been as honest with her as she'd thought.

She got up from her stool, carried her dishes into the kitchen, and dumped them into the slop sink. By the time she came back into the dining room, Angelica had gathered her manuscript and her purse and had her key out ready to lock up.

"When shall I tell Frannie you'll be over to talk to her?" Angelica asked, with just a touch of a sneer in her voice.

"I have no plans to talk to Frannie today."

"I'll tell her you'll see her tomorrow then, shall I?"

Tricia gave her sister a sour smile. "Thank you for the lunch. I'll see you later."

"Today? I thought your plan was to spend the evening with your cat and a book."

"I *am* a woman of mystery," Tricia reminded her.

"Since when?" Angelica asked as she ushered Tricia toward the door.

The answer was since she'd opened a mystery bookstore. And it had been a long time since she'd felt this awkward and unsure—high school, in fact. But Angelica seemed to have the knack to take her back to those feelings with only a couple of sentences.

"Has anybody ever accused you of being a bully?" Tricia asked, stopping dead.

Angelica nearly ran into her. "Of course. And I'm working on it."

"How's that? By bullying more or less?" Tricia asked.

"Go to the bank!" Angelica ordered, and pushed Tricia toward the door once again.

"Yes, ma'am."

"And don't call me ma'am!"

"Yes, Your Highness."

"That's better."

Angelica closed and locked the café's door.

The Bank of Stoneham was filled with customers, people eager to deposit their paychecks and obtain cash for the weekend, when Tricia entered. Elizabeth waited for her, sitting in a chair reserved for those in line to speak to a customer service rep. All of them were busy, so it was Billie Hanson, the bank's stocky manager, who called them to her office and personally took care of them.

"That does it for the paperwork," Billie said at last, and held up a finger, indicating they should wait a moment before leaving. "Let me get you a folder to put your deposit slips and other papers in. I'll be right back." She rose from her chair and left Tricia and Elizabeth sitting in the two visitor chairs in front of her desk.

Elizabeth turned to Tricia and wiped a few tears from her eyes. "I can't thank you enough, for everything you've done for us. Mr. Everett has already been such a help—and now this for Davey." She pulled a wadded tissue from her purse and pressed it against her nose. "I can't believe everything that's happened since yesterday. And to make matters worse, David's already accepted an offer on Deborah's store."

"Oh, Elizabeth. I'm so sorry."

"My daughter has only been dead twenty-six hours and already that man has sold off her most valuable asset."

"How could anyone be so cold?" Tricia asked, and yet she had to voice the question that was burning on her tongue. "Was it to—?"

"Nigela Racita Associates," Elizabeth finished with a nod and a scowl.

"Shouldn't you have done an inventory first? Shouldn't there have been—"

"David asked me last night for a ball-park estimate on what the store was worth. Apparently, they offered fifty thousand more than my figure."

"That is generous." Especially since Deborah's store hadn't been all that profitable. If nothing else, no one could say Nigela Racita Associates wasn't at least giving fair-market value for the assets it obtained. Picking up the Happy Domestic meant that in the space of two months, the development company now owned three local enterprises. Perhaps it was time to find out a little more about the firm. Tricia made a mental date for later that evening with her computer and Google.

Tricia glanced at her watch. "I'd better get back to my store. I've been missing half the day. Ginny's probably . . ." She hesitated. *Happy about it*, she thought, but aloud she finished, "Wondering if I fell off the planet." She stood.

"Thank you again, Tricia."

Tricia bent down and gave Elizabeth a hug before leaving the cubicle.

Billie met her halfway to the door, and paused to speak to her. "It's a good thing you're doing, Tricia, setting up that trust fund for Davey Black. The whole village will be behind you."

"The whole village?" Tricia asked.

Billie shrugged. "I know some of the villagers don't like the booksellers, but nobody likes to think of a baby losing his mother. I think you'll find the people of Stoneham have large hearts."

"I hope you're right."

"I'd better get back to Elizabeth," Billie said, and sketched a wave good-bye before heading back to her cube.

Tricia watched her, then started when someone touched her on the shoulder. She whirled. A woman who looked about thirty, with short-cropped dark hair, stood in front of her. "Excuse me, but I couldn't help overhearing you talking about a bank account for Davey Black."

"Yes. After what happened to his mother, her friends and colleagues want to establish an education fund for her son."

"I didn't know Mrs. Black well. Davey was with us for only six weeks."

Tricia looked at the woman, puzzled. "I'm sorry, I don't understand."

The woman gave a tired smile. "I'm Brandy Arkin. My sister and I run Tiny Tots Day Care over on Fifth Street."

"Oh." Tricia *had* heard of their business. Deborah had placed Davey in their care—and that's where he'd broken his arm, falling from a piece of outdoor play equipment.

Deborah felt the owners had been negligent, and while she decided not to sue, she had filed a complaint with the county.

"We'd like to make a contribution to the fund. Can I write you a check?" Brandy asked.

"Um, sure." Tricia said.

Brandy stepped over to the customer counter, set her purse down, rummaged through it, and pulled out a checkbook. She scribbled for a few moments before handing Tricia a check. Ten dollars. It wasn't a lot, but it was something—especially as Deborah and Tiny Tots Day Care hadn't parted on happy terms. "Thank you. I'm sure Deborah would've been pleased."

"I wish it could be more, but under the circumstances . . ."

The economy had picked up some, but Tricia knew a lot of small businesses were still suffering. And laid-off workers didn't send their children to day care.

"It was very nice meeting you, Ms.—"

"Arkin," the woman supplied. She smiled. "See you around the village."

Tricia watched as the woman headed for the door. She turned back for the counter and picked up a deposit slip. She may as well add the check to the new account.

Five minutes later, she exited the building and headed back to Haven't Got a Clue, dreading that she'd have to walk past the park yet another time.

Steve Marsden was still on site, only now he sat on one of the park benches that had been pushed to the side, balancing a laptop on his knees. In front of him stood Captain Baker. He saw Tricia, turned back to Marsden, and mouthed a few words before hurrying to intercept her.

"Hi," he said.

"Hi."

"How are you doing?" he asked, concern coloring his voice.

She shrugged. "Okay, I guess." Her gaze drifted to the uneven ground and dry dirt where only yesterday had been healthy lawn.

"I was wondering, do you have anything planned for this evening?" Captain Baker asked. She shook her head. "I was thinking . . . maybe you'd like to go out to dinner?"

Tricia sighed. Baker was just as bad as Russ when it came to issuing last-minute invitations.

"I've got something to tell you," Baker continued, "and I'd rather do it in person than over the phone. Now isn't a good time." He looked back at Marsden for a few seconds.

What could he possibly have to tell Tricia? That his estranged wife's condition had worsened and he needed a shoulder to cry on. Or maybe he was retiring from the Sheriff's Department and taking a job in Florida or Timbuktu.

Or maybe he was just lonely and wanted a sympathetic ear.

She could be that person. Heck, she'd *been* doing that for almost a year now.

"Sure, I had nothing planned for this evening." The whole truth and nothing but the truth.

"Fine. I'll pick you up at seven thirty. Why don't you wear that peachy-colored dress."

It was the nicest dress Tricia owned. So, this dinner engagement—she couldn't really call it a date; they hadn't had one of those in a long, long time—was to feature more than just diner fare. "I'll see you then," Tricia said, and smiled as Baker tipped his hat before turning back to Marsden.

Tricia started down the street again but decided that instead of crossing, she'd stop at the Coffee Bean. Haven't Got a Clue's coffee supply was getting low.

She entered the Coffee Bean and inhaled deeply. She never tired of the rich, mingled aromas of coffee on offer. She'd picked a good time to stop in—the store was empty, which meant its owners would have time to talk.

Alexa and Boris Kozlov had emigrated from Russia to the United States a decade before. Alexa reminded Tricia of the Soviet women weightlifters of old; tall, muscular, and a little bit more than androgynous, with a rather husky voice to go with the package. Tricia always envisioned someone with the name of Boris to be big, beefy, and jovial, but this Boris was none of those things. Alexa had worked hard to eradicate her accent; Boris had not. Alexa joked with her customers, making them feel at home. Boris brooded and seldom looked his patrons in the eye.

Tricia preferred to deal with Alexa.

"Good to see you, Tricia," Alexa said. "What can I get you?"

"I'll take two pounds of the French roast ground coffee and a cup of it to go, please."

"Coming right up," Alexa said, and stepped over to the big rack that housed at least twenty different flavored coffees. She poured the beans into a specialty bag with the Coffee Bean logo emblazoned on it and then transferred them to the coffee grinder to her left. "What's new?"

"I'm collecting money for an education fund for Deborah Black's son, Davey. Would you like to donate something?"

Alexa hesitated.

"*Nyet,*" Boris growled, and let go of a case of their store's paper cups. It banged against the side of the counter. "Why should we give a ting to that *dura*?"

Tricia didn't speak Russian, but she knew an epithet when she heard one.

"Boris!" Alexa admonished, and looked embarrassed.

"Something wrong?" Tricia asked in all innocence.

Alexa's face colored. "Our neighbor was not our favorite person."

That didn't seem right. Everyone loved Deborah.

"That *vor dura,*" Boris snarled, and for a moment Tricia thought he might accentuate that statement by spitting. Bewildered, she bounced her gaze between the husband and wife.

Again, Alexa hesitated before speaking. "We had a problem. . . ." She paused, as though trying to think of a polite way to phrase something unpleasant. "Garbage."

Tricia blinked, startled. "Garbage?"

"That *dura* always put her trash in our Dumpster," Boris said, his voice rising. "Then she'd lie about it. She'd blame her help, she'd blame teenagers."

Alexa nodded in agreement. "We set up a camera to catch her. Even when we showed her the video, she still denied she did it,"

"She was a thieving *dura* and a liar," Boris growled.

Deborah's business did generate a lot of boxes and packing material, and Tricia seemed to remember seeing garbage totes behind the Happy Domestic—much smaller and cheaper than the Dumpsters behind Haven't Got a Clue. Deborah had been struggling to cut costs for a long time. Was it possible she'd literally dumped the majority of her garbage in her neighbor's backyard?

"How long has this been going on?" Tricia asked.

"Since the day that *dura* opened her store," Boris said.

That was at least three years, and in that time Tricia had never heard about it. She said so.

"We keep our business to ourselves," Alexa said.

"If we'd said something, we might have shamed her into keeping her garbage to herself," Boris added.

That didn't exactly make sense, but Tricia got the gist of his complaint.

Alexa bagged Tricia's purchase, handed her the cup of coffee, and rang up the sale.

"I'm very sorry to hear that you and Deborah didn't get along. I'm also a little confused."

"We're hearing the store will be sold quickly," Alexa said. News sure got around fast. "We hope our new neighbor will respect our Dumpster."

"If they don't—" Boris swiped his index finger across his throat, like a knife slash.

Tricia swallowed, glad she didn't have the Kozlovs as her neighbors. As she left the store, she wondered if Deborah had ever felt the same way.

SIX

 Ginny was with a customer when Tricia finally returned to Haven't Got a Clue. Miss Marple greeted her as though she hadn't seen her in years, and demanded to be made a fuss over. All that petting produced a lot of cat hair, and Tricia had to seek out the lint roller from under the cash desk to keep her pretty white blouse from looking like a gray angora sweater.

Along with the day's mail, Ginny had left several catalogs on the counter. During the last week, they'd talked about making lists of items they might like to feature during the upcoming Christmas season. Ginny had made out her wish list and clipped it to the top of the pile. Tricia ran a finger down items and smiled. They were all things she also had thought of ordering. It pleased her that Ginny was so in tune with the things she wanted for the store, which only made Ginny's complaint earlier in the day so painful to recall. She'd have to get to Stoneham Hardware to have an extra key made for the store and give it to Ginny, and then she'd take Angelica up on her offer of an early dinner one night to show Ginny that she trusted her. That night was out of the question, as Baker wasn't picking her up until after closing.

Tricia sorted through the letters on top of the stack of mail. Bills and junk mail. On the bottom was a bubble-pack envelope. She glanced at the return address and sighed. It belonged to her ex-husband.

She pulled at her collar to touch the chain around her neck. She still wore the locket he'd sent for her birthday two months before and suddenly realized what tomorrow's date signified. It would have been their thirteenth wedding anniversary. They'd only lasted ten years, and she couldn't even count that last year together as married bliss. Christopher's midlife crisis had caused him to leave his stockbroker's job—and Tricia, too—to go find himself in the Rocky Mountains of Colorado. Since he left, they'd spoken only once on the telephone. Tricia had sent a brief thank-you note for the locket. It held a picture of Miss Marple. Christopher's note had said, "To remind you of the one you love best." It still irked her. After all, she hadn't left *him* for a cat.

She reached for the pair of scissors she kept in a coffee mug on the counter, along with an assortment of pens and pencils. Cutting the package open, she wondered what he had sent this time. Another locket? A bracelet?

She cut through the extra bubbled plastic wound around a small green velvet jewelry box but hesitated before opening it. Was there a card? She looked inside the padded envelope. Sure enough, a small card remained at the bottom. She used the scissors to slice open the top. The picture was a watercolor of a swan swimming on a peaceful pond. Water lilies broke the surface of the water, and all was serene. Inside, Christopher had written: *Ahh, for what might have been. Christopher.*

What might have been!

Christopher had been the one who didn't want to go through marriage counseling.

Christopher had been the one to propose divorce.

Christopher had been the one to leave.

Tricia fought the seething anger that coursed through her. At that moment, she wanted nothing more than to toss the card and the gift straight into the trash. How could the man be so . . . so insensitive?

Or maybe he was just stupid.

Alone, in the mountains—with another long winter ahead of him—maybe Christopher had mellowed. Maybe he was expecting her to make some kind of grand gesture.

Come home, darling, all is forgiven.

Ha! Fat chance of that happening.

Tricia wrenched open the velvet jewelry box. This time he'd sent stud earrings. They sparkled like diamonds—but had to be cubic zirconium. No one in their right mind would send diamonds in a plain padded envelope without benefit of insurance and a return receipt.

Cubic zirconium. Yes, their marriage had been a pale imitation of the real thing, too. At least, that was how she looked at it in retrospect.

And how had Deborah Black viewed her marriage? She'd complained about David on numerous occasions but had she loved him as much as Tricia had loved Christopher? And did any of that matter now that she was dead?

Eventually, Ginny and her customer approached the

register. Tricia forced a smile, moved the catalogs aside, and bagged the purchase after Ginny had rung up the sale.

"I know you're going to love that Josephine Tey. It's one of my favorites," she said, and the woman gave her a quick thank-you before heading out the door. As soon as the door closed, she slumped against the counter. "Was the store busy while I've been gone?"

"Off and on," Ginny said. "That was an awful long lunch."

"I'm sorry I left you on your own so long, especially as Mr. Everett is down at the Happy Domestic. But I ended up at the bank with Elizabeth. We opened a scholarship account for Davey."

"What a great idea. And don't worry. Nothing came up that I couldn't handle." Ginny bent down to straighten the bags under the counter.

"I'm so sorry about this morning, too," Tricia said, feeling guilty all over again. "But—"

"Let's forget I ever mentioned it." Ginny frowned. "In fact, there's something I need to talk to you about." She bit her lip, hesitating.

"Is something wrong?" Tricia asked.

"Not wrong, exactly. It's just that since we talked this morning, I've . . . I've been offered another job," she said, her voice no more than a whisper.

"Oh?" Tricia asked, dreading what she was about to hear.

"You see, Antonio—"

She didn't need to say more. Good old aggressive Nigela Racita Associates had struck again!

"He offered you the job of managing the Happy Domestic," Tricia said, some part of her noting how flat her voice sounded.

Ginny nodded, her eyes brimming with tears. "How did you know?"

"Elizabeth told me that David had accepted an offer." Tricia swallowed but had to ask. "What did you tell him?"

"That I had to think it over."

"What's to think over?" Tricia said, trying to muster some enthusiasm.

"Leaving you. And Miss Marple. And Mr. Everett. And, of course, Haven't Got a Clue. Tricia, I love working here."

"Ginny, don't be so sentimental," Tricia said, though it was hard to keep emotion out of her voice. "This is a wonderful opportunity for you. I'm assuming you'll make more money—"

Ginny nodded.

"And it's the kind of experience you need so you can learn every aspect of running a business—so that you'll be ready to open your *own* business one day."

"Yes, but—"

Tricia shook her head. "No buts."

A tear trailed down Ginny's cheek.

"It's hard to leave what you know and take on a new challenge, but I don't know anyone else who could do a better job taking over for Deborah than you."

"But I don't know her stock," Ginny protested.

"It'll take you a week—if that—to learn it," Tricia amended.

"I wouldn't know what to order, or the quantities—"

"You. Will. Learn."

Ginny's lower lip quivered. "What will *you* do without *me*? I've been here almost since the day you opened."

"I'll have to hire someone else," Tricia said reasonably.

"But not everybody knows about mysteries—especially *vintage* mysteries."

"You didn't know a thing about them before you came to work here," Tricia reminded her. She made sure to keep her voice steady as she asked her next question. "Now, when will you take over running the Happy Domestic?"

"If I accept the job, as soon as the paperwork goes through. Antonio thinks it'll be a couple of weeks—maybe a month."

"You *will* accept the job. And it gives me plenty of time to find someone to take your place."

"What about Mr. Everett? Couldn't he work more hours—?"

Tricia shook her head. "He isn't interested in working a full-time job."

"That's right," Ginny said quietly. "I suppose you'll have to call an employment agency."

"I suppose," Tricia said. She knew putting up a HELP WANTED sign in the window wouldn't work. At least it hadn't worked for Angelica when she'd been looking for help at the Cookery. But times were different. With so many jobs being shipped overseas, the locals seemed a tad more interested in the shops along Main Street and the retail work they offered. Before she made one call, though, she'd ask Frannie. She was still the best source of information in the village, and she might know of someone who'd like to take the job. And it would give Tricia an excuse to talk to Frannie about Deborah.

So there, Angelica!

Tricia turned her mind back to the problem at hand. "What will happen to Elizabeth?"

Ginny sighed. "Antonio says she can stay on as long as she likes—part-time, of course. I think that'll suit her, as she intends to stay a part of Davey's life. That is, if David will let her."

"Have you spoken to her?"

Ginny shook her head. "Antonio was going to do that."

"When?"

She glanced up at the clock. "Right about now. I don't think she'll be very happy about the situation. I have a feeling she hoped she'd be kept on to manage the store. But would she have the stamina to do that and take care of Davey, too?"

"You're probably right," Tricia said, and felt even worse for Elizabeth. First losing her daughter, then her daughter's store. And was there the chance David might take little Davey away from Stoneham?

Tricia stood. "I think I'll head over to the Cookery to see if Frannie knows anyone looking for a job. I'd like you to train whoever takes your place."

"Oh, sure," Ginny said, and Tricia noticed the tears had dried. Well, did she expect Ginny to pine and wail over her decision to leave Haven't Got a Clue? If she was honest, Ginny had put her career on hold to stay at this job for far too long.

Tricia took three steps toward the door before Ginny's voice stopped her. "Tricia?"

She turned.

"I just wanted to say how grateful I am for everything you taught me about running a business. It's because of you I want to make this my life's work. You're my role model."

Tricia's smile was halfhearted. She'd lost Deborah, and now she'd lose Ginny, too.

Some days it didn't pay to get out of bed.

* * *

Frannie stood behind the Cookery's cash desk, waiting on a customer. "Oh yes, Ms. Miles's next cookbook will be out early next year. Here, would you like a bookmark?"

The man accepted it and gave a parting smile before he turned to exit the store.

"Tricia, what's up?" Frannie said in greeting.

"Sad news, I'm afraid."

"Oh, no," she said, with a catch in her voice. "After yesterday, I don't think I can take much more bad news."

"Sad," Tricia corrected her, "not bad. Ginny's leaving Haven't Got a Clue."

Frannie's hand flew to cover her mouth. "Oh no! What happened?"

"She's been offered another, better job."

"What could be better than working for you?"

Tricia smiled at that. "Managing the Happy Domestic."

Frannie frowned. "I thought Elizabeth was taking over for Deborah."

"Apparently Deborah's husband has already made a deal to sell the store."

"But Deborah's only been dead a day," Frannie protested.

"That was my reaction, too."

"I'm happy for Ginny, but . . ." She paused, studying Tricia's face. "You don't look happy."

"I'm happy for Ginny, too, but I'm not happy to be losing such a wonderful assistant."

"She knows her stuff," Frannie admitted. "I'm sure she'll do a terrific job for the new owner."

"Nigela Racita Associates bought the store."

"Who else?" Frannie said with chagrin. "Whoever owns that company has deep pockets. Mark my words, it's out to buy the whole village."

"I've had that same thought," Tricia admitted.

"You're not the only one," Frannie said. "Too bad I don't go to the Chamber of Commerce meetings anymore. I'll bet more than a couple of the members will be getting nervous."

"Or looking for a bailout?" Tricia suggested.

"That, too." Frannie frowned. "Was there something else you wanted to tell me?"

"Ask. I'd like to hire someone here in Stoneham to take Ginny's place rather than go to an employment agency. Do you know of anyone looking for a job?"

"Only Cheryl Griffin, but I know Deborah wasn't very happy having her as an employee. You wouldn't like her, either." Frannie leaned forward, lowered her voice, and spoke conspiratorially. "She's a nut case." That was easy to believe after the conversation Tricia had had with Cheryl earlier in the day. Frannie straightened. "I'll let you know if I think of anyone else."

"Thanks." Tricia sighed. How was she going to bring up Deborah's name again?

Frannie reached a hand out and touched Tricia's arm. "We're all sorry about poor Deborah." She shook her head and frowned. "That husband of hers."

The perfect opening.

"I heard they used to fight a lot."

Frannie leaned forward. "Almost every night lately and always over her store or his *supposed* work."

"Deborah said he worked two jobs."

Frannie scowled. "If you could call what he did work."

"I thought he was a welder," Tricia said.

"Yes, but that second job of his doesn't really bring in any income. He does bad iron sculptures of birds with their wings extended and other weird-looking things. Their backyard is full of them—all rusty and ugly. If I'd been Deborah, I'd have been afraid to let little Davey out in the yard for fear he'd fall over one, cut himself, and get tetanus."

Deborah had never mentioned that David saw himself as some kind of artist. Just that his second job didn't pay well. Had she been ashamed of his art? Had she seen it the same way Frannie did?

"These arguments—do you think Deborah and David were close to divorce?"

Frannie shrugged. "I can't say. But more than once he stormed out of the house and didn't return home until the wee hours. A couple of times, he never came home at all."

Tricia's heart sank, and she wasn't sure if it was because Deborah's marriage had been foundering, or because Deborah hadn't confided in her more. How well had she really known Deborah?

The door at the back of the store opened, and Angelica emerged from the stairwell that led to her loft apartment. "Aha!" she called. "Didn't I predict you'd be here to see Frannie this very day?"

Tricia sighed. "I came to ask Frannie if she knew of anyone who needed a job. Ginny's turned in her resignation."

"Oh dear," Angelica said, suddenly full of concern.

A customer entered the store, and Frannie straightened, ready to spring into action. "May I help you?"

Angelica didn't wait to hear the customer's reply but grasped Tricia's arm, steering her toward the door to the stairwell. "Why don't we go talk about it upstairs. I'll make you a nice cup of tea. Or something stronger, if you prefer."

Tricia found herself shuffling up the stairs behind her sister, feeling totally downcast. She followed Angelica inside the apartment and down the hall to the kitchen. The afternoon sun streamed through the windows and felt warm on her back as she took a seat at the large table.

"It's a bit warm for hot tea," Angelica said, and instead opened the refrigerator and took out a glass jug filled with homemade ice tea. She snagged a couple of tumblers from the cupboard, filled them with ice from the freezer, and poured the tea. She set a glass on the table in front of Tricia. "Why are you moping around? I thought you were behind the idea of Ginny furthering her career."

"I am. I just hate to lose someone I trust so much."

"Wasn't it just this morning Ginny was complaining that you didn't trust her enough to let her open and close your store? That you didn't let her go to the bank for you. That—"

"Okay, maybe I should have given her a little more authority. I'm not standing in her way. I just wish, well, that she could've stayed forever. She's not only a good assistant, she's a good friend."

"And good friends don't stand in the way of one of them getting ahead. Look at you. You've already achieved your life's dream."

"You make it sound like I should just give up and quit—or die."

"I'm not saying that at all. I'm just wondering, will you always be happy selling books? Isn't there *anything* else you aspire to?"

Tricia hadn't given that much thought in the past few years. Her goal had always been to open Haven't Got a Clue—or something very like it. She was happy here in Stoneham. She couldn't imagine going back to her old life in Manhattan. And yet . . . could she imagine climbing all those steps to her loft apartment some twenty years in the future? Paper books might be a thing of the past the way e-books were proliferating. Was her chosen way of life doomed? She'd already had to stock items besides books to keep the customers satisfied. Edgar Allan Poe and other famous author coffee mugs, bookmarks, blank journals, key chains, and the like.

"Hello!" Angelica called.

Tricia looked up. "I'm sorry. I was lost in thought."

"Are you burned out?" Angelica asked, yet it sounded more like an accusation.

Tricia shook her head sadly.

"Maybe you need to be more like me," Angelica said with the hint of a devious smile touching her lips. "Diversify a little bit."

"How?"

Angelica shrugged. "I don't know. Make a few investments. I've already got the Cookery, the café, and a writing career. Maybe you could start a day spa. We could sure use one around here."

"Why would I want to run a day spa?"

"For fun! That's why I opened Booked for Lunch."

"Are you crazy? You've had nothing but problems since you opened the café. From thieving employees to a dead body in your garbage."

Angelica waved an impatient hand in the air. "Just a few speed bumps on my way to success. Look at me—less than two years after coming to Stoneham and already I'm a successful businesswoman and a bestselling cookbook author. And look at you."

"I am *not* a failure. I've just chosen different goals than yours."

"The bar doesn't get much lower."

"Hey! I'm a successful businesswoman, too. I don't choose to live a life as manic as yours."

"No, you get your ya-yas finding bodies every couple of months. Maybe there's a reason they call you the village jinx."

Not that again. And it hurt that Angelica would be the one to bring it up. Talk about bullying!

Suddenly Tricia was once again the unwanted second child. No matter what she'd accomplished, there was always something in the back of her mind that reminded her that she'd been an inconvenience to her parents—and Angelica—and how they'd probably wished they'd used more effective forms of birth control. How it still haunted her that during some stupid argument about a boy, her mother had blurted out, "We never expected to have another child." From that day forward, Tricia had viewed all slights and reprimands with a different perspective. Was it a surprise she'd clung to her loving, all-forgiving grandmother rather than her parents?

"Penny for your thoughts," Angelica said.

"I don't think you find them worth it," Tricia muttered, and got up from the stool. "I need to get back to my store. I have a ton of work to do before my date tonight."

"Oooh! Who's the lucky man?"

"Captain Baker is taking me to dinner."

"It's about time," Angelica said.

"He said he has something to tell me."

Angelica frowned. "Good or bad?"

Tricia shrugged. "He asked me to wear my peach dress."

"That sounds promising. Of course, this is you we're talking about. Call me if the whole thing's a fiasco and we'll commiserate."

Not on your life, Tricia refrained from saying aloud.

"But don't stay out too late, either," Angelica warned as Tricia headed for the door to the stairs. "We've got Deborah's funeral in the morning. Do you want to drive, or shall I?"

"I'll do it. Elizabeth said to be at the funeral home by nine. Why don't you meet me at my shop at eight forty-five and we'll go on from there."

"Got it," Angelica said.

As Tricia reached for the door handle, Angelica touched her shoulder. Tricia hesitated.

"I know you're unhappy to lose Ginny, but you did a wonderful job training her, and now she'll go on to have a successful career. You would've made a great teacher, Trish. You're so patient and kind and giving. I really think you missed your calling. And I wouldn't be where I am today, as a businesswoman, if I hadn't learned from your example. I know it didn't sound like it earlier, but I'm so proud of you, little sister." She threw her arms around Tricia, who didn't know what to say. Instead, she wrapped her arms around Angelica and allowed herself a smile.

SEVEN

It had been several weeks since Tricia had even driven by the Brookview Inn, and the changes since Nigela Racita Associates had taken over were readily apparent—and decidedly for the better. Captain Baker parked his car in the nearly full lot out back, then got out to open the door for Tricia. It had been a long time since a man had done that for her. Christopher, her ex-husband, as a matter of fact. She couldn't remember Russ ever opening the door of his pickup for her.

They walked around the inn to the front entrance. Back in June, there'd been no flowers bordering the walkway. The building had also needed a fresh coat of paint, which it had received in the not-too-distant past. Now several shades of pink begonias flanked the concrete. Colorful geraniums in shades of pink filled the window boxes on the front porch, and the dozen or so quant rockers also sported fresh paint. Baker held the door for her, and they entered the inn's lobby. New carpeting had replaced the shabby rug that had been there back in June, and the walls sparkled with more fresh paint and bright sconces.

"Wow," Baker said, taking in all the changes.

"Wow is right," Tricia agreed.

A muffled ring tone sounded, and Baker reached for the leather holder attached to his belt. He retrieved his cell phone, glanced at the number, and frowned. "I'm sorry, Tricia, but I'd better take this. I'll be right back."

"I'll be here," she said, resigned to a long wait, and watched him retreat to the porch. Then she turned back to the lobby and studied it more closely. Even the artwork had been spruced up. Had the original oil paintings been cleaned? That took money. Nigela Racita Associates had done a wonderful job of restoring and refurbishing, without putting too bold a stamp on the place. It pleased her, and that was about as effusive as she was likely to get about the company that seemed poised to take over Stoneham.

Eleanor, the inn's receptionist, waved at Tricia, motioning her to join her at the main desk. "Well," she asked, her voice filled with pride, "what do you think?"

"The whole place looks lovely. Has business picked up yet?"

"For the weekend trade. Until they finish building the dialysis center across the street, I'm afraid our weekday trade will suffer. But it's only supposed to be another couple of weeks until they begin finishing the inside of the building. It'll be a lot quieter when they do. But we're already booked solid for the Milford Pumpkin Festival in October."

"That's great."

"I'm so grateful to the new management," Eleanor said.

"Without them, we might have had to close our doors before the end of the summer."

"Have you met the top dog yet?"

"Ms. Racita? No, she's never been to the inn. But Mr. Barbero has been wonderful to work with." She pointed to the office door to the right of the reception desk. On it hung a polished wooden sign with gold leaf lettering:

MANAGER
ANTONIO BARBERO
NIGELLA RACITA ASSOCIATES, INC.

"He's on site every day, even weekends," Eleanor gushed. "The staff all love him. He's so easy to work with. And even though he's just a young man, somehow he always has the answer to every problem."

Ginny could have done worse picking a mentor—and boyfriend.

"What brings you to the inn?" Eleanor asked.

"I'm having dinner with a friend."

"I hope you made a reservation. Since Mr. Barbero hired the new chef, we've had to turn people away—even on weeknights."

"I don't know if he made reservations," Tricia said thoughtfully. Did this mean yet another meal at the Bookshelf Diner? She'd resigned herself to just that when Baker reentered the lobby and made his way across to her.

"Sorry about that," he apologized. "I asked the office not to call me again unless it's a real emergency."

Tricia gave him a weak smile.

Baker nodded his head toward the dining room. "Shall we?"

"See you later, Tricia," Eleanor said, her eyes twinkling.

Tricia gave her a quick wave and let Baker steer her toward the restaurant. The hostess checked the reservations log and quickly showed them to their table. Baker pulled out Tricia's chair, and she sat down.

"Can I take your drink order?" the hostess asked, and passed them each a leather-clad menu.

"I'll have a Geary's," Baker said.

"Chardonnay," Tricia said, and opened her menu. It had undergone quite a transformation since the last time she'd dined at the inn. Before she could peruse it much further, she looked up and saw Antonio Barbero seated at a table across the room from them. With him were David Black and a woman she didn't know. David was dressed as she'd never seen him before, in a suit and tie. The woman looked older than him but was still a striking beauty. The sleeveless mauve linen dress clung to her lithe figure, and her prematurely white hair was pinned with an exquisite gem-encrusted butterfly hair clip that dripped diamonds. Beside Antonio was a champagne bucket. He held the bottle and poured the wine into flutes his guests held.

"My God," Tricia breathed, feeling the blood drain from her face.

Baker leaned forward and touched her hand. "Are you okay, Tricia? You look like you've just seen a ghost."

"I wish I had." She shook herself. "Grant, that's David Black and some strange woman sitting over there drinking champagne with the inn's manager."

"Black? Husband of the woman who was killed yesterday?" he asked.

"Yes."

Baker half turned, looking in the same direction as Tricia. He faced her again. "What do you think that's about?"

"Deborah's mother said David was selling her shop to the development company that bought the empty lot where History Repeats Itself used to be. They've also invested heavily in this inn."

Baker shrugged. "It's crass but not illegal to be out in public a day after your wife's death."

"Deborah hasn't even been buried yet. And toasting the sale of her business. It stinks! The whole village will be talking about it tomorrow."

"That's his lookout, not yours," Baker said quietly.

Tricia pursed her lips and trained her gaze on her menu, although she couldn't focus on the words in front of her, and she'd suddenly lost whatever appetite she'd had.

"The sea bass looks good," Baker said, perusing his own menu.

Tricia set hers aside.

Baker looked up. "You're not going to let seeing Black ruin your evening, are you?"

At least he didn't say *my* evening.

"Deborah was my friend. I know she and David were having marital problems, but to be seen in public so soon after her death . . ."

"There's nothing you can do about it," Baker insisted.

She sighed. "You're right. I'm sorry. I'm just . . . upset." She remembered he had something to tell her. Would she be further upset?

"I was going to wait until later to mention this to you," Baker said, leaving the sentence hanging.

Here it comes, the old dumperoo. And yet that was hardly applicable to their situation. They were friends. Not even good friends. Still, Tricia steeled herself to hear the worst.

Baker sighed. "My divorce will be final in two weeks."

Tricia blinked. That wasn't what she'd thought he'd say. "Oh? I take it Mandy went into remission."

"Yes. And she's planning to move to North Carolina to be closer to her sister."

Tricia's spirits rose a little. Did that mean . . . ?

"How does that make you feel?" she asked, trying not to sound too eager.

Baker sighed. "Relieved. We'd planned to divorce before she became ill. And then, I just couldn't leave her to fight the cancer alone. If nothing else, at least we remained friends."

Tricia was well aware of that fact. She nodded, waiting for the other shoe to drop.

"I've been thinking a lot about my future," Baker continued.

Tricia leaned closer, but just as Baker was about to say more, the hostess appeared with a tray and their drinks. She set down embossed cocktail napkins, then a glass and a bottle of beer for Baker and Tricia's wine. "I'll send your waitress right over to take your order."

"Thank you," Baker said, and gave her a small smile. He turned his attention back to Tricia. "I told you a few months ago that I was going to be retirement eligible in January."

Here it came. The other shoe.

"And what have you decided?" Tricia asked.

"I'm going to take it."

Tricia eyed him. He looked devastatingly handsome in his navy blazer with a pale blue opened-necked dress shirt beneath it. The gray at his temples made him look distinguished, and somehow, despite the years of police work, his face was remarkably unlined. Did that mean he hadn't had much to smile about in all that time?

"Somehow I don't think retirement will suit you," she said.

"I don't either, but I'm ready for a change. I've already talked to a headhunter. He's put my name out there and has already had a few bites."

"So you'll be leaving Manchester?" Tricia asked, then picked up her glass and took a sip in an effort to hide her disappointment.

"I might even be leaving the state," he said, his voice soft.

Tricia couldn't bear to look at him and shifted her gaze to David Black. With champagne flute in hand, his attention was focused on his dinner companion, and he laughed at something she said.

Tricia swallowed hard, thinking of Deborah's naked, lifeless body under a sheet in a morgue drawer. No, if the service was tomorrow, she might already be lying in a coffin—or worse, mere ashes. She struggled not to burst into tears.

Baker misinterpreted her damp eyes. "It's not like we've been all that close, but I thought I should tell you in person."

Tricia took a steadying gulp of wine, carefully set down the glass, and picked up her menu once again.

"I was thinking," Baker continued. "Until I have to leave—which isn't a given—that we could see each other. You know, on a regular basis."

"You're asking me to give you my heart so I can have it broken when you leave?" Tricia asked. Been there, done that.

"Not at all," he said. "We could enjoy each other's company for however long—"

"Not much of a bargain, is it?" she cut him off.

Baker picked up his menu. "This isn't exactly how I thought the evening would go."

"I'm sorry not to turn handsprings at your news. My best friend was killed yesterday, I'm losing my top employee, and now you're probably going to be leaving the area. Excuse me, but I don't have a lot to celebrate, do I?"

David Black laughed once again, and this time both his dinner companions joined in on the joke.

The waitress appeared, dressed in a black uniform with a pristine white apron tied around her waist. "Ready to order?" she asked, sounding incredibly perky.

Baker nodded for Tricia go first. "I'll have the chef's salad," she said with defeat in her voice.

"You will not," Baker said, and then spoke to the waitress. "The lady will have the saffron shellfish risotto. I'll have the filet mignon with wild mushrooms. And we'll both have poppy seed dressing on our salads." He hesitated. "That is still your favorite, isn't it, Tricia?"

Tricia nodded but refused to look at him or the waitress.

"Excellent choices," the waitress agreed, gathered up their menus, and turned away.

Tricia let out a pent-up sigh and glared at Baker. "What if I don't like shellfish?"

"I've seen you eat it before."

Damn him!

"I thought you were going to have the sea bass," she said.

"I changed my mind."

Tricia sighed and her gaze strayed once again to the trio across the room.

"Will you stop looking at them?" Baker said, annoyed.

"Don't you think it's the least bit suspicious that David Black is out with another woman before his wife is even decently buried?"

Baker sipped his beer. "If this were my case, I might. But it's not up to me to investigate Deborah Black's death."

"You could at least speak with the NTSB investigator, tell him about this?"

"What bearing would that have on his investigation?"

Tricia opened her mouth to answer and then realized she had no logical retort.

Baker leaned closer and rested his hand on Tricia's arm. "I know you lost your friend, and you want someone to pay for it. But the person responsible—the pilot—has already paid the ultimate price—his life. There's not much left to do but bury the dead and move on."

"Do you know how cold that sounds?" she asked accusingly.

"Tricia, I've seen a lot of death in the past twenty years. Nobody in my line of work can afford to take each and every victim to heart. We'd lose our objectivity, and our sanity. You've read a lot of police procedurals—you, better than most, should understand that."

She didn't want to understand it. She wanted to hold on to her anger. And he was right, she wanted someone to pay.

And right now, that someone was David Black.

EIGHT

 Tricia awoke the next morning to gray skies and thundering rain. Somehow that made the idea of a funeral service more palatable. She hated to think of Deborah missing a glorious, sunny summer day.

After her usual run on the treadmill and a shower, Tricia retired to her kitchen for coffee and the morning paper. She thumbed through to the obituaries and found a listing for Montgomery (Monty) Capshaw. It hadn't been in the previous day's paper; had Mrs. Capshaw waited until the weekend to list it, a time when more people bought the newspaper?

Tricia read the entry. *Suddenly*—that was true enough—*August 8. Predeceased by his parents, Richard and Margaret Capshaw, and brother, Lawrence. Survived by his loving wife of twenty-eight years, Elaine; and nieces Brenda and Cara. Private interment at the family's convenience.*

As prearranged, Angelica showed up at precisely eight

forty-five, suitably dressed in black. Fleeing under the cover of their umbrellas, they hurried to the municipal parking lot. Tricia drove while Angelica rode shotgun to the Baker Funeral Home. Grant Baker's cousin Glenn was the owner. He stood near the door, directing the mourners to leave their wet umbrellas in stands in the foyer before ushering them into the large open room to the right.

Tricia led the way with Angelica following. The long line of mourners stood in a bottleneck at the lectern with the guest book just inside the door. It seemed like nearly all the Chamber of Commerce members had turned out for the early-morning service. At least David had done one thing right, she thought again, by scheduling the service early enough so that most of the booksellers didn't have to close their stores to attend.

Finally Tricia stepped up to the lectern, reached for the provided pen, and scribbled in both hers and Angelica's names while her sister scoped out the crowd. She put the pen down and nodded for Angelica to follow. They stepped inside the viewing room.

"This is going to take forever," Angelica groused with a sigh. She squinted and leaned in to look at Tricia. "New earrings?" she asked.

Tricia reached up to touch her left earlobe and Christopher's latest gift. "Just something I picked up. They're only cubic zirconium."

"Yes, it's best not to wear the good stuff when you're on the job. Although, I must say, they look really nice. They sparkle like the real thing. Where'd you get them? Maybe I should get a pair."

Tricia bit her lip. Should she tell Angelica about the package in the mail? That could open the floodgates of teasing. Either that or Angelica would annoy her to contact Christopher—maybe in hopes of a reconciliation—as if that would ever happen.

"I don't remember where I got them," she lied. "I must've had them for ages."

Lies, lies, lies!

Angelica nodded, accepting that explanation. "Who do you want to hang with?" she asked under her breath.

"There's Grace and Mr. Everett," Tricia said, and waved to them. She nodded for Angelica to follow.

"Good morning, Grace." Tricia leaned forward and kissed the elderly woman's cheek.

"Lovely to see you, Tricia, but terrible under these circumstances." Grace sighed. "Deborah was such a lovely person."

Tricia nodded.

"At least she got a good turnout," Mr. Everett said, taking in the crowd.

"Too bad she can't appreciate it," Angelica commented.

Tricia felt like jabbing her sister with an elbow, but Angelica conveniently stood out of reach.

"How sad," Mr. Everett said, shaking his head. "This is the second bookseller whose memorial service we've attended in as many months."

"Let's hope we don't have any nasty surprises like we did then," Angelica said. Tricia gave her a sour look. Angelica hadn't even attended Jim Roth's memorial service.

"Where's the receiving line?" Angelica asked, gazing around the room.

Until she'd mentioned it, Tricia hadn't noticed that lack of propriety. David stood to one side of the room, and Elizabeth was on the other—as far apart as they could possibly be.

"There doesn't seem to be one," Grace said. "Oh look, there's Deborah's mother. We should pay our respects," Grace told Mr. Everett, who nodded. "We'll talk to you later, dear." Mr. Everett reached for Grace's hand and led her toward the head of the room and an easel with a poster board filled with pictures. Most of them were of Deborah as a child and teenager. No wedding picture. None with David in them, and only a few of Deborah with Davey. Perhaps Elizabeth, instead of David, had contributed them for the gathering.

Angelica grabbed Tricia's arm and spoke low in her ear. "What's wrong with Mr. Everett's lip?"

"Wrong?" Tricia asked.

"I think he missed a big patch while shaving this morning."

Tricia stifled a giggle. "He's trying to grow a moustache."

"What for?"

"So he can walk around the village incognito. He's aiming for one like Tom Selleck's."

"That's a tall order for such a little guy. Maybe he should set his sights a bit lower. Like maybe Charlie Chaplin?"

"Shhh! He'll hear you."

"He will not. He's halfway across the room."

Muriel Dexter sidled her way through the crowd, followed by her twin sister, Midge. As usual, the elderly sisters were dressed alike, in matching black dresses, hose, shoes, and pillbox hats with tiny veils that almost covered their foreheads, and had probably come from a nice department store some forty or fifty years before.

Muriel waved to Tricia, who sighed. Talking to the sisters could be an ordeal.

"Tricia, good to see you, although under sad circumstances," Muriel said. She waited for her sister to catch up before she began conversing in earnest.

"How have you ladies been?" Tricia asked politely.

"Worried," Midge admitted, and looked around the room as if expecting to find a Russian spy behind a pillar. She lowered her voice. "There's talk about the village that we're ripe for the picking by alien invaders," Midge said earnestly.

"Do you ladies honestly believe that?" Angelica asked, startled.

Both heads bobbed solemnly, and Tricia's gaze traveled to the wall where Cheryl Griffin stood, her furtive glances taking in all in attendance. Probably looking for a Romulan centurion. "If you think about it, it makes perfect sense," Midge continued. "Here we are in the wilds of New Hampshire—and everybody knows aliens only show up in rural areas—"

"Never in highly populated areas like New York City or Chicago or Los Angeles," Muriel chimed in.

"We are *doomed*," Midge said, and exhaled a weary sigh of defeat.

Tricia cleared her throat and avoided looking at Angelica for fear she'd burst out laughing.

"We were thinking we should sell off everything we own and move to a tenement in New York City. It might be a lot safer," Muriel said, and shook her head, heaving yet another sigh.

A tenement?

It was Tricia's turn to exhale wearily. "Ladies, ladies— please, think about it." She paused. It wasn't likely they would honor *Star Trek*'s Mr. Spock and think the situation through logically. It would be up to her to provide the voice

of sanity. And yet there was no way she could convince
them that their beliefs were . . . crazy-nutso-bananas!

"Ladies," Tricia began again, "I want to assure you that
you will not be targeted by extraterrestrial slavers."

"Oh?" Angelica asked, with great interest.

"No?" Muriel asked, hopeful.

"I don't mean to sound morbid, but if you think about it
from a purely business perspective, any alien slave master
is going to go straight for the young and the brawny. That
means teenagers and young men and women of childbear-
ing age. They'll not only want individuals who can put in a
sixteen- or eighteen-hour workday but who will make ideal
breeding stock, too. This is one instance when I think you
can count your lucky stars that you're not only collecting
Social Security but safely past menopause."

Muriel's smile was positively beatific. "Well, if you put
it *that* way."

Midge gave a huge sigh of relief. "Oh, sister—finally
there's a reason to rejoice in being *old!* I think we should
go to the Brookview Inn tonight and celebrate with a great
big steak dinner!"

"I'm for that," Muriel said, and turned to face Tricia
again, grabbing her hand. "Thank you, Tricia. Not only
have you made our day, but you've made our week, month,
and year, too!"

The sisters turned in unison. "Well, that's a load off of
my mind," Muriel muttered

"Mine, too," Midge agreed, as they walked away, heading straight for Cheryl Griffin, who Tricia suspected was
about to get an earful.

"Nice move," Angelica said. "I didn't know you were so
well versed in intergalactic business policies."

"I went through a phase reading science fiction, too, you know."

"*Star Wars* era?"

"And a little before," Tricia admitted. "Of course, if all the aliens want is a food supply, we're all skunked." Once again she let her gaze travel the room, noticing there was no coffin. Instead, a small, six-sided cherry cask apparently held Deborah's earthly remains on a small dais at the front of the room near the easel. The way David had been behaving, she was surprised he had sprung for even that indulgence instead of the standard plastic container that came with a bottom-end cremation. Then again, who said the cherry cask wasn't just a prop for the service. Was he going to bury it or scatter Deborah's ashes at a later date? No one had mentioned David's plans for his wife's remains.

"That cheap sonofabitch," someone behind Tricia hissed. She turned to find Elizabeth Crane standing behind her.

"You mean David?" she asked.

Elizabeth nodded. Her face was pale and drawn, and her mascara was smeared. "He didn't even let us have a last good-bye with her before he had her cremated. He never even phoned to tell me what the plans were for today," she said with a catch in her voice.

Too busy wining and dining someone else at the Brookview Inn, Tricia thought, but didn't dare utter it.

"I'm glad I phoned Mr. Baker last night, or there wouldn't even have been pictures of Deborah on display," Elizabeth continued. "That wonderful man put this whole thing together this morning."

Tricia noticed the dark TV screen in the corner. Lately the funerals she'd attended had had some kind of slideshow to chronicle the deceased's life. There probably hadn't been time to assemble one.

"David wasn't even going to spring for remembrance cards, either. I paid for them. I don't want people to forget my baby." She shook her head. "I didn't approve of Deborah marrying David, but I never thought he'd be so callous toward her—or us."

Tricia wondered which of the unidentified women in the crowd were Deborah's two sisters. She exchanged an uncomfortable look with Angelica, who for once seemed at a loss for words.

"Oh my God," Elizabeth hissed. "What are *they* doing here?"

Tricia looked behind her to see the woman she'd run into at the bank. Brandy somebody. She'd mentioned having a sister. "Paying their respects?" Tricia offered.

"That surprises me, after the words the fat one had with Deborah after Davey broke his arm." The woman standing beside Brandy was tall and what Tricia would call ample, but the bulk appeared to be more muscle than fat.

"Water under the bridge at this point, I suppose," Tricia said.

"What words?" Angelica asked, making a show of staring at the woman.

"Shhh!" Tricia admonished.

"Will you stop shushing me!" she hissed.

"I'll explain later."

"I've been trying to track down Davey's missing blanket and I'm sure it was left at the day care center the day he broke his arm," Elizabeth continued. "Brandy has to have it and is keeping it out of spite."

"Did you ask her about it?" Tricia asked.

"Yes. She denies she's got it—the bitch. But that's the only place it can be. Without his mother and his blankie, the poor baby is inconsolable."

Davey was nowhere to be seen. Had Elizabeth found a babysitter for the morning?

A woman Tricia didn't know waved to Elizabeth, who turned and said, "Excuse me," before she left them.

The large viewing room was filled to capacity, and Mr. Baker had turned the air-conditioning up high to accommodate the crowd, but instead of comfortable, Tricia felt chilled. She shivered, wishing she'd worn a sweater, and noticed Cheryl still standing at the side of the room all alone, looking decidedly out of place. She didn't seem to be mingling with the rest of the mourners, just holding up a wall.

Angelica scanned the crowd. "Where's Ginny?"

"I don't know. I thought she'd be here."

"I don't see Alexa and Boris Kozlov, either," Angelica said.

"And you probably won't. They had a beef with Deborah over garbage."

"Garbage?" Angelica asked skeptically.

"It seems Deb needed to cut some corners to stay afloat and sometimes"—here she was stretching the truth—"put some of the Happy Domestic's trash in the Coffee Bean's Dumpster."

"That's as good as stealing," Angelica said, aghast.

"That's the way Alexa and Boris feel, too." Tricia frowned. "I didn't realize Deb had so many . . ." She paused, struggling to come up with a descriptor.

"Enemies?" Angelica supplied. "If we hadn't all witnessed the accident, one might think someone had bumped her off."

Tricia pondered that statement. Of course the plane crash had been an accident. It had simply run out of fuel. Besides, nobody in their right might would deliberately crash a plane into a crowd just to kill off one person.

And what if Monty Capshaw hadn't been of sound mind?

"Who is that woman in the tight black dress? I'd never seen her before last night," Tricia whispered. "In fact, she had dinner at the Brookview Inn with David Black and Antonio Barbero."

Angelica craned her neck, looked the woman up and down, and raised an eyebrow. "Her name's Michele something. I met her at some cocktail party Bob dragged me to in Nashua. If I'm not mistaken, she owns a gallery in Portsmouth. Didn't you say David welded god-awful metal sculptures?"

"Yes. I heard he wanted to quit his regular job and do it for a living."

"Ha! Retail is precarious enough. Trying to make a living in the arts is just about impossible."

"Which is why he's still got a day job. Well, two actually."

"When does he find time to do sculptures?" Angelica asked.

Tricia shrugged. "According to Frannie, making his art *is* his second job." She thought about it. The Blacks had always been in financial distress. Had David just told Deborah he held a second job while he did his sculptures for the gallery? And if that was true, where had he done the work? Deborah had said he kept none of his welding equipment in their garage. She was afraid he'd set the place on fire. Had he fabricated them at his day job? That didn't seem likely. Could he have rented a studio somewhere?

"We ought to go check out David's work—to see if it was any good," Angelica suggested.

"When?"

"How about tonight? Michele may take time out to go to a funeral, but I'm sure she isn't going to close the gallery because one of her artists' wives died. I mean, it's just not good business."

Did Angelica realize how cold she came off at times?

"Well?" she demanded.

"I guess," Tricia said.

"Ginny's been moaning for you to give her more responsibility. Let her close Haven't Got a Clue and we'll go to the gallery and then have a lovely dinner. I heard about this amazing Italian restaurant I've been dying to try."

"What about the Cookery?" Tricia asked.

"I have no problem with Frannie closing for me. And besides, you've been awfully depressed about Deborah's death. It might cheer you up to get out of Stoneham for an evening. I know I could sure use it."

It had been two years since Angelica had relocated to New Hampshire, and Tricia still couldn't get over the fact her sister felt comfortable with Stoneham's small-town charm. And of late, she'd spent nearly all her off time working on the new cookbook. Too much time. Despite the friction the night before, Tricia had missed their regular gab fests.

Angelica glanced at her watch. "What's taking so long? Shouldn't they have started the service by now?"

An impassive Mr. Baker still stood on the sidelines. Tricia crossed the room to join him. "Mr. Baker, when is the service supposed to start?"

Baker frowned and looked uncomfortable. "I'm afraid

there is no formal service scheduled. Mr. Black decided against it. He thought a gathering of friends would be adequate."

Tricia gaped at the man, whose disapproving gaze seemed to be riveted on David Black and the gallery owner. Tricia shook herself, and managed a shaky "Thank you" before turning to rejoin Angelica. "There's no service. This is it."

"This is what?"

"A gathering," Tricia explained.

"What idiot came up with that bright idea?" Angelica asked.

"David."

Angelica glanced at her watch again. "I need to go."

"But I'm not ready."

"That's okay. I've got my umbrella. I won't melt. I'll call you later about tonight."

"But, Ange—"

There was no stopping Angelica once she'd made up her mind about something. Tricia watched as her sister said good-bye to Elizabeth and then headed toward the exit.

David had finally extricated himself from the gallery owner and was speaking with Russ Smith, who bore an expression of surprise. No doubt David had just told him there'd be no ceremony.

Tricia marched across the room to stand before David. He didn't even acknowledge her. "I'm not paying for anything formal. If you want to run an obituary, that's up to you," he told Russ.

Tricia tapped David's shoulder. He finally turned. "I can't believe it. I can't believe how little regard you seem to feel for your poor dead wife. This"—she waved her hand at the room at large—"is not what Deborah would have wanted."

"And how would you know?" David challenged. "You were friends with her for what—two years?"

"Almost three," Tricia said, bending the truth just a little. It was more like two and a half years.

"Well, I was married to her for six years—and knew her for two years before that. I think I knew my wife much better than you did."

"Not the way she spoke."

David's head snapped up, his eyes blazing. "The subject is closed." He gestured toward the door. "Now, if you don't mind."

Several other mourners were obviously eavesdropping, but Tricia was so angry that she didn't care. She leaned closer and kept her voice low. "But I *do* mind. If I didn't know better, David, I'd say everything you've done for the past few days screams involvement in Deborah's death."

David's eyes grew even wider. "Get out."

Tricia met his gaze. "Gladly."

NINE

From her perch behind the cash desk, Miss Marple glared at the rain that continued to beat against Haven't Got a Clue's front display window. *"Yow,"* she said in what sounded like annoyance.

Tricia, sitting on a stool below the cat, looked up from the book she'd been trying to read. "You said it," she agreed. Movement to her right caught her attention. Someone at the door was closing an umbrella. The door opened and a figure stepped inside and pulled off the hood of a yellow slicker. "Feels more like November than August," Ginny said, and wiped her feet on the bristle welcome mat.

"Good morning," Tricia said, grabbed a bookmark, and closed the copy of Ellery Queens's *Double, Double*, setting it beside the newspaper she hadn't yet had time to finish reading. "Although by the looks of the weather, we might not have many customers today."

"The perfect time to seek out a nice cozy murder mystery, sit down with a cup of cocoa, and put your feet up. Sounds like heaven."

"To me, too."

"Speaking of heaven, how did Deborah's service go? You're back a lot earlier than I would've thought. I was going to try to make it, and then . . ." She let the sentence hang, and sighed. "I didn't want it to look like I was too eager to take over her store. You know, gloat over the body and everything."

"There was no body," Tricia said, and picked a gray cat hair from her black sweater. Since the day was so gloomy, she hadn't bothered to change out of her mourning attire. "There *was* no service. What is it with this town that people keep deciding there's no need for the rituals surrounding death?" she asked. "First Jim Roth, now Deborah."

"What?" Ginny asked, aghast, and struggled out of the sleeves of her still-dripping slicker.

Tricia crossed her arms. "David Black decided not to hold a ceremony. He thought a *gathering* would be enough. The cheapskate isn't even going to spring for a paid death notice in the *Stoneham Weekly News*. And worse—worst of all—he showed up to the funeral home with another woman in tow."

Ginny's mouth dropped. "A date? You're kidding!"

"No, I'm not. She was older than him, too. Angelica says she owns an art gallery in Portsmouth."

"Angelica certainly gets around," Ginny said, and headed toward the back of the store to hang up her jacket.

Tricia shrugged off the comment and then let out an exasperated breath. "What do you know about David Black's sculptures?" she called.

Ginny returned to the front of the store. She tucked a loose strand of her hair behind her left ear. "I saw some of them on display last month on the Milford oval. It was some kind of local starving artists' display. Antonio wanted to see if he could find some local paintings to decorate the Brookview Inn."

"I heard David's sculptures are rusty and ugly."

Ginny crossed her arms, rubbing them for warmth. "Rusty and rustic. I guess it's an acquired taste."

"Did he sell much?"

"I have no idea. We came late to the sale. In fact, most of the artists were already packing up. Antonio got a couple of paintings for a reduced price simply because the artists didn't want to drag them home."

"Shrewd businessman," Tricia said flatly.

Ginny nodded at the newspaper on the cash desk. "Did you read the article about the pilot who crashed the plane?"

Tricia looked up sharply. "No." Ginny made a dive for the paper, but Tricia beat her to it. "Where is it?"

"Inside the front section."

Tricia thumbed through the paper until she found an article at the bottom of page four. She scanned it, but it really didn't say anything she didn't already know— except for Monty Capshaw's address. She pursed her lips, thinking . . .

Ginny struck a pose, plastering her splayed fingers to her forehead, threw her head back, and squinted at the ceiling. "I predict you're going on a very short journey. To Milford. To Olive Road. Where you will visit Elaine Capshaw and talk about the death of her husband and your dear friend Deborah."

Tricia leveled an icy stare at Ginny. "That's not funny, Ginny."

Ginny laughed. "You may call me Madam Zola."

Tricia carefully refolded the newspaper. "As it happens, I have a lunch date. Would you mind watching the store?"

"Not at all," Ginny said.

"Not only that," Tricia said, "but Angelica and I have an appointment later this afternoon. Do you think you could close for me?"

Ginny's eyes widened. "I'd be very happy to do so. I just need—"

Tricia turned for the cash desk, opened the register, and took out a key on an Edgar Allan Poe keychain. She was glad Stoneham Hardware opened early. She'd had the key made on her way back from the funeral home. "I should have given this to you ages ago."

Ginny sobered and grasped the key, holding it tight in her palm. "I'll have to give it back to you in just a couple of weeks."

"If you're good, I'll let you keep the keychain," Tricia said.

Ginny laughed. "I'll treasure it always. You'd better get going. You don't want to keep Mrs. Capshaw waiting."

"I told you, I have a lunch date."

"At ten o'clock in the morning?"

"Did I say lunch? I meant brunch."

"Sure," Ginny said, drawing the word out for at least ten seconds.

Head held high, Tricia collected her still-damp raincoat and umbrella from the back of the store. "I'll see you in an hour or so."

Ginny, who had taken her station behind the cash desk called out, "Bring me back a burger and fries, will you?"

Tricia stood before the front door that needed painting on 87 Olive Road, unsure of what she might say should anyone actually answer. The small Cape Cod home had seen happier days. An aura of neglect seemed to permeate the place.

Plucking up her courage, Tricia transferred her umbrella to her left hand and pressed the plastic doorbell with her right. From somewhere inside came the muffled sound of barking. After thirty seconds with nothing happening, she tried again. And waited. The barking continued.

Tricia glanced in the driveway. A green Honda was parked there. Perhaps Mrs. Capshaw had been bothered by the press and had simply given up answering her door.

Just as Tricia was about to walk away, the door jerked open. A tired looking woman in her late fifties stood before her, struggling to hold on to a small, wiggling white dog. Her red-brown hair looked straggly, with a white stripe down the middle where she hadn't colored it in months.

"Mrs. Capshaw?" Tricia asked.

"I have nothing to say to the press," the woman said, and began to shut the door, but Tricia jammed her purse between the door and the casing. The little dog growled.

Tricia stepped back but held her purse in place. "Please, I'm not a reporter, and I witnessed the crash."

Mrs. Capshaw opened the door just enough to show her face. "What do you want?" she asked suspiciously.

"To talk to you about what happened."

"My husband crashed his plane. He's dead. There's nothing more to talk about."

She went to shut the door again, and Tricia blurted, "My best friend was killed."

Mrs. Capshaw's lower lip trembled, and her eyes filled with tears. She opened the door, stepped back, put the dog down, and ushered Tricia inside. "Come on in. Watch out for Sarge. He's small, but he bites."

The small fluffy dog sniffed Tricia's ankles but didn't seem about to attack, and Tricia gingerly followed the dog's mistress into the living room.

"Sorry about the mess," Mrs. Capshaw apologized. "Since Thursday, I haven't felt much like cleaning."

As she said, newspapers, with pictures of the crashed plane prominently displayed, lay across the coffee table in disarray, accompanied by dirty coffee mugs and several plates littered with crumbs. Mrs. Capshaw gestured for Tricia to take an empty seat, while she picked up and folded a colorful granny square afghan and tossed it onto the far side of the couch before taking a seat. She picked up a remote and muted the old black-and-white movie showing on her no-longer-new television. Sarge sat on his haunches between the two women, looking as fierce as a dog his size could manage.

"What do you want me to say—that I'm sorry your friend died? Well, I'm sorry my husband died. I'm not sure I have enough pity for anyone else. I'm pretty much wallowing in it."

"I understand completely." Tricia sighed. "How . . . how could this have happened? How could your husband's plane have run out of gas?"

"Monty might have lost track of time. Maybe his

credit card had been refused, but he thought he would squeeze a few more minutes in the air with what he had in the tank. He could have just forgotten to fill the tank—he'd been forgetting a lot of things lately." She shrugged and shook her head, leaning farther back into the worn leather couch.

"What kind of things?" Tricia asked, trying not to sound too pushy.

Mrs. Capshaw sighed once again. "He'd go to the store and forget why he went. Stupid things like that. It was a side effect from his meds."

Tricia's eyes widened. "Meds?"

Mrs. Capshaw nodded. "Monty hadn't been well. Sometimes I wondered if he should even be flying, but he said the doctor hadn't told him to stop, and he figured if he could still make money at it . . ."

Did Mrs. Capshaw really believe that? Something in her voice seemed to belie that.

"How ill was your husband?"

"Cancer," she admitted. "But he's been in remission for a while now. What we originally thought was a death sentence has turned out to be more of a chronic disease." She seemed to realize she'd spoken in the present tense and looked away. "We always thought the cancer would kill him, not flying. He really was a damned good pilot."

Tricia leaned forward, causing a wary Sarge to stand his ground, but at least he didn't growl. It was then she noticed several envelopes on the coffee table. The return address was New Hampshire Mutual. Was Mrs. Capshaw checking up on her husband's insurance policy? There was no tactful way to ask. Instead, she said, "Tell me about your husband."

Mrs. Capshaw sighed, her expression growing wistful. "He was a devil back when we were dating. He took me flying on our first date, complete with barrel rolls." She stifled a laugh. "I threw up. That certainly made am impression on him. But he asked me out again the very next night, and this time we stayed firmly on the ground."

Tricia smiled. "Go on," she urged.

"He'd make me so angry I'd threaten to break up with him—and then he'd do something silly and sentimental and I'd fall for him all over again."

"How long did you date?"

Mrs. Capshaw managed a weak smile. "Two months. We were married for thirty-eight years. In all that time, we never spent a night apart. Until now."

Never?

"He was the sweetest man who ever lived. Wouldn't hurt a fly." She sighed, and her face went lax.

Tricia studied the woman's face. For a couple so devoted, she didn't seem as bereft as one might have expected after suffering such a devastating loss. Or was it the fact that the cancer had shadowed their lives for so long—like a noose loosely wrapped around Capshaw's neck—that when the end came his wife was grateful for the extra years they'd managed to eek out—and to be rid of the stress of waiting for the end?

Mrs. Capshaw sighed again. "You seem awfully understanding for a woman whose friend was killed in this accident. I've received a couple of nasty calls, threatening you might say, from people professing to be friends of Deborah Black."

"I can't imagine any one of her friends being so . . . so . . ." Words failed her. The idea of someone like Nikki,

Frannie, or Julia doing something so callous or disrespect-
ful was unthinkable. "Male or female?"

"It was a woman."

"Have you told the police?"

She nodded. "The calls were made from a pay phone."

Not many—if any—of those left in Stoneham. Tricia
would have to keep an eye out for one. "I'm so sorry."

"To tell you the truth, I only let you in here so I could
listen to your voice. But I'm sure it wasn't you."

Thank goodness for small favors.

"But you could be in danger."

Mrs. Capshaw managed a weak smile, cocking her head
to gaze at her dog. "I have Sarge to protect me."

Tricia eyed the compact dog, still staring intently at her.

"Don't you have any family you can rely on?"

Mrs. Capshaw shook her head. "We never had children.
Monty had a couple of nieces and nephews, but I was never
close to them. Or, I should say, they never wanted to be
close to me. We'd get Christmas cards from that side of the
family, but didn't have much other contact."

"Do they live out of state?"

"No. Everyone lives within twenty or so miles of here.
We just never found reasons to get together. Look, I don't
want to appear rude, but . . ."

Tricia took the hint and stood. "I'm sorry to have troubled you."

"Just tell me you aren't planning on suing Monty's estate. His illness took a toll on our finances. This house is
mortgaged to the hilt. I've got nothing left."

The poor woman looked on the verge of tears. And
hadn't someone—Bob Kelly?—already said David Black
had threatened to sue? She wouldn't be surprised if he'd

already consulted a lawyer. After this morning, nothing he did would surprise her.

Tricia made her way to the front door, but turned to speak to Mrs. Capshaw. "Thank you for seeing me. I'm so sorry for your loss—and for all your troubles."

Mrs. Capshaw scooped up Sarge. "I'll probably lose my house," she said, and sighed. She looked over her shoulder into the shabby interior of her home. "I'm sure some people would say it isn't much of a loss, but . . . it's all I've got left now." She looked into the eyes of her adoring little dog. "Except for Sarge."

Tricia figured she'd better leave before both of them burst into tears. "Good-bye, Mrs. Capshaw."

Mrs. Capshaw closed the door. Tricia hesitated for a few moments, and soon she heard the muffled sound of the television.

As she drove back toward Stoneham, Tricia contemplated her next move. Who on earth would blame Monty Capshaw's widow for him crashing his plane? And a woman making threats? That didn't make sense. It couldn't have been Elizabeth . . . could it? And how could one gracefully ask a woman in mourning if she'd been making threatening phone calls?

Tricia clenched the steering wheel. No, she refused to believe Elizabeth would be so crude. That said, Deborah did have two sisters. Could one of them have been upset enough to make a threatening call? Darn—why hadn't she made a point to talk to them at the funeral? Tricia wasn't even sure if they'd be staying in town another day or two. That was something she could ask Elizabeth.

In the meantime, she needed more information. Much as she didn't even like to *speak* to Russ Smith these days, digging into Capshaw's background might be something she'd have to get him to do for her. Being a former big-time reporter, he knew the kinds of people to ask, where to find the information she might need.

Need for what? To quench some insatiable nosiness within you? Why do you even care—let it go!

But she couldn't let it go. It nagged at her. It wasn't so much the manner of Deborah's death that bothered her now but that she'd died at all.

TEN

The rain had stopped, but the day was still gloomy as Tricia prepared to leave for the day. The whole idea of letting Ginny close Haven't Got a Clue made her feel like a new mother abandoning her newborn to a teenager's care. She'd left a minimum of cash in the till, locking the rest of the day's receipts in the safe. Miss Marple had a litter box in the shop's washroom, and Ginny had agreed to feed the cat before she locked up for the night.

"Honest, Tricia, I can do this," Ginny assured her, with more than a little irritation evident in her voice.

Tricia sighed. "I know you can. And I'm sorry. It's not that I don't trust you to do a good job, it's just . . ."

Ginny shook her head, a wry smile lighting her face. "Haven't Got a Clue is your baby, and—"

"Exactly! You know, it won't take long before you feel the same way about the Happy Domestic."

"Except that it won't really be mine."

"It's the first big step in the process. I'll bet in a couple of years you'll be presenting a business plan for your own shop to Billie Hanson at the Bank of Stoneham."

"Oh, sure, I was just starting to feel okay about all this new responsibility, and now you have to ruin it by reminding me that one day it'll be me in that financial hot seat."

Tricia wasn't fooled by Ginny's words. "No pain, no gain."

Ginny smiled. "Get out of here. Your cat and your shop will be fine when you get back later tonight."

"I'm going," Tricia declared, and grabbed her purse from behind the counter. She headed for the door. "See you tomorrow."

"Good night," Ginny called.

As Tricia went out, a customer came in.

"Hi. Welcome to Haven't Got a Clue. I'm Ginny. Let me know if you need any help finding a book."

The door closed and Tricia squared her shoulders and marched over to the Cookery, determined not to look back.

Frannie stood behind the register, helping a customer when Tricia entered. She hadn't stepped more than four feet into the shop before she saw Angelica pass through the door marked PRIVATE that led to her loft apartment. Angelica checked her watch. "Right on time, Tricia. Let's move." She turned her attention to Frannie as she neared the front of the store. "See you tomorrow."

Frannie nodded and finished ringing up the sale.

Angelica trounced through the door without a care while Tricia meekly followed in her wake. Once outside, Angelica stopped short. "Come on, let's go," she urged.

Tricia caught up to her. "You make it look so easy."

"Make what look easy?" Angelica asked shortly.

"Leaving your store—your livelihood—in someone else's hands."

Angelica gave a bored sigh. "Until I hired Frannie, I was stuck with incompetent boobs. She and I just clicked. Except for Darcy, who I hired out of desperation, I've had pretty good success."

That was an understatement. Angelica had hired and fired five or more assistants at the Cookery before she'd found success with Frannie. Since then, she'd seemed to have mastered the art of hiring competent employees. Meanwhile, though Tricia trusted both her own and Miss Marple's lives to Ginny and Mr. Everett—she wasn't sure she entirely trusted them to take care of her beloved store.

She tried to put it out of her mind.

The sisters approached Tricia's car, parked in Stoneham's municipal lot. "I met Mrs. Capshaw this morning—widow of the pilot who crashed the plane on Thursday," Tricia said as casually as she could, and pressed the button on her key fob.

"Don't tell me you went and bothered the poor woman," Angelica said accusingly.

"I did, and . . . I'm afraid she literally *is* poor. She said they were in terrible debt. Monty Capshaw had been sick with cancer for some time, but he'd been in remission. Still, his illness nearly wiped them out. She's afraid she's going to lose her house."

"The poor woman," Angelica said, and opened the passenger side door. She climbed inside.

Tricia did likewise. "I felt so sorry for her and her little dog."

"Dog?" Angelica asked.

Tricia nodded. "What are those dinky, cutie-pie white dogs that look like toys?"

"Bichon frise?" Angelica suggested.

"Yeah, that's the kind. His name is Sarge."

"Sarge? Isn't that what you'd name a German shepherd?"

"It seems to fit the little guy. He was very protective of Mrs. Capshaw," she said, and turned the key in the ignition.

"Well, of course he was. She's his mom. My little Pom-Pom was very protective of me, too. He would've given his life to save mine." She sighed. "I still miss him every day."

Tricia steered the car toward the lot's exit. "She also said she'd received a couple of threatening phone calls. Who'd be so mean as to harass someone in her circumstances?"

"Let's play devil's advocate," Angelica said. "David Black—or maybe Deborah's mother. Those two had the most to gain."

"Mrs. Capshaw said it was a woman's voice on the phone, but I can't believe Elizabeth could be so cruel."

"Why not? Her daughter died. Most women will fight tooth and nail for their children."

"So says the childless woman."

"Hey, I may never have had kids, but I've got plenty of maternal instinct."

"If you say so," Tricia said, hoping her decision to agree with Angelica had been the right one. Sometimes Ange could be such a witch—arguing just for the sake of it.

Tricia approached Route 101 and slowed, tapping her right-hand turn signal. "I assume you know where we're going."

"Turn here and keep going. I'll give you further instructions as we approach our destination."

"Gosh, why would I ever need a GPS system when I have you in my front seat?"

"Just drive," Angelica ordered.

This could be a very long evening, Tricia decided.

Angelica did know where she was headed, and very soon she'd directed Tricia to park on one of Portsmouth's lesser-known streets. Or at least it hadn't been known to Tricia until that moment.

The Foxleigh Gallery was housed in an old Victorian building in a not-quite-shabby neighborhood near the waterfront. The sandblasted brick and nineteenth-century architectural details lent old-world charm. The red crosswalks done in pavers were charming, but not good for three-inch heels and Angelica definitely wobbled as she walked. Tricia was glad she'd worn sensible flats, as they'd had to park a block away.

They stepped inside the brightly painted door and into the dim interior. A buzzer sounded, alerting someone that they'd entered. "Is there anything more obnoxious than that noise?" Angelica hissed.

"Shhh. Someone will hear you."

"Do I care?"

The narrow building was completely devoid of potential customers. Its walls had been stripped back to the bare brick, with task lighting over each of the works of art that lined the walls at intervals. All but the load-bearing walls had been removed, making the space look a bit like a maze.

Tricia took a few more steps forward, cocked an ear, and stopped, with Angelica running into her back. She whirled. "Ouch!"

Angelica poked her in the ribs and nodded toward the back of the cavernous space. Footsteps forewarned that someone was approaching. As expected, it was the woman they'd seen at the funeral parlor that morning. She was still dressed in the tight-fitting black dress, but now she'd added costume jewelry to the ensemble, which made it seem more like cocktail attire than mourning wear.

"Hello. Can I help you?" the woman asked, with just the touch of an English accent.

"Yes," Angelica said, stepping around Tricia. "We understand the gallery is featuring some of David Black's sculptures."

The woman studied Angelica's face. "Didn't I see you earlier today at—?"

"Yes, you did. I'm Angelica Miles, and this is my sister, Tricia. We were friends of Deborah's."

"Michele Fowler. I own Foxleigh Gallery," she said and shook her head. "Such a tragedy. David's handling it well, though, don't you think?"

"Yes," Tricia said, her voice sounding colder than she'd meant.

Michele either missed it or chose to ignore it. "How tragic that she'll never get to see her husband's success as an internationally famous sculptor."

Was the woman delusional? Did she know David's last showing was an outdoor sale on the Milford oval?

"If you'll follow me, I'll take you to David's master-piece."

Angelica gave Tricia another dig in the ribs, stifling a laugh. "Masterpiece," she whispered.

Michele led the way to the back of the gallery, where they passed various smaller bronze sculptures of horses with incredibly delicate legs, life-sized wooden carvings in the shape of various hats—top hats, tams, berets, and many more that Tricia didn't quite catch, because at the back of the room stood a gigantic piece of metalwork that took her breath away.

"*Triumph*, by David Black," Michele announced, waving her arm like Vanna White in front of a letter board.

Tricia gasped, her mouth falling open as she gazed up at David's magnificent sculpture.

Several track lights from the ceiling pointed down on the formidable steel gate. It stood at least ten feet high and was at least twelve feet wide. The dull metal structure seemed to suck up the available light. From the vertical bars trailed colorful ribbons of metal, painted in playful pastels of pink, green, and blue, with just the hint of gold on the edges. Though static, the ribbons almost seemed to dance in some unseen breeze. Formidable yet . . . beautiful. What could have stood as a strong barrier was open and inviting.

A flush of exhilaration coursed through her, and Tricia found it hard to speak. "It's . . . it's—"

"Gorgeous," Angelica supplied. "Who knew David had so much talent?"

"I did," Michele said, sounding smug.

Tricia turned to face her. "It's magnificent. Surely this belongs—"

"In a bigger, more impressive gallery than mine?" Michele challenged, turning her gaze back to the massive gate. She sniffed. "Yes, I suppose it does. I don't imagine it'll sell—not here in Portsmouth. But if someone from Boston sees it, it could lead to a commission. I'm sure I'm just the first stepping-stone to a very successful career for David Black."

Angelica raised an eyebrow. "How do you feel about that?"

Michele sniffed again. Did she have allergies? "It never hurts to be the one who first discovers genius."

Tricia found she couldn't take her eyes off the piece. And some part of her yearned to own it. Thoughts flew through her mind. Could she get David to do a smaller scale steel gate for her own shop? Could he do something that would mesh with the store's mystery theme? Perhaps a raven?

For a moment, she forgot how much she disliked the man and how angry he'd been when they'd last spoken.

A telephone rang from somewhere within the gallery. "If you'll excuse me," Michele said, and headed back toward the front of the building.

"Not bad," Angelica said, circling the massive gate. "Not my taste of course, but it's a pretty significant piece of art."

Tricia frowned. "Deborah always spoke of David's hobby as though it were a joke—a waste of time. Ginny and Frannie made fun of his yard sculptures, too."

"Then the joke was on all of them," Angelica said. "Do you think Deborah ever saw this piece?"

"She would've had to change her tune if she did." Tricia studied the heavy black gate. Her English professor had loved to find symbolism in everything. Did this work of art represent oppression—or the shackles of marriage? But the gates were parted, with no sign of a lock. And why did the colorful ribbons seem to scream *freedom*?

Tricia remembered what Julia Overline had said the day Deborah died. She'd overhead a telephone call that had upset Deborah, and Julia distinctly remembered Deborah mention the word *gate*. Who had she been speaking to—David?—or perhaps Michele? Had she been angry or perhaps jealous of David's friendship with the gallery owner?

The Blacks had not been a happily married couple. They fought about money. They fought about the time Deborah spent in her store, and the time David devoted to his art. Could they have fought about Michele, too?

Deborah was dead.

David was now free . . . to pursue his art . . . to quit his job . . . to do whatever he wanted.

For a terrible moment, the word *murdered* flittered in Tricia's brain.

"What are you thinking?" Angelica asked, taking in Tricia's vacant expression.

"A very nasty thought."

"About David? I'm not surprised," Angelica said.

"What if . . . he wanted Deborah dead? What if that plane crash wasn't an accident?"

Angelica sighed and did a theatrical eye roll. "Oh, you *do* read *way* too many mysteries."

"I'm not kidding."

"Darling Tricia, you were *there*. You saw what happened with your own eyes. The plane ran out of gas. It crashed. End of story."

Footsteps heralded Michele's return.

"We'll talk after we're out of here," Tricia whispered.

"It had better be over a couple of glasses of wine and dinner," Angelica hissed.

Michele halted in front of the sisters. "I don't suppose you're going to purchase anything this evening." Not the best example of customer service Tricia had ever witnessed.

"Not tonight," Angelica agreed, "although"—she looked beyond Michele—"I'd like to take a closer look at those bronze horse sculptures. They're marvelous. Can you tell me about the artist?"

"He's from Western New York and sells a lot in Chicago and Philadelphia. I can give you a brochure," Michele said, her demeanor softening at the prospect of a potential future sale.

Tricia dutifully followed them, her mind whirling with possibilities. She could use the time during Michele's sales pitch to think things through before she shared her thoughts with Angelica, who was likely to tear her newborn theory to pieces.

Angelica swirled the pinot noir around in her glass, took a sip, and leveled her gaze at Tricia. "You're definitely certifiable."

Tricia picked up her own wineglass. "I think I make a pretty compelling argument."

"In what universe?" Angelica abandoned her glass and turned her attention back to her dinner. Pasta with sausage, artichoke hearts, sun-dried tomatoes, mushrooms, garlic, and lightly drizzled with olive oil. It smelled heavenly and tasted delicious. Tricia knew because she'd ordered the same dish, although she'd been too busy talking to eat much of the meal. Thank goodness for doggy bags—even if one didn't own a dog.

"It all fits," she insisted.

"Only in your warped mind." Angelica speared a piece of pasta, chewed, and swallowed. "You know, I think I could improve on this recipe."

"I'm serious," Tricia insisted. "I wonder if Elizabeth might agree with my conclusions."

"You're not seriously thinking of sharing them with the poor woman. She just lost her daughter. Leave her alone."

"But if Deborah was to confide in anyone, it would've been her mother."

"I don't confide in *our* mother," Angelica exclaimed.

"She's not the most nurturing woman on the planet," Tricia agreed. "But Elizabeth might know if Deborah's life was insured."

"So what if it was? She had a son. Most people with children make those kinds of arrangements."

"With Deborah gone, David gets everything he wanted. He's shed of the Happy Domestic, a headstrong wife, and he can quit his jobs and dedicate his life to his art."

"If Deborah had died any other way, you might have a case."

"That plane circled around and around the village square. What if the pilot was sizing up the best angle of approach? What if he deliberately let his tanks run dry and at the last moment—*pow!*—plowed right into the gazebo?"

"But no pilot is going to deliberately crash into a stone gazebo to take out the head of the Founders' Day celebration, wreck his plane, and kill himself in the process," Angelica said and speared a mushroom. "If you're thinking murder, why not blame Alexa and Boris Kozlov?"

"Why?"

"You said Deb tossed her trash in their Dumpster. I imagine that would piss off anyone."

"Enough to kill?" Tricia asked.

"Why not? What if Alexa and Boris were fugitives?"

Angelica asked, warming to her blossoming theory. "Maybe. . . ." Her eyes widened, as though a lightbulb had gone on over her head. "Maybe they were members of the Russian mafia. I mean, where did they ever get the money to open their own business?"

"Don't be ridiculous," Tricia said. "I'd never believe that of Alexa."

"Ah," Angelica said, raising her right index finger as though to prove a point. "But you *would* believe it of Boris."

Tricia frowned and shook her head. "Your mind is full of tommyrot."

"Admit it, you have to have noticed he can't look anyone in the eye. A born sneak, if ever I saw one."

"You think Boris arranged to have Deborah killed because she illegally dumped her garbage in the Coffee Bean's Dumpster?"

"You're the idiot who believes Deborah was murdered, not me. But that doesn't mean Boris isn't guilty of *something*."

Tricia mulled that over. Angelica had a point. That gave her two very good suspects. She did a mental shake of the head. Did she sound like the protagonist in a bad mystery if she tried to twist the facts to mesh with her version of events? Who killed over garbage? David was still her main suspect. Still, maybe what she needed to do was find out more about that pilot. And she thought she knew who to tap for that information.

ELEVEN

Tricia parked her Lexus in front of Russ Smith's house at almost ten o'clock that Saturday night. The rain had made a repeat appearance but was now diminishing to a fine mist. Tricia grabbed her umbrella after parking at the curb outside his home. She'd have to be careful how she phrased her request for help—otherwise he'd think he might have another shot at a relationship with her and that was the last thing she wanted.

Before Tricia could raise her hand to press the doorbell, the door opened and a delighted Russ stood before her. "Tricia, what brought you to my doorstep tonight?"

"Deborah Black's death. Do you have a few minutes to talk?"

For a moment Russ looked panicked. He glanced over his shoulder toward the living room. Tricia could hear the roar of a crowd. A Red Sox game? Russ turned back. "Uh, sure. Come on in." He held the door for her and she stepped into the small, familiar entryway.

"Hang up your coat," Russ said, and dashed into the living room. Seconds later, the room went silent, and she heard the rustle of newspapers as he did a slap-dash cleanup. She took her time hanging up her coat and standing her damp umbrella in the corner so it could dry. When she turned, she found Russ standing uncomfortably close by.

"This way," he said, as though she hadn't been in his home at least a hundred times, and ushered her into the living room. He gestured for her to sit on the couch, but she steered for the leather club chair instead. Russ perched on the edge of the couch, as though ready to leap up at any moment.

"I was surprised to see you at my door. I thought you didn't like me anymore," Russ said.

"I never said that."

"You sure haven't been friendly toward me for the last few months."

"You seem to forget it was *you* who dumped *me*."

"I've apologized at least a hundred times."

"Yes, well, I've forgiven you for that. But we can't have the kind of relationship we once had." *And I'd prefer that we had none at all*, she refrained from saying. But she needed him right now. Did that make her a terrible person, using him like this?

Probably. But she thought she could live with herself. Maybe.

She didn't want to think about that just now, and pressed on.

"How would you like to scoop the *Nashua Telegraph*?"

He looked at her skeptically. "Have you been snooping around in this plane crash business?"

"Not snooping. Just ... asking some judicious questions. I've got the beginnings of a theory."

Russ threw up his hands and turned away. "Theory? You can't possibly think Deborah was murdered."

"Why not?"

"Because it's ludicrous. You were there. You saw what happened."

Tricia kept her cool, shrugged, and stood. "Okay, I'll just call Portia McAllister."

Russ scowled. She'd definitely hit a nerve. Portia was a reporter with Channel 10 in Boston and had covered the Zoë Carter murder some eighteen months before. Russ was jealous of any reporter in a larger city—especially since his plans to resume his career as a crime reporter in a larger city had fizzled out the previous year.

"Okay, I'll bite. What's your theory?" Russ asked.

Tricia sat once again. She leaned forward and looked him straight in the eye. "Monty Capshaw had cancer. His wife was surprised that he hadn't had his license lifted for health reasons, especially since his medication left him forgetful."

"Forgetful enough not to fill his gas tank?" Russ asked.

"That's something for *you* to find out."

"And what if he *was* flying with a suspended license?"

"The ramifications from that ought to be obvious." *Even to you*, she felt like adding, but refrained.

Russ nodded. "If I were Bob Kelly, I'd be pretty damned worried. What else have you got?"

"How soon do you think you can find out about Capshaw's license?"

"I might have something tomorrow. I'll let you know. Maybe we could get together for lunch or dinner and discuss it."

"Why don't you just call me, and we'll go from there."

Russ sighed. "All right. Whatever I find out, I'll share with you. Deal?" He held out his hand.

Reluctant as she was to shake on it, Tricia accepted his hand. As expected, he didn't want to let go. She had to yank her hand free and glared at him.

"Rumor has it that David Black intends to sue anyone he thinks he can get a nickel out of," Tricia said.

"Which sounds reasonable under the circumstances."

"Frannie Armstrong lives a few houses from the Blacks. She says they fought almost every night."

"About?"

"Money, for one. It seems that Deborah's life was heavily insured and David is her only beneficiary," she bluffed, since she hadn't yet had time to ask Elizabeth about it.

"That's not unusual."

"But even more telling—David was seen on Friday evening at the Brookview Inn with the same woman he brought to the funeral parlor. They were drinking champagne, no doubt celebrating the sale of Deborah's store."

"Yeah, I heard Ginny's going to manage it," Russ said as he sorted through the magazines and papers on the coffee table, coming up with a steno pad and pen. "What's the woman's name?"

"Michele Fowler. She owns the Foxleigh Gallery in Portsmouth. David is exhibiting some of his metal sculptures there."

"How does all this relate to the pilot who was killed?"

"Monty Capshaw had been sick for a long time. He was

heavily in debt. What reasonable man would want to leave his wife in that situation? He flew that plane in circles around the village until he ran out of gas. Why didn't he steer for the Half Moon Nudist Camp? It's not far from the village and he could have landed safely instead of destroying a village landmark and killing himself and Deborah—as well as putting scores of other people at risk."

"Are you saying he committed suicide for an insurance payout?"

"It may have been the only way he could be sure his wife was financially secure."

Russ shook his head. "I still don't get what this has to do with Deborah's death."

"Double jeopardy. Someone could also have paid him to crash the plane. Someone who knew Deborah would be at that place and that time."

"Her husband?" Russ shook his head. "Sounds pretty farfetched to me. And even if it was true, how could you prove it?"

Tricia bit her lip and frowned. She didn't have a clue.

The status of Monty Capshaw's pilot's license wasn't the only thing on Tricia's mind. The fact that the name Nigela Racita Associates kept popping up in Stoneham was beginning to grate on her. Why was this particular firm so focused on this one little village in New Hampshire? Did they have other holdings, and if so, where were they?

Tricia settled at the desk in her living room and powered up her laptop. Miss Marple jumped onto her lap and head butted her chin. "Now now, Miss Marple," Tricia scolded, and gently set the cat down on the floor. Miss Marple circled the chair and jumped up from the opposite side, landing on Tricia's lap with a very pleased *"Brrrp!"*

Tricia reached around the cat to type a URL into her browser. Seconds later, the Google home page appeared. She typed in the words *Nigela Racita Associates* and hit enter. The last time she'd Googled the firm, only one entry, for its Website, appeared. This time, however, the entire screen was filled with entries, most of them either press releases or links to articles in the Web version of the *Nashua Telegraph*.

Miss Marple butted Tricia's hand, knocking it away from her wireless mouse. She disliked using the laptop's built-in mouse pad, preferring something with a little more heft. Miss Marple saw it as a toy and more than once had batted it off the desk and onto the floor. "Don't be naughty," Tricia admonished, but Miss Marple continued to nudge her hand with her cool, damp nose.

Despite the cat's persistence, Tricia clicked the top link and the NRA Website popped up on her screen. Like the acronym for the National Recovery Act, Nigela Racita Associates had cribbed a version of the winged motif as its logo. The site still boasted only a few pages and had no information on its owner or its local rep, Antonio Barbero, and clicking the contact us link only brought up a blank e-mail form addressed to contact@NRAssociatesNH.com.

Tricia clicked on the Current Projects page. It, too, had been updated, to include the Brookview Inn and its renovation, with a picture and a link to that dedicated Website. Of course, it was too early for the company to list the Happy Domestic among its assets, and nothing was posted except the address of the empty lot where History Repeats Itself had once stood.

She closed the page, frustrated. There must be other sources of information she could tap. But if the company was privately held, it had no obligation to the public to make any kind of disclosures.

Tricia clicked on each of the rest of the links and read through the news reports but found nothing new or of particular interest. Talking to Antonio had not been productive in the past. Could he have confided company chitchat to Ginny? If so, was there a possibility she might be willing to discuss it? Tricia vowed to ask Ginny the next morning.

It was getting late. Tricia shut down her computer, lifted the cat from her lap, and placed her on the floor. Miss Marple let out a disgruntled *"Yow!"* but Tricia rose from her chair before the cat could jump on her again.

"Time for bed," Tricia said, and Miss Marple trotted off toward the bedroom. Five minutes later, an exhausted Tricia climbed between the cool sheets on her bed and turned off the light. She didn't feel like reading and lay in the dark staring at the ceiling.

It bothered her that everyone dismissed her belief that Deborah had been murdered. The stars just didn't align to bring one person—David Black—that kind of good fortune. Not unless they had help. He was taking a little too much pleasure from his so-called loss, and no one but Tricia seemed the least bit suspicious.

TWELVE

Tricia wasn't the only one up early the next morning. When she went down to the shop to retrieve her morning paper, she saw Elizabeth Crane, with little Davey straddling her hip, unlocking the door to the Happy Domestic.

The Coffee Bean was already open, so she grabbed a ten from the cash drawer, locked the store, and headed across the street. A couple of minutes later, she took the two cups of coffee she'd purchased and knocked on the door to the Happy Domestic. "We're closed," Elizabeth called out, her voice muffled.

"It's Tricia. I brought you some coffee." She had to yell three times before Elizabeth came out of the back of the store, saw her, and hurried to open the door. "Goodness, you're up early," she chided, and took the offered cup. "I think I have some cookies in the back. They might not be at their best—"

"Nothing for me, thanks," Tricia said. Once again, Tricia saw Davey behind the childproof gate, already playing with some wooden blocks—or rather, hurling them against the wall, each of them leaving a dent. Elizabeth didn't seem to notice. She pulled a stool out from behind the counter and sat on it, leaving Tricia to stand.

"Have you heard anything from the investigators?"

Elizabeth shook her head. "I don't expect to. But I don't like the rumors going around town about David and that Fowler woman."

"I went to her gallery last evening to see David's sculpture."

"Junk—all of it," she said, bitterly.

"I haven't seen his yard sculptures, but the piece I saw there was truly magnificent."

Elizabeth scowled and took another sip of coffee. She looked around the tidy shop with its cheerful merchandise and the lovely displays. "David can't wait to unload this place. I should have bought into the business when I had the chance—right when Deborah started it. Later, when she was in a tight financial spot, she couldn't let me. She didn't want to be responsible for me losing my nest egg should the business—fold. And now David's selling it right out from under me," she said bitterly. "It's like he wants to erase all trace of Deborah."

Tricia had to bite her tongue not to spill her suspicions about David. *Now isn't the time*, she reminded herself.

"And worst of all—I've heard the new owners have hired your Ginny to be the manager. *She's* younger than Deborah was. How can I take orders from her when I know the shop and its stock better than she ever will?"

"Please don't blame Ginny for any of this. She was offered the job and it was in her best interests to take it. I've worked with her for two and a half years. She's good. And she'll do right by Deborah's store."

"I know. It's just"—Elizabeth grabbed a tissue from a box under the counter and pressed it to her leaking eyes—"it's all happened so fast. Four days ago, Deborah and I were making lists for our holiday orders. Now she's dead, and the store has been sold, and I'll be relegated to part-time assistant. That is until the new owners decide I'm excess baggage and get rid of me altogether."

Tricia didn't know what to say, how to comfort the woman. She looked away, taking in the tall spindle card rack. It was turned so that the sympathy cards faced her. She'd been so busy she hadn't thought to send Elizabeth—or David—a sympathy card. And would it be in bad taste to buy one from Deborah's own store?

Elizabeth took a shuddering breath. "I'm so sorry to dump all this on you, Tricia. I simply don't have anyone else to talk to about it."

"What about your other children?"

"They say I should walk away from the store—let David do what he wants to do and not make a fuss. They're afraid if I make waves he'll keep me from seeing Davey—and none of us want that."

"Do you think David would actually be that cruel?" Tricia asked.

Elizabeth sighed. "I don't know what to think. I've already lost Deborah. I don't want to end up without Davey in my life, too."

"But you've had Davey since—" She bit her tongue to keep from reminding Elizabeth about Deborah's death. "Since Thursday, right? Hasn't he spent any time with his father?"

Elizabeth shook her head. "But that doesn't mean David

might change his mind in an instant and take him away from me."

"Shouldn't he be with his father?" Tricia asked.

"David *never* wanted children," Elizabeth spat.

That wasn't what Deborah had said. Earlier in the summer, she'd told Tricia that David wanted more children and that she was the one who wasn't prepared to have another child. Had she shared that information with her own mother?

"Please don't tell Ginny my real feelings about her taking over the store," Elizabeth said.

"I won't," Tricia promised, but Ginny was perceptive. She'd know exactly how Elizabeth felt. Still, managing a staff—or in this case one part-time person—was what Ginny needed to learn if she was either going to climb the Nigela Racita Associates corporate ladder—or own her own store one day.

Elizabeth drained her cup and stood, which seemed like a not-so-subtle hint that it was time for Tricia to leave.

She took it. "I'd better be off. It's sure to be a busy day."

"Yes," Elizabeth said, and tossed her cup into the trash. "I have a lot to accomplish before David yanks the store out from under me. I'd better get to it. I'm sure I'll see you around, Tricia."

Tricia forced a smile at the dismissal and headed for the door.

She had liked Elizabeth's daughter much better than she liked Elizabeth.

No sooner had Tricia returned to Haven't Got a Clue than the phone rang. Tricia picked up the receiver. "Haven't Got a Clue. This is Tricia. How can I—?"

"Tricia, it's Russ. Can you meet me for coffee—in Milford?"

"What's wrong with your office?" she asked, suddenly annoyed.

"I'm already here. I've got an emergency appointment with my dentist in forty-five minutes."

Tricia glanced at the clock on the wall. "Oh, all right, but I've got to wait until Ginny comes in. I'll be there as soon as I can."

"Okay, but make it fast. I've got some news I think you'll want to hear." He gave her the directions and then hung up.

Tricia replaced the receiver and frowned. "Why couldn't he have just told her over the phone whatever he'd found out? Why all the intrigue?

As she'd hoped, Ginny arrived early and Tricia flew out the door.

The little diner Russ chose for their informational rendezvous was in a strip mall on Nashua Street, not far from the Milford Oval. The small restaurant was rather nondescript with pale yellow or beige walls (Tricia wasn't sure quite what the color was), and a few halfhearted attempts at decor, like the fake flowers in glass bud vases on every table. Russ was ensconced in one of the back booths. The diner's menu boasted the best seafood chowder in the state. Since Tricia had had no breakfast that morning, she asked about it, and was assured that at eleven forty-five it was readily available. In the meantime, she sipped her coffee.

"Nice place," she said, her voice dripping with sarcasm.

"You won't be so smug once you taste that chowder," Russ said.

"So what dental calamity has befallen you since last night?' Tricia asked.

"I've got a bridge ready to collapse and I want it fixed before it drops out of my mouth while eating a marshmallow."

"I didn't realize your teeth were so fragile."

"I'm joking about the marshmallow. But a friend of mine lost a bridge while eating a soft dinner roll. I don't want that to happen to me, and I'm willing to pay Sunday rates to see that it doesn't."

Tricia wasted no more time on small talk. "So what have you found out about Monty Capshaw and how on earth did you do it so fast?"

Russ leaned back in the booth, "I've got friends in high *and* low places, and a lot of them owe me favors—like you will after we talk." He really must have dental problems, she decided. Every time he said something with an *s*, his tongue seemed to slip so that he spoke with a slight lisp.

Tricia leveled her gaze at him. What he'd said was not the words of a man hoping for a reconciliation. "And when were you thinking of calling in this favor?"

"Some time in the future. And don't worry, it won't be something you can't deliver." He sounded so damned smug. But before she could reply, the waitress arrived with her soup and a package of oyster crackers. Tricia plunged her spoon into the creamy chowder and took her first mouthful. Her eyes widened as she let the soup lie on her tongue for a moment to savor the taste.

"Didn't I tell you?" Russ asked, rubbing it in.

The menu hadn't been bragging. This *was* the best seafood chowder she'd ever eaten—even topping Angelica's, which was saying something.

Tricia swallowed. "I *will* be coming back here on a regular basis. Angelica has got to try this."

Russ positively grinned. But Tricia hadn't forgotten why the two of them were really there. "Monty Capshaw," she reminded him.

Russ leaned forward and dropped his voice. "The man was broke. He was days away from having his plane repossessed."

"What about the cancer? His wife said he was in remission."

Russ shook his head. "Not according to some of his buddies at the airfield. He didn't want his wife to know that the cancer had come back. He was told he had three months."

"When was this?"

"A couple of weeks ago. And he was looking for a way out of his money situation. That's why he took the job flying the banner for Founders' Day."

"Was he fit to fly?"

Russ shook his head. "Not in the opinion of his cronies. They predicted something like this would happen."

Tricia shook her head. "I might think that if the plane hadn't run out of fuel. You saw how he circled the village until his tanks were dry."

"You're still trying to tie this into Deborah's death, aren't you?"

"It just seems very convenient for David Black that his wife's death suddenly opens so many doors for him."

"Like what?"

"Out of a marriage that wasn't working. Into the arms of a lover who can introduce him to the bigwigs in the art world. He'll also get insurance money and the money from the sale of the store."

"So, he got lucky," Russ said with a shrug.

Tricia glowered at him before spooning up another mouthful of soup. "What about Capshaw—was he insured?"

"To the hilt. He told his buddies that he would never leave his wife high and dry. And it looks like he didn't."

"Too bad you couldn't get a look at his bank accounts."

"Don't be too sure I can't."

"Russ!" she admonished.

"What I mean," he clarified, "is that I might know someone who can."

"That's illegal," she hissed, hoping no one nearby had heard his boast.

"What are you looking for? Some kind of large payment to his savings or checking account?"

Tricia frowned. "Something like that."

"I think I can find out."

"And what's in it for you?" Tricia asked.

"I think you may be right. There's more to David Black than meets the eye."

"I know there is. I checked out his art at the Foxleigh Gallery in Portsmouth last night. He's got a piece there that blows away everything he's done before."

"His lawn art really sucks—but he *has* made money at it," Russ said.

"How would you know?" Tricia asked.

"I ran a piece on him last summer in the *Stoneham Weekly News*."

"I must have missed it," Tricia said, and scraped the last of her chowder from the bowl. The truth was, she rarely read the local weekly news rag. "Did David mention he was trying new things?"

"As a matter of fact, yes. But he wasn't willing to talk about it at the time."

"I'd like to read the piece. Have you still got copies?"

"Not hard copies. Call over to the office and ask one of the girls to e-mail it to you."

"Thanks."

"What else have *you* got on David Black?" Russ asked.

"He doesn't seem very interested in his son. His mother-in-law says he hasn't been with the boy since Deborah died."

Russ frowned. "He's a rotten little kid. I can't say I blame David."

"Davey's just a baby," Tricia said, taken aback.

"Hitler started out as a child, too."

Tricia shook her head, pushed her bowl away, and wondered if she could get an order of the chowder to go. "Are you going to keep pursuing the story?"

"I've got a business to run. You could do some of the legwork yourself."

"Like what?" Tricia asked.

"Find out what else David Black has on his plate."

"And how am I supposed to do that? Stake him out?"

"Why not? You're also chums with the biggest gossips in the village. Frannie, for one."

"Ah, but she's been closemouthed about some things lately."

"That's something you could explore as well." Russ looked at his watch and frowned. "There's a dentist's chair waiting with my name on it." He reached for his wallet and peeled out a couple of ones. "You don't mind paying for your soup yourself, do you?"

Tricia shook her head. As a matter of fact, she didn't.

This meant she owed him nothing—except some favor in the vague future. She didn't like that—not one bit.

"Call me tomorrow," Russ said, got up from the booth, and left the diner.

Tricia signaled the waitress, ordered soup to go, vacated the table, and paid the check. It took only a minute or two for her to-go order to arrive before she, too, left the diner. She was halfway to her car when she spied a jewelry store on the other side of the strip mall. A neon sign winked OPEN. *Tacky*, she thought, and instinctively reached for the post in her left ear. On the spur of the moment, she decided she could use some exercise. She and her little take-out bag headed for Maxwell & Sons.

A small bell tinkled in greeting as she opened the door. No other customers loitered around the small, sedately decorated showroom, and in seconds a salesman stepped through a dark velvet curtain at the back of the shop. "May I help you?"

Tricia stepped up to the glass showcase. "I hope so. I was wondering, can you tell cubic zirconium from a genuine diamond?"

"That's quite easy to determine. Do you have something you'd like checked?"

Tricia touched her left earlobe, twisting the stud earring a quarter turn. "I got these earrings from a friend, and . . ."

"Ah," the gentleman said, and nodded in understanding. "Customers come in here all the time wanting to know the value of gifts they receive."

"Oh, it's nothing like that," Tricia said. "I just wanted to make sure for . . . for . . ." Her mind whirled. "For insurance purposes."

The salesman's placid expression never wavered. "Very good."

Tricia set her purse and the soup on the counter. She carefully removed her earring and handed it to the jeweler, who collected it in a soft gray shammy. He rubbed the stone for several seconds before he popped a loupe onto his eye and examined the earring. "Hmm."

Tricia felt her stomach muscles tense. Was that a good or bad "hmmm"?

"May I take a look at the other?"

Tricia removed and then handed him the second earring. He examined it with the same poker face, before removing the loupe. He pulled out a small scale and weighed each. "A full carat each."

"Cubic zirconium," she stated.

"Diamonds, ma'am. They're both exquisite—and beautifully cut."

"*Real* diamonds?" Tricia asked, her throat tightening.

"Did you want to sell them?"

"No!" But did she want to keep such an expensive gift?

Yes! Too bad they'd come from a man who'd unceremoniously dumped and then divorced her.

And yet . . . why had Christopher now sent her two gifts of jewelry? She fingered the chain on her neck. On impulse, she unfastened the catch and handed the chain to the jeweler. "Is this chain real gold?"

He inspected the chain, and then had a look at the locket. "Both fine specimens." He opened the locket. "Pretty kitty."

"Thank you," Tricia managed. Her head was spinning. What was she supposed to make of these gifts and the reason behind Christopher sending them?

The jeweler handed back the necklace and Tricia refastened the chain, hiding the locket beneath her sweater once more. She put the earrings back on, too.

"Were you interested in purchasing anything while you're here?" the salesman asked.

Tricia looked around the showroom. The man had been so nice about checking her jewelry, and since Ginny was leaving, maybe she should buy her a nice gift while she was here. It might be hard to get away from the shop once Ginny started working at the Happy Domestic and Tricia only had Mr. Everett working for her part time. "Yes. I'm looking for a gift. A friend of mine is about to start a new job and I thought it might be nice to get her something. Maybe a watch?"

Ten minutes later, Tricia left the store with her purse, her take-out bag of chowder, and a gift-wrapped watch for Ginny.

And a whole lot more on her mind than when she'd entered the store.

THIRTEEN

The words *the Happy Domestic* were beginning to grate on Tricia's nerves, so much so that she decided to spend her three or four dollars for a good-bye card for Ginny at the convenience store up near the highway instead of patronizing what was once Deborah's store. She picked up a couple of condolence cards, too, although she still wasn't sure she wanted to send one to David.

Traffic was light, and all too soon she found herself heading back from Stoneham's municipal parking lot toward Haven't Got a Clue. As she passed the Patisserie, she decided to stop in and buy a treat for Ginny. She loved cupcakes, especially those made and decorated by Nikki Brimfield, their friend and the Patisserie's owner.

Several customers stood in line to be waited on, and Tricia grabbed a ticket with a number from the little machine just inside the door. The heavenly aromas of bread, cookies, and pastries nearly lifted Tricia off the ground. She'd buy some of the raspberry thumbprint cookies Mr. Everett liked, too. Then she remembered that Mr. Everett was spending the day with Elizabeth Crane at—she winced— the Happy Domestic. Still, her customers would probably appreciate them.

Tricia studied all the wonderful desserts in the large refrigerated case and decided to get a cupcake for herself, too. Since she'd begun allowing herself the occasional sweet treat during the past two months, she found she'd gained three pounds. She still ran four miles on the treadmill every morning, and her clothes still fit, save for one pair of slacks that felt a little too tight for all-day comfort. Was she letting herself go—or was it the inevitable middle-age spread? No doubt Angelica, who'd always battled her weight, would laugh at the idea of being three pounds overweight.

Tricia took stock of her life as the line grew shorter. Was she too worried about what men thought of her appearance? And what for? Grant Baker wanted a companion with no long-term commitment. Russ Smith still kind of pursued her, although for some reason had dropped the solicitous act this morning, which was good, as she couldn't bear the thought of being with him ever again. And her ex-husband, Christopher, was sending her conflicting signals. He hadn't wanted to stay married but now he was sending her expensive gifts. What did that mean?

Nikki called out the next number, and the line dwindled yet again.

Apple turnovers, date bars, iced cut-out cookies, or whole wheat oatmeal raisin cookies—were they really a toboggan ride to diet hell? Did eating comfort food somehow make you an inferior human being, or was it a red flag that should send one to the nearest shrink in search of the catalyst for such behavior? Grant-Russ-Christopher and all that each man represented could be the reason Tricia had indulged. No doubt about it, she wasn't getting what she wanted or needed in a relationship, and an occasional cupcake or an extra cookie a day had somehow found its way into her usual routine. And honestly, three pounds wasn't the be-all and end-all of life. In fact, it was just an extra forty-eight ounces. A two-liter bottle of soda was heavier.

Okay, if the weight gain continued for too long, there could be trouble, but Tricia found the idea of a coconut cupcake now and then far too good to resist.

"Fifty-eight," Nikki called out, and Tricia realized that it was her turn to order. She raised her hand, stepped forward, and discarded her paper ticket in the little wicker basket atop the tall glass display case.

"Hi, Tricia," Nikki said brightly. Did her voice sound unusually high?

"Hey, Nikki. It looks like it's a coconut cupcake day. I'll take two. And a dozen of your raspberry thumbprint cookies." *And an apple turnover—or four!* something inside her wanted to shout, but she exercised all her self-control and let the order stand.

Nikki placed the items in a white bakery box, well insulated with baker's tissue. She tied the box with string and rang up the sale. Tricia handed her a ten-dollar bill, and Nikki made change. It was only then that Tricia realized there was no one behind her and that she and Nikki were the only ones in the shop.

"Wasn't Deborah's send-off yesterday a drag?" Nikki

asked, sounding more like her usual self. "And what was with David bringing a date? The man has no shame."

"I agree. And she's older, too."

"A real cougar, I hear," Nikki said snidely. "It seems Ms. Fowler makes a habit of seeking out younger *artists*." She added the last with contempt. "Still, I don't think she's the love of David's life; more like a stepping-stone to somewhere else."

"Oh?" Tricia asked. Hadn't Michele Fowler said the same thing . . . more or less?

Nikki nodded. "Seems to me I heard that David was fooling around with someone more close to home, but I can't think who—or even where I heard it."

"Frannie?" Tricia suggested.

Nikki shook her head. "Since Frannie was the source of so much gossip back in June and before, she seems to have handed off her Queen of the Rumor Mill title."

That made sense, as Frannie herself had been the object of scandal when her relationship to a murdered man had become public knowledge. Still, in the past, Frannie had been a wonderful source of information, and Tricia hated to see that source dry up. Then again, maybe it was a temporary thing. As Tricia's grandmother was fond of saying, "a leopard doesn't change its spots."

"I heard Ginny's going to be taking over as manager when the sale of the Happy Domestic goes through," Nikki said.

"Yes. And I'll be losing the best assistant in Stoneham."

"That's true. But this also gives someone else the opportunity to be the *next* best assistant. Have you got anyone in mind?"

Tricia shook her head. "If you know of anyone looking

for a job that you think might be a good fit, I'd be glad to interview her."

"Or him?" Nikki asked.

Tricia laughed. "Or him." She looked at her watch. "I'd better get back to work."

"Thank you," Nikki said, with what seemed like extra cheer, although the degree of her smile didn't quite match.

Tricia gave her a wave, exited the shop, and started down the sidewalk. As she passed the Cookery, she saw Frannie waiting on a customer. She raised her bakery-box-encumbered hand in a half wave but doubted Frannie even saw her. By now she was overloaded with purse, soup, watch, cards in a plain white grocery bag, and now the bakery box, and she had to juggle them all to open the door to Haven't Got a Clue. She backed into the store, which was empty except for Ginny, who stood behind the cash desk.

"Do you need help?" Ginny asked, and a sleepy Miss Marple looked up from her comfy spot on one of the chairs in the reader's nook.

"No, thanks," Tricia said.

Ginny spied the bakery box. "Nothing says lovin' like something from the Patisserie's oven."

"I bought us some coconut cupcakes," Tricia said, and trucked across the carpet to join Ginny.

"Oh, yum. And just in time for lunch."

"I've sort of already eaten mine, so this will be dessert. Hang on while I go put this in my fridge," she said, brandishing the bag with the soup in it and hoping Ginny wouldn't ask about the other bags. She left the bakery box and trudged up the stairs to her loft apartment, with Miss Marple following in her wake. Of course, that meant Tricia had to give the cat a kitty snack before she could put away her purchases, but Miss Marple had finished by the time Tricia was ready to head back downstairs. She sat patiently at the door to the stairs while Tricia called Angelica at Booked for Lunch to tell her not to save a tuna plate for her.

"I've already eaten—the world's best seafood chowder—and I brought some home for you, so don't eat lunch. I'll bring it over at the usual time."

"*Nothing* compares to *my* chowder recipe," Angelica declared.

"You might change your mind once you taste this."

"If you say so," Angelica said, and sounded distinctly bored.

Tricia hung up the phone and headed for the door. Perhaps to echo Angelica, Miss Marple gave her a bored *"Yow"* in passing.

Ginny was waiting for Tricia at the coffee station. She'd put on some cheerful Southwest-inspired new age music, and had placed the cupcakes on small paper plates that Tricia kept for just such purposes. "I waited for you to come down before I poured the coffee," Ginny said.

The hackles rose on Tricia's neck at Ginny's solemn tone. Was something unpleasant and smelly about to hit the proverbial fan?

Ginny didn't wait long to share her anxiety. "I'm beginning to have second thoughts about taking the new job," she admitted, and picked at the paper skin on her cupcake.

"Whatever for?" Tricia asked, reaching for her coffee.

"Deborah could never really make the Happy Domestic pay for itself. What if I can't make it pay, either? I'm younger than she was—this is a lot of responsibility. Antonio has let me know that his boss doesn't tolerate failure."

"Has Antonio ever failed Ms. Racita?"

"Not so far," Ginny said, and took a bite of her cupcake.

"He's not much older than you, and he seems to have good business sense. I doubt he would have picked you to take over the Happy Domestic if he didn't think you could handle it."

"But I'm his *girlfriend*," she said, sounding mortified. "I could put *his* job in jeopardy if I fail."

Tricia sighed. It was bad enough she was going to lose Ginny, who truly was the best assistant she could have wished for. How easy—and selfish—it would be for her to encourage Ginny in these flights of doubt. Instead, she donned an almost maternal expression of pride. "I predict you will flourish at the Happy Domestic. I have so much faith in you, and I regret not showing it more often. This whole business with me not giving you a key to Haven't Got a Clue wasn't that I didn't trust you. It's just that I . . ." Tricia stopped for a moment, unsure how to continue. "Haven't Got a Clue is what I longed for. Dreamed of. Worked so hard to obtain and years to achieve. I'm afraid I wasn't willing to share it with anyone." She had to stop herself for a moment, to swallow down the emotion that threatened to choke her.

And it wasn't Ginny she was thinking of—it was all the hurt she felt when Christopher told her he wanted out of their marriage. It was the months she'd lived alone in the aftermath of his rejection. Then a friend mentioned meeting Bob Kelly and told her of his efforts to recruit booksellers to some little backwater of a town in New Hampshire. The friend thought only a sucker would risk their financial future on opening a used bookstore in the middle of nowhere. But Tricia had been intrigued by Bob's grand plans to re-create a piece of the little Welsh village of Hay-on-

Wye in the not so wilds of southern New Hampshire. And Tricia's business hadn't just survived—it had thrived. And in many respects, so had she.

"Ginny, this is the next step in your life. You weren't sure you'd survive what happened with Brian, and look at you now. You've got a new man in your life, you've got a wonderful new job. Things can only get better."

Ginny nodded, and nibbled at her cupcake.

"I have faith in you. Antonio has faith in you. And Nigela Racita must have faith in you, too."

Tricia had just about run out of cheerleader commentary and was grateful when the door opened and a couple of customers entered the store. Tricia greeted them and then paused to think of something she ought to do—to give Ginny an opportunity to forget about her frets.

"Can you handle things here, Ginny? I've yet to canvass the neighborhood for donations for Davey Black's education fund."

"Sure," Ginny said, and straightened.

Tricia retrieved her list, an envelope, and traded spots with Ginny. Tricia gave Ginny a smile and a wave, then set off.

The first name on her list: By Hook or By Book.

Tricia rarely made it to the craft bookstore. The truth was, she just didn't have time for hobbies. In fact, her hobby, repairing old, tattered books, had taken a backseat since she'd opened Haven't Got a Clue. And while she'd refinished a couple of pieces of furniture, the results had not been all that pleasing, and she'd had to pay someone to fix what she'd nearly ruined.

Mary Fairchild was By Hook or By Book's second owner, having taken over after the original proprietress had nearly gone bankrupt during the worst of the great recession. An incredibly sharp businesswoman, Mary had a seemingly endless supply of crafting talent. She painted, knitted, crocheted, quilted, reupholstered, gardened, and baked heavenly concoctions that rivaled Nikki Brimfield's best pastries. Added to all that, she was also one of the nicest people Tricia had ever met. And best of all, she had turned out to be one of Tricia's most frequent customers. If Tricia wanted to talk about mysteries, she only had to go next door for a visit.

The little bell over Mary's door tinkled sweetly as Tricia entered By Hook or By Book. Mary, dressed in one of her quilted vests, sat behind her cash desk, crochet hook in hand, whipping off what looked like another shrug—a shawl with arms. She sold them from a rack beside the register and was no doubt stocking up for the cool weather that would soon be upon them.

"Tricia, what brings you out and about on this lovely summer day?"

"I'm collecting money for Deborah Black's young son."

Mary frowned. "I'm so sorry I didn't get to the funeral service yesterday. Then again, from what I gather, there really *wasn't* a service."

"No. I feel like I was cheated out of saying good-bye to Deborah."

Mary nodded sympathetically and gazed out the shop's front display window. The empty lot where History Repeats Itself had once stood always reminded Tricia of a smile with a missing tooth. She thought about Russ's loose bridge and wondered if his dentist had recemented it. "I'll be so glad when they start to rebuild," Tricia said.

"Yes, and from what I understand, it won't be long before they start. I heard there might be an announcement at tomorrow night's Board of Selectmen's meeting. I know I'm going to be there. How about you?"

Tricia shook her head. "It's not my cup of tea, I'm afraid."

"I'm more interested in who is going to make the announcement. There's talk that Nigela Racita herself might be at the meeting," Mary said with a wily grin.

"You're kidding," Tricia said. Suddenly she was more interested in attending what was usually a very long, boring meeting. "Where did you hear this?"

"I had dinner last night at the Brookview Inn. You know how Eleanor loves to gossip."

She hadn't mentioned anything so compelling to Tricia on Friday night. But then, Tricia had been preoccupied by first Grant Baker's threat to talk over something serious, and then later by Antonio dining with David Black and Michele Fowler.

"What do you know about this woman?" Tricia asked.

"Very little," Mary admitted, "and I've asked around, too."

"I tried Googling the firm but got nowhere fast," Tricia said.

"The corporate headquarters is a lawyer's office on a side street in Flemington, New Jersey," Mary said.

"How did you find that out?"

"My sister lives there. I asked her to look up the address, which is just a few blocks from her office building."

"That's strange. Antonio always gave the impression that the firm had offices in Manhattan."

"They might have incorporated in Jersey to save

money—they may well have offices somewhere else. Private companies are so hard to pin down," Mary said. "They don't have to make their balance sheets public, and from what I can tell, the only place they've invested is right here in Stoneham."

"Why Stoneham?" Tricia asked.

"Maybe the same reason I came here. It's a quaint little New England town. We've got a pretty good tourist trade, and we're close enough to Boston to make a great escape to civilization when the mood strikes."

"I'm dying to know more about the mysterious woman who runs the company. Why does Antonio do all her bidding? Why doesn't she show up in person?"

Mary shrugged. "According to Eleanor, Ms. Racita chose all the new linens and paint colors for the inn, even though all she'd seen were pictures of the place. She seems to have good taste, if nothing else."

"Yes, but is she old, young, middle-aged? She's got to have bags of money to invest if she could buy the lot across the street, invest in the inn, and now buy the Happy Domestic."

"Yes, Eleanor mentioned that to me, and I hear your Ginny is going to run it. She'll be perfect as manager. She's so good with customers."

"I hate losing her," Tricia confessed. "I hope I have luck finding someone as good as her." She sighed. "I'm sure to see Antonio before tomorrow. I'll make sure to ask him if his employer will be at the meeting."

"Good, then you can let me know, because I'll want a seat up front to check her out. Now, didn't you say you were collecting money for Deborah's son?" Mary asked.

Mary had a heart of gold, and though she hadn't known Deborah well, she wrote out a check for fifty dollars.

Tricia wished the rest of the shopkeepers were as generous, but as she left each shop, she couldn't condemn them for smaller donations, either. Not everyone's balance sheet had recovered from the great recession. Still, everyone she'd spoken to had made a donation and lamented Deborah's passing. Yet none of them had known her well—some barely knew who she was. "That smiling woman with the long hair," Joyce Widman from the Have a Heart romance bookstore had said.

And, of course, Tricia bypassed the Coffee Bean while on her mission to obtain donations.

By the time she'd made the rounds, she noticed Booked for Lunch had closed for the day. After making a stop at Haven't Got a Clue to retrieve her take-out container of chowder, Tricia headed across the street to the café to hit up the last person on her list of shopkeepers. After all, Angelica had been willing to donate days before.

"Soup's on," Tricia called as she entered the empty café. Once again, Angelica sat at the counter surrounded by manuscript pages. "Still not finished with that?"

Angelica frowned, taking in the container. She shook her head and sneered at the offered chowder. "I've got three weeks before I have to turn in the book. I'm going to polish it until it sparkles."

"I thought you weren't happy writing another *Easy-Does-It* cookbook. Why get so stressed over it?"

"I'd rather be turning in my Italian cookbook—which is finished and ready to go—but I've got to give them what they contracted for. And besides, it'll have my name on it. I'll be damned if I'll put out an inferior product."

Tricia felt duly chastised. "Besides bestowing the gift of chowder, I'm collecting for Davey Black's education fund."

"Oh, yes," Angelica abandoned the soup and grabbed her purse from behind the counter. She wrote out a check and handed it to Tricia. "Now, finally, I can eat." She picked up the container and headed for the café's tiny kitchen. "I thought I might go to the Board of Selectmen's meeting tomorrow night. Want to come?" Angelica asked, removing the lid from the container and smelling the chowder. She didn't pull a face, which Tricia took to be a good sign.

"You know I'm not interested in local politics." Tricia said. "Besides, they'll likely only talk about the plane crash and the village's liability. I really don't care to have it all hashed out again."

Angelica patted her shoulder. "I don't blame you. I'm not all that interested myself, but I promised Bob I'd go with him to keep him company. Besides, he hinted there might be an announcement on the repurposing of the empty lot two doors down from me."

"Mary over at By Hook or By Book said the same thing."

"Don't you want to know about it?" Angelica asked.

Tricia shrugged. "Antonio knows."

"Yes, and apparently he's not saying anything. I mean, if Ginny had mentioned it to you, wouldn't you have said something about it to me?" Angelica asked, and dumped the soup into a small saucepan.

"Definitely."

Angelica lit one of the burners on the big commercial stove and transferred the pot from the counter to it. "So come to the meeting tomorrow."

"I don't want to go. Although it's said Nigela Racita herself might show up.

Angelica's eyes widened and she almost grinned. "Really?"

Tricia nodded. "But it's only a rumor. I'm not sure I want to waste my time without proof. You can tell me what happened on Tuesday."

"Oh, all right," Angelica said with a shrug. She sighed. "What's gotten into you lately? You're almost as grumpy as me."

It was Tricia's turn to sigh. Maybe it was time to level with Angelica about at least one thing that was bothering her. She took another breath to work up her courage and forged ahead. "Ange, there's something I've been keeping from you."

Angelica looked stricken. "My God, Tricia—you're not dying, are you? Is that why you went into town this morning? To see a doctor?"

Tricia's heart skipped a beat. "No! Why would you even think that? Besides, it's Sunday. No doctor I know has office hours on Sunday." Then again, Russ *had* gotten his dentist into the office only hours before.

Angelica leaned against the counter and fanned her face with her hand. "Don't scare me like that. And what on earth could you have ever kept from me? Your life is an open book—and it's not a mystery."

Tricia sighed, and reached beneath the collar of her sweater to pull out the chain and the locket attached to it. "Look at this."

Angelica stepped close, lifted the locket with its calla lily motif, and gazed at it. "Pretty. Where did you get it?"

"You won't believe this, but from Christopher—for my birthday in June."

"And you didn't tell me?" Angelica accused.

"I wasn't sure what to make of it."

Angelica opened the locket and frowned. "Why is there a picture of Miss Marple in there?"

"The note that came with it said, 'To remind you of the one you love most.'"

"*Is* Miss Marple the one you love most?" Angelica asked, looking and sounding offended.

"Besides my family? I guess so. Not that I would admit that to anyone but you."

"Trish, Miss Marple is a cat."

"Duh!"

"Was Christopher jealous of your pet?" Angelica asked.

"I never thought so. The last time I spoke to him, he said he missed her."

"And when was that?"

"Almost two years ago."

Angelica sighed, closed the locket, and gently replaced it on Tricia's chest. "Weird." She grabbed a wooden spoon from out of a crock holding utensils, and stirred the soup.

"You want double weird? Those earrings you admired yesterday—" Tricia began.

"The cubic zirconia?"

"They're not."

"Not what?"

"Cubic zirconium. I had them checked by a jeweler in Milford this morning. They're the real thing—one-carat diamonds. Christopher sent them."

Angelica smiled. "Not bad. What was the occasion?"

"What would have been our thirteenth wedding anniversary."

"Why would a man who dumped you suddenly start sending you gifts?" Angelica asked, paused in her stirring, and sampled the soup. She frowned.

"Guilt?" Tricia suggested.

"Wouldn't flowers be a lot cheaper?" Angelica asked.

Tricia shrugged.

Angelica's eyes widened and she positively grinned. "Maybe he's trying to win you back."

"I hardly think so. I mean, if he was that interested, wouldn't he call—or at least send an e-mail?"

"He sent the jewelry snail mail?"

Tricia nodded. "Without insurance—or even delivery confirmation."

"Well, that's was just plain dumb. Have you contacted him to say thank you?"

Tricia shook her head. "I'm not sure I should encourage him."

" 'Good manners above all,' " Angelica said, quoting their long-dead grandmother.

"I know. But what's his agenda?" Tricia asked. "He dumped me and moved two thousand miles away."

"You said it, guilt!" Angelica reiterated in a singsong cadence.

"And I repeat—what am I supposed to do?"

Angelica shrugged. "Say thank you, wear the jewelry, and move on."

"But why is he doing this?"

"Didn't you just hear what I said? The man feels guilty for leaving you. He always did buy you jewelry, right?"

Tricia nodded.

"So wear it in good health and get on with your life."

"You make it sound so easy," Tricia said, suddenly feeling weary.

"It doesn't have to be difficult. Look at me. I've had to move on four times. And I'm wondering if it's time to move on from Bob, too." She grabbed a bowl from the stack of dishes on the shelf behind her, and transferred the soup to the bowl. "Do you want anything?"

Tricia shook her head. "I've noticed you haven't been seeing much of Bob lately. So why are you going to the Board of Selectmen's meeting with him?"

Angelica shrugged. "Maybe I don't like to be the first to leave."

"And maybe it's about time you changed that habit."

"Maybe." Angelica grabbed a spoon and pushed the swinging doors that separated the small kitchen from Booked for Lunch's dining room. Tricia followed her to the counter where they both sat down. Angelica grabbed a paper napkin from the stainless-steel holder, tucked one in the collar of her blouse, picked up her spoon and scooped up a mouthful. For a moment she held it on her tongue and then swallowed. Her frown deepened and she looked squarely at Tricia. "I hate to admit it, but you're right. This *is* the best seafood chowder I've ever eaten. Where did you say you got it?"

"At some little diner in Milford."

Angelica spooned another mouthful, closed her eyes, and groaned in ecstasy. "I must go talk to the cook. I've got to have this recipe for my next cookbook."

"It's their signature dish. They're hardly likely to just give it to you."

Angelica leveled her steely gaze on Tricia. "Never underestimate the power and reach of Angelica Miles."

Tricia didn't. Still, she had to stifle a laugh. The great and powerful Angelica? She'd been even more unlucky in love than Tricia.

"So, what else have you been up to today?" Angelica

asked, and plunged her spoon into the chowder once again.

Tricia related her meeting with Russ and told of her efforts to collect money on Davey Black's behalf.

"You've been a very good girl," Angelica said. She wiped her mouth and folded her napkin. Tricia could hear the *but* in Angelica's voice. She didn't have to wait long for it to come, either. "But you're expending an awful lot of time and energy on all of this. Is it a wise time investment?"

Tricia wasn't sure how to answer. The Deborah she'd learned about since Thursday bore little resemblance to the woman she thought she'd known for over two years.

"If something happened to me that you found suspicious, would you trust law enforcement to figure it out?"

Angelica shook her head. "I'm still not convinced anything suspicious happened to Deborah. I witnessed her death. What you suggest seems incredible. And I think you were probably a much better friend to her than she ever was to you."

"But if it *was* me, would you push to find out the truth?"

Angelica's eyes narrowed. "If anything suspicious ever happened to you, I'd move heaven and earth to get to the bottom of it. No one messes with my loved ones—ever."

The vehemence in Angelica's voice startled Tricia, but it also pleased her.

"Then we're on the same page."

Angelica nodded. "You bet your life."

Tricia smiled. "I hope I don't ever have to."

FOURTEEN

 Sundays were usually the worst day of the retail week, and this day had been no different. Still, Tricia was grateful for Ginny's company as the day wore on. She caught up on paperwork as Ginny waited on and charmed the few customers they did have. Tricia admitted she would terribly miss Ginny when she moved on and was grateful she'd have several weeks to get used to the idea—and to search for someone to replace her.

"More and more I think I should adjust our hours of operation," Tricia said, closing her laptop for the day.

"Yeah, the last hour of the day sometimes seems like a big waste of time," Ginny agreed. "I'm going to talk to Antonio about it. But first I'll see how things go at the Happy Domestic for the first month or so."

"I think I'll bring the whole hours discussion up at the next Chamber meeting," Tricia went on. "I don't see any

reason to remain open past five during nonpeak months."
That meant most of the winter and spring. Summer, leaf-
peeping season, and Christmastime were when the tourists
visited the most.

Tricia was casting about for something to read when the
door burst open, and a smiling Antonio bounded into
Haven't Got a Clue. "It's mine!" he shouted, and charged
toward the coffee station, where Ginny stood. He scooped
her up in a whirl.

"Whoa!" she called out. "What's going on?"

"I have just taken possession of the Happy Domestic,"
he said, set her down, and pulled a set of keys from his suit
jacket pocket. "You know what that means?"

Ginny's smile wavered as her gaze darted to Tricia. She
shook her head, but Antonio was too wound up to notice.
"You are now the official manager of the Happy Domestic.
Congratulations, Ms. Wilson. You start tomorrow."

Tricia's heart sank.

"I can't do that," Ginny said, lowering her voice. "I only
gave Tricia my notice on Friday. You said it would be at
least a month before the deal went through."

"Mr. Black wanted to expedite the sale. My team of law-
yers worked overtime to draft the settlement, and I've just
come from handing Black a cashier's check. Aren't you
happy?"

"Yes, but—"

"It's okay, Ginny," Tricia assured her, forcing a smile.
"You've got to do what you've got to do."

Ginny looked doubtful. "I wouldn't feel right leaving
you in the lurch like this."

"It's all right," Tricia said. "I'll take back Mr. Everett
tomorrow, and we'll go on from there." It was amazing

how she managed to keep her voice sounding downright cheerful, when she felt anything but happy about the situation. A change of subject was definitely called for. "How did Elizabeth take the news?" she asked Antonio.

He frowned. "I haven't yet spoken with Mrs. Crane. From what Mr. Black tells me, she will not take the news well."

"He's going to let *you* break it to her?" Tricia asked. Typical cowardly behavior on David's part.

"*Sí,*" Antonio said, and looked uncomfortable. "As my employer says, 'It's why I make the big bucks.'"

"When will you do it?" Tricia asked.

Antonio glanced at the clock. "I should do it now—to get it over with."

Ginny nodded. "What do you want me to do tomorrow?"

"We can talk about this over dinner. I will take you anywhere you want to go—as long as it's the Brookview Inn," he said with a laugh.

Ginny giggled. "That would be lovely."

"You should go home and change—make yourself beautiful, for a beautiful evening," he amended.

"I've still got half an hour to go before we close," Ginny said.

"It's okay. You can go," Tricia said.

Ginny shook her head. "I wouldn't feel right. This is . . ." Her voice caught in her throat. She swallowed before continuing. "It's my last day here at Haven't Got a Clue." A tear leaked from her left eye and she brushed it away.

"You are destined for bigger things, *amore mio,*" Antonio said softly. He put an arm around Ginny's shoulder and pulled her close. She held on to him for a long moment, and Tricia was glad there weren't any customers in the shop. In fact, she felt like she was intruding on their private moment, but it was *her* shop, after all. She cleared her throat.

Ginny pulled back. "You go ahead. I'll meet you at the Brookview in an hour."

Antonio kissed her. "I'll call ahead and have them put champagne on ice. Nothing is too good for the newest team member of Nigela Racita Associates."

"When do we get to meet your elusive leader?" Tricia asked.

Antonio shrugged, his smile sly. "One of these days."

"So she won't be at the Board of Selectmen's meeting tomorrow?"

Antonio shrugged again but said, "She has not said so." He turned back to Ginny. *"Ciao, mi amore."* He gave her another quick peck on the lips and was gone. The sound of the slamming door seemed to echo off the tin ceiling.

Tricia and Ginny looked at each other for a long moment.

"I'm sorry, Tricia. I didn't plan for this to happen so quickly," Ginny apologized.

"I understand." *And I wish I'd called that employment agency before this.* She glanced at the clock on the wall and sighed. The agency wouldn't open again until eight in the morning.

"I'll go get the vacuum cleaner and run it over the carpet before I—"

"Don't bother," Tricia said. "You may as well hang up your apron for the last time and take off."

Ginny grabbed the apron strap that hung from her neck.

"I was kind of hoping to keep it . . . as a souvenir. Would that be okay?"

"Of course," Tricia said. It wasn't much good to anyone else, since Ginny's name was embroidered on it.

Ginny reached into her apron pocket and withdrew the key to the store. "I guess I'd better return this to you." She sighed. "I only had it for two days."

Tricia took the offered key and removed it from the ring, returning that to Ginny. "Keep the ring as a reminder of your time here."

Ginny smiled. "Thanks."

"And don't think you're going to get away without some kind of a party to celebrate your new job."

"Oh, I don't want to put you to any trouble," Ginny said.

"It's no trouble at all. We'll do it on a Sunday—after our stores close—and we'll invite all the other shopkeepers and anyone else you'd like to attend."

"Thank you, Tricia. I can't tell you how grateful I am for everything I've learned here."

Tricia waved the praise aside. "Now, shoo! I'm sure we'll talk in the next couple of days."

"I'd like that, too. In fact, would you mind if I called you if I have any problems? Just for the first few days."

Tricia didn't have to fake a smile this time. "Of course you can. I feel honored you value my opinion so highly."

Ginny laughed. Tricia was going to miss that sweet sound. "You're my idol," Ginny gushed, and suddenly lunged forward to give Tricia a hug. Despite the fact she was losing the absolute best assistant in all of Stoneham, Tricia smiled again.

Ginny pulled back and wiped another tear from her eye. "I'd better leave now, before I start bawling."

Tricia sniffed. "Me, too. And it's not like we won't see each other. Maybe we'll even sit together at some Chamber of Commerce breakfasts."

"That would be great."

Ginny retrieved her purse from under the counter and headed for the door. She paused before opening it and turned back to take in Haven't Got a Clue. "I'll miss you, old mystery bookstore."

"Go," Tricia said, and laughed.

Ginny smiled, opened the door, and left, without a backward glance.

"*Yow!*" Miss Marple said, from her perch behind the cash desk.

"Yes, I'll miss her, too. We seem to witness a lot of people leaving our lives, don't we, Miss Marple?"

The cat jumped down from the shelf and was soon nuzzling her head against Tricia's arm as if to say, *I won't leave you.*

The words on Christopher's birthday card to her came back with a poignant pang: *The one you love most.*

"*Yow!*" Miss Marple said again, and Tricia turned back to the register to start her end-of-day tasks. She caught sight of her list of booksellers to hit for Davey Black's education fund and realized she'd missed her opportunity to hit up Antonio for a donation.

Before she had a chance to berate herself, the shop door burst open once again. Mr. Everett stood there, wild-eyed. "I quit!" he said with disgust.

"What happened now?" Tricia asked, wearily.

"Mrs. Crane and I had a disagreement over trash," he said.

That got Tricia's attention. "Oh?"

He stepped inside, closing the door behind him. Once again, Tricia was glad there were no customers in the store. He walked up to the cash desk, and Miss Marple transferred her attentions from Tricia's arm to Mr. Everett's welcoming hand.

"Earlier this afternoon," he began, "Mrs. Crane asked me to take out the trash but to put it in the Dumpster behind the Coffee Bean. I protested, but she assured me that Mrs. Black and the Kozlovs had an agreement. I did as I was told, and Mr. Kozlov came thundering out the back of the Coffee Bean. I thought for a moment he might hit me."

"Oh dear," Tricia said, and winced.

"I repeated what Mrs. Crane said, but he told me in no uncertain terms that they did not have any agreement about the trash. He also said if he caught me putting trash in their Dumpster again, he would call the Sheriff's Department and report me," he said with indignation.

Tricia sighed. "What did Elizabeth say when you went back inside the Happy Domestic?"

"That Mr. Kozlov was wrong. Deborah's agreement was with Mrs. Kozlov, and I was to wait until after closing to put the remainder of the trash in the Coffee Bean's Dumpster. I refused."

"As well you should have," Tricia said. "I prefer to think Elizabeth is mistaken rather than that she lied to you. But Alexa was just as upset about the whole situation as her husband. She would have told me if she'd had an agreement with Deborah."

"My refusal was not acceptable to Mrs. Crane. She called me insubordinate. She called me several other unflattering names as well."

"Elizabeth did that?" The thought of anyone picking on Mr. Everett appalled her.

"I understand the woman is in mourning. I understand she's under stress, but there really is no call to stoop to profanity when dealing with an employee—especially when that employee is being paid by a third party," he continued.

"I'm so sorry, Mr. Everett. I had no idea when I asked to you to work at the Happy Domestic that it would lead to . . . to this."

"May I come back to work for you tomorrow?"

"Yes, you certainly may. And please forgive me for sending you to the Happy Domestic. I had no idea it would be so uncomfortable for you. If it's any consolation, Ginny will be taking over as manager tomorrow."

"She should be told about the trash situation. Perhaps she can convince the new owners to pay for a proper-sized Dumpster."

"I'm sure she will."

Mr. Everett stared at Tricia for a few long moments. "This was Ginny's last day?" he asked, his mouth drooping. He rubbed at the bristles of the growing mustache under his nose.

"The purchase went through on the Happy Domestic much faster than anyone could've anticipated."

"So that's why Mr. Barbero came to the Happy Domestic."

Tricia nodded. "He's breaking the bad news to Elizabeth."

"When he arrived, she dismissed me for the day. I daresay that was a stroke of luck for me. I wouldn't want her to take out any more of her anger on me."

"I'm so sorry I put you into that position, Mr. Everett. It won't happen again. And I'll speak to Elizabeth about the way she treated you."

He shook his head and raised a hand to stop her. "That won't be necessary. She's no longer in charge of the store. And I have confidence Ginny would never treat her employees as Mrs. Crane treated me." Mr. Everett smiled once again. "I'll look forward to coming to work tomorrow, Ms. Miles. Now, I'd best get home to Grace. She's making meat loaf for dinner."

"Sounds wonderful." And what was Tricia going to have for dinner? It was grocery night—the task she hated most. Maybe Angelica had some leftovers in her fridge she'd be willing to share. As long as the cabinet was well stocked with cat food, Tricia saw no need to hit the grocery store for at least another week.

Mr. Everett waved from the door and closed it behind him.

Tricia glanced at her watch. The store was officially open for another fifteen minutes, but a glance out the front window informed her the sidewalks of Stoneham were about ready to roll up for the night, and she flipped the OPEN sign to CLOSED.

As Tricia went through the rest of her list of end-of-the-day chores, her mind kept wandering back to the scene that might still be going on at the Happy Domestic. Poor Elizabeth. Poor Antonio.

Her fury rose. David Black was a bully, a coward, and a cad. Angelica had said Deborah was afraid of him. Tricia couldn't quite picture that. But from what she'd seen during the past few days, the man certainly fit her picture of a prime suspect in Deborah's death. He'd known she was going to be at the Founders' Day opening ceremonies. He had to have known the timing of her speech. Could he and Monty Capshaw have been in cahoots?

Monty was dying. Would his insurance have paid if he'd died from the cancer, or would it have paid a lot more if he'd died while flying his plane?

The cliché "hitting two birds with one stone" seemed like it was meant for this scenario.

"I'm going to confront him," she said aloud.

"Yow!" Miss Marple protested.

"Deborah might have been afraid of David, but I'm not," Tricia asserted, and grabbed her purse.

"Yow!" Miss Marple warned more strenuously, but Tricia's mind was made up. "I'll be back in a while. You're in charge!" And she closed and locked the door behind her.

David Black's car sat in the driveway of the neat, white-painted home he and Deborah had shared on Oak Street. At least, she assumed it was his car. She hadn't seen Deborah's minivan since the day she'd died. It had been parked in the municipal parking lot. Had David already sold it, too?

Tricia parked behind the late-model Acura. She supposed he couldn't have afforded a Hummer. That would better fit the macho image he seemed to have of himself. Of course, now that they no longer made them, maybe his next vehicle would be a Mercedes.

Tricia marched up to the door. What was she going to say to him? They hadn't parted on good terms the day before. Would he even open the door?

She ascended the stairs and pressed the door bell. From

inside, she could hear an electronic version of the Westminster chimes. It hardly seemed to go with the humble abode, but then maybe it had been Deborah's idea of a joke.

The door opened and David stood before her, dressed in a holey gray sweatshirt and grubby jeans. Could the holes have come from sparks from welding? If so, shouldn't he have worn some kind of protection over his clothes?

"What do you want?" David asked, sounding weary. Dark circles shadowed his eyes. He looked like he hadn't slept. Was it guilt that kept him from peaceful slumber?

"We need to talk. About Deborah," Tricia said.

"There's nothing to say."

"David, please."

He sighed. "What the hell," he said, and walked away from the door.

Tricia entered the home. She'd never actually been inside the house before, although she'd often dropped Deborah off after one of their Wednesday night girls-only dinners. The descriptor that came to mind was . . . cutsey-poo. The living room sported all-white slip-covered furniture, with not a sign that a small child lived in the home. The accent colors were pastel, and the walls were filled with shabby-chic accessories. Not the real thing but the kinds of pictures and knickknacks Deborah sold at the Happy Domestic. And while Deborah was herself a bookseller, there were no signs of any books or magazines cluttering up the room.

Was the rest of the house so precious? Or had Deborah given David—and little Davey—rooms for themselves?

"Sit if you want," David said.

"Are you going to stand?"

"Deborah doesn't like me sitting on the furniture in my work clothes."

"Deborah isn't here," Tricia pointed out.

David looked at her in what looked like disbelief and then laughed. "That's right. I can do what I damn well please now."

"It seems that's all you've done since she died," Tricia pointed out.

His expression hardened. "Don't start on me."

"Someone needs to. You've sold your wife's store, her car—" She paused, waiting for David to deny it, but he didn't. "You didn't hold a ceremony to mark her death. And you've totally neglected your own son."

"That you've got wrong," he said with a sneer. "Davey isn't my child."

Tricia blinked, taken aback.

"You mean you hadn't noticed he doesn't look a thing like me?" David accused.

"He takes after Deborah's family," Tricia said, but suddenly realized that wasn't true, either.

"It's pretty easy to determine these things nowadays. All I had to do was wipe a swab on the inside of Davey's cheek and do the same to myself. I sent them to a lab. Do you want to read the report yourself, or will you take my word on it?"

Tricia opened her mouth to speak but could think of nothing to say. Finally she blurted, "How long have you known?"

"A little over a year."

Tricia's knees felt wobbly and she sank onto one of the slip-covered chairs. David towered over her.

"But Deborah said you wanted more children."

"Stupid of me, wasn't it? I thought if we had our own child, maybe we could save our marriage."

"Then who . . . ?"

"Who's Davey's father? Some jerk she met at one of those gift shows she went to in New York. Believe me, when she told him, he disappeared fast. He was smarter than me."

Tricia had known Deborah during most of her pregnancy. She hadn't let on at that time that she and David were having marital problems. That had come later—after Davey's birth. About the same time David found out he wasn't the boy's father?

"You're not totally innocent yourself," Tricia bluffed. "You and Michele Fowler . . ."

"We're friends," he said, and then a sly smile crept onto his lips. "And maybe just a little more. Deborah cheated first—and Davey's the living proof."

But it had been only a couple of months since Deborah had said David wanted more children. Had their marriage soured that much in just mere weeks? Could that be a reason for him wanting to rid his life of her?

"You've made out well since her death. I heard the shop sold for more than it was worth. What will you do now? Open a studio?"

"It's really none of your business—any of this—but yeah, I intend to buy a place up on the highway that I've had my eye on. Now I have the means to do it. I'm putting in my two weeks' notice at work tomorrow."

"How generous of you," Tricia said with contempt. Then again, Ginny had reluctantly given less than a day's notice.

"Look, I've got things to do. It's time you left."

"But—"

David grabbed her arm and pulled her up from the chair, pushing her toward the door. "It's been a nice visit. Don't hurry back. In fact, if we never speak again, it'll be fine with me."

"But Deborah—"

"Is dead, and it's time we both moved on."

Did he realize how guilty his attitude made him look? Here he was the classic cuckold husband wanting revenge. What better excuse was there for murder?

"Good night," David said, pushed Tricia over the threshold, and closed the door behind her.

Tricia stalked back to her car, got inside, and pulled her cell phone from her purse. She punched in Elizabeth's number and waited. After four rings, it rolled over to voice mail, so she left a message asking Elizabeth to call her. Elizabeth may have been too upset by Antonio's visit to be taking calls. Tricia couldn't blame her. But she needed to do something and she had an idea of what that might be.

She hit the speed dial for Angelica, who answered on the second ring. "What have you got planned for the evening?"

"I'm working on the manuscript," Angelica answered.

"Can you spare a couple of hours?"

"Why? What did you have in mind?"

"It's time to play stakeout again."

"Oh goody," Angelica squealed. "I'll bring the snacks." She paused. "Just who are we going to be watching?"

"David Black."

"Delicious. When can you get here?"

"Give me five minutes."

"I'm packing the Cheez Doodles right now."

FIFTEEN

Angelica stared out at the darkened street and sighed. Tricia had counted at least ten bored sighs since they'd followed David Black from his house more than an hour before, right after Tricia had returned to the municipal parking lot, parked her car, and got in the passenger's side of Angelica's car. Then they'd returned to Oak Street, parked in Frannie's driveway—cleared in advance, of course—and waited to see what David would do.

Sure enough, just after dark he'd left the home he'd shared with Deborah. Tricia had expected to follow him to Portsmouth, where she presumed he'd meet up with Michele Fowler, but instead, he'd driven three blocks to a large home on Fifth Street. The sign out front said TINY TOTS DAY CARE. Across the front, the wording had been partially obliterated by hand-painted lettering that said CLOSED.

"What kind of person names their child Brandy?" Tricia asked, still puzzled by David coming here.

"An alcoholic?" Angelica suggested, and tipped the Doodles bag upside down. Not a crumb remained. "For all we know, she's a fine girl, and a good wife she might be."

Tricia glared at her sister, who shrugged and sat back in her seat. "I *don't* think she's married."

Angelica checked the bottle of ice tea that sat in the beverage restraint device just under her car stereo. It, too, was empty. "I'm bored. We've been sitting here for over an hour and nothing has happened."

"Nothing that we can see, at least." Tricia corrected.

"Tell me this blankie story again," Angelica asked.

"It could be a reason for David being here. Elizabeth thinks little Davey left his beloved blankie at the day care center the day he broke his arm. He's been howling for it ever since."

"It doesn't take an hour and a half to negotiate the return of a hostage blankie," Angelica muttered.

No, it didn't. And since David had had little to no contact with Davey, the theory seemed implausible. Tricia stared at the former day care center, not liking what she'd been speculating for the past ninety minutes.

"Do you believe in flying saucers?" Angelica asked, breaking the quiet.

"Don't tell me you've been talking to Cheryl Griffin or the Dexter twins again," Tricia said.

"No, Frannie."

"I hope they haven't suckered *her* into believing that garbage."

"Of course not. She's not *that* gullible. She did tell me the Dexters were still worried, though."

"Are they still thinking about buying a tenement?" Tricia asked.

Angelica stifled a chuckle. "Those ladies are pretty single-minded. I wouldn't be surprised if they manage to get Stoneham the police force they've been campaigning for."

The sisters were known for carrying clipboards and getting the villagers to sign petitions every six months or so for just that reason. Every year they got closer to convincing the Board of Selectmen that it would be a good idea. Was this the year it would go through?

Angelica cocked her head to one side and squinted in the darkness. "Isn't that Russ's pickup?"

"Where?" Tricia asked, peering out the passenger window.

"There. At Nikki Brimfield's house."

The lack of light made it impossible to tell the color of the truck, but it did look like Russ's.

"I'm going to go have a look," Angelica said, and before Tricia could stop her, she'd opened the driver's door and escaped into the night.

Okay, what did this mean? That Russ and Nikki were a twosome? And if so, how come nobody had mentioned it to Tricia? Not that she cared. And if Russ was seeing Nikki, why had he mentioned taking her to lunch or dinner just the evening before?

And why did she suddenly feel hurt? She had no feelings for Russ. But maybe it wasn't feelings *for* him; perhaps it was the feeling of being left out.

His attitude was certainly different this morning. Had he and Nikki come to some kind of decision about their relationship between last night and this morning? That didn't seem right—not if he was afraid of Nikki seeing him without his bridge. He'd paid extra to make sure he didn't lose it. They must still be at a stage where appearances counted.

The driver's door opened and Angelica ducked back in. "Yup, it's Russ's truck all right. And all the lights are off inside the house. I think he must be warming Nikki's bed."

Tricia said nothing.

"I must say, I thought Nikki had better taste," Angelica said. "But then, it must be a relief to you. At least with him seeing Nikki, he won't be bothering you anymore."

"That's true," Tricia said, and yet on some level it did bother her. She stared out the passenger's window into the dark night and remembered how nervous Russ had been when she'd visited his house last evening. Had Nikki been there, too? Tricia hadn't seen any evidence—like glasses or plates for more than one—on the cocktail table. Had Nikki been hiding in the kitchen or upstairs perhaps—warming *Russ's* bed? Russ hadn't been in a hurry to get rid of Tricia, either.

It didn't make sense.

"While I was creeping around, I snuck up to Brandy's window and peeked in."

"Ange! That makes you a peeping Tom."

"Peeping Thomasina, maybe," she corrected.

"So what did you see?"

"Nothing. I think they went to bed, too. And that's probably where we should go. It's getting late."

But Tricia didn't want to go home. "I wish there were some kind of after-hours place here in Stoneham. Maybe a club that played jazz and served drinks."

"And whom would they serve? The sidewalks roll up at

dark. The problem is there's a real lack of hotel space in the area."

"But the Brookside Inn—" Tricia began.

"Isn't within walking distance," Angelica countered.

"Eleanor was worried someone would buy out the Full Moon Nudist Camp and Resort and put up a motel."

Angelica shook her head. "It won't happen. That place is a gold mine. But if the village could offer other amenities, it could attract the fully clad nudists in the evenings. And it wouldn't hurt if Stoneham had a day spa, an antiques joint, and a jeweler. Those are the kinds of businesses that cater to the tourist trade. There are a lot of huge Victorian homes here in the village that would make wonderful bed-and-breakfast inns. The Chamber ought to try to convince some of the owners to convert their properties."

Tricia laughed. "Have you told Bob all this? Surely he could recruit those kinds of businesses. I mean, he's done it before."

Angelica shrugged. "Bob's vision only extends to the properties he owns, which are all rented. But there's plenty of land on both ends of the village that could be rezoned as commercial property. It just takes someone with vision to pull it off."

"And why shouldn't you be that person?" Tricia suggested, with a laugh.

Angelica shook her head. "I've got enough on my plate. But don't be surprised if Antonio Barbero and Nigela Racita Associates don't pull it off first."

Tricia thought about it. The way things were going, such development might be possible. "I heard that a small village in Canada—Niagara on the Lake—got just such an infusion of cash from a mysterious woman back in the 1990s. It made all the difference in the world."

"Have you ever been there?" Angelica said with a sly smile.

Tricia shook her head.

"I have, and it's spectacular. Everything you want without losing that small-town charm. And they've got scads of wineries within a ten- or fifteen-minute drive, plus a historical fort and a marvelous theater. And in the summertime, there are flowers everywhere. It's just gorgeous."

"When did you go to Canada?"

"Years ago, with Drew," she said with a wave of her hand. Drew had been her fourth husband.

Tricia leaned back against her seat, wishing she was anywhere else in the state—the country, the planet—than staring at Nikki Brimfield's darkened house. How she longed to escape her life. She hadn't had more than a day off—at Christmas—since she'd opened Haven't Got a Clue. And now, with Ginny gone, she had no hope of having a day's respite until she'd fully trained someone else. And since she hadn't felt comfortable enough giving Ginny a key, would she be as restrictive with whomever she hired to take Ginny's place? Part of her hoped she'd learned her lesson. The other part wasn't so sure.

"You're being awfully quiet," Angelica said. "Is it because Russ is seeing Nikki?"

Tricia shook her head. "It's just one thing piling on top of another. Deborah's death, losing Ginny . . . What else can happen?"

In the dim light, Tricia could see the ghost of a smile light Angelica's face. "It's that old Chinese curse. . . ."

"May you live in interesting times," Tricia recited. "Yeah, I know all about it."

"Interesting doesn't necessarily mean good—or bad," Angelica said. "Just different."

She turned the key in the ignition and steered away from the curb, waiting until they were half a block from Nikki's house before she switched on the car's headlights.

Tricia was tired of living a different life. She wanted her old life back. No, that wasn't right, either. She wanted parts of her old life back, and she wanted them to neatly mesh with the life she'd built for herself since Christopher had left her. That wasn't going to happen.

It was time for a new plan.

Too bad she had no idea where to start.

SIXTEEN

At nine o'clock Monday morning, the sun was up and the temperature was already near eighty. It would be a hot one. When Tricia opened the door to Haven't Got a Clue to retrieve her newspaper, she saw Elizabeth Crane at the door of the Happy Domestic. She paused to watch as Elizabeth became more and more frustrated as she juggled keys, a coffee cup, and tried to keep little Davey from struggling out of his stroller.

Tricia tucked the paper under her arm and looked both ways before crossing the street to join her. "Something wrong?" she asked as she approached.

"Did you know the sale of the Happy Domestic has already gone through?" Elizabeth said, her voice shrill.

"I heard," Tricia said sympathetically.

"Look at this!" Elizabeth said, and pointed to the shiny brass keyhole. "The locks have been changed. I'm shut out," she cried in despair, and then burst into tears.

Tricia gathered her in a hug, patting her back.

"Nana, Nana!" Davey cried, yanking on Elizabeth's sweater.

Elizabeth pulled back and wiped at her eyes. "I apologize for losing it. I just can't believe how insensitive that Barbero man could be."

"He did tell you about the sale last night," Tricia said.

"Yes, but he said nothing about changing the locks."

"Nana, Nana!" Davey insisted, and Elizabeth turned her attention to her grandson.

This was Tricia's first chance to look at the boy since David's revelation about his paternity the night before. No doubt about it, Davey looked nothing like David Black, and she'd been right in thinking he didn't resemble Deborah's side of the family, either. Not with that nose and coloring.

"Did you get my message last night?" Tricia asked.

"What? Oh, yes. Sorry. I was upset. I didn't feel up to making calls. I intended to speak to you this morning, after I opened the store."

"But Ginny's supposed to be in this morning."

"I wanted to get here first, to clean up some of the paperwork, and be on hand to welcome her." She rummaged through the diaper bag and came up with a box of animal crackers.

There was no easy way to broach the subject other than to just do it. Tricia took a steadying breath before speaking. "I had a rather disturbing conversation with David last night."

"I haven't had a decent conversation with him for months," Elizabeth said, and handed Davey a few of the crackers.

"Did you know David wasn't Davey's father?" Tricia asked.

Elizabeth's mouth dropped, and for a moment Tricia thought she might burst into tears once again. But then she pursed her lips and looked away. Finally, she nodded.

"Do you know who Davey's biological father is?"

She nodded again, looking down at the child. "But that doesn't matter. David has more or less said I can keep Davey. I'm more than willing to dedicate my life to bringing him up, but according to the law, David is the boy's father. He's responsible for child support until Davey's eighteen. And I'm going to see to it that he pays."

"Why?"

"To punish him. If he'd been a better husband, Deborah wouldn't have felt the need to look for affection from other men."

There'd been more than one man? "Oh, Elizabeth, that's so unfair—to David, and to Davey."

"Feeling sorry for him? Well, don't. He's made out like a bandit. Not only has he sold the store, but he's going to sue the village, that pilot's widow, and anyone else he thinks he can shake a nickel out of. He had Deborah heavily insured. I found the paperwork in the store."

So, Tricia *had* been right. "Is it still there?"

Elizabeth shook her head. "I took it home on Friday. If I hadn't seen the crash with my own eyes, I would swear that David had my baby killed for the money."

"Have you told the NTSB investigator this?"

"He doesn't care about possible motives. All he cares about is the crash. The Sheriff's Department won't listen. 'Not in our jurisdiction.'"

Davey thrashed around in his stroller. "Cookies, cookies!" he hollered.

Elizabeth grabbed a fistful of animal crackers from the

box she still held and practically threw them at the child. He seemed delighted and picked up a miniature lion, biting off its head.

"Will you one day tell Davey about his real father, or would you rather he hear it from David?"

"He never has to know."

"You don't think David will be bitter enough to tell him?"

Elizabeth straightened, and her expression hardened as she crossed her arms over her chest. "I can handle David."

Tricia had never seen this side of Elizabeth—so cold-hearted. Had Deborah carried the same trait—and just kept it better hidden?

"You know that's not fair." Why was she suddenly feeling sorry for David Black?

Elizabeth leveled an angry glare at Tricia. "Whoever said life was fair? If it were, my daughter would still be alive. Now I don't have her, and I don't have her beautiful store. Instead, it was ripped from me and given to some punk kid who knows nothing about the business."

The slur against Ginny caught Tricia off guard. "Oh, Elizabeth—that's so unfair."

"I thought you were Deborah's friend—*my* friend," she sneered. "Now I see you're just as rotten as David." She grabbed the handles on the stroller and turned it, nearly smashing it into Tricia's shins. "Get out of my way."

Tricia stood back as Elizabeth strode down the street, head held high, Davey's childish laugh echoing off the buildings along the empty street.

Shaken, Tricia returned to Haven't Got a Clue. Miss Marple sat near the door and greeted her with a cheerful *"Yow!"*

"Glad you think so," Tricia said. She deposited the newspaper on the sales counter and headed for the beverage station. She needed a jolt of caffeine—STAT! She grabbed the pot, got water from the washroom tap, and filled the coffeemaker's reservoir before placing the filter and ground coffee in the machine and hitting the on switch. Now to wait the five or six minutes it would take to brew.

She felt torn. While she felt sorry for Elizabeth being locked out of the Happy Domestic, she'd been shocked by her attitude about Davey's paternity. Of course she was upset—she had reason to be. Life had not been kind to her these past few days. Lashing out at David had to be a reaction to his selling the store and not giving her a chance to buy it. While the entire conversation had been upsetting, she could see why Elizabeth would be angry. She'd give her the benefit of the doubt and ask Ginny about the locks and Elizabeth's status at the Happy Domestic.

She glanced at her watch. Knowing Ginny, she'd arrive early at her new job—she was probably already in transit. Tricia moved to the front of the store to look out the window, intending to wait for Ginny to arrive.

By the time the coffee had finished, she saw Ginny walk down the sidewalk toward the Happy Domestic.

Tricia poured two cups of coffee into the paper coffee cups intended for her customers, capped them, and headed out the door.

Ginny had already opened the door to the shop by the time Tricia arrived. Tricia knocked on the door, and seconds later Ginny appeared. She noted the coffee in Tricia's hand and a smile lit her face. "What a wonderful sight on my first day on the job. Come on in," she urged, and stood by to let Tricia inside.

Tricia handed one of the cups to Ginny. "Just how you like it."

"I always said you were the best boss. Maybe one day I can be, too."

"That's kind of why I came over to see you. Ginny, did you know the locks had been changed since Antonio broke the news to Elizabeth last night?"

Ginny didn't answer for a long moment. "It wasn't something Antonio planned on doing."

"I don't mean to sound judgmental, but wasn't that uncalled for?" Tricia asked.

"Please don't blame him," Ginny said. "His boss told him to do it last night, right after he talked to Elizabeth. She didn't take the news well that he'd already taken possession of the store. She was extremely upset—screaming at him. It was David she was angry at, but she took it out on Antonio. He said he'd keep her on, but she grabbed her purse and Davey and stormed out of the store without even closing for the day. Antonio had to call in a locksmith from Nashua and pay double to change the front and back locks. We never did get our celebratory dinner at the Brookview Inn," she added with a twinge of resentment.

Tricia shook her head and exhaled a long breath. "What about Elizabeth? Shouldn't she have been told about the locks?"

"That wasn't my decision," Ginny said, sounding defensive. "It was—"

"Don't tell me—Antonio's boss who decreed it."

Ginny nodded. "Look at it from Antonio's perspective. He didn't think Elizabeth would be coming back to work after all the nasty things she said." Ginny frowned. "I had hoped my first day would be pleasant. I hoped Elizabeth would at least tell me how things operated, who the suppliers were—that kind of thing. Now I'll either sink or swim."

"You'll do fine." Tricia braved a smile. "There's still a little time before you have to open. I should get going so you can take a look around and get familiar with your store."

Ginny managed a weak laugh. "My store," she repeated, and shrugged. "Well, as good as, anyway." Ginny bit her lip. "There is something I noticed when I was poking around last night that I didn't mention to Antonio. There are a lot of empty boxes in the back room."

"Mr. Everett said they've been having trash difficulties."

"Yes, but that's not the problem. The figurines are supposedly worth more if they're in mint condition and in their original packaging. I don't think Deborah or Elizabeth would sell the Dolly Dolittles without the boxes, and if someone buys them as a gift, they'd naturally ask for a box."

"Do you think they were stolen?"

"I wouldn't know who to point the finger at if they were."

Tricia frowned. "Mr. Everett helped out at the store for two days. He might have some insight to share. When he comes in, I'll send him over. He's welcome to stay if he wants to help out, but I'll need some coverage for lunch."

"That would be great. I'm sure going to miss working with him—and you, of course."

"If nothing else, having Mr. Everett on the register will give you time to check the inventory against your stock. That really should have been done before the store changed hands."

"Don't I know it," Ginny said. "We could have a real

mess on our hands come tax time. But Nigela Racita Associates seems to have every contingency covered, so I'll just putt along as best as I can for now."

"Do tell Antonio about it as soon as you can. You wouldn't want his boss to think you were hiding anything."

"Right," Ginny agreed.

"I'll leave you to it, then," Tricia said, and headed for the door.

"Thanks," Ginny called. "For everything."

Tricia smiled and exited the store. The smile was short-lived. As she crossed the road, she considered her earlier encounter with Elizabeth Crane. She'd said she wanted to get inside the store and clean up some of the paperwork. Had she instead intended to get rid of some paperwork? Maybe remove the evidence of all the empty boxes—and all before Ginny arrived?

Elizabeth had reason to hate David for selling off Deborah's store. Reason enough to steal from the store, too? But that didn't make sense, either. The figurines were far more valuable in their original packaging. Unless . . . one sold them cheap.

It was time to get out the old laptop and have a look at what was selling on eBay.

Business was slow, which gave Tricia time to do her Internet searches. Sure enough, someone in southern New Hampshire was selling a boatload of Dolly Dolittle figurines, but every one of the postings was without a picture, and each one listed the item as having no original box. Still, Tricia had no way of knowing who the seller could be. Worse than that, she had no way of proving the figurines were stolen property. All in all, it was pretty much a dead end.

The bell over the shop door jingled as someone entered. Tricia looked up from the computer screen to see Russ Smith striding toward the cash desk. "Good morning, Tricia."

Tricia straightened. "To what do I owe the pleasure?"

Russ's smile was jubilant. "I like the sound of that. Always happy to hear a pretty woman thinks it's a pleasure to see me."

Tricia folded her arms and straightened. "Russ, I know about you and Nikki."

Exit one smile, with bridge intact.

"Why did you invite me out to dinner the other night, when you were already in a new relationship?" she asked.

Russ looked uncomfortable. "I wanted to tell you myself."

"You've had several opportunities since then to tell me. Why didn't you? And look at the way you came in here just now, as though you were willing to continue with the ruse."

Russ's gaze was now focused on the top of the cash desk. "I'm sorry, Tricia. I don't know what it is about you that brings out the jerk in me."

Tricia raised an eyebrow, but didn't comment on that. Instead, she asked, "Is what you have with Nikki serious?"

"It could be. If I don't blow it."

"Good. I'm happy for you."

"Thanks. We've been keeping a low profile because . . . well, just because."

"You don't owe me any explanations."

"No, but I do owe you an apology. Actually, quite a few.

I was pretty arrogant, and now I can see how it might have come off as threatening."

"Apology accepted."

"Can we go back to being friends?" he asked.

"Sure." However, Tricia didn't offer him her hand to shake on it. She didn't trust him that much . . . yet.

"So, what brings you to Haven't Got a Clue?"

"This." He offered her a folded piece of paper—a photocopy of a story from the *Stoneham Weekly News*. "I asked Gail if you'd called for a copy of the piece we did on David Black. She said no, so I—"

"I completely forgot about it. Thank you," she said, unfolding the paper. The accompanying photo was of David standing next to one of his rusty bird sculptures.

"I also have some news about Monty Capshaw's bank account."

"Russ—you didn't hack into it, did you?"

"Of course not. But I have a friend who did." He held out his hands in submission. "Don't even ask. A good reporter never reveals his sources."

Tricia frowned, disapproving, though eager to know exactly what he had found out. "Well?" she demanded.

"A sizable deposit was made the morning the plane crashed."

"How big is sizable?"

"Ten thousand dollars."

"Sounds cheap, when you consider Capshaw paid with his life."

"Hey, he was dying, anyway," Russ said with a shrug.

"What about insurance?" Tricia asked, remembering the envelopes she'd seen on Elaine Capshaw's coffee table.

"To the max. His wife was the primary beneficiary."

"Elizabeth Crane told me Deborah was also heavily insured, with David as the sole beneficiary."

"So you said. Interesting. It wouldn't be the first time people have been killed for profit."

"Yes, but how can we prove it? Can you find out who wrote the check Monty deposited?"

He shook his head. "It was a cash deposit."

"To leave no paper trail?" Tricia asked.

"That's my guess."

Tricia looked down at her laptop on the counter. "Do you think your hacker friend can find out who a seller on eBay is?"

"What's that got to do with Monty Capshaw?"

"Probably nothing. But something odd is going on at the Happy Domestic." She told him about the missing inventory and the empty boxes piled in the back room.

Russ shrugged. "eBay is pretty secure. Why don't you just buy one of the things? That way you'd know for sure who the seller is."

Tricia felt like smacking herself in the head. "Of course. Why didn't I think of that?"

"Because you read too many mysteries. You think everything has to be so god-awful complicated."

Tricia frowned. "Thanks for that."

"You're thinking a theft at Deborah's store is tied in with both their deaths, but I don't see how. Selling those figurines sounds more like an inside job to me."

"Hey, with what I found out about Deb and some of her shady doings, it's possible she could've been behind the thefts, making an insurance claim and selling the stuff off cheap."

"Shady doings?" Russ inquired.

Tricia told him about unloading trash in the Coffee Bean's Dumpster.

Russ shook his head. "Dumping your trash in someone else's receptacle and petty theft aren't usually motives for murder."

"All these listings were made before Deb died," Tricia pointed out.

"So what? If it wasn't Deb, who do you think that might implicate?"

"How about her mother?"

Russ shook his head. "Elizabeth thought the sun rose and set on Deborah. My money's on David."

"He did have keys to the shop," Tricia admitted. "And their relationship had deteriorated enough for him to do something like that out of spite." Tricia wondered if she should tell Russ about both Deborah and David's lack of fidelity, but decided to hold back for now. She could always clue him in later.

Russ glanced at his watch. "I need to get back to my office. Keep me posted on what you find out—and I'll do likewise."

"Okay."

Russ started for the door, then paused and turned to face her again. "I am sorry about the way I treated you for the past year. I hope you can forgive me."

"Should your relationship with Nikki fizzle, don't pull the kind of crap on her that you did on me."

"I don't think you have to worry on that account. I think she's the one."

"The *one*?"

"Yeah. Forever."

Hadn't he thought that about the two of them, too?

"I'll see you," Russ said, and headed out the door.

Tricia watched him cross the street and go back to the *Stoneham Weekly News*. She wasn't sure she believed him.

She shook her head and opened her laptop once again. Russ was right. She should just buy one of the figurines. She pulled up the bookmarked page and was about to finalize the purchase when she stopped herself. Buying it outright would alert the buyer that she was on to him/her/them. Instead, she reached for the phone and dialed a long-distance number. It rang several times before it was picked up.

"Hi, Nancy. It's Tricia Miles. Yes, long time no hear from. Look, are you still an eBay power seller? Good—good. Listen, can you do me a favor . . . ?"

SEVENTEEN

Come Tuesday morning, Haven't Got a Clue seemed terribly lonely without Ginny and Mr. Everett. Even Miss Marple appeared to sense the wrongness of their new situation and had stayed close to Tricia all morning, offering comforting looks and damp-nosed head butts whenever Tricia paused for a minute or more.

Too bad for Tricia, the day seemed to drag when there were no customers and no one to talk to. She wondered how the shopkeepers who had no employees kept their sanity. Between customers, Tricia called the employment agency in Nashua and was told to go online to fill out a form. So, out came the laptop once again. She had just begun to fill out the form when a customer came in looking for a first edition copy of Aaron Elkins's *Old Bones*. Luckily, she had one.

The bell over the door rang, and Cheryl Griffin stepped

over the threshold. This day she had on black slacks that hovered just above her ankles, and a pink long-sleeved knit top that looked too warm for the weather. Tricia rang up her customer's purchases, keeping an eye on Cheryl as she flitted around the store, picking up books, looking them over, and then replacing them on the shelves. When Tricia bid her customer a good afternoon, Cheryl hightailed it to the cash desk.

"Hello," Tricia greeted her. "What can I do for you today, Cheryl?"

"I hear you've lost an employee. I'm here to fill out an application for the job."

Application? Tricia hadn't thought that far ahead. "I don't have any forms to fill out," she began, but Cheryl cut her off.

"I've got a résumé," she said, dipping into her purse to retrieve a piece of paper. She handed the creased document to Tricia. It had seen better days.

Tricia skimmed each entry on the error-ridden typed page. The poor woman had never worked anything but minimum wage jobs, and either her typing or her spelling was atrocious.

"I won't give my Social Security number unless you actually hire me," Cheryl said. "I worry about having my identity stolen."

She didn't need to fear it from Tricia. Masquerading as Cheryl Griffin would be the last thing on Tricia's to-do list.

"I haven't even listed the job with an employment agency yet. But I'll certainly keep you in mind," Tricia said, and bent to place the résumé under the counter.

"That's the only one I've got," Cheryl said. "Why don't you make a copy of it?"

This woman didn't have a clue how to approach a prospective employer. Rather than give her a lecture on the subject, Tricia turned on the all-in-one printer under the cash desk and copied the paper. She handed the original back to Cheryl.

"What does the job pay?" Cheryl asked.

"It's minimum wage, I'm afraid."

Cheryl frowned. "Deborah Black told me that you paid Ginny Wilson at least five bucks an hour more than that. I'd expect the same."

Ginny had been an exceptional employee who had started at minimum wage and quickly proved to be worth far more than that. And why had Deborah disclosed that kind of information, anyway?

"I'm sorry. That's all I can offer at this time."

"That doesn't seem fair," Cheryl grumbled, and refolded the résumé. "When are you going to make a decision? I really need this job."

"Ginny only left yesterday. I haven't given it too much thought." *And if you're the only job candidate, I might not replace her at all*, Tricia thought. "I do still have another employee who is willing to cover for Ginny's absence."

"I guess," Cheryl said, none too graciously. "But as you can see, I've worked a lot of retail jobs."

"So I see, but what do you know about mysteries?"

"What's to know? Somebody always gets killed."

"Many of my customers ask for recommendations. I like my staff to be knowledgeable about the genre."

Cheryl shrugged. "Just tell me what books you want me to push, and I'll push them."

"I'm afraid I don't work that way," Tricia said, using every bit of tact she possessed to keep her voice level with this alien from the planet Nimrod.

"I watch a lot of television. Do you sell books based on the *CSI* series?"

"I'm afraid my stock is mostly classic mysteries. Agatha Christie, Josephine Tey, Dorothy L. Sayers . . ."

"Never heard of them." Cheryl looked thoughtful for a moment and then brightened. "Maybe you could give me a couple of books and I could read them before I start work. Being unemployed, I have a lot of time on my hands."

"Yes, I'll bet you do," Tricia said.

Cheryl stood there, staring at Tricia. "So, what books do you think I should read?"

"Why don't we wait and see what happens first. I wouldn't want you to waste your time."

Cheryl's expression darkened. "It sounds like you don't want to hire me."

"As I told you, I'm not even sure I'm going to be hiring anyone."

"But you said the job paid minimum wage."

"If there *were* a job, that's what it would pay."

Cheryl's lips were now a thin line, and her brows had furrowed. "It doesn't sound like you really know how to run a store. Is that why you paid Ginny so much, because she was really the brains behind the business?"

The door opened and a customer walked in before Tricia had an opportunity to answer the question. "Good afternoon. Welcome to Haven't Got a Clue. I'm Tricia. Let me know if I can help you with anything."

"I'm looking for some Rex Stout first editions," the man said.

"Let me show you where they are." She turned back to Cheryl. "I'm sorry, but I really must help this customer. I have your information and will call and let you know if I can use you."

Cheryl tightened the grip on her purse strap and stalked across the store to the door. She didn't say good-bye.

"I'm sorry, I hope I didn't interrupt anything," the gentleman offered.

Tricia conjured up her most winning smile. "Not at all. Now, let me show you our Nero Wolfe collection."

All too soon the shop was empty once again, and Tricia ducked behind the counter seeking Miss Marple's company. "Were we this lonely when we first opened the store?" she asked the cat.

Miss Marple opened one sleepy eye, regarded Tricia for a couple of seconds, and then flopped back to doze in the afternoon sunshine.

The door handle rattled, the bell overhead jingled, and in walked Elaine Capshaw. She was dressed casually, in a white, scoop-necked shirt and green capri pants and sandals, with a massive straw purse thrown over her left shoulder. Angelica probably had a similar purse stashed in one of her closets. She, too, liked them big. Elaine had also colored her hair since the last time they'd met, which made her look less weary—more like a woman ready to get on with her life.

"Mrs. Capshaw," Tricia greeted. "Welcome to Haven't Got a Clue. What brings you to Stoneham?" Too late, Tricia noticed the woman's eyes were red-rimmed and that she'd obviously been crying. "Can I get you some coffee?" she asked, feeling like a heel.

"That would be nice. Thank you."

Tricia hurried over to the beverage station and poured a cup. Elaine followed. She set her purse on the floor and accepted the cup. Tricia pushed the nondairy creamer and sweeteners toward her, but Elaine shook her head. She took a sip. "Nice blend."

"I get it from the Coffee Bean across the street."

"Can you believe it? I've lived in Milford for the past twenty years and never ventured into Stoneham before today."

"From what I hear, until the last few years—when the booksellers arrived—there was no reason to."

Elaine nodded and took another sip. She frowned. "I had to see where Monty died. At first I told myself it wasn't necessary, but—I didn't think I could move on until I did."

Tricia wasn't quite sure what to say to that—so she said nothing.

"I was surprised," Elaine continued. "There's not much to see. Just some missing lawn and the crumpled gazebo. I'm sure the grass will soon grow back and they'll repair the gazebo, and in a couple of years no one will ever remember that two people died there."

Tricia had tried hard to put the memory of the crash out of her mind, but she was sure she would never forget the horror of seeing the small plane smash into the gazebo, killing her friend.

"I'll remember," she said quietly.

Elaine's mouth trembled and she took another sip of coffee. "I understand there are five stages of grief, but I'm afraid I haven't got time to go through them. My financial situation . . ." She let the sentence trail off.

Tricia's eyes widened. Was Elaine unaware of the ten-thousand-dollar deposit that had been made in her—or was it only her husband's—bank account? She bit her lip to keep from asking about it. And Russ had said Monty was insured to the hilt—did she know that, too?

Looking into Elaine's grief-stricken eyes, Tricia doubted she was aware of her upcoming economic windfall.

"Do you have a plan?" she asked.

Elaine sighed. "I need to find a job. I've been out of the job market for quite a while; my skills are pretty rusty."

"What were you thinking of applying for?"

"I used to be a secretary, but that was before employers wanted you to know every software program on the planet, plus do their accounting, *and* make coffee *and* scrub the toilet, too. I'll probably have to settle for a retail position."

Tricia bit her lip. Should she offer Ginny's job to Elaine Capshaw? So far, she'd liked what she'd seen of the woman. She was mature, probably more than capable. "Do you like mysteries?"

Elaine gave a halfhearted laugh. "I read them all the time. I'm constantly nagging the director over at the Wadleigh Memorial Library in Milford to buy more of my favorite authors."

"Does she?" Tricia asked.

Elaine smiled. "You bet. I love cozy mysteries, and Mary Jane Maffini is one of my favorite authors. I just love her Charlotte Adams mysteries—but the library carries her Canadian titles, too. I like the classics, too. I've always loved Josephine Tey's books, and I think I have every one of them. And then there's the queen of mystery, Agatha Christie. Nobody did it better."

Tricia mulled it over for all of ten seconds before asking, "Elaine, how would you like to come and work for me?"

"Here?" she asked, surprised.

"It just so happens my full-time employee was offered the manager's job for a business across the street." She didn't bother to tell Elaine that her husband had killed the former owner. That would come out in its own good time.

"Oh, well. I . . . I don't know what to say."

"Think about it," Tricia said. "You don't have to make a decision today."

"But I can't leave you hanging."

"Take a couple of days. If it seems like something you'd like to try, we'll give it a go."

"Thank you, Ms. Miles."

"Tricia," she said, and offered her hand.

Elaine shook it. "Thank you, Tricia. She gazed out the window. I don't know if I could pass the place where Monty died every day. But"—she looked around the store—"I sure like what I see here."

"Think about it," Tricia said again.

Just then Elaine's purse moved, and a quiet "*yip*" sounded. Over at the cash desk, Miss Marple stirred, looking alertly around her. The purse moved again, and Elaine looked embarrassed. "I'm sorry. He doesn't usually make any noise when we go anywhere."

"You've got Sarge in your bag?" Tricia asked.

"He doesn't like to be alone," she admitted, and picked up the purse. As she did so, a small curly white head popped out of the top of the bag. "*Yip*," Sarge said again, cocking his head to one side. Tricia was sure the dog had been bred just to look cute.

Miss Marple jumped down from the cash desk, trotted over to the beverage station, committing a total breach of kitty etiquette, and jumped onto the counter. She glared at Sarge, who wasn't quite sure what to make of the cat. Had he ever seen one before?

The fur along Miss Marple's back stood on end and she reared back and hissed at the dog.

"Miss Marple," Tricia admonished.

Sarge blinked at the cat, then lunged forward to lick her. Miss Marple jumped from the counter. Sarge made a mighty leap from the bag, but Elaine caught him before he could charge after the cat. She struggled to hold on to the wiggling dog, while Miss Marple beat a hasty retreat to the safety of the shop's washroom.

"I'm so sorry," Tricia apologized.

"No need. Cats and dogs are like oil and water—they don't mix all that well."

She placed the dog back into her purse, but Sarge began to whine, his eyes riveted on the spot where he had last seen Miss Marple. "I'm afraid I'll have to find some kind of doggy day care for Sarge before I can accept any kind of job. I certainly can't bring him with me to work."

That was a given.

She hefted the bag over her shoulder, and Sarge disappeared from sight.

"Doesn't he get heavy?" Tricia asked.

"He only weighs ten pounds. I've gotten used to lugging him around with me." She smiled. "Thanks for your hospitality. And I really will give the job offer some serious consideration. I'll let you know before the weekend."

Tricia extracted a business card from the holder on the counter. "That would be good, thank you."

Elaine tucked the card into the outside pocket of her bag. "Thanks again." The bell tinkled as she closed the door behind her.

As though sensing the danger had passed, Miss Marple poked her head around the washroom's door.

"It's okay, that big, mean dog is gone," Tricia called.

Miss Marple sauntered back through the shop to jump onto the cash desk, while Tricia got out the disinfectant spray and cleaned the beverage center's counter. "You were naughty," she admonished, but Miss Marple ignored her, instead turning her face to the afternoon sun, closing her eyes, and enjoying her sunbath as though nothing had happened.

Tricia tossed the paper towel into the trash, hopeful Elaine Capshaw would take the job. She liked Elaine, but it was asking a lot for the poor woman to have to face the site where her husband had died. Still, if Tricia had already found one likely candidate for the job, there had to be others. There was no way she could work with Cheryl Griffin.

The day dragged on. Customers came and went.

Tricia's stomach growled and she eyed the clock. With Mr. Everett working with Ginny for the day—possibly week?—there'd be no time for lunch. She'd have to call Angelica and tell her she wouldn't make it to Booked for Lunch for her usual tuna plate. But just as she reached for the phone, the door opened and Mr. Everett entered.

"What are you doing here?" she asked, pleased to see him nonetheless.

"Ginny thought you'd be ready for your lunch break about now. We've both had ours."

"Are you finished for the day over at the Happy Domestic?" she asked hopefully.

Mr. Everett shook his head. "Ginny's been studying the paperwork while I've taken care of the customers. She hasn't said anything to me, but she seems to be quite worried about something."

"Oh dear." Probably the missing inventory and those empty boxes she'd told Tricia about.

"I'll just get my apron, and then you can be off," Mr. Everett said, and headed for the back of the shop. A few moments later, he was back, and finished tying it around his waist before he took Tricia's former position behind the counter. He petted Miss Marple, who burst into spontaneous purring.

"I'll try not to be long," Tricia said, and headed out the door. Once outside, she looked both ways before crossing the street, and saw the Patisserie's sign. The last time she'd spoken to Nikki, she'd seemed nervous. Now Tricia knew why. Making a spur of the moment change of plans, she headed north down the sidewalk.

Only in the past couple of months had Tricia begun to really appreciate the smell of fresh baked goods, and when she entered the Patisserie she had to restrain herself from standing in the middle of the store and just breathing deeply.

Only one person stood at the counter. Nikki made eye contact but quickly looked away and continued to wait on her customer. Tricia had time to kill, so once again studied the contents of the refrigerated cases. She wouldn't buy any coconut cupcakes today. With Ginny gone, she had no one to share them with anyway. The idea of never working

with Ginny again saddened her, making her want that cupcake all the more.

Finally, Nikki made change and bid her customer a
good day.

Tricia stepped forward. "Hi."

"Hi," Nikki said, sounding nervous again.

"You can relax now. I know about you and Russ."

Nikki seemed to deflate. "Thank goodness. I feel like
we've been sneaking around for weeks."

"I still don't understand why you guys felt you had to
keep your relationship so hush-hush."

"I know you two had some problems. Russ had a hard
time letting go. Because of that, I asked him to see a coun-
selor before I would date him. He did."

"Do you know for sure?" Tricia asked.

"Yes, because I went with him."

Tricia blinked in surprise, but when she thought about it,
it made sense. Nikki had had enough heartache in her
life—from a lonely childhood, then a bad marriage, to a
lovesick admirer who would do anything—even kill—for
her love and admiration. It was no wonder she'd been cau-
tious before getting involved with anyone else. Especially
after the tales Tricia had told her concerning Russ.

"Thank you for being so candid," Tricia said.

"I wanted to say something, but Russ insisted he be the
one to mention it to you."

"I haven't had feelings for him for a long time," Tricia
said.

"I know. But the heart is a funny organ. It aches even
when it gets what it wants." She frowned. "That didn't
come out quite right."

"I know what you mean. I was surprised to hear about

the two of you. Maybe a little hurt—but only because I consider the two of us friends. If you're happy, then I'm happy for you."

"Actually, I'm quite happy. *We're* quite happy," she amended with a laugh. "You'd be surprised how much the bakery and news businesses have in common."

"You think?" Tricia asked.

Nikki laughed. "No. But it sounds good, doesn't it?"

Tricia smiled. Their friendship would withstand this small strain.

"What can I get you?" Nikki asked.

"A coconut cupcake. Actually, make it two. I think I deserve it."

"I think you do, too!" Nikki said, grabbed a white bakery bag, and carefully snagged two cupcakes, nestling them between crinkled-up baker's tissue.

Tricia paid for the cupcakes and took her change. "Will I see you at the next book club?"

Nikki looked skeptical.

Tricia nodded. "That's how things go when you're into a new relationship. You want to spend all your time with that person."

Nikki managed a laugh. "I guess those kinds of things never change."

"When you're ready to rejoin us, we'll be waiting."

"Thank you. And thank you for being so understanding."

"Gotta go. See you," Tricia said, and waved as she walked out the door. Back on the sidewalk, she glanced at her watch. Could she eat an entire tuna salad plate in under ten minutes? She'd have to try.

She crossed the street at the corner and headed south

down the sidewalk. As she passed the Happy Domestic, Tricia waved at Ginny, who was with a customer, and then she hurried on to Booked for Lunch.

"About time you got here," Angelica said from her perch at her usual counter seat. "I'd about given up on you."

"I brought a peace offering. One of Nikki's coconut cupcakes."

"Oh, great. I'll pour the coffee," she said, and got up from her seat, crossing to the coffee urn, and poured them both a cup. She set the coffee in front of Tricia, then grabbed the tuna plate from the undercounter fridge. "Anything interesting happen today?"

"I confronted Russ about his relationship with Nikki."

"Spill the juicy details," Angelica said with relish as she rested her elbows on the counter and her head in her hands.

"Not much to tell. Nikki's got his number, and even made him go to counseling before she'd date him."

"Good for her. And good for Russ, too. Maybe he isn't the world's biggest jackass after all. Anything else?"

"Russ found out a big deposit was made to Monty Capshaw's savings account the day he died. A *cash* deposit."

"You still don't think someone paid him to kill Deborah, do you?"

"You have to admit it looks suspicious."

"Maybe," Angelica reluctantly agreed.

"Elaine Capshaw came to visit me earlier," Tricia said, and took another bite of tuna. Oh, how she missed all those wonderful crunchies when Jake made it. She swallowed. "I asked her if she wanted to come work for me."

"You don't waste any time."

"Cheryl Griffin also came to visit just before that. Did I tell you she thinks she's about to be abducted by aliens?"

"If only it would happen," Angelica said wistfully.

"She wanted the job, too. I am *not* hiring her."

"You can hire anyone you like," she said, and straightened. "So, what's it like on your first day without Ginny?"

"Lonely. I loaned Mr. Everett to her for a couple of days. She wasn't happy with the way things were left at the Happy Domestic."

"How so?" Angelica asked.

"Missing inventory, for one."

"Oh. That doesn't sound good."

"She wasn't sure how to bring it up to Antonio. I told her to just tell him."

"Wise decision." Angelica studied Tricia's face. "What's wrong?"

Tricia looked away. "Nothing."

"Oh, yes there is. Now spill."

Tricia kept her gaze fixed on her plate. "I guess I'm not a big fan of change. You were right. I was in a nice, comfortable rut at Haven't Got a Clue. Ginny, Mr. Everett, and I made a great team. The business had done far better than I could have hoped. . . ."

"And you're afraid Ginny leaving is going to jinx that."

Tricia frowned and glared at her sister. "You know I don't like that word."

"No, but it's an accurate descriptor. Trish," she said, softening her voice, "the only thing certain in life is that nothing ever stays the same."

"I think I knew that."

"With your *mind*, but not your *heart*."

"Nikki said just about the same thing not ten minutes ago."

"She's a sharp lady." Angelica got up from the counter

and topped up their coffee cups. Then she reached into the bakery bag and extracted the cupcakes. She set one in front of Tricia and removed the paper from the outside of her own. "Carpe diem," she said, raised her cupcake in salute, and then took a bite. Loose coconut shards rained onto the counter and a smear of white icing clung to her lip. "Damn, that tastes good."

Tricia pushed her nearly finished tuna plate aside and picked up her cupcake, removing its paper and holding it aloft, too. "One thing in life *is* certain. There will always be cupcakes."

"Amen," Angelica said, and took another bite.

EIGHTEEN

Considering how boring the day had been, Tricia was looking forward to a quiet evening with a glass of wine, a good book, and Miss Marple's company. But as she went to turn the deadbolt on the shop door, she heard the muffled roar of an engine zooming up Main Street, the screech of brakes, and a scream. She yanked at the lock and wrenched the door open in time to see the taillights of the car heading north and what looked like a pile of clothes and a stroller on the sidewalk. A child screamed, and Tricia recognized the stroller. Could the pile of clothes be—?

"Elizabeth!" she nearly screamed, and ran toward the huddled mass on the sidewalk. She ran up the sidewalk, as other shop doors along the street also began to pop open.

"What happened?" Frannie called.

"Call 9-1-1!" Tricia hollered as she approached Elizabeth, who wasn't moving. She crouched beside her, noting her scraped cheek where her face had done more than just kiss the sidewalk. Davey continued to scream, but the stroller looked intact and he didn't appear to be hurt—just terrified.

"Elizabeth?" Tricia called, afraid there would be no answer. She was still breathing, which was a hopeful sign, and there was no sign of blood. Still, she could be badly hurt with internal injuries. Tricia decided not to touch her—just in case.

"Is she alive?" Tricia looked up into Nikki's worried face.

"So far. What's taking the rescue squad so long to get here? They're only up the street."

True to her words, she heard the sound of a siren and looked up to see the fire truck approach. It rolled to a halt, and in seconds the EMTs spilled from the cab.

"What happened?" one of them asked, crouching down to touch Elizabeth's neck, checking for a pulse.

"I heard the roar of a car, a squeal of brakes, and a scream."

"Did you see the car's make?" the second EMT asked.

Tricia shook her head. "It all happened so fast—I'm not even sure I could tell you the color." She stood, backing away to allow the men to do their work.

"Do you think she's going to—" Frannie didn't seem able to finish the sentence.

"Did someone deliberately try to run Elizabeth down?" Nikki asked.

"Hey, what happened?" Russ called from across the street, as he emerged from the *Stoneham Weekly News* with his Nikon slung around his neck. With no traffic in sight, he bounded across the road without even looking to the left or right. He stepped onto the curb and exchanged a worried glance with Nikki. For a moment, Tricia thought they might grab one another, kiss passionately, and then cling to each other, but then they both looked down at Elizabeth with concern. Russ showed great restraint by not photographing her at her worst.

Soon Elizabeth began to stir. Her first thoughts were of Davey, still strapped in his stroller. He'd ceased crying and now whimpered, arms outstretched, trying to reach his nana.

"Davey, Davey," Elizabeth called, which seemed to upset the boy even more.

"He's okay," the EMT assured her. "But you're going to the hospital to get checked out."

"Who'll take care of Davey?" Elizabeth wailed, her eyes wild with fright. "I'm all he's got!"

"We'll find someone," the second EMT said as he fastened a cervical collar around her neck.

Elizabeth's gaze roamed all the faces towering above her and finally focused on Tricia. "Tricia, you were Deborah's best friend here in Stoneham. Will you take care of Davey for me?"

"I . . . I . . ." was all she could get out as the EMTs rolled Elizabeth onto a backboard. She howled in pain.

The EMTs soon transferred her to a gurney and hustled her to the back of their ambulance.

"That poor woman," Nikki murmured. "First she lost her daughter, then the shop, and now this."

Someone—Russ?—pushed the stroller in front of Tricia. No one else seemed interested in taking charge of the toddler, and already the sidewalk seemed to be clearing. Tricia looked down at the whining child, wondering what she'd do with him. Had he had dinner? Was he potty-trained? The paramedics had grabbed Elizabeth's purse, but there didn't seem to be a diaper bag anywhere in sight. What had Elizabeth been doing walking down Main Street after business hours? Nothing was open. Shouldn't she have been at home getting Davey ready for bed?

Tricia glanced around and saw that Angelica had emerged from the Cookery and was conversing with Frannie, who nodded and stepped back inside. Angelica advanced on Tricia, who felt rather shell-shocked. What on earth was she supposed to do with a not-quite-two-year-old boy?

"Why would Elizabeth pick you to take care of the kid?" Angelica asked. "You never even earned your Girl Scout child care badge. Have you ever babysat in your entire life?"

"No," Tricia said, desperate to keep from panicking.

If nothing else, Angelica was quick on her feet. "Didn't Deborah have a playpen for Davey over at the Happy Domestic? Maybe it'll still be there."

Ginny had not been drawn to the accident scene. Could she still be at the store?

As the ambulance pulled away from the curb, Tricia pushed the stroller across the street, with Angelica following behind. They paused outside the darkened storefront. Still, they could see a light burning in the back of the shop.

Angelica pounded on the door.

"Maybe Ginny went home and just forgot to turn off the lights," Tricia said.

Angelica kept hammering on the door until Tricia was sure she'd rattle the glass loose.

"Stop, stop! You'll break something," Tricia said, but

instead a silhouette appeared in the doorway that led to the store's back room. It paused for what seemed a long time before darting forward.

Ginny fumbled to open the door. "We're closed!"

"We're not here to shop," Angelica said, and barged in, holding the door open for Tricia to come inside. "Is there still a playpen or crib in the back room?"

"Yes, but—" Ginny protested, but Angelica was like a steamroller and barreled forward, and Tricia followed without protest.

Angelica had a better memory than Tricia. The back room contained not only a small, colorful rectangular mesh and plastic playpen that could double as a crib, but a changing table, toy box, and a large package of disposable diapers—everything needed to take care of Davey for the next few hours until they could figure out something else.

"You can't be here," Ginny protested. "I've got tons of work to do and no time to mess around with a baby." She seemed to shake herself. "And what are you doing with Davey Black, anyway?"

"Elizabeth was hit by a car a few minutes ago. They've taken her to St. Joseph Hospital to get checked out. She wanted me—of all people—to take care of Davey."

"Whoa, she must have been desperate," Ginny blurted, and then seemed to realize she'd just insulted her boss. *Oops—former boss*, Tricia reminded herself.

"What else are we going to do with him?" Angelica asked. "We're not prepared to take care of a small child. Everything we need is here."

Davey seemed to sense the tension building and started to cry once again. Ginny, too, appeared on the verge of tears.

"It'll only be for a couple of hours," Tricia said.

"You hope," Angelica said, and Tricia felt like kicking her.

Tricia bent down to extricate Davey from the belt that held him in place. As she picked him up, she caught an unpleasant odor wafting from his nether regions. The poor kid must have literally had the crap scared out of him during this whole ordeal. She carried him over to the playpen and set him down. "Anyone know how to change a baby?"

"How hard can it be?" Angelica said.

"What am I going to tell Antonio?" Ginny insisted.

"Tell him you're being a good neighbor," Angelica said, and turned to Tricia. "Have you got David's phone number? The kid is his—he ought to be the one taking care of him."

Tricia winced. "Technically—David isn't Davey's father. Biologically, that is. He's more or less dumped the boy on Elizabeth."

"You're kidding," Ginny said, aghast.

Angelica threw her hands into the air. "Another man who can't—or won't—take care of his responsibilities."

"That's the thing—Deborah cheated on him and passed Davey off as David's son. That's one of the reasons they hit a snag in their marriage."

"This is all very interesting," Ginny said, "but I need to get some work done. I'm not terribly confident as it is, and all the distractions—"

Angelica turned to face her. "Why don't you show me what's got you bogged down? Maybe I can help. I do successfully run two businesses," she bragged.

Ginny brightened. "That would be great."

"Why don't we take the books out front and spread them

over the cash desk. We'll give Davey some privacy while Tricia changes him."

"Thanks a lot," Tricia groused.

Angelica hustled Ginny, along with the pile of papers she'd been working on, into the shop, leaving Tricia with Davey. The boy screwed up face as he plucked at the seat of his rompers.

Tricia swallowed and held out her hands to pick the boy up. "Come to Tricia," she said in what she hoped was a cheerful voice, "and I'll tell you about the *Ten Little Indians*—Agatha Christie–style."

The pizza had a chewy crust, double cheese, pepperoni, and onions. Angelica did the ordering, of course. She did consult Tricia and Ginny first but ordered what she wanted, anyway. It was tasty, so Tricia didn't see the need to complain. Aloud.

"Is that child asleep yet?" Angelica asked, wiping her mouth with a paper napkin.

Tricia stood between the door to the back room and the Happy Domestic's showroom. "Finally," she said, and tiptoed back to the chair she'd occupied just moments before. "It's a good thing I never had kids—I don't think I'm cut out for motherhood. Has there ever been a more important and yet less appreciated job?"

"Not in my experience," Angelica said.

Ginny didn't comment. With a pizza slice in one hand, she had her nose buried in the pile of spreadsheets in front of her. "If we can't figure out the passwords in the computer, it's going to take a long time to duplicate these data," she said with a worried frown.

"But at least you have an idea of what you're in for now," Angelica said cheerfully.

Ginny nodded. "Thanks to you. I don't think I would've been able to puzzle all this out."

"Call the local geek squad tomorrow, and I'm sure you'll be fine," Angelica said. She closed the lid on the pizza box. "Why don't you take it home, Ginny? I'm sure you'll make better use of this than Tricia or I would."

"Thanks. If I have a lot of late nights here at the store, my stove will probably sport cobwebs."

A banging on the door caused the three women to look up. Backlit by the picturesque gas lamps stood Elizabeth Crane. "Good grief," Tricia called, and hurried to open the door. "Elizabeth, come in, come in. We were so worried about you. Are you okay?"

Elizabeth stood rooted on the rush welcome mat. "I've been better," she said testily. "You might have at least put a note on your shop door to tell me where you'd be. I've been calling all over town trying to track you down. And after what I've been through tonight . . ."

"I'm sorry. It didn't occur to me to—"

Elizabeth cut her off. "I've come for my grandson. Will you please get him?"

Angelica stepped closer. "Are you all right, Elizabeth?"

"I'm fine." Could she have been more curt? But then, except for the brush burn on her cheek, she did indeed seem fine.

"Elizabeth, come in," Ginny said, coming up from behind.

"No, thank you," Elizabeth said more sternly. "I never want to set foot in this store again. Now will you please get my grandson, or do I have to call the Sheriff's Department?"

"I'll get him," Ginny said, and flew for the back room.

"Elizabeth, what's wrong?" Tricia asked. "How did you get back to Stoneham? Can one of us drive you home?"

"I don't need any of *your* help. You've done enough. You're all in this together, along with David. Conspiring against me, taking Deborah's store from me."

Had her brain been addled when the car hit her?

"Elizabeth," Tricia said, hurt.

"Tricia," Angelica said, in nearly the same tone as Elizabeth.

Before another word could be said, Ginny arrived with a sleeping Davey strapped in his stroller. Tricia and Angelica stepped aside so she could steer the stroller through the door. "He didn't even wake up," she said.

Elizabeth snatched the handles from her, jostling the boy, who awoke with a start and began to cry. She bent down and smoothed his sleep-tousled hair, which had the desired effect, and he settled down again. She looked up. "I'll send someone over to collect Davey's toys, the play-pen, and changing table, or did David sell them along with the rest of the inventory?"

Ginny shook her head.

"Really, Elizabeth," Angelica chided, "there's no need to be so nasty to us. If you want to be angry with David, be my guest. The man's a jerk. But we've tried to be your friends."

"Shut up," Elizabeth said, grabbed the stroller's handles, and started up the street.

Angelica blinked. It was rare that she didn't get the last word.

Tricia stepped forward and shut the door. The three women looked at one another and then turned back to the cash desk. "I'd say that put a damper on the evening," Tricia said.

Ginny straightened the papers, while Angelica searched for and found her purse on the floor.

"Did it feel like you've just been kicked in the teeth?" Angelica asked.

"Perhaps gratitude isn't in Elizabeth's lexicon," Ginny grumbled.

"Never mind," Tricia said. "She suffered a trauma, what with nearly getting killed earlier this evening. She'll probably get over it in a couple of days and come back and apologize."

"Or maybe with Deborah gone, Elizabeth will take Davey and move out of Stoneham. We can but hope," Angelica said.

"She does have other children," Ginny said, pausing to turn out the lights.

"But as far as I could tell, Deborah was her favorite. Will they want to take in their mother, when she let everyone know Deborah had the top spot in her heart?" Tricia asked.

"Who says she has to live with them?" Angelica pointed out.

"Very true," Tricia agreed.

Ginny closed and locked the door.

"We'll walk you to your car, Ginny," Tricia said.

"That won't be necessary. Stoneham is completely safe."

"How soon you forget. Let's see, who was murdered in the past couple of years?" Angelica asked. "The Cookery's former owner; that hot-shot *New York Times* bestselling author; Tricia's ex-roommate; Jim Roth—"

"And Deborah," Tricia put in.

"Okay, walk me to my car," Ginny said, surrendering. She and Angelica walked side by side up the sidewalk, with Tricia following. "Angelica, I don't mean to be a pain, but would you please explain again how you figured out that equation on the spreadsheet?"

"It's easy, really," she began, but Tricia tuned her out. It was Elizabeth and her spiteful attitude that whirled through her thoughts. Was she just rattled by her experience that evening, or was she serious about blaming them, along with David, for all of her problems? Either way, it left Tricia feeling troubled.

The entire situation left her feeling troubled. Angelica had the right attitude. Move on. She'd said it about Christopher, too.

It was often hard to take good advice, especially when it ran up against everything you believed. But for now, Tricia decided that Angelica was probably right on all accounts. She'd just never give her the satisfaction of saying so.

NINETEEN

 Tricia and sleepless nights were getting to be a common pair since she'd moved to Stoneham. Was it the fact that she'd experienced more death in thirty-six months than she had in more than thirty-six years, or was it just the fact no one shared her bed anymore?

There's more to life than just sex, she reminded herself, but early that morning she couldn't think of what it might be.

Four miles on the treadmill seemed like forty, so there was no way she'd make up for the missing miles from days before. It took two cups of coffee to perk her up before she and Miss Marple headed down the stairs to start their day at Haven't Got a Clue. When she'd heard the car roaring down the road that had hit Elizabeth Crane, she'd bolted from the store without doing her end-of-day tasks. And when she'd returned after midnight, she'd been too tired to tackle them. She still felt tired, but forced herself to haul out the Hoover and start to vacuum the carpet.

The phone rang. Since the store wasn't due to open for half an hour, Tricia thought about letting it go to voice mail, but on the fourth ring, she shut down the vacuum cleaner and grabbed the receiver—much to Miss Marple's relief. "Haven't Got a—"

"Oh, Tricia, we've been robbed—we've been robbed," Ginny sobbed.

For a moment Tricia couldn't understand why Ginny was so upset. A quick look around Haven't Got a Clue told her that everything was still in place as it had been the night before. Even the till, with its meager offerings, was intact. And then she remembered that Ginny no longer worked for her and in fact now managed her own store.

"What's missing?" Tricia asked.

"I don't know. I don't know the stock well enough yet to tell. But there's busted glass all over the floor. And there's a huge mess in the back room."

And everything had been in perfect order the night before.

"What about the alarm, did you set it last night before we left?"

"Elizabeth didn't give us the code, and the security company hasn't gotten back to us yet. Oh crap—I don't even know if the insurance will cover this. Antonio is in charge of all that."

"Did you call him?"

"His voice mail kicked in. He must be at a meeting."

"Did you call the Sheriff's Department?"

"I couldn't think what else to do, so I called you."

"Hang up. Call 9-1-1, and I'll be right over."

"Oh, thank you, Tricia." The line went dead and Tricia replaced the receiver in its cradle, her hands shaking. She couldn't remember any of the stores along Main Street being robbed—at least since the murder at the Cookery two years before. And even then, only one item had been taken—and there'd been no wholesale destruction. Poor Ginny having to face this on day two of her new job.

Grabbing her keys, Tricia locked the store and once again crossed the road for the Happy Domestic.

The shop door was ajar, and Tricia pushed it open with her elbow. She wasn't about to put her fingerprints in the mix—she knew enough about crime scene investigations to avoid that. As Ginny had said, the carpeted floor was covered with broken glass from several smashed display cases. The remnants of porcelain figurines and delicate Waterford crystal glassware lay among the overturned card carousel. Books had been pulled from the shelves, their dustcovers ripped to shreds.

Whoever was responsible had been mighty angry.

And who had been furious the evening before?

Elizabeth Crane.

With her cell phone still in hand, Ginny came out from the back room, her face twisted into a grimace and tears streaming down her cheeks. "Oh, Tricia," she wailed, and rushed for her, throwing her arms around her.

"It's okay, it's okay," Tricia soothed, patting Ginny's back. And it would be okay. The person who'd made the mess had taken his—or her—aggression out on inanimate objects, not the new owner—or manager—of the store.

A tinny voice came from Ginny's cell phone. "Miss, Miss—"

Tricia pulled back. "Pull yourself together, and talk to

the dispatcher," she said firmly but with kindness. "We'll make this right. I promise."

Ginny nodded and wiped her eyes with the back of her hand. She raised the phone back to her ear. "I'm here," she said, her voice sounding stronger.

Tricia heard the sound of a siren, and looked out the store's display window to see a Sheriff's Department cruiser pull up outside. The driver's door flew open and Deputy Placer leapt from the car. "You reported a robbery?" he asked Tricia.

"The store's manager did," she said, indicating Ginny with a nod of her head. "It must have happened sometime last night—after midnight."

Placer frowned. Tricia could almost read his thoughts. *No action here!*

Through the window, she saw Boris and Alexa Kozlov standing on the pavement. They were soon joined with other rubberneckers who'd come to see what was happening.

"You don't belong here," Placer said to Tricia.

"Ginny—Miss Wilson—called me when she discovered the mess."

"Why don't you wait outside while I talk to her," Placer said.

Tricia frowned. Despite their many encounters, she and the deputy had never become buddies, and apparently never would, either. "I'll do that. Ginny, I'll be outside."

Ginny sniffed and nodded.

"What happened?" Alexa asked as Tricia stepped over the threshold.

"Last night, someone broke into the Happy Domestic and did a lot of damage."

"Hmm," Boris grumbled, and turned away, heading back for the Coffee Bean. For an instant Tricia wondered if he could've been responsible for the mess inside the store, but then she instantly dismissed the idea. Boris had been angry with Deborah and Elizabeth—not the new owner of the store. But then, did he *know* the store had already changed hands and was now owned by Nigela Racita Associates?

Tricia shook the thought away. She was letting her imagination run wild. Much as she hated to admit it, there was someone else with a much better motivation to ransack the store, and for some reason—maybe a misplaced sense of loyalty—she refused to consider it.

Whoever had vandalized the Happy Domestic had a score to settle. And, unfortunately, there was more than one possible suspect. The problem was, which one did it?

Time did not fly when there were few suspects to consider for the robbery at the Happy Domestic, and no sales at Haven't Got a Clue, either. Tricia had sent Mr. Everett across the street to help Ginny with the cleanup and, more important, for moral support. It pleased her that the two had such a good rapport. Of course, the Sheriff's Department investigators probably weren't letting him do much of anything yet, but she knew Ginny would appreciate his being there.

Sheriff's Department patrol cars lined the street, and did nothing to improve the morning's sales. Tricia hoped they'd clear off before the expected busload of tourists arrived at one thirty.

"Yow!" Miss Marple announced, startling Tricia from her reverie.

"Yes, it sure is lonely here without Ginny and Mr. Everett. We'll have to do something about that pretty soon. But if Elaine Capshaw turns down my job offer, I will *not* hire Cheryl Griffin," she reaffirmed. "You and I will run the store alone rather than put up with her and her threats of alien invasions."

Miss Marple almost seemed to nod before she set to licking her paw and rubbing her ear, the beginning of yet another prolonged bathing session.

Tricia sighed and closed the store's copy of Marjorie Allingham's *Death of a Ghost*. Even reading didn't appeal to her right now—she had too much on her mind.

Her attention turned back to the window, just as a uniformed officer stepped out of the Happy Domestic and looked in Haven't Got a Clue's direction. Why, it was none other than Captain Baker, whom she hadn't spoken to in five days. He looked to the right and left for traffic, and then jaywalked across the street, heading her way.

"Looks like we're about to get some company," Tricia told Miss Marple, who did not acknowledge the remark but began to lick her stomach.

Out on the sidewalk, Captain Baker removed his high-crowned hat before entering. Tricia wondered if he would grow his hair longer once he left the Sheriff's Department. It would better suit him than the buzz cut he now wore, she decided.

The shop door opened and Baker entered. "Hello," he called, looking around the store, apparently not seeing her standing behind the register.

"Over here," she called.

His head whipped around and he blushed, and then stepped over to the cash desk. "Slow day?" he asked, and nodded toward the lack of customers in the store.

"It won't be in another hour or so. No offense, but I hope you and your men will be long gone before the next tour bus arrives."

"They're finishing up now. Do you have any ideas on who might have broken into the Happy Domestic?"

"Ideas but not a shred of evidence."

"How about the former manager?" he asked.

"Deborah's dead. You mean her mother, Elizabeth Crane?" Baker nodded. "She was angry last night when she came to pick up her grandson at the Happy Domestic, but I can't imagine she'd actually break in and do that kind of damage. Her daughter loved that store and everything in it."

"And it was sold out from under Mrs. Crane by her son-in-law," he pointed out.

"I agree David could've waited a decent amount of time before doing that. I guess he needed the money for something. But I suspect he's got an alibi with at least one of the women he's currently bedding."

"Is that a touch of anger I hear in your voice?"

Tricia sighed. "This whole situation becomes more tangled every day." Baker seemed to be waiting for her to say more on the subject. Instead she asked, "When will you talk to Elizabeth?"

"As soon as we track her down. She wasn't at the number Ginny gave me. I'll drive by her house. If she's not there, I'll have one of my men stake out her home and wait for her to return."

Tricia nodded. "You did know someone tried to run her down last evening."

"Yes, Deputy Placer informed me. Did you see what happened?"

Tricia shook her head. "I found Elizabeth lying on the sidewalk, and the car speeding away."

He nodded.

There didn't seem to be much more to say on the subject.

Baker cleared his throat. "Uh, have you given any thought to our discussion the other night?"

"Quite a bit, actually," Tricia said. That was putting it mildly. It was among the many topics that had kept her awake these last few nights. "I still think it's unfair of you. You want all the perks of a loving relationship without the commitment."

"That's not what I proposed," he said, sounding hurt.

Tricia forced a laugh. "No, you made it quite clear that a proposal was never going to be part of the deal."

Baker frowned. "What are you talking about? I thought we could be friends—hang out together. Have some fun."

"Yeah, and then you'd leave."

"I never said I'd definitely be leaving, just that it was a possibility."

"Has that changed?" Tricia asked.

"As a matter of fact, yes. I've been offered a job here in southern New Hampshire. I'll probably relocate, but I anticipate moving closer to you—not farther away."

Tricia blinked in surprise. "When did this happen?"

"Yesterday."

"And what was your answer?" she asked.

Baker straightened. "I accepted the job. I'll be sworn in on January first."

"That's four months away."

"I'm committed to the Sheriff's Department until December thirty-first, and there are other obstacles that have to be cleared before the job becomes available. Plus it gives me time to put my house up for sale and find somewhere else to live. It ends up being perfect timing for me."

"What does this mean for us?" she asked.

"I was hoping you'd sound a little more enthusiastic about my new situation."

Tricia sighed. "I'd be willing to work at that."

Baker smiled. She liked the way his eyes lit up when that happened. "I should have a lot more free time in my next position."

"Weekends off?" Tricia asked.

"That depends on how many officers they hire to keep the peace."

"Will you have a say in that?"

Baker moved closer—much, much closer. "I sure hope so."

Tricia smiled and Baker jerked forward, planting a tentative kiss on her lips. He pulled back, as though to gauge her reaction.

She smiled. "I'd thought about not replacing Ginny. But now . . . I might need to delegate authority here at Haven't Got a Clue . . . if I'm going to be spending more time off, too."

"*Yow!*" Miss Marple seconded, and the two of them laughed.

"I think that sounds like a wonderful plan. Would you be willing to help me find a place to live—somewhere between here and Nashua?"

"House hunting," Tricia repeated, warming to the idea.

Baker nodded.

"Sounds like fun."

He edged closer again. "Mandy took most of our furniture. Maybe you could help me pick out some new stuff."

Tricia could feel the heat of his body. She leaned in closer for another kiss, and the door rattled, startling her so she jumped back. A couple of women entered the store and Baker settled his hat back on his head. He cleared his throat.

"And just remember, Ms. Miles—safety first."

Tricia nodded enthusiastically. "Yes, I'll do that."

"I'll call you later," Baker whispered, did a smart about-face, and headed for the door.

Tricia couldn't help but smile, her gaze lingering on the door long after he'd left.

The much-anticipated tourist bus arrived, and all too soon departed. Tricia barely had time to wait on the ten or so customers who'd patronized her store before the bus was outside, its driver hammering on the horn to get them moving. By the time the crowd had dispersed, it was well after three o'clock.

Tricia was tidying the cash desk when Mr. Everett returned. His moustache was beginning to fill in, even though he'd only been growing it a few days. Sadly, it would never rival the magnificent Magnum moustache, but she supposed he could dream.

"Ginny has sent me over to relieve you for a lunch break."

"Thank you, Mr. Everett. Everything cleaned up over there now?"

He nodded. "Mr. Barbero arrived and had Ginny order more display shelving. It should arrive by tomorrow morning. She'll also be getting some new stock shipped overnight. By tomorrow, no one should be able to tell the place was ransacked."

"I'm so glad. It was a terrible thing to happen Ginny's second day on the job."

"Yes, but she's handling it well. I think she'll be a grand success." He beamed with grandfatherly pride. "But now, it's time you were off for your lunch. I'll just go get my apron," he said, and tottered off to the back of the store.

By the time he returned, Tricia had gathered her purse and petted Miss Marple good-bye. With a wave of her hand, she was out the door. As she waited for traffic to abate, she noticed Ray's roach coach was parked outside the village square. Something different about the truck captured her attention. The chrome doors were just as shiny as ever, but now the back of the truck bore colorful vinyl graphics proclaiming EAT LUNCH and, under that, the words A DIVISION OF NIGELA RICITA ASSOCIATES. Was there no business in the village that Antonio and his employer wouldn't soon have their fingers in?

Tricia crossed the street in a hurry.

"Hello," Tricia said as she approached Ray, who was polishing the chrome with a tattered bit of rag.

"Hi," he said, barely looking up from his work.

Tricia studied the items on display. Gone was the Lucite box that held wrapped sandwiches. Instead, a small grill took its place. Alongside it were condiments, as well as containers filled with chopped onions, peppers, lettuce, tomatoes, and packages of wrapped cheese slices. The menu was now distinctly different, too. Burgers, hot dogs, Italian sausage, chips, and sodas.

"Uh . . . how much are the burgers?" Tricia asked.

Ray pointed to a sign to her left.

"I'll have one with lettuce, tomato, and mayo."

"Ketchup?" he offered.

"Of course."

"Coming right up, made to order," Ray announced, and abandoned his polishing. He donned a pair of plastic gloves and went to work on the grill, which already had a couple of burgers waiting in the wings. "Would you like a soda with that?"

"I'll have a bottle of ice tea and one of those big chocolate chip cookies." Tricia figured the more she bought, the more he might be willing to talk to her. Ray handed her the tea and cookie. She gave him a ten-dollar bill and waited as he made change.

"I see something new has been added to your truck," Tricia said, indicating the new graphics.

"Yup, I've been bought out," he said, but his words held pride, not shame.

"Had you been trying to sell the business?"

"Oh, no. I got a call from some Italian guy asking me if I'd be willing to talk. What he said made a lot of sense."

"What *did* he say?"

"That I would do better not to compete with the diners in the village. So I upgraded. Got the grill. He was right. Burgers and dogs sell much better than sandwiches."

"So now you work for them?"

"Yeah, and they're paying me really well to do it, too."

"Are you on salary?" she asked.

He nodded. "For the first time in twenty years. I'll tell you, lady, it's been tough these past couple of years, what with the economy and all. But now I have a five-year contract. If I decide to retire by then, well and good. Or maybe

I'll hang around for another five years. Who knows? Either way, this has been great for me."

Yes, it certainly had.

The burger was done at last, and he wrapped it in paper and put it in a sack before handing it to her. "Thanks for stopping by."

"Nice talking to you," Tricia said, and headed back down the street to Booked for Lunch. Angelica wasn't likely to be happy, but the money she'd spent was well worth the information she'd received. Now, what was she going to do with it?

Tricia pushed open the door café's door to find Angelica at the counter, her manuscript pages one again spread out before her. She looked up. "There you are. I was beginning to worry. What with Ginny being robbed and all, Stoneham is turning into crime central."

"You got that right. But she's okay, and Antonio authorized her to buy whatever she needs to get the store up and running again."

"What a guy," Angelica said, and then focused in on the bag in one of Tricia's hands, and the bottle of ice tea in the other. "What are you doing bringing food you purchased elsewhere into my café?" she demanded. "And for a third day in a row."

"I wanted to find out the dirt on Ray's roach coach," Tricia said, taking a seat at the counter.

"Dirt?" Angelica said, suddenly sounding interested.

"Ray has sold out."

"To whom?"

"Who else? Nigela Racita Associates."

"What?" Angelica cried.

"My sentiments exactly." Tricia unwrapped the burger

and took a bite. Not bad. She unscrewed the cap on her ice tea. "He's got a five-year contract."

Angelica frowned. "Okay, let's do a recap," she said, and counted off her points on the fingers of her left hand. "One, this Nigela Racita outfit bought the lot two doors down from me. Two, they've heavily invested in the Brookside Inn. Three, they've taken over the Happy Domestic. And now they've taken over Ray's roach coach. There can't possibly be any other businesses on the selling block . . . or can there?"

Tricia shrugged and took another bite of her burger. It was pretty tasty!

"Since we were at the Happy Domestic with Ginny, I missed the Board of Selectmen's meeting. Apparently Nigela Racita Associates was the talk of the town," Angelica said. "Mary Fairchild from over at By Hook or By Book ordered lunch delivered this afternoon—so naturally I took it over. She attended the meeting and was willing to tell all. She's worried this foreign outfit is going to take over the entire village. And she's not the only one, either."

"I don't blame her. It seems like the person behind that company is absolutely ruthless," Tricia said, and wiped ketchup from the corner of her mouth.

"What do you mean?" Angelica asked.

"Swooping in to snatch up the Happy Domestic within hours of Deborah's death. Locking out Elizabeth. Grabbing *my* best employee."

Angelica nodded thoughtfully. "That does sound pretty ruthless," she agreed. "I hope they don't come after me and mine—and that includes you."

"Haven't Got a Clue is not for sale—at any price," Tricia added, and took a sip of her ice tea.

"Likewise the Cookery and Booked for Lunch," Angelica piped up. "Still, I hear Ginny's boyfriend looked really sharp when he unveiled the plans for the empty lot."

"Oh?"

Angelica nodded. "Mary said he looked up old photos of Stoneham at the library and found there used to be a fire station here on Main Street. They're going to build the façade to look like the old station. I guess someone asked if they were going to put the fire pole in and he said yes! Doesn't that sound cool?"

"What are they going to use the space for?"

"On the bottom floor, a bar," Angelica said and squealed with delight.

"Here? In Stoneham?" Tricia asked, aghast.

Angelica nodded. "And what's wrong with that? At present, you either have to drink alone or risk a DUI arrest. And it'll be an upscale bar, maybe serve tapas. In keeping with the whole book-town theme, it'll be called the Dog-eared Page. The plan is to keep people in the village after the bookstores close for the evening."

"I'm all for that—if it works."

"Why shouldn't it work?" Angelica asked.

"There's nothing else for them to do. No theater, no movie house, and the only fine dining around here is the Brookside Inn, which isn't exactly within walking distance. What will the other two floors be used for?"

"Office space for Nigela Racita Associates."

"Will the big cheese herself show up, or will Antonio occupy it?"

"Mary didn't say."

"Did anything else happen at the meeting?" Tricia asked.

"The Board of Selectmen have retained a lawyer from Boston at three hundred and fifty dollars an hour, anticipating a wrongful death suit from Deborah's estate."

"That seems a reasonable precaution."

"Bob called. He's in an absolute tizzy. And since it might be years before the estate has to make a claim, he and the village could be living with the threat hanging over them for a long time."

"The way David Black sold the Happy Domestic mere hours after Deborah's death convinces me he isn't likely to wait before he files suit."

Angelica sighed. "What's with that guy juggling two women with his wife barely cold in the ground?"

"Far from cold. Remember, he had her cremated."

Angelica ignored that piece of information. "You know, I'll bet if we tried, we could squeeze more information out of Michele Fowler. Why don't we invite her for drinks?"

"Where?"

"Well, if the new tapas bar was open we could invite her here, but the timeline calls for it to open next summer. We'll have to go to Portsmouth. Have you got anything planned for this evening?"

Tricia pushed the last of her burger aside. "No." She frowned. "Something you said the other day has stuck with me."

"Darling Trish, everything I say should stick with you, but what pearls of wisdom are you referring to?"

"When you asked if selling books was to be my only future."

"And now it isn't?"

"Not necessarily. But I guess when I saw myself in the future, it wasn't alone. And yet—"

"The pickings ain't that good here in Stoneham," Angelica supplied.

"Exactly. Although . . . I spoke with Grant Baker this morning. He's going to be retiring from the Sheriff's Department at the end of December and taking a new job near here. He wants me to help him look for a house—maybe furnish it, too."

"That sounds promising."

"Maybe," Tricia said, and drained the bottle of ice tea.

Angelica gathered up her pages. "You don't have to stay in Stoneham. You could close shop here and reopen in Boston or New York."

Tricia shook her head. "I like it here. It's just that I would like it better if I were *with* someone. I mean, permanently."

"Well, if you don't want to wait for Captain Baker, there's always Internet dating," Angelica suggested.

Tricia glowered at her. "I didn't say I wasn't interested in him."

Angelica's grin was positively evil. "Maybe we should talk to Antonio and suggest Nigela Ricita Associates start a dating firm." The grin faded. "Heaven knows, I might be their first customer."

"Things still not right between you and Bob?"

"How can they be? He cheated on me," she said, the hurt evident in her voice. "I'm afraid all we can be now is friends. And how much can I trust a friend who's already lied to me?" She exhaled sharply. "Back to Ms. Fowler. Are you interested?"

Tricia shrugged. "Why not?"

"Right. I'll give her a call and set it up. What time? Eight okay for you?"

"Fine." Tricia got up and deposited her trash in the bin behind the counter.

"I have a feeling that what we learn tonight is going to radically change a certain someone's life—and *not* for the better," Angelica said, with hint of smugness.

"Do you know something you're not telling me?" Tricia asked, giving her sister a suspicious look.

"Who, little me?" Angelica said. "You know I always share all." Her evil grin was back again. "Well, almost all."

Tricia grabbed her purse. "I'll see you later."

"Tootles!" Angelica called.

As Tricia made her way back to Haven't Got a Clue, she thought about what Angelica had said. There was no way whatever she learned tonight would change anyone's life. Still, a shiver ran down her neck, and she wished Angelica hadn't decided to start making prophecies—especially negative ones.

In Tricia's experience, they had a tendency to come true.

TWENTY

 "That'll be one hundred ninety-six dollars and twenty-four cents," Tricia said, and waited for her customer to dig into her purse to extract a credit card.

"This is my first trip to Stoneham," the chubby, middle-aged woman exclaimed. "I've even booked a room at the Brookview Inn so I could spend a day or two just rummaging around all these lovely bookstores."

Rummage was the right word. The woman had practically examined each and every book on Haven't Got a Clue's shelves, refusing any help from Tricia. But she wasn't going to sneer at a nearly two-hundred-dollar sale, either. Customers like this were few and far between. But now the question was, how was she going to get all these books to the woman's car? Although it was near closing, Tricia hated to leave the shop unattended, even to help a customer carry books to the municipal lot. Especially when

236

she was hoping to shut down early to get ready for her . . . nondate . . . with Angelica and Michele Fowler. Well, it was the closest she'd gotten to a night out on the town in . . . okay, five days. But her dinner with Grant Baker at the Brookview could hardly be classified as a date. After their frank conversation, she'd hoped he would have called. That he hadn't . . .

"Would you mind if I left these books here and picked them up tomorrow?" the woman asked.

"Not at all," Tricia said. Yes! Problem solved!

"I'm going to have to rearrange the trunk of my car if I'm going to get all this stuff home, and I'm just too tired to tackle that tonight. Besides, I don't want to miss dinner at the Brookview. I hear the chef is magnificent."

"I've eaten his food, and it's pretty darn good." Oh, how she missed Jake's tuna salad!

"I'll just take my receipt and be back before noon tomorrow to pick up the books."

"They'll be waiting for you," Tricia said, and waved as the woman headed for the door.

She packed the books in a heavy-duty shopping bag and stowed them behind the counter. The shop door opened and for a moment Tricia thought her customer had returned, but instead it was Boris Kozlov. While Tricia had patronized the Coffee Bean on hundreds of occasions, neither Boris nor his wife had ever been inside Tricia's store. "This is a surprise," Tricia said in a wary greeting.

Boris looked around the shop before he approached the cash desk. He leaned in a little too close and lowered his voice, sounding like the villain in a cold-war flick. "I have someting for you." He set a thin, plastic CD jewel case on the counter and pushed it toward her.

"What's this?" Tricia asked.

"Someting you can use. Or at least someting your ex-employee and the new owner of the Happy Domestic can use." Good grief. He sounded just like the cartoon character Boris Badenov.

"You didn't answer my question," Tricia said, trying to keep her voice neutral.

"Is recording from video camera. I bought the equipment to film Deborah Black putting her trash in our Dumpster. I leave it on at night to see if her mother does the same ting. Last night it filmed more than trash. There's a twenty-minute section I thought you should see. The robbery next door to me."

Tricia's eyes widened. "You caught it on video?"

"Digital. I downloaded it to DVD for you."

Tricia picked up the thin plastic case. It was scratched as though it had been in circulation for quite some time. "Why are you giving it to me and not the Sheriff's Department?"

Boris shook his head and grimaced with distaste. "I don't like talking to the police. Bad memories from Russia."

"So you want me to be your go-between? They're still going to want to talk to you."

"Then they can talk to Alexa. I don't want to be involved, but I do want the *dura* who robbed the new owner of the Happy Domestic to go to jail—for a long, long time."

"You haven't told me who robbed the place."

"I tink you know," he said, and nodded. He straightened. "I go back to the shop now. Alexa can talk to the Sheriff's Department any time they need. Good night, Tricia."

There was something creepy about the way he said her

name. Almost like Bela Lugosi. She watched Boris slink out of the shop, grateful he wasn't wearing a black cape and didn't have fangs.

Tricia eyed the shiny, unmarked DVD inside the case. She did have an idea who might have robbed the Happy Domestic—the very idea being too upsetting to contemplate. She glanced at the clock. The store was due to close in another ten minutes, and as there were no customers—why wait? She'd watch the video and then call Grant Baker and report that she had the DVD in her possession.

Tricia set the jewel case back on the counter and headed for the door, turning the bolt and flipping the OPEN sign to CLOSED.

The phone rang. Tricia was going to let it go to voice mail, but technically the store was still open. She picked it up on the fourth ring. "Haven't Got a Clue. This is Tricia. How can I—"

"Ms. Miles? This is Elaine Capshaw. I hope I'm not calling at a bad time."

"Not at all," she fibbed. "Have you decided to take the job?" she asked hopefully.

"What? Oh. To tell you the truth I haven't given it a lot of thought."

Tricia sighed. "Then how can I help you?"

"I don't know who else to turn to."

That didn't sound good. "What's wrong?"

"I got another one of those phone calls a little while ago. From a woman. I still didn't recognize the voice. She said I shouldn't say anything about Monty to anyone— especially not the investigator from the National Transportation Safety Board."

"Steve Marsden," Tricia supplied.

"Yes. But I already have."

"Did you tell her that?" Tricia asked.

"No!"

Maybe you should have, Tricia thought with a pang of anxiety. "Did this woman threaten you?"

"She told me to keep my mouth shut—or else. I'm scared. I don't know what to do. I haven't got anyone, you see. And—"

"You should call the Milford police."

"I didn't want to be a bother."

"It's not a bother, especially if you feel threatened."

"I don't want them to think I'm some hysterical woman who's afraid to be alone after the death of her husband," she said, and yet Tricia could hear the fear in the older woman's voice.

"Would you like me to come over? I can call them for you. And I'll stay with you so that you'll have a friendly face around when they arrive," she asked.

"Oh, I'd appreciate that. Thank you. How soon can you make it?"

Tricia glanced again at the clock and winced. Could she get there and back to meet Angelica by eight o'clock? Maybe, if she called the Milford police and excused herself soon after they arrived. "I can be there in about fifteen minutes. Will you be okay that long?"

Elaine sniffed. "I think so. And I have Sarge here to protect me," she said, and gave a mirthless laugh. Somewhere in the background, the tiny dog barked as though agreeing with her.

"I'll be there as soon as I can," Tricia said, and hung up the phone. She grabbed her purse and, on impulse, shoved the DVD into it. She locked the door behind her, and jogged to the municipal parking lot and her car.

The drive from Stoneham to Elaine Capshaw's home on the outskirts of Milford took about ten minutes. Tricia parked her car at the curb, got out, and hurried up the walk to the house. Her stomach lurched when she saw the front door was open a crack.

She looked around, saw no sign of anyone lurking nearby, and rapped on the screen door. "Mrs. Capshaw? Elaine?"

Unlike the last time she'd arrived at the Capshaw home, there was no barking from within. "Elaine?" she yelled louder.

Still no answer.

"Sarge! Sarge!" she called. No sign of the dog, either. Elaine's car was still parked in the driveway, so unless she'd left in a hurry, she had to still be inside the house. Gripped with indecision, Tricia considered her options. Should she charge inside like the heroine in a bad mystery—and risk running into whoever had spooked Elaine—or call for backup and feel foolish if the woman had simply fled to one of the neighbor's homes to look for comfort?

Tricia deliberated for a full ten seconds before she turned away from the door and walked down the steps. She pulled out her phone and punched in 9-1-1. Within seconds a male voice answered: "Hillsborough County 9-1-1 Emergency. Please state your name and the nature of your emergency."

"Tricia Miles. I want to report a break-in." As she gave them the rest of the particulars, Tricia walked around the house, trying to peek in the windows, but as when she visited the first time, all the drapes had been drawn. She couldn't see a thing inside.

As she rounded the corner of the house, a Milford police cruiser pulled up to the curb. A young officer got out of the car, and seemed in no hurry. Tricia reported his arrival to the dispatcher and folded her phone.

"You called the police?" the officer asked. He wore his sandy-colored hair in a brush cut, looking like he'd stepped right out of the police academy—or boot camp.

Tricia nodded. "Mrs. Capshaw called me not more than fifteen minutes ago and asked me to come over. She'd received a threatening phone call. I saw the door was open and figured I'd better call the police."

"Did you go inside?"

She shook her head.

The officer nodded. "You stay here." He strode up to the front door, knocked, called inside, and then entered.

Tricia bit her lip as she waited. It seemed a long time before the pale, grim-faced officer came out of the house, holding a handheld radio, probably talking to his superiors or dispatcher. Another patrol car raced down the street, lights flashing but no siren, and came to a screeching halt at the curb. The officer jumped out the car and ran for the house. Both officers went back inside, and Tricia's stomach knotted as she feared the worst.

Before long, several more patrol cars and a fire rescue squad had arrived. Everyone along the chain of command took their shot at her and asked again and again why she was there, why she had called 9-1-1, and finally, confirmed that a woman inside the home was indeed dead. By then Tricia was so upset, it was all she could do to keep from crying. She had liked Elaine and hoped they could work together and become friends.

An older man in uniform approached her. "Ma'am? I'm Chief Aaron Strauss of the Milford Police Department. I'm sorry to have to ask, but we'd like you to come inside and make an identification. Do you think you could do that?"

It was the last thing Tricia wanted to do, but she found herself nodding and let him take her arm, guiding her up the steps and into the house.

Despite the fact that every light in the living room had been turned on, an aura of gloom penetrated each corner of the room. Tricia's nose twitched at the coppery tang of blood that filled the air.

"It's pretty gruesome," the burly police chief warned, as Tricia approached the prone figure that lay on the floor between the faded couch and the Formica coffee table.

Tricia steeled herself. She'd seen plenty of grisly corpses on television dramas—but they were actors—or dummies—with makeup and colored Karo syrup simulating injuries, not the real thing. She moved her gaze up the length of Elaine's body. She held something in her hand—but Tricia couldn't exactly see what it was. She dared look at the bloody mess that had been the back of Elaine Capshaw's head, gasped, and quickly turned away.

"That's her," she managed, and took a couple of gasping breaths to regain her control.

"Would you like to sit down, ma'am?" the officer with the brush cut asked.

"I'm okay," Tricia lied, and focused her attention on the framed print of a pot of red geraniums that hung on the opposite wall. "Chief Strauss, I think you ought to know that Mrs. Capshaw's husband died in the plane that crashed in the Stoneham Square on Thursday. The National Transportation Safety Board is looking into it, but there's a possibility her death is related to his."

The police chief scowled. "I doubt it."

Tricia bristled at this superior tone.

"What happened to her dog?" she asked the young officer standing next to the chief.

"He's hurt pretty bad, ma'am," the officer—Malcolm, by his name tag—said. "Whoever killed the lady of the house probably kicked the little dog like a football. Looks like traces of blood around his mouth. He may have bitten the attacker. We'll have the lab team take a swab."

"What will happen to him?" Tricia asked

"I'll see if one of the guys can take it to the vet," the chief said. "I'll also have one of my men check the hospitals for dog bite reports. But my guess is they'll have to put the dog down." He shook his head and turned away.

Tricia's hand flew to her throat—and instinctively she grabbed the locket's chain and thought of the picture of Miss Marple within it. "I'd hate for that to happen. Would it be okay if I took him to the vet?" she asked Officer Malcolm.

The officer eyed the chief, who hadn't seemed that interested. "I'll ask the sarge. He's a soft touch—has a whole menagerie at home."

Tricia shook her head at the irony. "That's the dog's name—Sarge."

The officer nodded. "The chief may have more questions for you later. Would you like to wait in the kitchen?"

Again she shook her head. "I'll wait outside, if that's okay." At his nod of approval, she exited the house, grateful to inhale the cool, crisp evening air.

Dusk had fallen by the time one of the firemen came out of the house with what looked like a bundle of towels. "Ma'am, one of the officers said you were willing to take the victim's dog to a vet?"

"Yes."

"I'll put him in your car. I don't think you should touch him."

"Will he bite?" Tricia asked.

He shook his head. "I've tied a makeshift muzzle around his jaws. When you get to the vet, let them come get him. They'll know best how to handle him so he isn't hurt further."

They walked toward Tricia's car and she opened the door to the backseat. With care, the fireman settled the dog, who whimpered softly. Sarge turned his sad brown eyes on Tricia. He seemed to be pleading, *Help me!*

The fireman handed Tricia a scrap of paper with an address on it. "I called the vet. They'll be waiting for you." He looked down at the dog and frowned. "Poor little guy. I hope he makes it." The fireman gave Tricia a weak smile and a parting nod and went back inside to join his comrades.

Chief Strauss approached Tricia once again. "Ma'am, where can we reach you if we have any further questions?"

Tricia opened her car door and retrieved her purse, extracting one of her business cards. She wrote her home and cell numbers on the back before handing it to him.

Strauss touched the bill of his cap in farewell and walked back to the house.

Tricia got in her car and started the engine. Before she put the car in gear, she glanced at the address on the slip of paper the fireman had given her. It was the same place she took Miss Marple for her annual shots, not far from the strip mall that housed the diner and jeweler she'd visited just days before. She turned to look at the little dog. His eyes were closed and he seemed to be panting very fast. "I'll get you some help, Sarge. I promise."

She started the car and pulled away from the curb, hoping she could keep her word.

TWENTY-ONE

It was long past eight o'clock when Tricia finally made it back to Stoneham, and she was ravenous. But as she hadn't done any shopping, there was still nothing of substance in her fridge, and the thought of yogurt or toast wasn't at all appetizing—not after what she'd been through that evening. Worse, she hadn't phoned Angelica to tell her she couldn't make their rendezvous with Michele Fowler. Oddly enough, Angelica hadn't called her, either.

Tricia pulled into the municipal parking lot, cut the engine, and pulled out her cell phone. Angelica answered on the first ring. "I hope I'm not interrupting anything important. Are you alone?"

"Absolutely!" Angelica said with chagrin.

"Then can I come over and mooch something to eat?"

"Sure. What's wrong?"

"I'll tell you when I get there. See you in a minute."

It took two minutes by the time Tricia let herself into the Cookery and made her way up the stairs to Angelica's loft apartment. Angelica met her at the door. "Is it a hot cocoa, wine, or something-stronger kind of funk you're in?"

"Wine sounds good."

"I just happen to have a couple of bottles. Red or white? Although it rather depends on what leftover you choose as your entrée. Come on in."

Tricia followed her sister down the corridor to the loft's kitchen that overlooked Main Street. Angelica hadn't bothered to draw the blinds, and the gas lights down below glowed, attracting an assortment of insects that buzzed around them.

Angelica opened the door to the fridge to survey its contents. "I've got tons of food—all recipes I've tested for the new cookbook."

"Good grief, is that an entire roast turkey in there?" Tricia asked in disbelief, peering over her sister's shoulder.

"What's left of one. I told you, I'm working on *Easy-Does-It Holidays*. My editor wants me to include a section on how to make use of Thanksgiving leftovers. Of course, I don't have any cranberry sauce, but if you don't mind it sliced cold, I could whip up a salad and some veggies or make you a turkey salad sandwich. Or would you rather have turkey tetrazzini or turkey curry?"

"How hot is the curry?" Tricia asked.

"Hot enough to curl your hair. And I'll zap a papadum in the microwave for you, too."

"I'll go for it. Now pour me a glass of white wine and I'll tell you a tale that might curl your hair, too."

"Oh, this sounds interesting," Angelica said, and snagged

a couple of glasses from the cupboard and the wine from the fridge. She poured.

"I got a phone call from Elaine Capshaw just as I was about to close the store."

"And?" Angelica dutifully prompted.

"She'd received another threatening call. I tried to convince her to call the police, but she asked me to come over to be with her when she did. It couldn't have been fifteen minutes from the time I left until—"

"Let me guess—you got there and she was gone," Angelica said, taking a plastic-wrap-covered bowl from the fridge.

"No, she was dead."

Angelica scowled, and with hands on hips demanded, "Don't tell me you found her?"

"Almost. Whoever called her made good on their threat before I could get there. She'd been bludgeoned to death."

Angelica winced as she transferred the curry to a saucepan.

"Her poor little dog suffered a similar fate," Tricia said.

Angelica's head snapped up. "Someone killed her dog?" she cried in anguish.

Tricia shook her head. "No, but it's badly injured. I ended up taking the little guy to the local vet—that's where I've been for the past two hours. He's already cost me half a grand, and it looks like I'm responsible for him, unless a relative or one of Elaine's neighbors claims him. If that doesn't happen, I suppose I'll call the Humane Society or maybe a dog rescue service to find him a home. *If* he recovers."

"Oh, no!" Angelica cried, distressed.

Tricia nodded. "According to the vet, Sarge's lungs

were bruised. He must've been kicked into a wall or some other solid object."

"Bruising is better than busted ribs," Angelica said, but she didn't sound convinced.

"Maybe, maybe not. There's a danger his lungs could fill with fluid, and then he'd probably—" Tricia stopped before saying the *D* word. Angelica had once had a poodle she'd loved. She'd said she'd never recovered from losing her little Pom-Pom. Hearing about Sarge's injuries might be too painful for her.

Angelica's bottom lip trembled, and she looked close to tears. "That poor, poor puppy."

Tricia frowned. "I've met him three times now, and he seems like a wonderful little dog. I wonder if Grace and Mr. Everett would like a pet—if he makes it, that is."

Angelica sighed. "They'd be good doggy parents," she agreed.

Tricia nodded. "I'll ask Mr. Everett in the morning."

"So what do you think happened to Elaine? It had to be a friend—or someone she knew, right? Why else would a frightened woman open the door?"

"That's what I figured—and so did the Milford cops. But she told me when we met on Saturday that she had no one to depend on and said it again tonight when she phoned me. I'm sure that's why she called me to come be with her."

"You were lucky the killer was already gone. Or should I say, smart not to barge in on a crime scene. Did you actually see the body?"

Tricia winced. "Yes. The police asked me to identify her."

"Was she in worse shape than Kimberly Peters?"

Kimberly, the niece of the late *New York Times* bestselling author Zoë Carter, had been hit in the mouth with a baby sledgehammer. It had been Tricia who'd found her. She'd survived the attack, although she'd required extensive dental reconstruction.

Tricia shook her head. "That *was* worse. Still, identifying a body·is not my favorite pastime."

"Here, you stir this, and I'll get that papadum going," Angelica said.

Tricia did as she was told, taking over at the stove, and watched as Angelica opened the cupboard and took a flat disc of what looked like yellow plastic from a cellophane bag. She squirted it with cooking spray, placed it in the microwave, and punched in twenty-two seconds. Tricia never tired of seeing a papadum transform from something flat and dull into a tasty, bumpy flatbread.

"You know, Elaine had something in her hand. I didn't really see it. But it looked like a knickknack or something."

"Why would she be holding a knickknack when someone was trying to kill her?"

Tricia shrugged. "She'd turned her back on this person. You wouldn't do that if you were afraid."

"So you think it was someone she knew?"

"It had to be."

Angelica grabbed a plate, a fork, and a serving spoon, and thrust them at Tricia. "Take as much as you want."

Tricia spooned the curry onto her plate while Angelica placed the finished papadum on another plate at the spot where Tricia usually sat. Tricia took her seat while Angelica refilled their glasses.

"How was your day?" Tricia asked, and plunged her fork into the curry, wishing it sat on a bed of Basmati rice.

"Oh, the usual. In fact, *more* boring than usual. I feel

like I'm awash in paperwork. Anything else happen to you today?"

Tricia tasted the curry and gasped. Angelica hadn't been kidding when she'd said it was hot. "Wow. Is *this* the recipe you're using in your book?"

"Of course not. I make it triple strength for myself. Americans are such wimps when it comes to adding spices."

Tricia grabbed her wine and took a healthy swig. Ahh— relief! "I take it you've never been to the Southwest."

"Of course I have. There are always exceptions to the rule."

Tricia took another mouthful of curry, and while volcanic, it did not displease her, but again she wished for rice. She bit into the papadum, which promptly shattered, sending shards across her place mat. It, too, was wonderful.

As she swallowed, she remembered her visit from Boris Kozlov. "Good grief! I almost forgot." She jumped up from her chair and grabbed her purse from the counter. Rummaging through it, she came up with the DVD Boris had given her hours before.

"What is that?" Angelica asked, swirling the wine in her glass.

"Video from the Coffee Bean's surveillance camera. Boris Kozlov set it up to catch Deborah tossing her garbage in his Dumpster. He told me it shows who robbed the Happy Domestic last night."

Angelica's eyes snapped wide open. She got up and grabbed the jewel box from Tricia's hand. "Let's watch it." Without waiting for an answer, Angelica headed for the living room and the DVD player.

Tricia tossed what was left of her papadum onto her plate and followed.

Angelica had the remote in her hand and the DVD drawer was already open by the time Tricia placed her dish on the coffee table and made herself comfortable on the leather couch. Angelica took the wing chair to her left, aimed the remote, and the drawer slid shut. The TV's blank screen flashed gray and the alley behind the Coffee Bean came into view. Nothing happened for what seemed an eon. Tricia dug back into her curry.

"I think Boris is playing a joke on you," Angelica said after a couple of minutes went by with no action on the tube.

"Give it a chance," Tricia said, scraping the bottom of her plate. As she swallowed the last mouthful, a car pulled into the frame.

"Okay," Angelica said with relish. "Now we're getting somewhere." But when the figure emerged from the car, its head was covered by the hood of a sweatshirt. "Damn!"

"Indeed," Tricia agreed.

The person walked out of camera range. Tricia picked up her wineglass and sat back. Nothing happened. Nothing happened. Nothing happened. Tricia wished the burglar would hurry up and make a reappearance. After all, how long did it take to trash a small book and gift shop?

"This is pretty boring," Angelica said, and got up from her chair, heading for the kitchen. "Do you want a refill?"

" 'I wouldn't say no,' " Tricia said, quoting a line from one of John Mortimer's Rumpole stories. It went right over Angelica's head.

Angelica returned to the living room with the wine bottle, topped up Tricia's glass, and made herself comfortable once again, before the hoody-clad figure returned to the TV screen, encumbered by a large carton.

"What do you suppose is in there?" Angelica asked.

"Your guess is as good as mine," Tricia said, studying the shape of the figure, which was not what she'd expected. She'd been expecting the person to be . . . rounder. More mature . . . more womanly. "Rats," she groused.

"What?" Angelica asked.

"I thought for sure the robber was going to be Elizabeth Crane. But the person we just saw weighed a lot less than Elizabeth."

"So who could it be?" Angelica asked.

Tricia shook her head as the figure disappeared from view once again. "Do you recognize the car?"

Angelica shrugged. "The only car I can identify, besides my own, is a Corvette, and Corvettes don't have trunks like the one on the screen."

"I'll bet Captain Baker knows a lot more about cars than we do. If he or one of his men can identify it, they should be able to use the state DMV computer to narrow down the search within the Stoneham zip code."

"What do you mean?"

"Well, whoever it was had to know about the stock within the Happy Domestic. It was targeted, after all."

"Didn't Elizabeth say her other children were in town? What if she encouraged one of them to break in?" Angelica asked.

"I don't want to speculate," Tricia said.

"Well, I think you should call Captain Baker and report this right now," Angelica said, and grabbed her wireless phone from its base, handing it to Tricia.

"But he'll be off duty. It can wait until morning."

"If Haven't Got a Clue had been robbed, and one of your neighbors knew about the crime, would you want them to wait another day to report it?"

Tricia sighed. "I suppose not."

"Call," Angelica commanded.

Tricia knew better than to disobey such a direct order, and she punched in Grant Baker's personal phone number. As she suspected, the call rolled over to voice mail. "Grant, it's Tricia Miles. The owner of the Coffee Bean has given me a copy of a surveillance tape that appears to show the person who robbed the Happy Domestic last night. I told him he should report it to the Sheriff's Department and that you would want to speak to him, but he pushed it on me, anyway. Please call me in the morning. Thanks."

She clicked the button to end the call. "There. Happy?"

"Yes." Angelica accepted the phone, replaced it on the base, and glanced at the clock. "It's getting late. I still have paperwork to finish and your cat is waiting for you, probably worried sick."

Tricia blinked at that comment. Angelica had never spoken of Miss Marple possessing humanlike emotions. No doubt little Sarge's predicament had reminded her of her long-lost Pom-Pom.

"I'm going. And I shall shower my cat with affection," she promised as she picked up her dishes and carried them to the sink. It was then she remembered the plans they'd made for the evening. "Good grief! Weren't we supposed to meet Michele Fowler tonight?"

"She couldn't make it, so I asked her about tomorrow. She said she'd meet us at some place called Nemo's. Have you heard of it?"

"No."

"I'll look it up online and get directions."

Tricia started for the door to the stairs. Angelica walked along with her. "Will you lock up downstairs?"

"Yes," Tricia dutifully answered. "Thanks for feeding me. See you tomorrow."

"Good night," Angelica called, and locked the apartment door behind Tricia.

As she made her way down the stairs and through the Cookery, Tricia thought again about the figure in the video. It had to be a woman. But if it wasn't Elizabeth Crane, who could it have been?

TWENTY-TWO

The nagging alarm clock kept ringing, even though Tricia had batted the thing several times. It took her a few foggy moments to realize that it wasn't the alarm that was ringing but the phone. She fumbled for the receiver and picked it up. "Hello?" she managed, still blinking.

"What are you doing?" Captain Baker demanded.

"I was trying to sleep." She squinted at the clock, which said six fifty-two.

"I got a report that you found Elaine Capshaw dead last night. And then I check my voice mail and hear you telling me you've got a video of who robbed the Happy Domestic. Tricia, this is police business—you're not supposed to be poking your nose into our cases. It's dangerous."

Tricia struggled to sit up, disturbing Miss Marple at the foot of the bed. "I wasn't poking my nose into anything.

Elaine Capshaw called me and asked me to come over to her house. When I got there, she was dead. And I didn't invite Boris Kozlov into Haven't Got a Clue—he came over of his own accord. He said he didn't want to get involved with the Sheriff's Department and asked me to pass on the video."

She exhaled, feeling tired, grumpy, and put upon. Why was he being so grouchy, and what had happened to the happy fellow who had visited her just the day before?

"I'm sorry," he said contritely, as though reading her mind. "I don't want anything to happen to you."

"Thank you."

"When can I come and pick up the video?"

"As soon as you want."

"How about now? I'm parked outside your store."

"What? It's not even seven o'clock. What time did you get up?"

"Five. I always get up early."

"Give me five minutes to put the coffeepot on, and I'll come down and unlock the door."

"Five minutes," he said, and the line went dead.

Tricia got out of bed, ran a comb through her hair, then grabbed her robe from the hook on the back of the door and staggered off for the kitchen.

Five minutes later, the coffee was brewing and she'd set out a couple of mugs, spoons, milk, and sugar, and headed down the stairs for the door to Haven't Got a Clue. Miss Marple didn't follow.

Captain Baker stood behind the door, holding Tricia's copy of the *Nashua Telegraph* and looking extremely impatient.

Tricia unlocked the door, and with a sweeping hand ushered the captain inside. He walked up to the beverage station. "I thought you were going to make coffee."

"I did. Upstairs. Come on."

It had been a while since she'd invited him to her loft apartment. He set his wide-brimmed hat on the counter and followed her up the stairs.

As Tricia topped the stairs, she saw Miss Marple sitting next to her empty food bowl, looking surly. *"Yow!"* she demanded.

"Yes, I will feed you now," she said to the cat. Turning to Baker, she said, "Help yourself. And pour me a cup, too, will you?"

Tricia picked up Miss Marple's dish, swished it under the faucet, and wiped it with a piece of paper towel, then opened a fresh can of cat food. All the while, Miss Marple rubbed against her bare legs, urging her to hurry.

Baker set a steaming mug of coffee on the counter and took a seat at the breakfast bar. "I want to hear everything that happened last night. Spare no details."

"Even the part where I went to Angelica's and bummed leftovers for dinner?"

"You can skip that part. Now, tell me about the call that took you to Milford and Elaine Capshaw's home."

She did, leaving nothing out, and even told him how much she'd spent at the veterinarian's office.

"Wow," he said, reacting to the vet's bill. "Is the little guy going to make it?"

"They said I could call after eight." A glance at the clock told her she still had fifty-five minutes before that would happen. "You wouldn't happen to want a dog, would you?"

"I'm barely home as it is."

"But you'll have more free time in your next job," she said, expecting validation.

"If I were going to get a dog, I'd get something a little more manly than a bichon frise."

"Dog bigot," she accused, but her tone was mild, and he smiled.

"What about that video?"

"It's on the coffee table in the living room. Why don't you watch it while I take a shower?"

He rose from his seat, grabbed his coffee, and without a word headed for the living room and the DVD player.

Tricia headed for her bedroom. No four miles on the treadmill this morning. She'd have to try to work in double that tomorrow. Maybe.

By the time Tricia returned to the living room some fifteen minutes later, Baker sat on her couch, and the TV sported a blank screen. Tricia took the adjacent chair. "So, what do you think?"

"I couldn't see the plates, but if it's licensed here in New Hampshire, we should be able to narrow down the owner by the make of the car."

"That's what I figured, too. Angelica and I don't know much about cars—other than they're transportation to get you from point A to point B."

"You showed this to Angelica?"

Tricia nodded. "Anything wrong with that?"

"I'd better call her and ask her not to talk about it—at least until we try to find the owner of that car. Don't you say anything, either," he warned, and rose.

She saluted. "Aye, Captain."

"I'm going to have a talk to Mr. Kozlov at the Coffee Bean."

Tricia followed him to the apartment door. He reached for the handle and paused. "I want you to promise me that this is the end of your sleuthing."

"I wasn't sleuthing. Boris gave me that DVD. He *wanted* me to give it to you. End of story."

Baker looked skeptical.

"Hey, you're being a little rough on me. What happened to the guy who wanted to be more than just my friend, and was that only yesterday?"

"It was, and I'm concerned because I care about you. So much that I want you to stay out of it. Can you do that?"

Tricia sighed. "I guess."

As if to prove his point, he leaned over and kissed the top of her head, then stood back, pointing a finger of warning at her. "Be good." He headed down the stairs.

Tricia wasn't sure if she should feel flattered or insulted. She chose the former.

Returning to the counter, she warmed up her coffee and sat down at the breakfast bar. Within seconds, Miss Marple appeared and levitated onto her lap. At least, that's what it always seemed like. One second she wasn't there—and the next she was, leaping up with no effort, and seemingly no weight, either.

"Yow," Miss Marple said, in what sounded like commiseration.

Tricia petted her cat and thought of the poor, battered little dog that had been so terribly abused while trying to defend his mistress. Sarge wasn't much bigger than Miss Marple—how could someone be so cruel?

Miss Marple seemed to purr all the louder as Tricia continued to stroke her head.

"Even though the animal hospital isn't officially open

until eight o'clock, I think I'll call to see how Sarge is doing."

Miss Marple closed her eyes and seemed to nod her head in assent, which seemed charitable after her reaction to meeting Sarge two days earlier.

Tricia reached across to grab the slim phone book on the counter to look up the number. She grabbed her phone and dialed, and was pleased when someone picked up the call.

"Milford Animal Hospital. This is Georgia. How can I help you?"

"Hi, it's Tricia Miles. My cat is one of your patients, but I'm calling about something else. I brought in a bichon frise last night. His name is Sarge. I was wondering how he was doing."

"Hang on. I'll find out," Georgia said, and the line went silent as she put Tricia on hold.

Tricia continued to stroke the fur on Miss Marple's head. She didn't complain.

Eventually, Georgia came back on the line. "Ms. Miles, we have good news. Dr. Arnold said Sarge had a good night and she anticipates he'll have a full recovery."

"Oh, I'm so glad to hear that."

"Even better news. Someone called late last night and left a message saying she'd like to claim the little guy. I've already spoken to her. She said she was a friend of Sarge's deceased owner and will take care of his medical expenses and adopt him when he's ready to leave our care. We've canceled the charges against your credit card and thank you for bringing him in."

Tricia frowned. The place wasn't officially open for the day and already someone had made arrangements to pick up the dog? And while she hadn't really considered adopting the dog—just looking at Miss Marple reinforced the reality that her cat would be forever offended if she brought a canine into their home—she'd kind of liked the idea of bringing Sarge home. No doubt about it, he was incredibly cute and had been unmistakably devoted to his now-departed mistress. Tricia didn't doubt that the poor dog would mourn the loss of his human mama.

"That's good . . . I guess."

"It *is* good," Georgia insisted. "This lady assures us she knows the dog and that she'll give him a happy life. She cried when I described Sarge's injuries, and she's eager to bring him home."

"When will that be?" Tricia asked, feeling an odd constriction in her throat.

"If he continues to improve, in a couple of days."

It sounded like Sarge had a happy future to look forward to, with someone who would love him as much as Elaine Capshaw had. Then why did Tricia feel so sad?

"Thank you," she said with false bravado. "I'm so glad everything will work out for him." Albeit with someone else.

"Is there anything else we can do for you today?" Georgia asked.

Tricia forced a smiled—extending it to her voice. "No, thanks so much."

"We'll send you a reminder in April when it's time for Miss Marple's booster shots."

"Thank you," Tricia said again, trying hard to sound cheerful. "Good-bye." She hung up the phone and stared at it.

How had one of Elaine Capshaw's friends heard about

the dog's fate? Was Sarge's benefactor one of Elaine's neighbors?

No matter. The situation was no longer any of Tricia's concern.

But somehow, she wished it was.

Tricia leaned over the sales counter and perused the headlines in the *Nashua Telegraph*, then glanced over the feature stories and found nothing of interest. It wasn't the newspaper's fault—the fault was squarely on her shoulders. Depression was an emotion she seldom let dominate her, but today it tried mightily. She remembered in vivid detail how on weekends her ex-husband would wake her with a fresh-brewed cup of coffee. How she'd loved drinking that first cup of the day in bed while reading the *New York Times*.

Those days were long gone. And why did the memory have to surface right now?

Tricia glanced up and saw Ginny pause in front of the Happy Domestic. She pawed through her keys, and opened the door. Ah! Company. If only for a few moments. Although if Ginny was arriving an hour before opening, it stood to reason she had work to do. But still, Tricia grabbed her keys, locked up, and headed for the Coffee Bean. Thankfully, Boris was not around, and Alexa waited on her with her usual good cheer.

"I see Captain Baker has left," Tricia said.

"*Ja, ja,*" Alexa said. "I told Boris it was foolish to involve you . . . but . . . men!" she said, and laughed, as though that explained everything. "Are you going next door to visit Ginny?"

"Yes."

"Mr. Everett tells me she's ordered a proper Dumpster."

"Yes, I believe she has."

Alexa nodded. "She will make a good neighbor."

Tricia held out a ten-dollar bill to pay for the coffee, but Alexa shook her head. "You tell her it's a very small welcome gift from me."

"That's very sweet of you. Thank you."

She bid Alexa good-bye and took the coffees next door. Once again, she had to knock several times before Ginny appeared from the back room behind the counter. As Tricia hoped, Ginny was smiling. Good. She didn't want her to think she was spying on her—or blatantly interrupting her.

"Coffee," Ginny said after opening the door. "You're a mind reader."

"It's from Alexa, actually. To welcome you to the neighborhood. And I just thought I'd come over to see how you're doing."

"How nice—on both accounts." Ginny waved a hand around the shop. "At least I didn't arrive to find chaos this morning."

Tricia took an appreciative look around the store. The merchandise sparsely decorated the shelves, but the place was tidy and still inviting. "You're in early."

Ginny took a sip of coffee and blushed. "I feel like I'm playing house. Come on in the back and sit down awhile."

Tricia dutifully followed Ginny into the back of the shop. Elizabeth must have made good her threat of having Davey's things collected, for the playpen, changing table, toys, and diapers were gone. In their place was a desk, file cabinets, a table with a coffeemaker and microwave, and a small refrigerator. Everything Tricia had collected for the employee break room on the floor above her shop.

Ginny sat at the desk and ushered Tricia to take the hard-backed chair to the side of it. "I'm already getting to know the stock," she said proudly. "And I like arranging stuff on the shelves. Thanks so much for loaning me Mr. Everett again yesterday. He's such a doll, and he can fix things, too. The card rack was all bent out of shape, but he managed to put it back into its original shape. And he's just as good with the customers here as he is at Haven't Got a Clue. I'm hoping to find someone as good as him to work for me."

Tricia smiled. "You're not going to try to woo him away from me, are you?"

"Would I do that?" Ginny asked in mock innocence.

They shared a laugh, and then sipped their coffee in contented silence. Ginny was the first to speak. "I'm going to be ordering the Christmas stock this morning. I spent all last evening going through the catalogs. I think Antonio was bored to death, but he pretended to pay attention. I mean, it is in his best interest to know what's going on here at the Happy Domestic."

"What are you ordering?"

"Christmas doilies, angels, a few really cute nativity scenes, Dolly Dolittles in Christmas garb, some specialty chocolates—"

"What does Dolly Dolittle look like?" Tricia asked. She'd done all that eBay research but hadn't yet seen the small china figurines and felt curious about them.

Ginny pawed through a stack of catalogs on the desk, picking one out and handing it to Tricia, who smiled in delight. Dolly Dolittle was an angel in Victorian garb. The cover shot showed a little girl in pastel blue, with a white fur collar. Her hands were thrust in a furry muff to match the collar, and the entire figurine was covered in iridescent sparkles. "She's adorable."

"Apparently they sell like crazy—especially at Christmastime. They're one of the few angels that outlived the craze a few years back. I think one of the reasons may be that they're still made here in the U.S. instead of China. They have a huge, loyal following."

For the past two Christmases, Tricia had confined her holiday decorations to Haven't Got a Clue, but as she studied the various Dolly Dolittles in the catalog, she thought she might make an exception and grace her shelves with a couple of the figurines. Each of them was named. Would that make it easy for prospective buyers on eBay to Google each one, so that the seller didn't need to put up a photograph in order to entice a willing customer?

"Were you able to find Deborah's inventory for the missing Dolly Dolittles?"

Ginny frowned and shook her head. "Except for the empty boxes, there's no way to prove they were ever part of the stock when the store was sold.

"That's too bad."

"I'm not going to worry about it. All I can do is move forward. There's no point in looking back and wondering what might have been."

"Sound reasoning," Tricia agreed. She glanced at her watch. "I'd better let you get back to work."

Ginny stood. "I know it's only been three days, and it was kind of nerve-racking dealing with Elizabeth, the missing inventory, and the break-in, but other than that, it's been a great couple of days. I already love this job."

"So you won't miss us over at Haven't Got a Clue?"

"Of course I will. But . . . this is what I want to do now."

Tricia smiled. "That's exactly how I felt when I opened my shop, too. And believe it or not, it gets even better."

Ginny positively grinned.

Tricia led the way to the shop entrance. "Well, have a good day."

"You, too," Ginny said, gave a quick wave, and shut and locked the door.

Tricia made her way back to Haven't Got a Clue. If she was honest with herself, she felt a bit envious of Ginny. But something about what she'd seen in the catalog filled with Dolly Dolittle figurines stayed with her, and she wasn't sure why.

TWENTY-THREE

The bell over the door rang and Tricia looked up to see Elizabeth Crane push Davey's stroller through the shop door. After the tongue lashing she'd received two nights before, she wasn't eager to talk to Deborah's mother. But it was a contrite Elizabeth who walked up to the sales counter.

"Hello, Tricia."

"Elizabeth." That was as gracious a welcome as Tricia could muster under the circumstances.

Davey grabbed at the items in the glass display case, quickly frustrated that he couldn't get his hands on the worn and fragile first editions Tricia kept under lock and key. Still, he left his sticky fingerprints all over the glass.

"I came here to apologize for my behavior the other night."

Tricia said nothing. If Elizabeth was intent on apologizing, she was going to let her do it.

"I was pretty stiff and sore when I got out of the ER. All I wanted was a hot bath and a nice strong drink. And when I couldn't find you to retrieve Davey . . . I may have let my temper get the better of me."

She sure had. Still, Tricia wasn't sure she wanted to let Elizabeth off the hook so easily. "I can understand that," she said.

Davey grunted his displeasure, and Elizabeth pulled a picture book from the catch-all at the back of the stroller. He squealed with delight at what must have been the familiar sight of fire engines.

"The last few days have been a nightmare. I saw Bob Kelly this morning about putting my house up for sale. After what happened the other night, I don't feel safe here in Stoneham anymore."

"Then you don't think it was an accident?" Tricia asked.

"I most certainly do not. That car came straight at me and Davey."

"But why?"

Elizabeth shrugged. "Who knows why crazy people do what they do."

Crazy people. Like Cheryl Griffin? "So you didn't see who was behind the wheel?"

Elizabeth shook her head.

"What were you doing walking down Main Street at that time of day, anyway?"

"I've been going back to the village park. I feel close to Deborah in the place where she died. Or at least I wanted to believe I would feel close to her. But she's not there. And for all I know, David dumped her remains in his garbage can. I must admit, I've thought about looking there. But their trash day was yesterday. If he disposed of her ashes that way, there's no way I'll ever find my baby's final resting place." A single tear cascaded down her cheek. She brushed it aside.

Davey pounded a picture of a Dalmatian with his chubby index finger. "Doggy, doggy!" he insisted.

"These past few days you've seen the worst of me," Elizabeth continued, "and learned the worst of Deborah. I'm her mother. I know she was no saint, but she was my daughter and I loved her unconditionally. Isn't that what a parent is supposed to do?"

"I always thought so," Tricia said quietly. She didn't want to think too hard on that statement. It was too painful a place for her to go.

Another tear leaked from Elizabeth's eye and she dabbed at it with the knuckles of her right hand. Tricia reached under the counter and brought out the tissue box, which seemed to be getting quite a workout this week.

Elizabeth took one and blew her nose.

"Where will you go?" Tricia asked.

"Back to Long Island. I have friends there, and my other girls aren't far away. Somehow Davey and I will build a new life." She gave a mirthless laugh. "We've got no other choice."

"Nana, Nana! Doggy," Davey insisted with the joy that only a small child can experience.

There didn't seem to be much else to say, so Tricia began with, "Good luck. If there's anything else I can do for you before you go, please let me know."

"I've already abused the friendship you had with Deborah." She took a deep breath and looked toward the door. "I'd best be going. I'm heading to the liquor store in Milford to see if I can scrounge up some boxes. I may as well start packing today." She grabbed the handles of the stroller and headed for the exit. She opened the door. "Wave goodbye to Tricia, Davey."

Davey looked up from his book, raised his hand, and opened and closed it several times. "Bye-bye."

Tricia waved back. "Good-bye, Davey."

Elizabeth gave Tricia a parting smile and left the store.

Miss Marple appeared at Tricia's elbow, giving her a loving head butt. "That was unexpected."

Miss Marple said, *"Yow!"*

The bell tinkled again as the shop door opened, but instead of a customer it was Angelica.

"Good morning, good morning!" she chimed, sporting a jubilant grin. As usual, she was dressed in her waitress uniform, but she carried two cups from the Coffee Bean. Unfortunately, Tricia was feeling coffeed out.

"You seem unusually happy," she said.

"I'm celebrating this morning. I've just come from the post office where I sent off my manuscript to my editor."

"I thought you still had a few weeks."

"When you've accomplished perfection, there's no reason to hang on to it a second longer."

"Perfection?" Tricia asked skeptically, accepting her cup.

"Of course, darling."

"Post office? I thought most authors turned in their manuscripts electronically these days."

"My contract says hard copy, and you know what a stickler I am for following the rules."

Tricia laughed, glad she hadn't had a mouthful of coffee when she heard that one. Snorting coffee was not a pleasant experience.

"Well, you're not the only one with good news. Someone's already claimed Elaine Capshaw's dog," Tricia said.

"Claimed him? I thought you were responsible for him." Angelica said.

"So did I. But when I called to check up on him this morning, they said he'd been claimed. Probably by a neighbor. I never even got to ask Mr. Everett if he wanted a little doggy friend."

Angelica shrugged. "It's probably for the best."

Tricia nodded. "More news. Elizabeth is leaving town and taking Davey with her."

"I thought I saw her leaving your store. Well, you won't see me shed a tear."

"She came here to apologize."

"It would have been nice if she'd apologized to Ginny and me, too," Angelica said in a huff.

"It was a blanket apology I'm supposed to pass on," Tricia fibbed.

"Oh, well, then all is forgiven. Did she have any idea who tried to run her down on Tuesday night?"

"No."

"It was probably just an accident," Angelica said, and sipped her coffee. She glanced up at the clock, and nearly choked. "Is that the time? Good grief. The lunch crowd will be over at Booked for Lunch any moment now."

"What crowd? It's been dead around here, thanks to the Founders' Day celebration being canceled."

"I know. You'd think we would've had at least the usual amount of tourists. It's like some kind of retail curse has been put on the entire village. But it can't last for long," she said, regaining her cheer. "Now don't forget, we're meeting Michele Fowler for drinks later."

"It looks like it'll be the highlight of my day," Tricia said.

"Now, now," Angelica admonished. "Let's not be bitter."

Tricia sighed. "I'll try."

Angelica turned for the door. "See you," she called, and as she left the store, Grace Harris-Everett entered. So far, not one paying customer had entered Haven't Got a Clue that day.

Still, the sight of Grace brought a smile to Tricia's lips. She'd lost her grandmother too many years ago, but she counted her friendship with Grace as in the same league, and hoped Grace somehow did the same.

"Hello, Tricia," Grace said. "And hello to you, too, Miss Marple."

Miss Marple jumped down from her perch behind the register to accept Grace's attention. She purred effusively and head-butted Grace's chin with almost wild abandon.

"My, my," Grace said, enjoying the feline attention. "I can see I must come and visit more often."

"What brings you here today?" Tricia asked.

"William tells me you've held the fort for two days now. It must be terribly lonely for you—both of you."

"I'm afraid he's right. I miss both him and Ginny terribly. I thought I'd found a wonderful replacement in Elaine Capshaw. . . ."

"Yes," Grace said, turning somber. "I've heard. But soon William will be back to Haven't Got a Clue. He does love working here, you know. Although no one has hounded him for his lottery winnings since he's been at the Happy Domestic." She leaned forward and whispered, "He thinks it's due to his new moustache."

Tricia tried to stifle a smile, with poor results. "I love having him work here," she said. "But you still haven't told me what brought you in today."

"I understand you've been collecting money for Deborah's son's education fund. The Everett Charitable Foundation fund would like to make a contribution." She dipped into her purse and withdrew a check.

"Thank you, Grace. That's very sweet of you both."

"We were quite fond of Deborah," she said, and handed the check to Tricia. One thousand dollars—the biggest contribution to date.

"Thank you very much, Grace," Tricia said. "I'll make sure this goes into Davey's account when I do my banking—probably tomorrow. Are you still enjoying the work you do for the foundation?"

"Heavens, yes," she said, her eyes lighting up. "Dear William suggested I take over my late husband's home office and make that our headquarters. It's worked out nicely. I so enjoy working on the Website and researching the requests. And we're going to establish a job bank in connection with the Food Shelf. Libby Hirt is coordinating the effort."

"It's something that's needed. Haven't Got a Clue may be the first to sign up. I'm going to need to replace Ginny, but I can't hire just anyone."

"We'd only send suitable candidates," Grace assured her.

"Whatever you do, please don't send me Cheryl Griffin. She's already interviewed—if that's what you could call it. I don't think she'd work well selling mysteries."

"Cheryl is looking for work?" Grace asked.

"Yes. She was working part time at the Happy Domestic, but Elizabeth had to let her go when Deborah died."

Grace nodded. "I see."

"I guess she's in pretty dire straits. She said she's about to be evicted."

"Oh my. Well, I'll have to see about the foundation giving her a helping hand. There's also an opening for a clerk at the Clothes Closet. Do you know her telephone number? Perhaps she'd like to interview for the job."

Tricia was about to say no but then remembered she had a copy of Cheryl's résumé. She bent down to look under the counter and came up with the paper. She scanned the text, but the telephone number had been crossed out. "Oh dear. It's not on her résumé." Perhaps Cheryl had her phone service cut off for nonpayment. How was an employer supposed to contact her if there was a job opening?

"Let me write down that address. Perhaps I can stop by her home and tell her about the job bank and how she can list herself."

"I don't need this résumé. You can have it," Tricia said, and handed Grace the paper.

She read it over. "My, with all this retail experience, it sounds like she'd be perfect for the Clothes Closet." She folded the résumé and placed it in her purse.

"How can I list my opening?" Tricia asked.

"Go to the Food Shelf's Website. There's a link for the job bank. Fill out the form, and Libby will contact you." She gave Miss Marple's head another pat. "Well, I must be off. Lots to do."

"I'm glad you stopped in. It's always so nice to see you."

"And you, too, dear." Grace gave a wave and headed for the door.

"Yow!" Miss Marple said in parting.

With Grace now gone, once again the store seemed . . . empty. The lack of customers was disconcerting. Tricia glanced at the clock. It was hours before she and Angelica were to meet with Michele Fowler. Hours and hours of not much to do, and lots of things she'd rather be doing.

Tricia was going to have to hire someone to take Ginny's place pretty darn quick. She brought out her laptop, followed Grace's instructions, and posted the opening on the job bank's site. Now to wait—and hope—she got more than just one referral.

As she closed her computer, Tricia happened to glance out the shop's front window. Bob Kelly was just leaving the Happy Domestic. Was he paying a courtesy call on Ginny, or had Deborah been behind in her rent and he'd come to nag for his money?

Bob bypassed the Coffee Bean. He was too cheap to pay for gourmet coffee, and no doubt the Kozlovs were current on their rent. He paused in front of Booked for Lunch, which had been closed for some time. Was that a wistful expression on his face as he turned away? His infidelity had been the cause for the less-than-warm reception Angelica had been giving him of late.

Bob's next stop was the Armchair Tourist; Chauncey Porter must be late with his rent. Back in June he'd told Tricia that times were hard.

With nothing better to do, Tricia stared at the storefront, waiting for Bob to leave. Miss Marple appeared at Tricia's elbow, took up the vigil beside her, and began to purr.

"I'll bet Bob knows more than he's telling about Monty Capshaw," she told Miss Marple.

"Yow!" the cat agreed.

"And he's sure kept a low profile since the Founders' Day celebration was canceled."

Miss Marple rubbed her head against Tricia's arm, as though in agreement.

"And why does he have Betsy Dittmeyer running interference for him over at the Chamber of Commerce?"

Miss Marple had no answer for that, either.

"I'm going to intercept him when he comes back down the street. Maybe I can get him to talk." She looked down at the cat, whose whiskers twitched skeptically. "I grant you, it's a long shot—but I'm sure somehow Bob knows something that could help us solve what happened to Deborah."

That was apparently too much speculation for Miss Marple, who jumped off the cash desk and trotted over to the reader's nook, settling herself on one of the comfortable chairs.

"'Oh, ye of little faith,'" Tricia quoted, and went back to waiting.

Bob certainly took his time—twenty minutes, in fact—before he exited the Armchair Tourist and started back up the street. Had all the booksellers on the east side of Main Street paid their rent, or did Bob have a sixth sense that told him Tricia would be gunning for him?

Tricia scurried around the counter and out the door. "Bob! Bob!" she called.

An eighteen-wheeled truck lumbered by, cutting off her sight of Bob. She waited for the truck to pass—but after it had, she couldn't even see Bob. At first. For a man who had no formal exercise routine, Bob jogged up Main Street at an astounding speed. "Bob!" Tricia hollered, but he didn't look back. As Tricia couldn't leave the store unattended, she stalked back to Haven't Got a Clue.

If ever a man looked guilty about something, it was Bob.

Tricia picked up the receiver. If she couldn't track him down in person, the next best thing was to try to get him on the phone.

The only question was—would he answer?

TWENTY-FOUR

 "He's deliberately avoiding me," Tricia said, and braked for a red light. "And I left messages for him at his home, his office, the Chamber of Commerce, and on his cell phone."

"Bob can be stubborn," Angelica admitted from the passenger's side of Tricia's car as she inspected the polish on her nails.

"Maybe you could call him and ask him to get back to me."

Angelica sighed, turning her attention to the road ahead of them. "Trish, how are you going to convince Bob—or the authorities—that Deborah's death was premeditated when you still haven't convinced me?"

"You could be a little more supportive," Tricia said, as the light turned green. At least traffic wasn't heavy at this hour.

"I set up this meeting with Michele Fowler, didn't I? That's got to count for something."

"It does," Tricia grudgingly agreed.

"I think the bar is down on the left. Snag that parking space just ahead, and we'll walk."

Tricia did as she was told, and the sisters got out of the car. Sure enough, the bar was only a couple of doors down. "How did you know?" Tricia asked.

Angelica gave a knowing shrug. "I drove it on my computer earlier this afternoon using Google Street View. A great little program."

They paused in front of the bar. Nemo's Deep Sea Dive sounded like it might be a dump, but instead it was a charming little tavern around the corner from the Foxleigh Gallery. Pseudo-portholes, lit from behind, suggested the life of the submariners depicted in Jules Verne's *Twenty Thousand Leagues Under the Sea*. That is, if they ate a lot of fried seafood and guzzled beer and cocktails on a regular basis. The lighting was subdued, but the ambience was welcoming, as was the painfully thin hostess with the skin-tight sailor suit and jaunty cap.

"We're meeting a friend. I believe she reserved a table. The name's Fowler," Angelica said.

"Oh, Mich. Yeah, she's one of our regulars," the young woman said, and grabbed three menus from the rack alongside the lectern that served as her post. "Right this way." With a flip of her index finger, she indicated they should follow. She led Tricia and Angelica to a table near the side of the room, away from the bar and the swinging door to the kitchen.

"Would you like to order something from the bar?" the hostess asked.

"We'll wait for our friend," Angelica said.

The hostess nodded and left them alone.

They didn't have long to wait. Michele arrived like a mini tornado. She stopped to say hello to every employee, who welcomed her like an old friend. Tricia suspected that everywhere she went, laughter soon followed.

Michele caught sight of them, fingered a wave, and rushed across the room to join them. "Am I terribly late?"

"Right on time," Angelica said.

The hostess lost no time in returning. "What can I get you ladies?"

"A glass of chardonnay," Tricia said.

"Chardonnay," Angelica echoed.

"Merlot," Michele said, and set her clutch purse on the table.

The hostess gave them a nod and headed toward the bar.

"Well, I suppose you want to know all the dirt about David Black and me," Michele said. Apparently she didn't see the need to waste time with idle chitchat.

"If you wouldn't mind," Tricia said.

"We've had sex exactly six times over the last two or three weeks. Marvelous it was, too."

"So your relationship is a pretty recent thing?"

"Definitely, although I've known David for almost a year now. He approached me about showing some of his horrible bird sculptures. Well, they're strictly for the amateur art show circuit, aren't they? I asked him if he was doing some serious work, and he showed me sketches for his beautiful gate—which was then a work in progress."

"How long have you had the finished piece in your gallery?" Angelica asked.

"Three weeks."

So, they'd celebrated the grand unveiling with a roll in the hay. Not very original, but if David was getting no kudos from his wife for his artwork—or anything else, apparently—and an attractive woman was all too willing to show her appreciation in some fashion, why wouldn't he succumb to temptation?

"Did you know David was seeing someone else?" Tricia asked.

Michele sighed. "Obviously, ours was never an exclusive relationship."

"Does it bother you?"

"Not a bit."

The hostess arrived with their drinks, setting them down on cocktail napkins. "Can I get you anything else?"

"No, thank you," Angelica said with a smile that said, *Go away so we can talk!*

She did so.

"I understand you had a conversation with David's wife the day she died."

Michele sighed. "I called to invite her to see David's work. I'm afraid she was rather rude to me."

"Did she know you were having an affair with her husband?"

"Possibly. But my intentions were sincere. I was hoping they'd get back together again."

"Why?" Angelica asked, incredulous.

"David's a very confused and unhappy man. Rather than gallivanting around with an incredibly attractive, older, sexy woman, I suspect he'd prefer to be home with a wife and family. Not that he ever mentioned it to me."

"But he *had* a family," Tricia insisted.

Michele raised a dark eyebrow. "I've since learned it was his wife who cheated on him—and a child that was not his own. Hard to pour on the love in a situation like that."

"And yet you called her," Angelica said.

"Men never know what's good for them. They may have had their differences, but at the heart of things, I believe David really did love his wife."

"And yet he was seeing you and Brandy Arkin."

"Yes, what about this other woman? Is she good breeding stock?" Michele asked with a quirky smile. "Because I suspect more than anything what David wants and needs is a new family."

"We don't know that much about her," Angelica said, "although until recently she owned a day care center. Sounds like that should make her the nurturing type."

Michele quirked an eyebrow. "Maybe. David has big plans for his future."

"Like opening a studio," Tricia stated.

"Yes. I've seen it. It's brilliant. And he intends to hire others to do welding jobs while he works on his sculptures. It's a sound business plan. Mark my words, the man is destined for greatness."

"And Deborah is dead," Tricia said sadly.

"Everybody dies, eventually," Michele said without judgment. "Let's hope none of us goes before our time." She raised her glass. Angelica did likewise. Tricia was slow to do so, but in the end, she did, too.

"Life is a journey," Michele said. "At this point in my life I've been called a cougar by some of the women I used to hang with, and they're right. But for the past five years I've had the time of my life, with a lot more action than I saw when I was in my so-called prime, if you know what I mean."

Angelica smirked, but Tricia only felt bewildered. She'd been cast in the good-girl role for so long, she wasn't sure she could break the mold—or even if she wanted to. And yet, on some level, she *was* extremely unhappy with her life. She missed loving somebody—and being loved in return.

"You girls are such fun. Something that's been distinctly lacking in my life of late." Michele took a swig of her drink and exhaled loudly. "There hasn't been much of an economic recovery when it comes to the arts." She stared at the lipstick staining the rim of her glass. "I'll probably have to shut the gallery and declare bankruptcy before the end of the year."

"Oh dear. What will you do?" Angelica asked.

"I'll probably go back to managing a restaurant. I've done it before. Right here, as a matter of fact." So that's why she'd greeted the staff with such enthusiasm. "The hours are hell and the pay stinks, but it's a living. That is, if I can find a job. A lot of restaurants and bars have gone under."

"A woman like you? You'll find something," Angelica said confidently.

"Keep your ears open. If you hear something, give me a call." She stood. "Sorry, girls, but I've got a business appointment with one of my artists." She waggled her eyebrows and grinned. "Thanks for the drink, and please do call me again, will you?"

"You bet," Angelica said.

Tricia gave a self-conscious wave and turned her attention back to her dwindling glass of wine.

Angelica leaned back in her chair and sighed. "When I grow up, I want to be Michele Fowler."

"Oh, please. She can't be more than five years older than you."

"And she's having a lot more fun, too."

Tricia frowned. "I'm surprised at you, Ange. You've been the wronged woman four times now, and yet you've taken to Michele, who thinks nothing of sleeping with other women's husbands."

"At least she's honest about it. To her it's just sex. She's not interested in a relationship."

"That makes a difference?"

"It shouldn't . . . but I guess it does." Angelica polished off the last of her wine.

Tricia did likewise. "It's too bad she's losing her job," Tricia said, and examined her empty glass, wishing there was just one more sip.

"She'll land on her feet. People like her usually do." Angelica rummaged through her purse, and then threw a few dollar bills on the table. "We'd better go."

The outside air was damp and brisk, with a hint of autumn yet to come. Tricia led the way to the car. "That was a waste of time."

"Oh, I don't know. We did find out a few things we didn't know before."

"The fact David wants a little wife at home and a family? I'm still angry at him for throwing it all away."

"It sounds like Deborah cheated first."

"And that sounds like you're blaming the victim," Tricia said.

"Deborah was a victim of the plane crash, *not* of a failed marriage. It seems as if she was just as much—if not more—to blame than David. And why are you so upset? Because Deborah wasn't the paragon of virtue you thought she was?"

Tricia sighed. "I'm afraid you're right, there. The

woman I've been hearing about for the past seven days bears no resemblance to the woman I thought I knew— from stealing Dumpster space, to having a child that wasn't her husband's. I can't help but feel there might be other secrets Deborah was hiding, and that we'll never know who she really was."

"Deborah's gone. It's time you let go of her."

"To move on like she was never here?" Tricia asked.

"The *real* Deborah never revealed herself to you."

"Which makes me question every friendship I've ever had."

"I wouldn't go that far. But you do seem to trust people too easily."

Tricia frowned. "So far, I haven't done too bad."

They reached the car, Tricia pressed the button on her key fob, and the doors unlocked. How come these conversations with Angelica always left her feeling depressed and dissatisfied with her life? It wasn't as though Angelica had a completely blissful life, either. With four failed marriages behind her, she was no authority on happiness. And yet, despite all the grief that had come her way, Angelica seemed to rise above the discontent and sail through it, whereas Tricia seemed to dwell on the misfortunes that hit her. Angelica wanted to be more like Michele, but Tricia wished she could be more like Angelica. And maybe . . . just maybe . . . she always had.

All the way back to Stoneham, Angelica gabbed about her favorite subject: herself. This time, she went on and on about her plans for her next cookbook launch and the self-promotion book tour she would undertake. That would mean that Tricia would have to keep an eye out for the Cookery and Booked for Lunch once again—which was *not* something she wanted to do. She didn't voice that opinion. Angelica wouldn't listen to her protests, anyway.

As she approached the municipal parking lot, Tricia saw flashing lights and noticed a Sheriff's Department patrol car parked at the north end of the alley that ran behind the Main Street stores on the west side. "Uh-oh. You don't suppose there's more trouble at the Happy Domestic, do you?" she asked, and pulled into the lot.

"There can't be," Angelica said. But the women hurriedly left the car and jogged across the street, circling behind the *Stoneham Weekly News* to end up in the mouth of the alley. The patrol car was empty and they bypassed it, heading down the eerily lit alley, their shadows bouncing against the brick walls, thanks to the patrol car's flashing blue lights.

"What do you think is going on?" Angelica asked.

"Hey, you ladies shouldn't be here," one of the deputies said. Henderson, if Tricia remembered right. Sure enough, a hooded figure was bent over the trunk of a car that looked a lot like the one in Boris Kozlov's surveillance video. Tricia watched as Captain Baker himself slapped handcuffs around the suspect's right wrist and then grabbed the suspect's left hand and cuffed it, too. He grabbed the person by the arm and hauled her (him?) forward. It was then Tricia recognized the suspect.

"Good grief, it's Cheryl Griffin!" Tricia cried, trying to keep up as Baker hustled Cheryl down the alley. "I thought you didn't have a car!"

"I borrowed it from my cousin," Cheryl called over her shoulder.

"There must be some mistake," Angelica said, following in Tricia's wake. "Why would Cheryl want to rob the Happy Domestic?"

"We caught her red-handed," Baker said. "And what are you doing here?"

Tricia hurried around them, causing Baker to halt. "We saw the lights on the patrol car." Tricia turned her attention back to Cheryl. "What happened? Why on earth would you want to rob the Happy Domestic?"

"Elizabeth Crane fired me and refused to pay me my last week's pay. I figured I'd take what she owed me in merchandise."

"But Elizabeth doesn't own the Happy Domestic. It's under new management," Tricia insisted.

"Like I care."

"You had a clean record. Why would you ruin your reputation, risk going to jail, for such a paltry sum?" Tricia asked.

"Maybe a week's pay means nothing to you, but I'm facing eviction. I have nowhere to go—no one to bail me out of my financial jam."

"But, Cheryl," Tricia protested.

"Don't you get it? I *want* them to send me to jail. I hope I get two, maybe three years. Let the state take care of me. At least I'd have a roof over my head and three square meals a day. Maybe I could even learn a trade so that when I got out I could find a good job."

And no one willing to hire you, Tricia thought. Well, perhaps Angelica. She had hired an ex-con, and that job had led to bigger and better things for Jake Masters. But it was more likely that Cheryl would get community service and an order to make restitution. That might drive her to commit even more—and more serious—crimes.

Baker shook his head and shoved Cheryl toward the waiting Sheriff's Department cruiser and placed a hand on her head as he guided her into the backseat of the car.

"Do you think you can recover the stolen items?" Angelica asked.

"If we can get her to tell us where they are. My guess is, she's already sold them."

"What if she put the items on eBay?" Tricia asked.

"I can ask one of the guys to check it out."

Tricia was about to tell him she'd bought a suspect figurine but decided not to. At this point, she had no clue who the seller was. She'd have to wait a couple of days until the figurine her friend Nancy had bought arrived in the mail. Then she'd know for sure if it was evidence the Sheriff's Department could use. It could wait.

"How did you come to arrest Cheryl?" Angelica asked.

Baker looked at his prisoner in the car. "We got a tip that someone was trying to break into the Happy Domestic. I wouldn't be surprised if we find that Ms. Griffin made the call herself."

"She's not likely to go to jail for a first offense, is she?" Tricia asked.

"It's possible—if she has a really crummy lawyer and if she gets a vindictive judge. More likely she'll be asked to do community service and make restitution." Just as Tricia had thought. He opened the driver's door. "I'll talk to you later," he said to Tricia, removed his hat, and climbed inside the cruiser.

Tricia bent down to speak to Cheryl through Baker's open window. "Cheryl, Grace Harris-Everett of the Everett Charitable Foundation has been looking for you."

"I don't *want* charity!" Cheryl declared.

"She may have a job for you at the Stoneham Clothes Closet."

Cheryl looked ready to cry. "*Now* you tell me!"

"Have Mrs. Everett call the county lockup. Maybe there's something she can do for Miss Griffin," Baker said, and put the cruiser in gear.

Tricia stepped back, and she and Angelica watched as Baker backed the patrol car into the street.

"So much for the great Stoneham robbery," Angelica said with a shrug.

Tricia shook her head. "Poor Cheryl just hasn't got a clue."

"Great name for a mystery bookstore," Angelica quipped.

"Very funny."

"It looks like this puts your little investigation right back at square one," Angelica said, and started walking again.

"I wasn't investigating anything. I'm just curious about the goings-on here in Stoneham."

"Curiosity killed the cat," Angelica reminded her. "Come on back to my place and I'll fix you something to eat. Preferably made of leftover turkey."

That wasn't exactly what Tricia was in the mood for, but the pickings were even slimmer in her own refrigerator.

She followed Angelica to her loft apartment and settled down at the big kitchen table. She wondered if Miss Marple was sleeping or missing her. If the latter, she knew she would get a stern scolding when she returned home. Angelica's home seemed so . . . empty without a cat. But it was useless to even bring up the subject of adding a feline friend to the mix. And honestly, Angelica was far too busy to take care of a pet.

"Penny for your thoughts," Angelica said, taking two wineglasses from the kitchen cupboard.

Penny. That was the name of Frannie's cat.

"You wouldn't want to know," Tricia said as Angelica poured. "It's too bad I know next to nothing about eBay."

"And why's that?"

"Because, I want to find out who's selling those Dolly Dolittle figurines that were stolen from the Happy Domestic. I'm almost sure they've shown up on eBay." She explained about her research and that she expected to receive one of the figurines in the mail.

"Frannie knows everything about anything," Angelica said. "Why don't you give her a call?"

"Do you have her home number?"

"On speed-dial," Angelica said, and handed Tricia the phone. Angelica turned back to the fridge to rummage, and Frannie answered on the second ring.

"Hi, Frannie. It's Tricia. I'm sorry to call so late, but do you have a couple of minutes?"

"Penny and I were just watching an old movie, anyway. What do you need?"

"If I wanted to sell something on eBay, and I didn't have a computer, where could I go to do that?"

"But you *do* have a computer. I've seen you use it."

"I'm speaking hypothetically," Tricia said, hoping she'd kept her impatience from her voice.

"There's a place in Milford that does it. They even pack

and ship the items—for a fee, of course. But if you wanted to stay local, I'd send you to Brandy Arkin."

"Brandy?" Tricia repeated, surprised. An eavesdropping Angelica raised an eyebrow as well.

"She's a power seller. And since the day care center closed, she's stepped up her online business. She's got to keep a roof over her head, you know."

"I take it you don't have to upload pictures of the items you're selling," Tricia said.

"There's a cost for everything. But who wants to buy something if you can't see a picture of it?"

Who, indeed. Cheryl wasn't the sharpest pencil in the box, and she was broke. What if she'd asked Brandy to list the Dolly Dolittle figurines but tried to save money by not posting pictures? It would be just like her.

But even if Brandy *did* post the items for sale, that didn't mean she knew they were stolen. And even if she suspected it, she probably wouldn't admit it.

And what good did any of this do, except to help prove Cheryl was guilty of breaking and entering the Happy Domestic and selling stolen items. It sure would help the prosecutor convict Cheryl, which was exactly what she wanted. She'd made a sloppy entry into a life of crime—just as she'd intended. Maybe she wasn't quite as vapid as everyone gave her credit for.

"You still there?" Frannie asked.

"Oh, sorry. I was thinking. I'll let you get back to your movie."

"Nice talking to you," Frannie said, and hung up.

Tricia handed the phone back to Angelica. "Frannie says Brandy Arkin is an eBay power seller."

"So what's that got to do with anything?" Angelica asked. She held a carving knife in her hand, and what was left of the turkey carcass sat on the counter.

"Nothing, I suppose." Tricia thought back on her day. "Bob still hasn't returned any of my calls. Why don't you call him, and then you can pass the phone to me and I'll talk to him."

"I am *not* calling Bob for you." She hacked off what was left of the turkey's thigh.

"I know you're angry with him, but if you want to annoy him, this is the perfect opportunity," Tricia said.

"If you must know, he's being punished." Angelica peeled off a bit of skin, and attacked what was left of the breast.

"By you?"

"Of course by me. I'm waiting for *him* to call *me*. Groveling wouldn't be a bad move on his part, either." Did she seem just a tad annoyed at what was apparently now her erstwhile boyfriend? Angelica hadn't turned back, so Tricia couldn't see her face to judge just how upset she was about her relationship with Bob.

"I thought you guys were finished."

"Not entirely," Angelica admitted.

"Maybe you left him hanging for just a little too long," Tricia suggested.

"I really don't want to talk about Bob. Now, what do you want to eat? A turkey club or a turkey salad sandwich? Or I could smother it in gravy with some leftover garlic mashed potatoes on the side."

"Turkey salad is fine. But only if you're making it with whole wheat bread and light mayonnaise."

"I do not have light *anything* in my kitchen, and I only

have a baguette from Nikki's Patisserie in the freezer, but it'll be better than any sandwich you've ever eaten at home."

Tricia sipped her wine. "Whatever," she said, and cringed at herself for using that hated expression.

Angelica took celery from the fridge's crisper drawer and began to chop up a rib.

"How long is this likely to take?" Tricia asked. "I'm going to go over to Bob's house after I leave here."

Angelica sighed. "You're like a terrier, you know that? You just don't let go of things."

"You could come with me, you know. Maybe it would help you and Bob smooth things over."

"More likely, he'd get angry with me. He doesn't like to be pushed. And you're a pusher!"

"I don't deal drugs," Tricia said wryly.

"And I don't go crawling back to people who've done me wrong," Angelica said bitterly.

"You could stay in the car."

"And do what? Listen to the radio? Watch out for aliens?"

"The Dexter sisters still think we're ripe for an invasion," Tricia reminded her.

"Ha!"

"Well, are you game?"

Angelica sniffed and gave the last piece of celery a vicious chop. "I suppose I could go along . . . just to keep you company.'

"Fine," Tricia said and nodded. More likely Angelica wanted to make sure Bob wasn't canoodling with someone else on the sly. "How's that sandwich coming?"

"Get the baguette out of the freezer and nuke it for about

thirty seconds. I'll have this turkey salad finished by the time you do that and get some plates out."

Tricia glanced at the clock. It was already well past nine o'clock. Would Bob still be up by the time they ate their makeshift dinner and drove to his house?

She sure hoped so, because at this point, she wasn't sure she wouldn't pound on his front door and wake him up if he had gone to bed.

This time, she would get some answers.

TWENTY-FIVE

Angelica hadn't finished her sandwich and had barely touched her wine before Tricia led her to the municipal parking lot to pick up her car. Was Angelica that worried Bob might be shacked up with someone else?

The drive to Bob's house was silent, and Tricia was glad she only had to endure it for two blocks. She pulled the car to a stop outside of Bob's home, put it in gear, and shut down the engine before killing the lights. "Do you want to come in with me?"

Angelica refused to look at her. "No. I told you, I only came along for the ride." But Tricia did notice that her sister's gaze was focused on Bob's driveway, where only his own car was parked.

"I won't be long."

"Take as much time as you want. I'm not going anywhere." It sounded like a threat.

Tricia got out of the car and walked up the concrete path that led to the porch and Bob's front door. The lights were still on in the living room, and Tricia snuck a peak through one of the windows. Bob sat on the couch, staring at the flickering television screen.

Tricia stepped back to the door and rapped on it hard enough to bruise her knuckles. For a long moment nothing happened, and she was about to dart back to the window to take another peek, when the porch light came on, the handle rattled, and the door opened.

"Tricia. What are you doing here at this time of night?" Bob asked, sounding genuinely surprised.

"I tried contacting you at least four times earlier today. Why didn't you return my calls?"

Bob frowned, sudden anger hardening his expression. "I'm a busy man. I don't have time to mess around with someone who thinks she's the reincarnation of Agatha Christie."

"I don't write mystery novels. I read and sell them. Now, why have you been avoiding me?" Tricia demanded.

"Because, you're a terrible nag—just like your sister," he blurted.

Tricia's eyes blazed, and Bob seemed to realize the *big* mistake he'd just made.

"Ohmigod, please don't tell Angelica I said that. She's been giving me the cold shoulder for months. I'd do anything to get back in her good graces."

"Anything?" Tricia asked.

Bob's eyes narrowed. "To a point." He sighed. "You'd better come in." He stood back, letting Tricia enter his tidy living room. She noticed a framed portrait of Angelica— her author photo—sitting on the fireplace mantel, but there was little else to personalize the room.

Bob directed Tricia to sit, but he chose to stand before the fireplace. Maybe he thought he'd be more intimidating if he stood, but Tricia wasn't afraid of him.

"What is it you want to know now?" he asked, with a bit of a whine.

"Bob, you've got to remember who recommended Monty Capshaw to fly over the Founders' Day opening ceremonies."

"How am I supposed to remember? It was weeks ago—maybe even a couple of months."

"Was it at a Chamber breakfast?" Tricia suggested.

"I don't know," he complained, and turned away.

Tricia grabbed him by the shoulder, forcing him to face her once again. "This is important, Bob. Whoever suggested you hire Capshaw wanted Deborah Black dead. I should think you'd want her death off your conscience."

Bob sighed, collapsed onto the couch, and hunched over, covering his face with his hands. "I just don't remember."

"What meeting did it happen in? Was it the first time the idea of hosting Founders' Day came up?"

He shook his head. "No—long after that."

"Did someone hand you a business card?"

Bob pulled his hands away from his face. "Yes. It was Monty's card for Capshaw Aeronautics." He leaned over, withdrew his wallet from his back trouser pocket, and opened it, shuffling through the contents until he came up with a battered business card. He handed it to Tricia. She studied it for a moment before giving it back to him.

Tricia considered how to approach her next question. "Think about the hand that gave you the card. Was it a man's or a woman's hand?"

Bob stared at the card, and then closed his eyes tight in

concentration. "A woman's. Now that I think of it, she was wearing a funny ring."

"Funny?" Tricia pressed.

"It was gold . . . with a heart and two hands."

"Sounds like a Claddagh."

"A what?"

Tricia indicated the computer that sat on the desk on the opposite side of the room. "Is your computer on?"

Bob nodded, and Tricia crossed the room, taking a seat at the desk. Bob followed her. Tricia tapped on the keyboard, brought up a Google search screen and typed in "Claddagh." The screen filled with links, and she chose one to Wikipedia, hitting enter. The screen flashed and brought up a page with a large picture. "Is this the ring you saw?"

Bob took a few moments to study the screen before nodding. "Yes, that's it."

"It's an Irish wedding band." She read through the entry. "It says here it can also be worn on the right hand if you're on the lookout for love. Which hand was the ring on?"

Bob frowned again. "It would've been the right."

"So, an unmarried woman looking for a relationship. Who in the Chamber is looking for love?" Tricia asked.

Bob shrugged, and looked embarrassed. "Most of the women members aren't married. You would probably have to contact every one and ask if they have the ring."

"Who's going to admit it?" Tricia shook her head. "Asking someone directly is too dangerous. If they were willing to get rid of Deborah, they might be willing to come after me—or you, if you step up to the plate."

"You're crazy. Monty ran out of gas. It was an accident. And don't look at me to help you find the woman who owns that ring," Bob declared. "I've run into enough danger this year."

Of course, he was referring to his part in saving Tricia's life at the hands of a killer just two months before. But the fact that he thought he might be in danger bolstered her beliefs.

Tricia stood. "I'll handle this, Bob."

"No, you won't. You've got to call Steve Marsden. He's in charge of the investigation."

"He only cares about *why* the plane crashed, not who put Monty up to crashing it," Tricia pointed out.

"Then tell your friend Captain Baker."

Tricia pursed her lips. He wouldn't be her first choice of confidant. "When's the next Chamber meeting?" she asked.

"Friday."

"That's too long to wait."

"What else can you do?" Bob asked.

"I assume Betsy can give me a list of all the current Chamber members."

"I was kidding when I said you should visit them all."

Tricia nodded. "I've got the perfect excuse; I'm still collecting for Davey Black's education fund."

Bob shrugged and moved toward the door—a hint that it was time to leave. "Better you than me. But if you find the woman wearing that ring, you'd better call Steve Marsden."

"Of course I will," Tricia said, not entirely sure it was a true statement. She looked back at the image of the Claddagh on the computer screen and suddenly felt quite charitable toward Bob for all his help. Of course, he had to go and spoil it.

"If something happened to you because of this conversation, Angelica would never forgive me, and I've been in the doghouse far too long," he said.

Tricia straightened and frowned. "I'm relatively sure you're on safe ground, Bob. I have no plans to do anything stupid."

"Well, see that you don't."

"Thank you for your help," Tricia said.

"I hope you're going to tell Angelica how I helped you. I need a good word from someone about now."

"You'll get it," she said as he opened the door for her. "Good night, Bob."

"Good night."

He didn't wait to see if she got back to her car all right, just closed the door with a bit of a bang. Tricia didn't look back.

"Well, what did he say?" Angelica said, once Tricia was back in the car.

"Bob remembers getting a business card for Monty's flying service and that it was a woman wearing a Claddagh ring who gave it to him."

"He remembered it was a woman, eh?" Angelica said sharply.

"Only that it was a woman's hand. He doesn't remember who actually gave it to him." Tricia frowned. "And do we know anyone who wears a Claddagh?"

"Maybe," Angelica said, sounding thoughtful.

Tricia blinked. "You remember seeing one lately?"

"Yes, but . . . I'm not sure when. It had to be within the past week or so, though. I thought maybe *I* should get one to wear on *my* right hand."

"Good. Bob's not good enough for you, anyway."

Angelica sighed theatrically. "Oh, I don't know. I still have some residual feelings for him—albeit buried deep."

Tricia started the car and eased away from the curb. She turned the corner onto Fifth Street and noticed that Brandy Arkin's house was lit up. She slowed the car.

"Why are you stopping?" Angelica asked.

"Do you think it's too late to talk to Brandy about the whole eBay scheme?"

"Definitely."

"But this might break the case."

"The case is broken," Angelica reminded her. "Your Captain Baker captured the thief red-handed."

"We could nail it shut for him." She turned off the engine. "Now, what pretense can I use to get in to see her?"

"How about asking, Are you selling stolen goods for Cheryl Griffin?" Angelica suggested.

"That's too obvious. I have to ease into the conversation."

"David's probably already told her to steer clear of you after your last altercation with him."

Tricia pursed her lips and thought about it. Then it came to her. "I've got it! Remember at Deborah's funeral gathering Elizabeth told us she suspected Brandy had Davey's security blanket? Maybe I could go to Brandy and ask her about it, appeal to her better nature."

"Anyone who'd deprive a baby of his security blanket is no candidate for a Mother Teresa award."

"That's the least of her personality faults, if she can stoop to selling stolen goods."

"This is where you call your buddy the captain and let him do the digging," Angelica ordered.

"What digging? All I have is theory—and all I want to do is just talk to her."

"You shouldn't go in alone."

"You think she's going to threaten me for asking about eBay?"

"You *are* about to accuse her of a crime," Angelica pointed out.

"But if she didn't *know* the goods were stolen, she's a victim, *not* a perpetrator."

"Whatever," Angelica said, causing Tricia to wince yet again.

"Besides, it looks suspicious enough with me showing up this time of night."

"Then I will wait in the car, and if you don't come out in a timely manner—"

"I do *not* want you to come and get me. If I'm in danger, you'd be in trouble, too."

"I have no intention of coming to save your skinny butt. I value my own hide too much. But I *can* dial 9-1-1 faster than anyone I know."

"Good, then it's settled." She opened the car door. "Wish me luck!"

"Good luck."

Tricia made her way up the walk to the house and paused to look into the night sky. She squinted, examining the twinkling lights in the sky. Could one of them be a mothership poised to swoop down on New Hampshire, capturing its entire population as slaves? She thought about the potential horror of such a situation—for all of five seconds—then said to herself, "Nahhhh."

Tricia hammered on the scratched oak door for a third time before he heard the muted sound of footsteps approach. The outside light snapped on, and she looked directly at the front door's peephole and braved a smile. The door jerked open. "What are you doing here at this time of night?" Brandy asked, sounding more than a little annoyed.

"I've come to ask you a huge favor. It has to do with Davey Black. Can I come in?"

Brandy heaved a sigh and stepped back. "I guess." She stepped aside and let Tricia enter before leading her into what must have once been a large parlor at a time when the house had been a stately home. All around the edges of the room were the bulky pink, green, and orange plastic toys that seemed like required equipment wherever a child was in residence, although the children in this house had been day boarders while their parents worked.

All the furniture had a scuffed, beat-up look to it—like it had survived college years and beyond. Perhaps if Brandy had invested everything she had in the now-defunct day care center, flea market and yard sale finds were all she could afford to furnish her home. Or was it that the children she'd taken care of were rough on everything?

Several self-built, flake-board cabinets lined the south end of the room, surrounding a flake-board computer desk. The computer was switched off. Nearby stood a table covered in white butcher paper. On it was a small red Pyrex bowl and a pocket digital camera—the tools of Brandy's eBay trade.

"Now, tell me why you're interested in Davey Black?" Brandy demanded, and leaned against one of the cabinets.

"His mother was my friend. Her mother, Elizabeth, is also my friend."

"Yeah, and Deborah Black put me out of business, so why should I want to help any of her relatives?"

"Davey's just a little boy. He misses his mother; *and* he misses his blanket. He cries himself to sleep every night."

"Is that sob story supposed to melt my cold heart? Listen, I've seen every kind of spoiled rotten kid on the face of the planet, and in about fourteen years there'll be a jail cell with that little hooligan's name on it."

Tricia was taken aback by the vehemence in Brandy's tone.

"I think you'd better leave," Brandy said.

"No, please. Do you have Davey Black's security blanket? He's heartbroken."

Brandy crossed her arms. "Look, I told the kid's grandmother I don't have it."

"But could you please look? I'd be willing to pay you for it," Tricia said, adding a bit of a lilt to her voice.

Brandy's eyes narrowed. "How much?"

"Fifty dollars," Tricia said.

Brandy frowned and shook her head. "Surely something that valuable is worth a lot more money."

Elizabeth had been right. Brandy Arkin was a bitch.

"One hundred?" Tricia suggested.

Again, Brandy shook her head.

"Two?" she tried. "Three?"

Tricia felt a flush rise up her neck to color her cheeks. "Five hundred."

"Now you're talking."

Tricia sighed. "Unfortunately, I don't carry that kind of cash around with me."

Brandy raised her eyebrows and cocked her head. "That *is* too bad. I mean, something could happen to widdle oohed Davey's bwankie," she said, in a simpering tone.

"Such as?"

"It might end up in the rag bag. Or the trash."

Tricia swallowed. "Would you take a check?"

"I will—but only as a retainer. You bring the cash to-morrow, I'll give you the blanket."

"I want something in return as well," Tricia said.

"I'll cut off a quarter of the blanket. You can have that as collateral."

"But—"

"It can be sewn back together. Believe me, the kid won't care."

"Very well," Tricia agreed.

"Fine. I'll go get it. You wait here."

She left the room with an awkward gait, like she had a sore foot, and Tricia heard her clomp through the house. How long would it take her to find scissors and chop out a chunk of the blanket? Probably no more than a minute or two. That didn't give Tricia much time for a search for the Dolly Dolittle figurines.

She started by opening the cabinets—which housed much more bric-a-brac than toys. Each item was tagged with a handwritten identifier, probably corresponding to the items listed for sale online.

Tricia abandoned the cabinets and glanced at the bookshelves, which held more clutter and very little to read, besides children's storybooks. What novels Brandy did own seemed to have been bought used from the Have a Heart romance bookstore—or yard sales. The spines looked like they'd seen some hard wear. The rest were cookbooks by Food Network chefs—and a copy of Angelica's *Easy-Does-It Cooking*. Tricia frowned. She wouldn't have thought Brandy would be a fan.

Tricia poked around the room, opening the armoire that hid the bulky old analog TV, with its dusty screen. Since it was hooked up to cable, it probably still functioned fine. A couple of pieces of stereo equipment also lived inside along with a stack of children's CDs and DVDs, which had probably been used to entertain the day care's clients. Tricia closed the doors once again, casting her gaze about the room.

A large unpainted toy chest was backed against the wall, next to stacks of colorful plastic chairs made for tiny bottoms. On a shelf above it sat several remotes, no doubt for the equipment in the armoire.

Tricia looked around. Still no sign of Brandy. She lifted the chest's cover an inch or so and peeked inside. It was too dark to make out the jumble of objects inside. Throwing caution to the wind, she lifted the lid. Instead of toys, she found several framed photographs that had been tossed on top of a bunch of small pillows and yoga mats. On top was a darling photograph of a little white dog. A familiar little white dog.

Tricia felt the hairs on her neck bristle: Sarge.

TWENTY-SIX

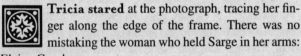 **Tricia stared** at the photograph, tracing her finger along the edge of the frame. There was no mistaking the woman who held Sarge in her arms: Elaine Capshaw.

Elaine had told Tricia that she and her husband weren't close to any of their local relatives. If so, what was Brandy Arkin doing with such a photo?

Footsteps approached and Tricia almost let the chest's lid slam. She tossed the photo back inside the chest, shut the lid and took several hurried steps away from it, trying not to look out of breath when Brandy reentered the room with a definite limp.

As promised, Brandy held a square of dirty, yellow polar fleece with little tractors driving across it. It had a crocheted yellow border, which now hung ragged on two ends. Was it possible the thing could be repaired to its former state? Maybe Davey wouldn't care what it looked like as long as he was reunited with it. Perhaps Mary Fairchild at By Hook or By Book could replicate the thing if Brandy destroyed the original.

"Where's that check?" Brandy demanded.

Tricia gave a nervous laugh. "Oh, sorry. I guess I should have written it out while you were gone."

Brandy frowned.

Tricia pulled her checkbook and a pen from her purse and proceeded to write out the check. She'd put a stop on it the minute the bank opened in the morning. She tore out the check and handed it to Brandy. And caught sight of a gold band on her right hand.

Not a band—a Claddagh.

Sweat broke out on the back of Tricia's neck, and she swallowed. It was Brandy who had given Bob Kelly Monty Capshaw's business card and encouraged him to give the pilot a call. And that sore leg? Sarge had bitten whoever attacked Elaine Capshaw. But why would Brandy threaten Elaine?

Brandy's frown increased as her gaze traveled around the room. "Something's different. Have you been poking around in my things?"

"Of course not," Tricia lied, as every muscle in her body tensed. She had to get out of there.

Brandy focused on the blanket chest and Tricia took a step to the left. The door was at least ten or twelve feet from where she stood. Had Brandy locked it behind her after she'd entered the house?

Brandy tossed the piece of blanket on the floor, stalked over to the blanket chest, grabbed the handle, and flipped open the lid. As she looked down at the contents, the color drained from her face.

Tricia bent down to retrieve the remnant of Davey's

blanket. "I'll bring you the cash first thing tomorrow morning," she said, already backing toward the door.

"You're not going anywhere," Brandy commanded.

"I don't understand," Tricia bluffed.

"You saw that picture. *You* know."

"What picture?"

"You were at my aunt's house the night she died," Brandy accused.

"I was?" Tricia said, hoping her voice hadn't already betrayed her.

"You took that miserable yappy dog to the vet."

No use denying that. But how did Brandy fit in? Elaine Capshaw was her aunt?

And then she remembered Monty Capshaw's obituary. It listed a couple of nieces: Brenda and Cara. Brandy was really Brenda?

"I've got to get going," Tricia said. "I'll see you in the morning, and then I think our business will be finished."

"You're not going anywhere," Brandy said, and reached for a slender wooden bat—the kind used for T-ball. Had Brandy bludgeoned Elaine Capshaw to death with something similar?

"There's someone waiting for me outside. If I don't turn up in the next couple of minutes, the Sheriff's Department will be called."

"I don't believe you."

"I'm telling the truth," Tricia insisted.

"Sure, like you told the truth when you walked in here saying you wanted Davey Black's blanket. Now, what do you *really* want?"

"I *was* going to ask you to list some things on eBay for me. I understand that's your new business."

Brandy shook her head. "David said you were suspicious about Deborah's death."

"He did?" Oh boy. Why did she have to open her mouth and voice that opinion to so many people?

Brandy tapped the end of the bat against her open left palm. "Deborah Black's death was an accident—plain and simple."

"You're right. I'm sure that's what the National Transportation Safety Board will decide. I mean, why would someone deliberately let his gas tanks run dry and then crash his plane into a stone gazebo? It just doesn't make sense. Unless . . ."

Brandy tapped the bat harder against her palm. That had to smart.

"Unless," Brandy said, picking up the story, "he was well paid to do it."

"Ten thousand dollars?" Tricia volunteered.

"Money that was supposed to come back to me when the will was read. That was the deal. But Elaine showed me the will—it had never been amended. I drove that miserable old fart to the attorney's office myself. But the lawyer made me leave the room when Uncle Monty supposedly signed it. He said it would prove I wasn't coercing the old man to make the changes."

"And did you coerce him?"

Brandy snorted. "My uncle was already living under a death sentence. All I did was suggest a way to make it easier on his darling Elaine."

"And now she's dead. I suppose under the terms of the original will, you and your sister would only inherit if Elaine were out of the picture."

"Yeah, and now I have to split my own ten grand with my sister," she grated.

"But now you get David. And isn't that what you really wanted all along?"

"I don't even get him. He's decided I'd be a liability in the hoity-toity art world. I'm not pretty enough, or thin enough, or educated enough for him. He's looking to step up—to that old hag Michele Fowler."

"She's far from a hag," Tricia said.

"She's twenty years older than me! And yet he'd rather be with *her* than me! After all I did to—"

"Set him free?" Tricia asked.

"Of Deborah—of that rotten kid. Did you know Deborah's mother plans to soak David for child support even though she knows the kid isn't his?"

"Is that why you tried to run Davey over the other night?"

Brandy's eyes grew wide, and she drew back her arm and swung the T-ball bat at Tricia.

Tricia ducked, and the momentum—and her sore leg— threw Brandy off balance. Tricia raced for the door but fell over her own feet, tumbling to the floor. Brandy took advantage and charged at her, but Tricia dove for cover behind the bulky pink plastic child-sized house.

The bat came down again and again, but the plastic was made to withstand the destructive power of ten small children. Still, Tricia cringed with each strike, her eyes darting to look for any avenue of escape. The former parlor, with its high ceilings, seemed almost cavernous.

Bam!

That split second of inattention cost her, as Brandy

slammed the bat into Tricia's upper arm. As Brandy drew back to strike again, Tricia scrambled to her left, but there was nothing there to hide behind.

She grabbed the handle of the flimsy cabinet, yanking it open—an instant shield against Brandy's fury.

Brandy's bat came down again and again against the door and the cabinet wobbled, the hinges pulling out of the flake board. Brandy screamed epithets as the bat hammered against the cabinet and it began to come apart in shreds.

Tricia had pulled the handle closer to her body, ducking her head to avoid the blow, when the cabinet tilted crazily forward and fell, squashing Brandy like a bug.

TWENTY-SEVEN

 Champagne chilled in a silver bucket, but Tricia felt like doing anything but celebrate. Still, she didn't think she'd succumb to tears, either. Ginny's leaving was just another sad passage in life. And it wasn't like she'd never see her onetime assistant again. Ginny would still live at the edge of town in her little cottage. She'd be working right across the street, and she might even show up at Chamber of Commerce meetings. But it would never be the same at Haven't Got a Clue. Life moved on, but sometimes it seemed like Tricia was always being left behind. She fingered the diamond stud in her left ear and thought about Christopher.

Had it only been days since the terrible events at the Tiny Tots Day Care? True, Brandy had not succumbed to her injuries, and Grant Baker assured Tricia she would have a long time to recover—in jail.

Worse yet, after Brandy revealed David Black's betrayal, a deputy had gone to Deborah's and David's home to find that Brandy had taken out her revenge on David, too. He would live. No doubt nursed back to health by Michele Fowler . . . until one or the other tired of the obligation.

The shop door opened, but before Tricia could tell the person behind it that the store was closed, in barreled Antonio Barbero with a large cardboard box. "Can you help, *per favore*?" he called.

Tricia reluctantly went to the door to hold it open, and was surprised to find three more people behind Antonio, all carrying what looked like rental equipment: tables, folding chairs, and a large coffee urn. "What's all this?"

"I hope you don't mind my arranging for some food and drink for your guests."

"Where do you want the table set up?" asked one of the men in white chef togs.

"Is this all stuff from the Brookview Inn?" Tricia asked.

Antonio nodded. "Set up along that wall," he told his minions. "There will be somewhere to plug in the coffee urn, will there not?" he asked Tricia.

"Yes," she answered, overwhelmed and a little annoyed that Antonio was hijacking her farewell party for Ginny. "You really didn't have to do this. I ordered—"

"Sweets for my sweet," Antonio said, directing the rest of his workers on where to set up other equipment. "I spoke to Nikki at the Patisserie. We coordinated the entire menu."

"Menu?" Tricia asked, aghast.

"But you must have hot hors d'oeuvres. Nothing is too good for Ginny," Antonio said, deadly serious.

Tricia could hardly complain because—he was right. But who was going to eat all the food his workers had brought?

As if reading her mind, Antonio reached into the breast pocket of his jacket and withdrew a linen envelope. Tricia lifted the flap and withdrew an engraved invitation.

Ms. Tricia Miles requests the honor of your presence . . .

Good grief, it sounded more like a wedding invitation than an after-hours farewell party.

She skimmed the rest of the note. "How many of these did you send out?"

"Only thirty or forty."

"Thirty or forty?" Tricia squealed. How would they ever fit thirty or forty bodies into Haven't Got a Clue?

Russ Smith walked through the still-open door. He hadn't been on Tricia's invitation list, but as though anticipating her intention of throwing him out, he brandished his invitation. "And where's the girl of the hour?" he asked with a grin.

"Girl," Tricia grated, wondering what she had ever seen in this Neanderthal of a man.

"Why, Ginny, of course."

"She should be here any—" Before she could utter the word *moment*, Ginny entered Haven't Got a Clue. She took one look around the room and her lips trembled. "Oh, Tricia, you didn't have to go to all this trouble for me."

Tricia threw a sour look at Antonio. "Well, I—"

"You have had the most wonderful employer. It is so sad you must leave this most welcoming place," Antonio said, his teeth nearly gleaming. Had he just had them whitened? "But, I'm sure Tricia cannot blame me for stealing you away from her. You are already marvelous as the manager for the Happy Domestic. Do you not agree?" he said, with a pointed look at Tricia.

She forced a smile. "Of course." She turned a more genuine expression on her now-former employee. "I can't take all the credit for—" She gestured toward the table now laden with food. "It was—"

"The work of all your friends," Antonio supplied.

Ginny covered her mouth with her left hand, her eyes swimming with tears. She seemed about to speak, but before she could, the bell over the door jingled, and Angelica stepped over the threshold, carrying a large wrapped gift, with one of her gigantic purses slung over her left shoulder.

"Well, doesn't it look nice in here," she said with an admiring smile at the food and the drink. "Tricia, I thought you said this was going to be a simple affair."

"Well, I—" But before she could elaborate, Nikki Brimfield from the Patisserie swooped in with a large tray piled high with cookies covered in plastic wrap.

"Happy new job, Ginny," she called. She looked fantastic in a tight black dress and heels, with her upswept hair pinned firm with a ruby-studded clip. She set the tray on the empty end of the long serving table and uncovered the cookies, before she doubled back and gave Ginny a warm hug. "Congratulations. This is a wonderful opportunity for you. I started out managing the Patisserie and now I own it. Maybe you'll have the same luck."

"Oh, I don't know," Ginny said shyly, but she seemed to like the notion just the same.

The bell over the door rang again, and this time it was Mr. Everett and his bride, Grace, who entered. "Congratulations, Ginny," Grace called, and hurried over to plant a grandmotherly kiss on Ginny's cheek, leaving the faintest imprint of red lipstick.

"Thank you, Grace. I'm already overwhelmed. I just hope I can live up to Antonio's expectations. And . . . Ms. Racita's, too, of course."

Mr. Everett held out his hands, taking both of Ginny's. "Miss Marple and I shall miss your sunny smile," he said, and this time it was Ginny who kissed him.

Mr. Everett actually blushed.

"I love your moustache," Ginny said. "What made you decide to go with the Poirot look instead of Selleck's?"

Mr. Everett cleared his throat. "It was Grace's request."

"And isn't he cute?" she gushed. "I had to order the moustache wax online."

"I think it looks very dignified," Tricia said, and Mr. Everett's blush deepened.

Grace turned a fascinated gaze on Antonio. "When do we get to meet this woman of mystery who's been buying up so much of Stoneham?"

Tricia trained her gaze on Antonio. This was a question she'd been dying to ask herself.

He shrugged. "Ms. Racita is so very busy. But I think she will have to come to Stoneham soon to see all that she has acquired. It would be in her best interests, I think."

Yes, Tricia thought. *It would*. But before she could voice that thought, the door opened again, and this time it was Bob Kelly. He held a cellophane-wrapped bouquet of red carnations—trust Bob not to spring for roses—but they were cheerful and he ignored the others and made a beeline for Ginny, handing her the flowers and lunging forward to plant a kiss on her cheek.

"Thank you, Bob," she said, with just a bit of a strain in her voice.

Angelica leveled a glare at Bob, who was standing much too close to Ginny, whose discomfort was quite evident. "Whoa, boy. Rein yourself in," Angelica ordered.

Bob turned, looking sheepish, and stepped back. "Hello, honey bun."

Hadn't he yet noticed that Angelica hated that particular term of endearment?

Angelica gazed at Ginny fondly. "You're almost like a part of the family. I'm sorry you're leaving Haven't Got a Clue, but I'm so proud of you for taking the next step in your career." She leaned in and gave Ginny an air kiss, then pulled back and smiled. She proffered her gift. "For your new home."

Ginny opened her mouth to protest—she'd had her home for over a year. But she accepted the gift and set it on the beverage counter. "Thank you, Angelica. I hardly know what to say."

"Open it," Angelica encouraged.

With the delight of a child at Christmas, Ginny ripped the paper and discarded the ribbon, lifting the lid on a beautifully crafted box, covered in gray silk organza, that looked more like a throw pillow. Ginny's mouth dropped as she first gazed inside the box and then reached for the gift inside.

"Oh, Angelica, it's beautiful. Where did you get it?" she asked, lifting the beautiful bronze sculpture of a horse— one Tricia recognized as having been for sale at Foxleigh Gallery.

"Just something I picked up on my travels," she said. Tricia had seen the price tag. It wasn't a Kmart blue-light special, by any means. She hadn't realized Angelica was that fond of Ginny.

"I'm overwhelmed by the kindness you've all shown me," Ginny said, as the door opened, and Cheryl Griffin stuck her head inside. "Oh, wow. Is this a party?"

Tricia hurried to the door. "Yes, but I'm afraid it's a private party."

"Oh, no sweat. I wanted to tell you that I can't take the job here at your store. I've got a job at the Clothes Closet, and they're going to help me with my legal problems, too."

"Congratulations," Tricia said, and tried to edge Cheryl out of the doorway, but then Cheryl caught sight of Grace. "Hey, there's Mrs. Everett. She's my friend." Cheryl pushed past Tricia, who shook her head and made to close the door, only to find Frannie, Julia Overline, Chauncey Porter, Mary Fairchild, and a bunch of the other Main Street booksellers approaching the store. Captain Baker was at the end of the line.

"Ah, here's the man of the hour," Bob announced once everyone had entered. "Or should I say, the new year?" he added with a laugh. "Congratulations, Captain, on being named Stoneham's new police chief."

Tricia whirled on Baker. "You didn't tell me you'd been offered the job as Stoneham's police chief," Tricia said, feeling hurt.

"I had to wait until the Board of Selectmen made a public statement—which was earlier today. Besides . . . you never asked where my new job would take me."

"Isn't this exciting! Our own police force," Frannie said, with delight. "How big a force will there be?"

"Just six officers to start. We'll see how that goes."

"This is all very nice," Antonio said, "but this is Ginny's

celebration. Captain Baker—may I be so bold as to suggest you hold your own party—somewhere else."

Baker opened his mouth to protest, but it was Angelica who stepped in to defend him. "Antonio, it was Bob who brought up the subject," she said, leveling a hard gaze at the Chamber chief.

"Sorry," Bob apologized.

From the vicinity of the floor came a low growl. Tricia looked around but saw Miss Marple on her perch behind the register. She wasn't good in crowds.

"What's that noise?" Bob asked, and bent down.

The growl grew louder, and then a white blur emerged from Angelica's purse, and soon attached itself to Bob's trouser leg.

"Sarge!" Tricia called, making a lunge for the tiny white dog. And though Sarge wasn't a terrier, he was tenacious. It took both Angelica and Tricia to pull the feisty bichon frise away from Bob. Angelica held him to her cheek, and the dog immediately calmed. "Be still, my little sweetheart, I won't let that big bad man hurt you."

Bob looked anything *but* a big bad man. He'd paled, shocked by the sudden attack.

"What are you doing with Sarge? The receptionist at the animal hospital told me that the woman who adopted him was well known to the dog."

"I had a dream that Sarge was my little Pom-Pom reincarnated. I could hardly let him be given to just anyone," she explained fervently.

Sarge licked her chin and made mewling noises reminiscent of a kitten. Ginny, Grace and Mr. Everett, and Frannie were suddenly clustered around Angelica, each of them hesitantly petting the dog, who seemed to lap up the attention.

"Have you thought this through? You lead a busy life. You can't bring a dog into Booked for Lunch. And before you know it, you'll be back on the road to promote your next cookbook."

"Oh, don't be such a stick in the mud. This dog *needs* me." She kissed the top of Sarge's head. "And I need him."

Tricia glanced back at Miss Marple, who seemed quite annoyed.

Still holding Sarge in the crook of her arm, Angelica nudged Frannie to pick up the tray filled with punch cups. Tricia took one. "Tricia, I think it's time for you to propose a toast." Angelica grabbed one of the glasses.

Tricia smiled, holding her cup aloft. "To Ginny. May this new step be the start of a wonderful career."

"Hear, hear," chorused the rest of the gathering.

"I have something else to announce," Ginny said, and Antonio beamed at her. She brandished the ring finger on her left hand, and on it was a gorgeous full-carat diamond solitaire. "Antonio and I are engaged."

"This really is a celebration!" Frannie squealed with delight, and rushed forward to give the bride-to-be a hug, nearly spilling her champagne punch.

Tricia stepped back and let the others surround Ginny to give their hearty congratulations. Some part of her felt wistful as she remembered announcing her own engagement to Christopher and the whirlwind of parties and arrangements that occurred afterward. It had been the best time of her life. That idea disturbed her now. Surely the life she had was one to be envied, and yet the thought that her best days might already be behind her . . .

Captain Baker stepped close and whispered in her ear. "Penny for your thoughts."

"Not a good bargain," she said, grateful she'd managed to keep her voice steady.

"We've both got new adventures ahead of us. You'll soon have a new employee to train, and I'll soon have a whole new life. I hope you'll be a big part of that life." He raised his glass, looking hopeful.

Tricia raised hers to clink against his.

Then again, who said the future didn't offer pleasures yet to come?

ANGELICA'S RECIPES

TURKEY CURRY

2 cups milk
2 chicken bouillon cubes
2 cups diced peeled apples
1 cup chopped onion
1 rib celery, chopped
¼ cup vegetable oil
2 tablespoons all-purpose flour
2 teaspoons curry powder *
½ teaspoon salt
¼ teaspoon freshly ground black pepper
1 tablespoon freshly squeezed lemon juice
4 cups diced cooked turkey or chicken
Hot cooked rice enough to serve four
2 hard-boiled eggs, diced (optional)

½ cup dry roasted peanuts (optional)
Minced cilantro (optional)

In a small saucepan, heat the milk and bouillon, stirring until bouillon is dissolved. Set aside.

In a large saucepan, sauté the apples, onion, and celery in oil until tender. Stir in the flour, curry powder, salt, and pepper until blended. Gradually add the milk mixture and lemon juice. Bring to a boil; cook, stirring until thickened, about 2 minutes. Add the turkey and heat through. Serve over rice. If desired, garnish with chopped egg, peanuts, and cilantro.

Serves 4

*If you're like me and prefer your curry hotter, use up to 2 tablespoons hot curry paste.

PASTA WITH SUN-DRIED TOMATOES AND ARTICHOKES

6 ounces uncooked penne
2 hot Italian sausage links
1 8.5-ounce jar sun-dried tomatoes packed in
    olive oil, oil reserved
1 8-ounce package of sliced mushrooms
3 tablespoons chopped scallions

*6 cloves garlic, peeled and chopped (we like a
     lot of garlic)*
1 14-ounce can artichoke hearts, drained

Cook the pasta according to package instructions until al
dente.

Partially cook the sausage links (about ten minutes), and then
cut into coins.

Pour half of the reserved oil from the sun-dried tomatoes into
a large frying pan and sauté mushrooms and garlic until soft.
Add the sausage coins and cook through (about another five or
ten minutes). Add the sun-dried tomatoes and artichoke hearts
to warm through. Add the pasta and mix thoroughly. Coat with
the remaining reserved oil. Top with the chopped scallions.

Serve warm with crusty Italian bread.

Serves 2

Turn the page for a preview
of Lorraine Bartlett's
next book in
the Victoria Square Mysteries . . .

THE WALLED FLOWER

Coming soon
from Berkley Prime Crime!

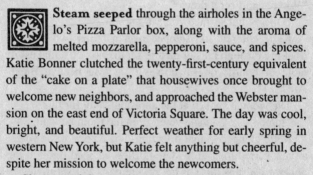**Steam seeped** through the airholes in the Angelo's Pizza Parlor box, along with the aroma of melted mozzarella, pepperoni, sauce, and spices. Katie Bonner clutched the twenty-first-century equivalent of the "cake on a plate" that housewives once brought to welcome new neighbors, and approached the Webster mansion on the east end of Victoria Square. The day was cool, bright, and beautiful. Perfect weather for early spring in western New York, but Katie felt anything but cheerful, despite her mission to welcome the newcomers.

She opened the sagging gate and stepped into the small front courtyard, which was littered with rocks, weeds, and the remains of rusty old garden urns. As she mounted the rather rickety wooden steps, Katie noticed the mansion's heavy oak door stood ajar. Katie paused in the doorway, squinting into the darkened interior. Yup, it was definitely *occupado*. Using her elbow, she knocked on the doorjamb, its blistered, peeling paint just another job awaiting completion on the list of renovation and restoration that was taking place at what was soon to be an upscale bed-and-breakfast.

"Anybody hungry?" Katie called.

A dirt-smudged face appeared around the door. Dusty blond bangs hung over a pair of light blue eyes. More wisps had escaped the faded red bandanna that was supposed to protect the rest of the woman's hair. Clad in a grubby T-shirt and jeans, she held a claw hammer in one hand, the knuckles on her other hand oozing blood.

"Pizza?" the woman said hopefully.

"The best," Katie assured her, proffering the box. "Where can I set it down?"

"On any flat surface you can find."

Katie entered and stepped over a fallen two-by-four, tracking through plaster dust to set the box on a makeshift table of boards on sawhorses. "Do you need a Band-Aid?"

The woman sucked at the abrasion. "Not for this."

"Janice," said a male voice from the room beyond.

Katie glanced in that direction. The owner of the voice, a dark-haired man in his late thirties, stepped through the doorway, just as dirty as his counterpart. Not surprising in the ruin of what, one hundred years before, had been a lovely home.

"Hi, I'm Katie Bonner. I manage Artisans Alley on the other end of the Square, and I'm president of the Victoria Square Merchants Association. Welcome to the neighborhood."

"Thanks," the man said, and moved to stand by the woman.

"I've seen you working here for the last couple of days and figured you might need a break," Katie said.

"Do we ever." The woman moved closer, setting the hammer down and offering Katie her hand. "Janice Ryan. And this is my husband, Toby."

Katie shook both their hands, then pulled a sheaf of paper napkins from the back pocket of her jeans. "Please, help yourself."

"Thanks," the couple chorused, and each dove for a slice.

Katie took a long look around the cavernous space. Bare studs gave the room a skeletal look. Lath and chunks of plaster from the ceiling filled plastic buckets, waiting to be emptied into the commercial Dumpster out back. A bare lightbulb hung from a cheap 1960s fixture. That, too, would eventually have to go.

"Wow, I can't believe how much you've already accomplished," Katie said.

Janice swallowed, her mouth flattening into a frown. "Sounds like you've been in here before."

Many times, Katie was tempted to blurt. She and her late husband, Chad, had tramped through the cold, uninviting place on dozens of occasions during the four years they'd saved to buy it. Then Chad had impulsively invested instead in Artisans Alley, a going concern quickly going downhill. Chad had passed away the year before—the victim of a car accident—and Katie was now the owner and manager. So far she hadn't made a nickel of the money back either.

"Once or twice," Katie said, forcing a smile. "What are your plans?"

Janice beamed. "We hope to open the Grand Victoria Inn in about three months."

A very ambitious plan, considering the state the building was currently in.

"We'll have seven guest rooms to start. The property comes with plenty of acreage to add guest cottages if we do well."

Katie had planned an extensive garden refit, perfect for outdoor weddings and corporate picnics. And if the weather didn't cooperate, she figured she could always tent such affairs. And she'd wanted a white-painted gazebo at the far end of the yard, flanked by a lovely cottage garden, with lots of pink and white cosmos.

Janice's eyes glowed with pride. "The entryway will be totally restored," she said, taking in the space with a sweep of her hand. "As you can see, we've just got that wall over there to remove. They divided the place into apartments, but that's good in a way, because we won't have to re-plumb the whole house for the guest rooms."

That was one of the things Katie had counted on, too. Her plan had been to renovate the old mansion and open the English Ivy Inn. Chad was to be the host, and Katie would manage the kitchen and the financial end of things. It was a solid plan. It was her life's dream. And now it was forever out of her reach.

"Toby's good at carpentry and has plans for a lovely oak check-in desk, over here," Janice said with a wave of her hand. "We've got wood salvaged from another site that'll be just perfect."

Katie already had a lovely oak reception desk sitting in a storage unit waiting to be stripped and refinished. She'd collected brass headboards, oriental carpets, dressers and nightstands, pedestal sinks, light fixtures, dishes, and silverware, too. Every month she wrote out a check to keep her treasures warehoused, and every month she debated getting rid of it all. Owning all that stuff was just another painful reminder that life wasn't always fair.

Katie's anger flared as she noted the sledgehammer resting against the wall. "Are you doing all the work yourself?"

"Just the preliminary demolition," Toby said, reaching for another pizza slice. "It'll save us three or four grand that we can better use elsewhere."

"There's a certain satisfaction in taking down a wall, especially when you can already visualize how perfect the space will be," Janice said. She laughed. "I've spent the last few months decorating this house in my mind. I can't wait until opening day when I can show it off to the world."

Katie, too, had imagined exactly how she'd renovate the old house. Replacement newel posts for the staircase, frosted glass sconces on the walls, delicate rose-patterned wallpaper, chair rails, and crown molding. For years she'd longed to swing a sledge and take out an extraneous wall or two.

She picked up and hefted the tool, nearly staggering under its weight. "Would you mind if I took a whack at that wall—just for fun?"

"Go for it," Toby said, grinning. He put down his pizza, grabbed a pair of work gloves, and accompanied Katie to the wall.

"I'd better cover the pizza," Janice said.

"We're taking down the plasterboard first, then we'll yank out the studs. It's not a load-bearing wall," Toby said, handing Katie the gloves and a pair of safety glasses.

That she already knew. Many an evening she'd pored over how-to books in anticipation of applying her own brand of sweat equity to the place.

Toby or Janice had already removed the baseboard molding at the bottom of the wall, leaving a three-inch gap that had never seen a coat of paint. An odd, gummy dark stain marred the middle of that section of pristine plasterboard.

Katie donned the gloves and glasses, grasped the sledge firmly, swung it high, and let its weight slam against the wall. Bang! A circular dimple marred the surface, but not enough to make a break in the drywall.

"Put your weight into it," Toby encouraged with a smile.

Clenching her teeth, Katie hauled off and swung again. Bang!

The anger blossomed inside her, threatening to engulf her.

This should have been *her* house!

Bang!

It would have been hers if Chad hadn't invested— without her knowledge—in that money pit Artisans Alley.

Bang!

The sledge careened through the air, smacking hard into the wall, taking a jagged hunk of plasterboard with it.

Katie swung again and again, her biceps complaining at the strain. Clouds of dust swirled in the air.

Hands on hips, Toby watched from her left. "You're doing great, Katie." He didn't sound as pleased as he had a few moments before.

Katie took another mighty swing, sending a fragment of plasterboard flying. She paused to yank a loose piece from the studs.

Janice gasped behind her.

Katie lost her grip on the sledge, nearly crushing her toes. She turned to see what Janice was fussing about.

Openmouthed and panting, a wide-eyed Janice frantically pointed at the gaping hole in the wall.

Confused, Katie turned to see the source of her distress.

Behind a heavy layer of plastic, empty eye sockets gazed at nothing; the jaw hung open as though in a scream. The remains of long blond hair were suspended like Easter grass among the bones, and a shiny silver locket dangled from the proximity of its neck.

Katie swallowed, her mouth going dry. "Well, this could ruin your day."

Yellow crime-scene tape barred the mansion's entrance. The east end of the Victoria Square parking lot was clogged with squad cars scattered with no regard to the orderly lines painted on the asphalt. Katie leaned against a paint-flaked column on the wide veranda, noting the rain damage at its base. It would be expensive to replace.

"This is a bad omen," Katie heard Janice complain for the hundredth time, from inside the house. "Who'll want to come to the inn knowing we found a body in a wall?"

The poor woman had no concept of marketing, Katie thought with a rueful shake of her head. A ghost was a great draw . . . if you had a good story to go with it.

She'd been glad to escape the crowd inside. As a material witness, Katie was compelled to stay until the law said she could leave. She glanced at her watch. It was going on two hours now.

She sighed, unsure why she hadn't felt as shattered as Janice and Toby at finding a skeleton walled up in what once might've been her home. Maybe because it *wasn't* her home and never would be. Then again, she'd seen Artisans

Alley's former owner/manager dead in a puddle of his own blood. She'd found one of the vendors dead with a broken neck from a fall. An anonymous skeleton wasn't half as scary. Or maybe she was just in denial. But it was obvious the person behind the wall had been dead a long—well, reasonably speaking—time, and it sure hadn't been an accident.

A crowd of rubberneckers ringed the cordoned-off area. Katie looked up to see her friend and Artisans Alley vendor Rose Nash among the crowd, clutching a card or paper, madly waving to her, trying to get her attention. Dyed blond curls bobbed around her anxious, wrinkled face. Katie took a step forward, but a hand on her shoulder made her turn.

Detective Ray Davenport of the Sheriff's Office homicide detail was once again on site, looking just as formidable and bad-tempered as the other times Katie had interacted with him.

"You seem to attract death, Mrs. Bonner," the balding, middle-aged cop said.

Katie straightened indignantly. "Me, attract death? Detective, that poor woman's been dead for decades."

"And how do you know it was a woman?" he asked suspiciously.

Katie frowned. "Long blond hair, a locket—it doesn't take a genius to figure out the gender."

Davenport glowered. "Just what were you doing here anyway, Mrs. Bonner?"

"Paying a friendly visit to my new neighbors on behalf of the Victoria Square Merchants Association. Believe me, I didn't want to find the remains of that . . . that poor person."

"Detective! Detective!" Rose called, elbowing her way through the crowd. "I heard they found a body."

"You'll have to read about it in the paper, ma'am," he said, ignoring the agitation in her voice as he turned back toward the mansion entrance.

"Was it a woman?" Rose persisted. "Blond hair, brown eyes? Did she have a locket?"

Davenport stopped dead, turned. "Locket?"

"Rectangular, sterling silver. Rhodium-plated with a bright-cut floral design," Rose cried in desperation. She held out a wallet-sized photo, waving it at him.

Davenport trudged down the steps, took the picture from her, studied it, and frowned. Then he lifted the crime-scene tape, motioning her forward.

Katie hurried to meet Rose, steadying the elderly woman as she climbed the six shallow steps into the mansion.

Portable work lights illuminated the crime scene. The room seemed claustrophobically small with so many deputies and technicians crowded in. As the trio entered, they stepped back, quieting as Davenport approached.

The wall had been taken down in one piece, thanks to a reciprocating saw, and now lay flat on the floor. The rest of the drywall had been removed, revealing the earthly remains—just bones—in situ, wrapped in clear plastic sheeting and lying on a fluffy pillow of faded pink Fiberglas. A petrified black substance—rat or insect dung, Katie surmised—was also visible. She shuddered at the thought of how it had gotten there and turned her attention to the wooden studs, which were twenty-four inches on center—not a lot of room. The body must have been wedged in at an angle—the shoulders were cocked, the wrists crossed in front of the pelvis. No remnant of cloth or flesh remained.

Rose blanched, and Katie felt her friend wobble in her grasp.

"Do you recognize the locket?" Davenport asked the older woman.

Tears filled Rose's eyes and she nodded, the movement causing her to sway. "It belonged to my niece." She took a shuddering breath and choked on a sob. "Oh, Heather, everyone thought you'd run off to New York—and you were here all along," she said, and collapsed in a dead faint.

THE NEWEST CHAPTER IN THE
NEW YORK TIMES BESTSELLING
BOOKTOWN MYSTERIES FROM

LORNA BARRETT

CHAPTER & HEARSE

Mystery bookstore owner Tricia Miles has been spending more time solving whodunits than reading them. Now a nearby gas explosion has injured Tricia's sister's boyfriend, Bob Kelly, the head of the Chamber of Commerce, and killed the owner of the town's history bookstore. Tricia's never been a fan of Bob, but when she reads that he's being tight-lipped about the "accident," it's time to take action.

M770T0910

THE *NEW YORK TIMES* BESTSELLING
BOOKTOWN MYSTERIES FROM

LORNA BARRETT

CONTINUES WITH

BOOKPLATE SPECIAL

Bookstore owner Tricia Miles has put up—and
put up with—her uninvited college roommate
for weeks. In return, Pammy has stolen one
hundred dollars. But the day she's kicked out,
Pammy's found dead in a Dumpster, leaving
loads of questions unanswered.

penguin.com